‘ sion of the Bristol Riots, ascribed to Arthur Vaughan, was actually played by Major, afterwards Sir Digby, Mackworth, aide-de-camp to Lord Hill. Major Mackworth, though present in an unofficial capacity, took upon himself to give the order to charge, which in the opinion of many saved the city.’

Author’s Note

CHIPPINGE began ‘a trilogy on life in the first decade of the nineteenth century. Sir Keith Feiling, in a volume of biographical essays called *In Christchurch Hall,* evaluates this as Weyman’s best work. He also rates highly *The Castle Inn*.’

F. Seymour Smith, *An English Library*

‘I made a collection once of what I called the key books in my life which included Anthony Hope, Rider Haggard, Stanley Weyman, Captain Gilson, and I do occasionally re-read them. Stanley Weyman in particular.’

Graham Greene in an interview with
Ronald Bryden, BBC, April 1970

By the same author in Pan Books

THE CASTLE INN
A GENTLEMAN OF FRANCE

STANLEY J. WEYMAN

CHIPPINGE

UNABRIDGED

PAN BOOKS LTD · LONDON

First published 1906 by Smith, Elder and Co.
This edition published 1971 by Pan Books Ltd,
33 Tothill Street, London, S.W.1

ISBN 0 330 02599 6

Printed in Great Britain by
Richard Clay (The Chaucer Press), Ltd, Bungay, Suffolk

CONTENTS

CHAPTER I

The Dissolution

Boom!

It was the twenty-second of April, 1831, and a young man was walking down Whitehall in the direction of Parliament Street. He wore shepherd's plaid trousers and the swallow-tailed coat of the day, with a figured muslin cravat wound about his wide-spread collar. He halted opposite the Privy Gardens, and, with his face turned skywards, listened until the sound of the Tower guns smote again on the ear and dispelled his doubts. To the experienced, his outward man, neat and modestly prosperous, denoted a young barrister of promise or a Treasury clerk. His figure was good, he was above the middle height, and he carried himself with an easy independence. He seemed to be one who both held a fair opinion of himself and knew how to impress that opinion on his fellows; yet was not incapable of deference where deference was plainly due. He was neither ugly nor handsome, neither slovenly nor a *petit-maître*; indeed, it was doubtful if he had ever seen the inside of Almack's. But his features were strong and intellectual, and the keen grey eyes which looked so boldly on the world could express both humour and good-humour. In a word, this young man was one upon whom women, even great ladies, were likely to look with pleasure, and one woman – but he had not yet met her – with tenderness.

Boom!

He was only one among a dozen who within the space of a few yards had been brought to a stand by the sound, who knew what the salute meant, and in their various ways were moved by it. The rumour which had flown through the town in the morning, that the King was about to dissolve his six-month-old Parliament, was true, then! So true that already in the clubs, from Boodle's to Brooks's, men were sending off dispatches, while the long arms of the semaphore were carrying the news to the Continent. Persons began to run by Vaughan – the young man's name was Arthur Vaughan; and behind him the street was filling with a multitude hastening to see the sight, or so much of it as the vulgar might see. Some ran towards Westminster without disguise. Some, of a higher station, walked as fast as dignity and their strapped trousers permitted; while others again, who thought themselves wiser than their neighbours, made quickly for Downing Street and the different openings which led into St James's Park, in the hope of catching a glimpse of the procession before the crowd about the Houses engulfed it.

Nine out of ten, as they ran or walked – nay, it might be said more truly, ninety-nine out of a hundred – evinced a joy quite out of the common, and such as no political event of these days produces. One cried, 'Hip! Hip! Hip!'; one flung up his cap; one swore gaily. Strangers told one another that it was a good thing, bravely done! And while the whole of that part of the town seemed to be moving towards the Houses, the guns boomed on, proclaiming to all the world that the unexpected had happened; that the Parliament which had passed the People's Bill by one – a miserable one in the largest House which had ever voted – and, having done that, had shelved it by some shift, some subterfuge, was meeting the fate which it deserved.

No man, be it noted, called the measure the Reform Bill, or anything but the Bill, or, affectionately, the People's Bill. But they called it that repeatedly, and, in their enthusiasm, exulted in the fall of its enemies as in a personal gain. And though here and there amid the general turmoil a man of mature age stood aside and scowled on the crowd as it swept vociferating by him, such men were but as straws in a backwater of the stream – powerless to arrest the current, and liable at any moment to be swept within its influence.

That generation had seen many a coach start laurel-clad from St Martin's, and listened many a time to the salvoes that told of the victories in France or Flanders. But it was no exaggeration to say that even Waterloo had not flung abroad more general joy, nor sown the dingy streets with brighter faces, than this civil gain. For now – now, surely – the

People's Bill would pass, and the people be truly represented in Parliament! Now, for certain, the Bill's ill-wishers would get a fall! And if every man – about which some doubts were whispered even in the public-houses – did not get a vote which he could sell for a handful of gold, as his betters had sold their votes time out of mind, at least there would be beef and beer for all! Or, if not that, something indefinite, but vastly pleasant. Few, indeed, knew precisely what they wished or what they were going to gain, but

Hurrah for Mr Brougham!
Hurrah for Gaffer Grey!
Hurrah for Lord John—

Hurrah, in a word, for the Ministry, hurrah for the Whigs! And, above all, three cheers for the King, who had stood by Lord Grey and dissolved this niggling, hypocritical Parliament of landowners.

Meanwhile the young man who has been described resumed his course, but slowly, and without betraying by any marked sign that he shared the general feeling. Still, he walked with his head a little higher than before; he seemed to sniff the battle; and there was a light in his eyes as if he saw a wider arena before him.

'It is true, then,' he muttered. 'And for today I shall have my errand for my pains. He will have other fish to fry, and will not see me. But what of that? Another day will do as well.'

At this moment a ragamuffin in an old jockey cap attached himself to him, and, running beside him, urged him to hasten.

'Run, your honour,' he croaked in gin-laden accents, 'and you'll 'ave a good place! And I'll drink your honour's health, and Billy the King's! Sure he's the father of his country, and seven besides. Come on, your honour, or they'll be jostling you!'

Vaughan glanced down and shook his head. He waved the man away.

But the lout looked only to his market, and was not easily repulsed.

'He's there, I tell you,' he persisted. 'And for threepence I'll get you to see him. Come on, your honour! It's many a Westminster election I've seen, and beer running, from Mr Fox – that was the gentleman, and always a word for the poor man – till now, when maybe it's your honour's going to stand! Anyway, it's down with the mongers!'

A man who was clinging to the wall at the corner of Downing Street waved his broken hat round his head.

'Ay, down with the borough-mongers!' he cried. 'Down with Peel! Down with the Dook! Down with 'em all! Down with everybody!'

'And long live the Bill!' cried a man of more respectable appearance as he hurried by. 'And long live the King, God bless him!'

'They'll know what it is to balk the people now,' chimed in a fourth. 'Let 'em go back and get elected if they can. Ay, let 'em!'

'Ay, let 'em! Mr Brougham'll see to that!' shouted the other. 'Hurray for Mr Brougham!'

The cry was taken up by the crowd, and three cheers were given for the Chancellor, who was so well known to the mob by the style under which he had been triumphantly elected for Yorkshire that his peerage was ignored.

Vaughan, however, heard but the echo of these cheers. Like most young men of his time, he leant to the popular side. But he had no taste for the populace in the mass; and the sight of the crowd, which was fast occupying the whole of the space before Palace Yard, and even surging back into Parliament Street, determined him to turn aside. He shook off his attendant and, crossing into Whitehall Place, walked up and down, immersed in his reflections.

He was honestly ambitious, and his thoughts turned naturally on the influence which this Bill – which must create a new England, and for many a new world – was likely to have on his own fortunes. The owner of a small estate in South Wales, come early to his inheritance, he had sickened of the idle life of an officer in peacetime; and after three years of Service, believing himself fit for something higher, he had sold his commission and turned his mind to intellectual pursuits. He hoped that he had a bent that way; and the glory of the immortal three who thirty years before had founded the

Edinburgh Review, and, by so doing, made this day possible, attracted him. Why should not he, as well as another, be the man who, in the Commons, the cockpit of the nation, stood spurred to meet all comers – in an uproar which could almost be heard where he walked? Or the man who, in the lists of Themis, upheld the right of the widow and the poor man's cause, and to whom judges listened with reluctant admiration? Or, best of all, highest of all, might he not vie with that abnormal and remarkable man who wore at once the three crowns, and whether as Edinburgh Reviewer, as knight of the shire for York, or as Chancellor of England, played his part with equal ease? To be brief, it was prizes such as these, distant but luminous, that held his eyes, incited him to effort, made him live laborious days. He believed that he had ability, and though he came late to the strife he brought his experience. If men living from hand to mouth and distracted by household cares could achieve so much, why should not he who had his independence and his place in the world? Had not Erskine been such another? He, too, had sickened of barrack-life. And Brougham and the two Scotts, Eldon and Stowell. To say nothing of this young Macaulay, whose name was beginning to run through every mouth; and of a dozen others who had risen to fame from a lower and less advantageous station.

The goal was distant, but it was glorious. Nor had the eighteen months which he had given to the study of the law, to attendance at the Academic and at a less ambitious debating society, and to the output of some scientific feelers, shaken his faith in himself. He had not yet thought of a seat at St Stephen's; for no nomination had fallen to him, nor, save from one quarter, was likely to fall. And his income, some six hundred a year, though it was ample for a bachelor, would not stretch to the price of a seat at five thousand for the Parliament, or fifteen hundred for the Session – the quotations which had ruled of late. But a seat some time he must have – it was a necessary stepping-stone to the heights he would gain. And the subject in his mind as he paced Whitehall Place was the abolition of the close boroughs, and the effect which the transfer of electoral power to the middle class would have on his chances.

A small thing – no more than a quantity of straw laid thickly before one of the houses – brought his thoughts down to the present. By a natural impulse he raised his eyes to the house; by a coincidence, less natural, a hand, as he looked, showed itself behind one of the panes of a window on the first floor, and drew down the blind. Vaughan stood after that, fascinated, and watched the lowering of blind after blind. And the solemn contrast between his busy thoughts and that which had just happened in the house – between that which lay behind the darkened windows and the bright April sunshine about him, the twittering of sparrows in the green, and the tumult of distant cheering – went home to him.

He thought of the lines, so old and so applicable:

Omnes eodem cogimur, omnium
Versatur urna, serius, ocius,
Sors exitura, et nos in aeternum
Exilium impositura cymbae.

He was still rolling the words on his tongue with that love of the classical rhythm which was a mark of his day, and which returns no more than the taste for the prize-ring which was coeval with it, when the door of the house opened and a man came heavily out, closed the door behind him, and, with his head bent low and the clumsy gait of an automaton, made off down the street.

The man was stout as well as tall. He wore his hat pulled awry over his eyes, his dress was slovenly and disordered, and his hands were plunged deep in his breeches pockets. Vaughan saw so much. Then the door opened again, and a face, unmistakably that of a butler, looked out.

The servant's eyes met his, and though the man neither spoke nor beckoned, his eyes spoke for him. Vaughan crossed the way to him.

'What is it?' he asked.

The man was almost blubbering. 'Oh Lord!' he said. 'My lady's gone not five minutes, and he'll not be let nor hindered! He's to the House! and if the crowd know him he'll be murdered. For God's sake, follow him, sir! He's Sir Charles

Wetherell, and a better master never walked, let them say what they like. If there's anybody with him, maybe they'll not touch him.'

'I will follow him,' Vaughan answered. And he hastened after the stout man, who had by this time reached the corner of the street.

He was surprised that he had not recognized Wetherell. For in every bookseller's window, caricatures of the 'Last of the Boroughbridges', as the wits called him, after the pocket borough for which he sat, were plentiful as blackberries. Not only was he the highest of Tories, but he was a martyr in their cause; for, Attorney-General in the last government, he had been dismissed for resisting the Catholic Claims. Since then he had proved himself, of all the opponents of the Bill, the most violent, the most witty, and, with the exception of Croker perhaps, the most rancorous. At this date he passed for the best-hated man in England; the representative to the public mind of all that was old-fashioned and illiberal and exclusive. Vaughan knew, therefore, that the servant's fears were not unfounded, and with a heart full of pity – for he remembered the darkened house – he made after him.

By this time Sir Charles was some way ahead and involved in the crowd. Fortunately the throng was densest opposite Old Palace Yard, whence the King was in the act of departing; and the space before the Hall and before St Stephen's Court – the buildings about which abutted on the river – though occupied by a loosely moving multitude, and presenting a scene of the utmost animation, was not impassable. Sir Charles was in the heart of the crowd before he was recognized; and then his stolid unconsciousness and the general good-humour, born of victory, served him well. He was too familiar a figure to pass altogether unknown; and here and there a man hissed him, and one group turned and hooted after him. But he was within a dozen yards of the entrance of St Stephen's Court, with Vaughan on his heels, before any violence was offered. There a man whom he happened to jostle recognized him and, bawling abuse, pushed him rudely. The act might well have been the beginning of worse things, but Vaughan touched the man on the shoulder and looked him in the face. 'I shall know you,' he said quietly. 'Have a care!' And the fellow, intimidated by his words and his six feet of height, shrank into himself and stood back.

Wetherell had barely noticed the rudeness. But he noted the intervention, by a backward glance. 'Much obliged,' he grunted. 'Know you too again, young gentleman.' And he went heavily on and passed out of the crowd into the court, followed by a few scattered hisses.

Behind the officers of the House who guarded the entrance a group of excited persons stood talking. They were chiefly Members who had just left the House and had been brought to a stand by the aspect of the crowd. On seeing Wetherell, surprise altered their looks.

'Good God!' cried one, stepping forward. 'You've come down, Wetherell?'

'Ay,' the stricken man answered, without lifting his eyes or giving the least sign of animation. 'Is it too late?'

'By an hour. There's nothing to be done. Grey and Bruffam have got the King body and soul. He was so determined to dissolve, he swore that he'd come down in a hackney-coach rather than not come. So they say!'

'Ay!'

'But I hope,' a second struck in, in a tone of solicitude, 'that as you are here, Lady Wetherell has rallied.'

'She died a quarter of an hour ago,' he muttered. 'I could do no more. I came here. But as I am too late – I'll go back.'

Yet he stood a while, as if he had no longer anything to draw him one way more than another; with his double chin and pendulous cheeks resting on his breast and his leaden eyes sunk to the level of the pavement. The others stood round him with shocked faces, from which his words and manner had driven the flush of the combat. Presently two Members, arguing loudly, came up, and were silenced by a glance and a muttered word. The ungainly attitude, the ill-fitting clothes, did but accentuate the tragedy of the central figure. They knew – none better – how fiercely, how keenly, how doggedly he had struggled against death, against the Bill.

And yet, had they thought of it, the vulgar caricatures that had hurt her, the abuse that had passed him by to lodge in her bosom, would hurt her no more!

Meanwhile, Vaughan, as soon as he had seen Sir Charles

within the entrance reserved for Members, had betaken himself to the main door of the Hall, a few paces to the westward. He had no hope that he would now be able to perform the errand on which he had set forth; for the Chancellor, at this crisis, would have other fish to fry and other people to see. But he thought that he would leave his card with the usher, so that Lord Brougham might know that he had attended, and might make a fresh appointment, if he still wished to see him.

Of the vast congeries of buildings which then encased St Stephen's Chapel and its beautiful but degraded cloisters, little more than the Hall is left to us. The Hall we have, and in the main in the condition in which the men of that generation viewed it, as Canning viewed it, when with death in his face he paced its length on Peel's arm, and suspecting, perhaps, that they two would meet no more, proved to all men the good will he bore his rival. Those among us whose memories go back a quarter of a century, and who can recall its aspect in term-time, with three-score barristers parading its length, and thrice as many suitors and attorneys darting over its pavement – all under the lofty roof which has no rival in Europe – will be able to picture it as Vaughan saw it when he entered. To the bustle attending the courts of law was added on this occasion the supreme excitement of the day. In every corner, on the steps of every court, eager groups wrangled and debated; while above the hubbub of argument and the trampling of feet, the voices of ushers rose monotonously, calling a witness or enjoining order.

Vaughan paused beside the cake stall at the door and surveyed the scene. As he stood, one of the two men who were pacing near saw him, and with a whispered word left his companion and came towards him.

'Mr Vaughan,' he said, extending his hand with bland courtesy, 'I hope you are well. Can I do anything for you? We are dissolved, but a frank is a frank for all that – today.'

'No, I thank you,' Vaughan answered. 'The truth is, I had an appointment with the Chancellor for this afternoon. But I suppose he will not see me now.'

The other's eyebrows met, with the result that his face looked less bland. He was a small man, with keen dark eyes and bushy grey whiskers, and an air of hawk-like energy which sixty years had not tamed. He wore the laced coat of a serjeant-at-law, powdered on the shoulders, as if he had but lately and hurriedly cast off his wig.

'Good God!' he said. 'With the Chancellor!' And then, pulling himself up, 'But I congratulate you. A student at the Bar, as I believe you are, Mr Vaughan, who has appointments with the Chancellor has fortune indeed within his grasp.'

Vaughan laughed. 'I fear not,' he said. 'There are appointments and appointments, Serjeant Wathen. Mine is not of a professional nature.'

Still the Serjeant's face, do what he would, looked grim. He had his reasons for disliking what he heard.

'Indeed!' he said dryly. 'Indeed, but I must not detain you. Your time,' with a faint note of sarcasm, 'is valuable.' And with a civil salutation the two parted.

Wathen went back to his companion. 'Talk of the old one!' he said. 'Do you know who that is?'

'No,' the other answered. They had been discussing the coming election. 'Who is it?'

'One of my constituents.'

His friend laughed. 'Oh, come,' he said. 'I thought you had but one, Serjeant – old Vermuyden.'

'Only one,' Wathen answered, his eyes travelling from group to group, 'who counts or, rather, who did count. But thirteen who poll. And that's one of them.' He glanced frowning in the direction which Vaughan had taken. 'And what do you think his business is here, confound him?'

'What?'

'An appointment with old Wicked Shifts.'

'With the Chancellor? Pheugh!'

'Ay,' the Serjeant answered morosely, 'you may whistle. There's some black business on foot, you may depend upon it. And ten to one it's about my seat. He's a *broom*,' he continued, tugging at the whiskers which the late King had stamped with the imprimatur of fashion, 'that will make a clean sweep of us if we don't take care. Whatever he does, there's something behind it. Some bed-chamber plot, or some intrigue to get A out and put B in. If it was the charwoman's place he wanted, he'd not ask for it and get it. That wouldn't please him. But he'd tunnel and tunnel and tunnel – and so he'd get it.'

'Still,' the other replied, with secret amusement – for he had no seat, and the woes of our friends, especially our better-placed friends, have their comic side – 'I thought that you had a safe thing, Wathen? that old Vermuyden's nomination at Chippinge was as good as an order on the Bank of England?'

'It was,' Wathen answered dryly. 'But with the country wild for the Bill, there's no saying what may happen anywhere. Safe!' he continued with a snarl. 'Was there ever a safer seat than Westbury? Or a man who had a place in better order than old Lopes, who owned it, and died last month; taken from the evil to come, Jekyll said, for he never could have existed in a world without rotten boroughs! It's not far from Chippinge, so I know – know it well. And I tell you his system was beautiful – beautiful! Yet when Peel was there – after he had ratted on the Catholic Claims and been thrown out at Oxford – Lopes made way for him, you remember? – he would not have got in, no, by God, he wouldn't have got in if there had been a man against him. And the state in which the country was then, though there was a bit of a Protestant cry, too, wasn't to compare with what it will be now. That man' – he shook his fist steadily in the direction of the Chancellor's Court – 'has lighted a fire in England that will never be put out till it has consumed King, Lords, and Commons – ay, every stick and stone of the old Constitution. You may take my word for it. And to think – to think,' he added still more savagely, 'that it is the Whigs have done this. The Whigs! who own more than half the land in the country; who are prouder and stiffer than old George the Third himself; who wouldn't let you nor me into their Cabinet to save our lives. By the Lord,' he concluded with gusto, 'they'll soon learn the difference!'

'In the meantime – there'll be dead cats and bad eggs flying, you think?'

Wathen groaned. 'If that were the end of it,' he said, 'I'd not mind.'

'Still, with it all, you are pretty safe, I suppose?'

'With that fellow closeted with Brougham? No, no!'

'Who is the young spark?' the other asked carelessly. 'He looked a decentish kind of fellow. A little of the prig, perhaps.'

'He's that!' Wathen answered. 'A damned prig. What's more, a cousin of old Vermuyden's. And what's worse, his heir. That's why they put him in the Corporation at Chippinge and made him one of the thirteen electors. Thought the vote safe in the family, you see? And cheaper?' He winked. 'But there's no love lost between him and old Sir Robert. A bed for a night once a year, and one day in the season among the turnips, and glad to see you back, my lad! That's about the position. Now I wonder if Brougham is going to try— But, Lord! there's no guessing what is in that man's head! He's fuller of mischief than an egg of meat!'

The other was about to answer when one of the courts, in which a case of some difficulty had caused a late sitting, discharged its noisy, wrangling, perspiring crowd. The two stepped aside to avoid the evasion, and did not resume their talk. Wathen's friend made his way out by the main door near which they had been standing; while the Serjeant, with looks which mirrored the gloom that a hundred Tory faces wore that day, betook himself to the robing room. There he happened upon another unfortunate. They fell to talking, and their talk ran naturally upon the Chancellor, upon old Grey's folly in letting himself be led by the nose by such a rogue; finally, upon the mistakes of their own Party. They differed on the last topic, and in that natural and customary state we may leave them.

CHAPTER II

The Spirit of the Storm

THE COURT OF CHANCERY, the preserve for nearly a quarter of a century of Eldon and Delay, was the farthest from the entrance on the right-hand side of the Hall – a situation which enabled the Chancellor to pass easily to that other seat of his labours, the Woolsack. Two steps raised the Tribunals of the Common Law above the level of the Hall. But as if to indicate that this court was not the seat of anything so common as law, but was the shrine of that more august conception, Patronage, and the altar to which countless divines of the Church of England looked with unwinking devotion, a flight of six or eight steps led up to the door.

The privacy thus secured had been much to the taste of Lord Eldon. Doubt and delay flourish best in a close and dusty atmosphere; and if ever there was a man to whom that which was was right, it was 'Old Bags'. Nor had Lord Lyndhurst, his immediate successor, quarrelled with an arrangement which left him at liberty to devote his time to society and his beautiful wife. But the man who now sat in the marble chair was of another kind from either of these. His worst enemy could not lay dullness to his charge; nor could he who lectured the Whitbreads on brewing, who explained their art to opticians, who vied with Talleyrand in the knowledge of French literature, who wrote eighty articles for the first twenty numbers of the *Edinburgh Review*, be called a sluggard. Confident of his powers, Brougham loved to display them; and the wider the arena the better he was pleased. His first sitting had been graced by the presence of three royal dukes, a whole Cabinet, and a score of peers in full dress. Having begun thus auspiciously, he was not the man to vegetate in the gloom of a dry-as-dust court, or to be content with an audience of suitors, whom equity – blessed word! – had long stripped of their votes.

Again and again during the last six months, by brilliant declamation or by astounding statement, he had filled his court to the last inch. The lions in the Tower, the tombs in the Abbey, the New Police – all were deserted; and country-folk flocked to Westminster, or to Lincoln's Inn, not to hear the judgements of the highest legal authority in the land, but to see with their own eyes the fugleman of reform – the great orator, whose voice, raised at the Yorkshire election, had found an echo which still thundered in the ears and the hearts of England.

'I am for Reform!' he had said in the castle yard of York, on a day long to be remembered. And the people of England had answered: 'So are we; and we will have it, or—'

The lacuna they had filled, not with words, but with facts stronger than words – with the flames of Kentish farmhouses and Wiltshire factories; with political unions counting their members by scores of thousands; with midnight drillings and vague and sullen murmurings; above all, with the mysterious terror of some great change which was to come – a terror that shook the most thoughtless and affected even 'the Duke', as men called the Duke of Wellington in that day. For was not every crown on the Continent toppling?

Vaughan did not suppose that, in view of the startling event of the day, he would be admitted. But the usher, who occupied a high stool in the gloom outside the great man's door, no sooner read his card than he slid to the ground.

'I think his lordship will see you, sir,' he murmured blandly; and he disappeared.

He was back on the instant, and, beckoning to Vaughan to follow him, he proceeded some paces along a murky corridor, which the venerable form of Eldon seemed still to haunt. Opening a door, he stood aside.

The room which Vaughan saw before him was stately and spacious, furnished with grave richness. A deep silence, intensified by the fact that the room had no windows, but was lighted from above, reigned in it – and a smell of law-calf. Here and there on a bookcase or on a pedestal stood a marble bust of Bacon, or Selden, or Blackstone. And for a moment Vaughan fancied that these were its only occupants. On advancing farther, however, he discovered two persons, who were writing busily at separate side tables; and one of them looked up and spoke.

'Your pardon, Mr Vaughan!' he said. 'One moment, if you please!'

The speaker was almost as good as his word, for less than a minute later he threw down the pen, and rose – a gaunt figure in a black frock-coat, and with a black stock about his scraggy neck – and came to meet his visitor.

'I fear that I have come at an untimely moment, my lord,' Vaughan said, awed in spite of himself by what he knew of the man.

But the Chancellor's frank address put him at once at his ease.

'Politics pass, Mr Vaughan,' he answered lightly, 'but science remains.'

He did not explain, as he pointed to a seat, that he loved, above all things, to produce startling effects; and to dazzle by the ease with which he flung off one part and assumed another.

Henry Brougham – so, for some time after his elevation to the peerage, he persisted in signing himself – was at this time at the zenith of his life, as of his fame. Tall, but lean and ungainly, with a long neck and sloping shoulders, he had one of the strangest faces which genius has ever worn. His clownish features, his high cheekbones, and queer bulbous nose are familiar to us; for, something exaggerated by the caricaturist, they form week by week the trailing mask which mars the cover of *Punch*. Yet was the face, with all its ugliness, singularly mobile; and the eyes, the windows of that restless and insatiable soul, shone, sparkled, laughed, wept, with incredible brilliance. That which he did not know, that which his mind could not perform – save sit still and be discreet – no man had ever discovered. And it was the knowledge of this, the sense of the strange and almost uncanny versatility of the man, which for a moment overpowered Vaughan.

The Chancellor seated himself opposite his visitor, and placed a hand on each of his widespread knees. He smiled.

'My friend,' he said. 'I envy you.'

Vaughan coloured shyly. 'Your lordship has little cause,' he answered.

'Great cause,' was the reply, 'great cause! For as you are I was. And,' he chuckled, as he rocked himself to and fro, 'I have not found life very empty or very unpleasant. But it was not to tell you this that I asked you to wait on me, Mr Vaughan, as you may suppose. Light! It is a singular thing that you at the outset of your career – even as I thirty years ago at the same point of mine – should take up such a parergon, and alight upon the same discovery.'

'I do not think I understand.'

'In your article on the possibility of the permanence of reflections – to which I referred in my letter, I think?'

'Yes, my lord, you did.'

'You have restated a fact which I maintained for the first time more than thirty years ago! In my paper on coloursss, read before the Royal Society in – I think it was '96.'

Vaughan stared. His colour rose sharply. 'Indeed?' he said, in a tone from which he vainly strove to banish incredulity.

'You have perhaps read the paper?'

'Yes, I have.'

The Chancellor chuckled. 'And found nothing of the kind in it?' he said.

Vaughan coloured still more deeply. He felt that the position was unpleasant.

'Frankly, my lord, if you ask me, no.'

'And you think yourself,' with a grin, 'the first discoverer?'

'I did.'

Brougham sprang like a boy to his feet, and whisked his long, lank body to a distant bookshelf. Thence he took down a much-rubbed manuscript book. As he returned he opened this at a place already marked, and, laying it on the table, he beckoned to the young man to approach.

'Read that,' he said waggishly, 'and confess, young sir, that there were chiefs before Agamemnon.'

Vaughan stooped over the book and, having read, looked up in perplexity.

'But this passage,' he said, 'was not in the paper read before the Royal Society in '96?'

'In the paper read? No. Nor yet in the paper printed? There, too, you are right. And why? Because a sapient dunderhead who was in authority requested me to omit this passage. He did not believe that light passing through a small hole in the window-shutter of a darkened room impresses a view of external objects on white paper; nor, that, as I suggested, the view might be made permanent if cast on ivory rubbed with nitrate of silver!'

Vaughan was dumbfounded, and perhaps a little chagrined. 'It is most singular!' he said.

'Do you wonder now that I could not refrain from sending for you?'

'I do not, indeed.'

The Chancellor patted him kindly on the shoulder, and by a gesture made him resume his seat.

'No, I could not refrain,' he continued; 'the coincidence was too remarkable. If you come to sit where I sit, the chance will be still more singular.'

Vaughan coloured with pleasure. 'Alas!' he said, smiling, 'one swallow, my lord, does not make a summer.'

'Ah, my friend,' with a benevolent look. 'But I know more of you than you think. You were in the Service, I hear, and left it. *Cedant arma togae*, eh?'

'Yes.'

'Well, I, too, after a fashion. Thirty years ago I served a gun with Professor Playfair in the Volunteer Artillery at Edinburgh. God knows,' he continued complacently, 'if I had gone on with it, where I should have landed! Where the Duke is, perhaps! More surprising things have happened.'

Vaughan did not know whether to take this, which was gravely, even sentimentally spoken, for jest or for earnest. He did not speak. And Brougham, seated in his favourite posture, with a hand on either knee, his lean body upright, and the skirts of his black coat falling to the floor on either side of him, resumed.

'I hear, too, that you have done well at the Academic,' he said, 'and on the right side, Mr Vaughan. Light? Ay, always light, my friend, always light! Let that be our motto. For myself,' he continued earnestly, 'I have taken it in hand that this poor country shall never lack light again; and by God's help and Johnny Russell's Bill I'll bring it about! And not the phosphorescent light of rotten boroughs and corrupt corporations, Mr Vaughan. No, nor the blaze of burning stacks, kindled by wretched, starving, ignorant – ay, above all, Mr Vaughan, ignorant men! But the light of education, the light of a free Press, the light of good government and honest representation; so that whatever they lack henceforth they shall have voices and means and ways to make their wants known. You agree with me? But I know you do, for I hear how well you have spoken on that side. Mr Cornelius,' turning and addressing the gentleman who still continued to write at his table, 'who was it told us of Mr Vaughan's speech at the Academic?'

'I don't know,' Mr Cornelius answered gruffly.

'No?' the Chancellor said, not a whit put out. 'He never

knows anything!' And then, throwing one knee over the other, he regarded Vaughan with closer attention. 'Mr Vaughan,' he said, 'have you ever thought of entering Parliament?'

Vaughan's heart pounded, and his face betrayed his emotion. Good Heavens! was the Chancellor about to offer him a Government seat? He scarcely knew what to expect or what to say. The prospect, suddenly opened, blinded him. He muttered that he had not as yet thought of it.

'You have no connexion,' Brougham continued, 'who could help you to a seat? For if so, now is the time. Presently there will be a Reformed Parliament and a crowd of new men, and the road will be blocked by the throng of aspirants. You are not too young. Palmerston was not so old when Perceval offered him a seat in the Cabinet.'

The words, the tone, the assumption that such things were for him – that he had but to hold out his hand and they would fall into it – dropped like balm into the young man's soul. Yet he was not sure that the other was serious, and he made a tremendous effort to hide the emotion he felt.

'I am afraid,' he said, with a forced smile, 'that I, my lord, am not Lord Palmerston.'

'No?' Brougham answered, with a faint sneer. 'But not much the worse for that, perhaps. So that if you have any connexion who commands a seat, now is the time.'

Vaughan shook his head. 'I have none,' he said, 'except my cousin, Sir Robert Vermuyden.'

'Vermuyden of Chippinge?' the Chancellor exclaimed, in a voice of surprise.

'The same, my lord.'

'Good God!' Brougham cried. It was not a mealy-mouthed age. And he leant back and stared at the young man. 'You don't mean to say that he is your cousin?'

'Yes.'

The Chancellor laughed. 'Oh dear, dear!' he said. 'I am afraid that he won't help us much. I remember him in the House – an old high-and-dry Tory. I am afraid that, with your opinions, you've not much to expect from him. Still – Mr Cornelius,' to the gentleman at the table, 'oblige me with Oldfield's *House of Commons*, the Wiltshire volume, and the private Borough List. Thank you. Let me see – ah, here it is!'

He proceeded to read in a low tone, skipping from heading to heading: 'Chippinge, in the county of Wilts, has returned two Members since the twenty-third of Edward III. Right of election in the Alderman and twelve capital burgesses, who hold their places for life. Number of voters, thirteen. Patron, Sir Robert Vermuyden, Bart, of Stapylton House.

'Umph, as I thought,' he continued, laying down the book. 'Now what does the list say?' And, taking it in turn from his knee, he read:

'In Schedule A for total disfranchisement, the population under 2,000. Present Members, Serjeant Wathen and Mr Cooke, on nomination of Sir Robert Vermuyden; the former to oblige Lord Eldon, the latter by purchase. Both opponents of Bill; nothing to be hoped from them. The Bowood interest divides the Corporation in the proportion of four to nine, but has not succeeded in returning a Member since the election of 1741 – on petition. The heir to the Vermuyden interest is—'

He broke off sharply, but continued to study the page. Presently he looked over it.

'Are you the Mr Vaughan who inherits?' he asked gravely.

'The greater part of the estates – yes.'

Brougham laid down the book and rubbed his chin. 'Under those circumstances,' he said, after musing a while, 'don't you think that your cousin could be persuaded to return you as an independent Member?'

Vaughan shook his head with decision.

'The matter is important,' the Chancellor continued slowly, and as if he weighed his words. 'I cannot precisely make a promise, Mr Vaughan; but if your cousin could see the question of the Bill in another light, I have little doubt that any object in reason could be secured for him. If, for instance, it should be necessary in passing the Bill through the Upper House to create new – eh?'

He paused, looked at Vaughan, who laughed outright. 'Sir Robert would not cross the park to save my life, my lord,' he said. 'And I am sure he would rather hang outside the White Lion in Chippinge market-place than resign his opinions or his borough!'

'He'll lose the latter, whether or no,' Brougham answered, with a touch of irritation. 'Was there not some trouble about his wife? I think I remember something.'

'They were separated many years ago.'

'She is alive, is she not?'

'Yes.'

Brougham saw, at this stage, that the subject was not palatable, and he abandoned it. Altering his bearing abruptly, he flung the books from him with the recklessness of a boy, and he raised his sombre figure to its height.

'Well, well,' he said, 'I hoped for better things; but I as Tommy Moore sings –

He's pledged himself, though sore bereft
Of ways and means of ruling ill,
To make the most of what are left,
And to stick to all that's rotten still!

And, by the Lord! I don't say that I don't respect him. I respect every man who votes honestly as he thinks.' And grandly, and with appropriate gestures, he spouted –

'Who spurns the expedient for the right
Scorns money's all-attractive charms,
And through mean crowds that clogged his flight
Has nobly cleared his conquering arms.

'That's the Attorney-General's. He turns old Horace well, doesn't he?'

Vaughan coloured. Young and candid, he could not bear the thought of taking credit where he did not deserve it.

'I fear,' he said shyly, 'that would bear rather hardly on me if we had a contest at Chippinge, my lord. Fortunately, it is unlikely.'

'How would it bear hardly on you?' Brougham asked, with interest.

'I have a vote.'

'You are one of the twelve burgesses?' in a tone of surprise.

'Yes, by favour of Sir Robert.'

The Chancellor smiled and shook his head. 'No,' he said,

'no. I do not believe you. You do yourself an injustice. Leave that sort of thing to older men. To Lyndhurst, if you will, damned Jacobin as he is, preening himself in Tory feathers, and determined whoever's in he'll not be out. Or to Peel. Leave it! And, believe me, you'll not repent it. I,' he continued loftily, 'have seen fifty years of life, Mr Vaughan, and lived every year of them and every day of them, and I tell you that the thing is too dearly bought at that price.'

Vaughan felt himself rebuked; but he made a fight. 'And yet,' he said, 'are there no circumstances, my lord, in which such a vote may be justified?'

'A vote against your conscience – to oblige someone?'

'Well, yes.'

'A Jesuit might justify it. There is nothing which a Jesuit could not justify, I suppose. But though no man was stronger for the Catholic Claims than I was, I do not hold a Jesuit to be a man of honour. And that is where the difference lies. There! But,' he continued, with a quick change from the lofty to the confidential, 'let me tell you a fact, Mr Vaughan. In '29 – was it in April or May of '29, Mr Cornelius?'

'I don't know to what you refer,' Mr Cornelius grunted.

'To be sure you don't,' the Chancellor replied, without any loss of good-humour; 'but in April or May of '29, Mr Vaughan, the Duke offered me the Rolls, which is £7,000 a year clear for life, and compatible with a seat in the Commons. It would have suited me better in every way than the Seals and the House of Lords. It was the prize, to be frank with you, at which I was aiming; and as, at that time, the Duke was making his right-about-face on the Catholic question, and was being supported by our side, I might have accepted it with an appearance of consistency. But I did not accept it. I did not, though my refusal injured myself, and did no one any good. But there, I am chattering.' He broke off, with a smile, and held out his hand. 'However,

Est et fideli tuta silentio
Merces!

'You won't forget that, I am certain. And you may be sure I shall remember you. I am pleased to have made your acquaintance, Mr Vaughan. Decide on the direction, politics or the law, in which you mean to push, and some day let me know. In the meantime follow the light! Light, more light! Don't let them lure you back into old Giant Despair's cave, or choke you with all the dead bones and rottenness and foulness they keep there, and that, by God's help, I'll sweep out of the world before it's a year older!'

And still talking, he saw Vaughan, who was murmuring his acknowledgements, to the door.

When that had closed on the young man, Brougham came back, and, throwing wide his arms, yawned prodigiously.

'Now,' he said, 'if Lansdowne doesn't effect something in that borough, I am mistaken.'

'Why,' Cornelius muttered curtly, 'do you trouble about the borough? Why don't you leave those things to the managers?'

'Why? Why, first because the Duke did that last year, and you see the result – he's out and we're in. Secondly, Corney, because I am like the elephant's trunk, that can tear down a tree or pick up a pin.'

'But in picking up a pin,' the other grunted, 'it picks up a deal of something else.'

'Of what?'

'Dirt!'

'Old Pharisee!' the Chancellor cried.

Mr Cornelius threw down his pen, and, turning in his seat, opened fire on his companion.

'Dirt!' he reiterated sternly. 'And for what? What will be the end of it when you have done all for them, clean and dirty? They'll not keep you. They use you now, but you're a new man. What, you – *you* think to deal on equal terms with the Devonshires and the Hollands, the Lansdownes and the Russells! Who used Burke, and when they had squeezed him tossed him aside? Who used Tierney till they wore him and his fortune out? Who would have used Canning, but he did not trust them, and so they worried him – though they were all dumb dogs before him – to his death. Ay, and presently, when you have served their turn, they will cast you aside.'

'They will not dare!' Brougham cried.

'Pshaw! You are Samson, but you are shorn of your

strength. They have been too clever for you. While you were in the Commons they did not dare. Harry Brougham was their master. So they lured you, poor fool, into the trap, into the Lords, where you may spout, and spout, and spout, and it will have as much effect as the beating of a bird's wings against the bars of its cage.'

'They will not dare!' Brougham reiterated.

'You will see. They will throw you aside.'

Brougham walked up and down the room, his eyes glittering, his quaint, misshapen features working passionately.

'They will throw you aside,' Mr Cornelius repeated, watching him keenly. 'You are a man of the people. You are in earnest. You are honestly in favour of retrenchment, of education, of reform. But to these Whigs – save and except to Althorp, who is that *lusus naturae*, an honest man, and to Johnny Russell, who is a fanatic – these are but catch-words, stalking-horses, the means by which, after the dull old fashion of their fathers and their grandfathers and their great-grandfathers, they think to creep into power. Reform, if reform means the representation of the people by the people, the rule of the people by the people, or by any but the old landed families – why, the very thought would make them sick!'

Brougham stopped in his pacing to and fro. 'You are right,' he said sombrely.

'You acknowledge it?'

'I have known it – here!' And, drawing himself to his full height, he clapped his hand to his breast. 'I have known it here for months. Ay, and though I have sworn to myself that they would not dare to treat me as they treated Burke, and Sheridan, and Tierney, and as they would have treated Canning, I knew it was a lie, my lad; I knew they would. My mother – ay, my old mother, sitting by the chimneyside, out of the world there, knew it, and warned me.'

'Then why did you go into the Lords?' Cornelius asked. 'Why be lured into the gilded cage, where you are helpless?'

'Because, mark you,' Brougham replied sternly, 'if I had not, they had not brought in this Bill. And we had waited, and the people had waited, another twenty years.'

'And so you went into the prison house shorn of your strength?'

Brougham looked at him with a gleam of ferocity in his brilliant eyes.

'Ay,' he said, 'I did. And by that act,' he continued, stretching his long arms to their farthest extent, 'mark you, mark you, never forget it, I avenged all – not only all I may suffer at their hands, but all that every slave who ever ground in their mill has suffered, the slights, the grudged meticulous office, the one finger lent to shake – all, all! I went into the prison house, but when I did so I laid my hands upon the pillars. And their house falls. I hear it – I hear it falling even now about their ears. They may throw me aside. But the house is falling, and the great Whig families – pouf! – they are not in the heaven above, or in the earth beneath, or in the water that is under the earth. You call Reform their stalking-horse? Ay, but it is into their own Troy that they have dragged it; and the clatter of strife you hear is the knell of their power. They have let in the waves of the sea, and dream fondly that they can say where they shall stop and what they shall not touch. They may as well speak to the tide when it flows; they may as well command the North Sea in its rage; they may as well bid Hume be silent, or Wetherell be sane. You say I am spent; and so I may be. I know not. But this I know! Never again will the families say "Go!" and he goeth, and "Do!" and he doeth, as in the old world that is passing – passing this minute, passing with the Bill. No,' he continued, throwing out his arms with passion, 'for when they thought to fool me, and to shut me dumb among dumb things behind the gilded wires, I knew – I knew that I was dragging down their house upon their heads.'

Mr Cornelius stared at him. 'By God!' he said. 'I believe you are right. I believe that you are a cleverer man than I thought you were.'

CHAPTER III

Two Letters

THE HALL was empty when Vaughan came forth into it; and as the young man strode down its echoing length there was nothing save his own footsteps on the pavement to distract his mind from the scene in which he had taken part. He was excited and a little uplifted, as was natural. The promises made, if they were to be counted as promises, were of the vague and indefinite character which it is as easy to evade as to fulfil. But the Chancellor had spoken to him as to an equal, and treated him as one who had but to choose a career to succeed in it, and to win the highest prizes which it could bestow. This was flattering; nor was it, to a young man who had little experience of the world, less flattering to be deemed the owner of a stake in the country, and a person through whom offers of the most confidential and important character might be properly made.

He walked to his rooms in Bury Street with a pleasant warmth at his heart. And at the Academic that evening, where owing to the events of the day there was a fuller house than had ever been known, and a fiercer debate, he championed the Government and upheld the Dissolution in a speech which not only excelled his previous efforts, but was a surprise to those who knew him best. Afterwards he recognized that his peroration had been only a paraphrase of Brougham's impassioned 'Light! More Light!' and that the whole owed more than he cared to remember to the same source. But, after all, why not? It was not to be expected that he should at once rise to the heights of the greatest of living orators. And it was much that he had made a hit; that as he left the room he was followed by all eyes.

Nor did a qualm worthy of the name trouble him until the morning of the 27th, five days later – a Wednesday. Then he found beside his breakfast plate two letters bearing the postmark of Chippinge.

'What's afoot?' he muttered.

But he had a prevision before he broke the seal of the first. And the contents bore out his fears. The letter ran thus:

Stapylton, Chippinge

DEAR SIR, I make no apology for troubling you in a matter in which your interest is second only to mine, and which is also of a character to make apology beside the mark. It has not been necessary to require your presence at Chippinge upon the occasion of former elections. But the unwholesome ferment into which the public mind has been cast by the monstrous proposals of Ministers has nowhere been more strongly exemplified than here, by the fact that, for the first time in half a century, the right of our family to nominate the Members for the Borough is challenged. Since the year 1783 no serious attempt has been made to disturb the Vermuyden interest. And I have yet to learn that – short of this anarchical Bill, which will sweep away all the privileges attaching to property – such an attempt can be made with any chance of success.

I am informed, nevertheless, that Lord Lansdowne, presuming on a small connexion in the Corporation, intends to send at least one candidate to the poll. Our superiority is so great that I should not, even so, trouble you to be present, were it not an object to discourage these attempts by the exhibition of our full strength, and were it not still more important to do so at a time when the existence of the Borough is at stake.

Isaac White will apprise you of the arrangements to be made and will keep you informed of all matters which you should know. Be good enough to let Mapp learn the day and hour of your arrival, and he will see that the carriage and servants meet the coach at Chippenham. Probably you will come by the York House. It is the most convenient.

I have the honour to be
Your sincere kinsman,
ROBERT VERMUYDEN

To Arthur Vermuyden Vaughan, Esquire,
17 Bury Street, St James's

Vaughan's face grew long, and his fork hung suspended above his plate, as he perused the old gentleman's epistle. When all was read he laid it down and whistled.

'Here's a fix!' he muttered. And he thought of his speech at the Academic; and for the first time he was sorry that he had made it. 'Here's a fix!' he repeated. 'What's to be done?'

He was too much disturbed to go on with his breakfast, and he tore open the other letter. It was from Isaac White, his cousin's attorney and agent. It ran thus:

High Street, Chippinge, April 25th, 1831

Chippinge Parliamentary Election

Sir, I have the honour to inform you, as upon former occasions, that the writ in the above is expected and that Tuesday the 3rd day of May will be appointed for the nomination. It has not been needful to trouble you heretofore, but on this occasion I have reason to believe that Sir Robert Vermuyden's candidates will be opposed by nominees in the Bowood Interest, and I have therefore, honoured Sir, to intimate that your attendance will oblige.

The Vermuyden dinner will take place at the White Lion on Monday the 2nd, when the voters and their friends will sit down at 5 PM. The Alderman will preside, and Sir Robert hopes that you will be present. The procession to the Hustings will leave the White Lion at ten on Tuesday the 10th, and a poll, if demanded, will be taken after the usual proceedings.

Any change in the order of the arrangements will be punctually communicated to you.

I have the honour to be, Sir,
Your humble obedient servant,
Isaac White

Arthur V. Vaughan, Esq (late HM's 14th Dragoons),
17 Bury Street, London

Vaughan flung the letter down and resumed his breakfast moodily. It was a piece of shocking ill-fortune, that was all there was to be said.

Not that he really regretted his speech! It had committed him a little more deeply, but morally he had been committed before. It is a poor conscience that is not scrupulous in youth; and he was convinced, or almost convinced, that if he had never seen the Chancellor he would still have found it impossible to support Sir Robert's candidates.

For he was sincere in his support of the Bill; a little because it flattered his intellect to show himself above the prejudices of the class to which he belonged; more, because he was of an age to view with resentment the abuses which the Bill promised to sweep away. A government truly representative of the people, such as this Bill must create, would not tolerate the severities which still disgraced the criminal law. It would not suffer the heartless delays which made the name of Chancery synonymous with ruin. Under it spring-guns and man-traps would no longer scare the owner from his own coverts. The poor would be taught, the slave would be freed. Above all, whole classes of the well-to-do would no longer be deprived of a voice in the State. No longer would the rights of one small class override the rights of all other classes.

He was at an age, in a word, when hope invites to change; and he was for the Bill.

'Ay, by Jove, I am!' he muttered, 'and I'll not be set down! It will be awkward! It will be odious! But I must go through with it!'

Still, he was sorry. He sprang from the class which had profited by the old system – that system under which some eight score men returned a majority of the House of Commons. He had himself the prospect of returning two Members. He could, therefore, enter in a measure – at times in a greater measure than he liked – into the feelings with which the old-fashioned and the interested, the prudent and the timid, viewed a change so great and so radical. But his main objection was personal. He hated the necessity which forced him to cross the wishes and to trample on the prejudices of an old man whom he regarded with respect: a solitary old man, the head of his family, to whom he owed the very vote he must withhold; and who would hardly be brought, even by the logic of facts, to believe that one of his race and breeding could turn against him.

Still, it must be done. The sooner, therefore, it was done, the better. He would go down to Stapylton while his courage was high; and he would tell Sir Robert. Then, whatever came of it, he would have nothing with which to reproach himself. In the heat of resolve he felt very brave and very virtuous; and the moment he rose from breakfast he went to the coach office, and finding that the York House, the fashionable Bath coach, was full for the following day, he booked an outside seat on the Bristol White Lion coach, which also passed through Chippenham. From Chippenham, Chippinge is distant a short nine miles.

That evening proved to be memorable. For the greater part of London was illuminated by the Reformers in honour of the Dissolution; not without rioting and drunkenness, violence on the part of the mob, and rage on the side of the minority. When Vaughan passed through the streets before six next morning, on his way to the White Horse Cellars, traces of the night's work still remained; and where the early sun fell on them, showed grisly and menacing. A moderate Reformer might have blenched at the sight, and questioned – as many did question – whither this was tending. But Vaughan was late, and his coach, one out of three which were waiting to start, was horsed. He had only eyes, as he came up, for the seat he had reserved behind the coachman.

It was empty, and so far his fears were vain. But it annoyed him to find that his next-door neighbour was a young lady travelling alone. She had the seat on the near side.

He climbed up quickly; to reach his place he had to pass before her. The space between the seat and the coachman's box was narrow, and as she rose to allow him to pass she glanced up. Their eyes met; Vaughan raised his hat in mute apology, and took his seat. He said no word. But a miracle had happened, as miracles do happen, when the world is young. In his mind, as he sat down, he was not repeating, 'What a nuisance!' but was saying, 'What eyes! What a face! And, oh Heaven! what beauty! What blush-rose cheeks! What a lovely mouth!'

For 'twas from eyes of liquid blue
A host of quivered Cupids flew,

And now his heart all bleeding lies
Beneath the army of the eyes.

He gazed gravely at the group of watermen and nightbirds who stood in the roadway below, waiting to see the coach start. And apparently he was unmoved. Apparently he was the same Arthur Vermuyden Vaughan who had passed round the boot of the coach to reach the ladder and his place. But he was not the same. His thoughts were no longer querulous, full of the haste he had made, and the breakfast he had to make; but of a pair of gentle eyes that had looked for one instant into his, of a modest face, sweet and shy, of a Quaker-like bonnet that ravished as no other bonnet had ever ravished the most susceptible!

He was still gazing at the group of loiterers, without seeing them, when he became aware that an elderly woman plainly but respectably dressed, who was standing in the roadway, was looking up at him and trying to attract his attention. Seeing that she had caught his eye, she spoke:

'Gentleman! Gentleman!' she said, but in a restrained voice, as if she did not wish to be generally heard. 'The young lady's address! Please say that she's not left it! For the laundress!'

He turned and made sure that there was only one of the sex on the coach. Then – to be honest, not without a tiny flutter at his heart – he addressed his neighbour.

'Pardon me,' he said, 'but there is someone below who wants your address.'

She turned her eyes on him and his heart gave a perceptible jump.

'My address?' she echoed, in a voice as sweet as her face. 'I think that there must be some mistake.' And then for a moment she looked at him as if she doubted his intentions.

The doubt was intolerable. 'It's for the laundress,' he said. 'See, there she is!'

The girl rose to look over the side of the coach, and perforce leant across him. He saw that she had the slenderest waist and the prettiest figure – he had every opportunity of seeing. Then the coach started with a jerk, and if she had not steadied herself by laying her hand on his shoulder, she must have relapsed on his knees. As it was, she fell back into her seat. She blushed.

'I beg your pardon,' she said.

But he was looking back. He had his eye on the woman, who remained in the roadway, pointing after the coach and apparently asking a bystander some question respecting it – perhaps where it stopped.

'There she is!' he exclaimed. 'The woman with the umbrella! She is pointing after us.'

His neighbour looked back, but made nothing of it. 'I know no one in London,' she said, a little primly – but with sweet primness – 'except the lady at whose house I stayed last night. And she is not able to leave the house. It must be a mistake.' And with a gentle reserve which had in it nothing of coquetry, she turned her face from him.

Tantivy! Tantivy! Tantivy! They were away, bowling down the slope of broad empty Piccadilly with the four nags trotting merrily, and the April sun gilding the roofs of the houses, and falling aslant on the verdure of the Green Park. Then merrily up the rise to Hyde Park Corner, where the new Grecian Gates looked across at the equally new arch on Constitution Hill; and where Apsley House, the residence of 'the Duke', hiding with its new coat of Bath stone the old brick walls, peeped through the trees at the statue of Achilles, erected ten years back in the Duke's honour.

But, alas! what was this? Wherefore the crowd that even at this early hour was large enough to fill the roadway and engage the attention of the New Police? Vaughan looked and saw that every blind in Apsley House was lowered, and that more than half of the windows were shuttered. And the little French gentleman who, to the coachman's disgust, had taken the box-seat, saw it too; nay, had seen it before, for he had come that way to the coach office. He pointed to the silent, frowning mansion, and snapped his fingers.

'That is your reward for your Vellington!' he cried, turning in his excitement to the two behind him. 'And his lady, I am told, she lie dead behind the broken vindows! They did that last night, your *canaille*! But he vill not forget! And when the refolution come – bah – he vill have the iron hand! He vill be the Emperor and he vill repay!'

No one answered; they received his outburst with silent British scorn. But they one and all stared back at the scene, at the grim blind house in the early sunshine, and the gaping crowd – as long as it remained in sight. And some, no doubt, pondered on the spectacle. But who, with a pretty face beside him, and before him a long day's drive by mead and shining river, over hill and down, under the walls of grey churches and by many a market-place and cheery inn yard – who would long dwell on charges past or to come? Or fret because in the womb of time might lie that 'refolution' of which the little Frenchman spoke?

CHAPTER IV

Tantivy! Tantivy! Tantivy!

THE WHITE LION coach was a light coach carrying only five passengers outside, and merrily it swept by Kensington Church, whence the travellers had a peep of Holland House – home of the Whigs – on their right. And then in a twinkling they were swinging through Hammersmith, where the ale-houses were opening and lusty girls were beginning to deliver the milk. They passed through Turnham, through Brentford, awakening everywhere the lazy with the music of their horn. They saw Sion House on their left, and on their right had a glimpse of the distant lawns of Osterley – the seat of Lady Jersey, queen of Almack's, and the Holland's rival. Thence they travelled over Hounslow Heath, and by an endless succession of mansions and lawns and orchards, rich at this season with apple blossom, and framing here and there a view of the sparkling Thames.

Vaughan breathed the air of spring, and let his eyes dwell on scene after scene; and he felt that it was good to be young and to sit behind fast horses. He stole a glance at his neighbour, and judged by the brightness of her eyes, her parted lips and rapt expression, that she felt with him. And he would have said something to her, but he could think of nothing worthy of her. At last:

'It's a beautiful morning,' he ventured, and cursed his vapidity.

But she did not seem to find bathos in the words. 'Beautiful!' she answered, with an enthusiasm which showed that she had forgotten her doubts of him. 'And I,' she added simply, 'have not been on a coach since I was a child!'

'Not on a coach?' he cried in amazement.

'No. Except on the Clapham Stage. And that is not a coach like this.'

'No, perhaps it is not,' he said. And he thought of her, and – oh, Lord! – of Clapham! And yet after all there was something about her, about her grey, dove-like dress, and her gentleness, which smacked of Clapham. He wondered who she was and what she was; and he was still wondering when she turned her eyes on him, and, serenely unconscious, sent a tiny shock through him.

'I enjoy it the more,' she said, 'because I – I am not usually free in the morning.'

'Oh yes!'

He could say no more; not another word. It was the stupidest thing in the world, but he was tongue-tied. Seeing, however, that she had turned from him and was absorbed in the view of Windsor rising stately amid the trees, he had the cleverness to steal a glance at the neat basket which nestled at her feet. Surreptitiously he read the name on the label.

MARY SMITH,
Miss Sibson's,
Queen's Square, Bristol

Mary Smith! Just Mary Smith! For the moment – it is not to be denied – he was sobered by the name. It was not a romantic name. It was anything but high-sounding. The author of *Tremayne*, or *De Vere*, nay, the author of *Vivian Grey* – to complete the trio of novels which were in fashion at the time – would have turned up his nose at it. But what did it matter? He desired no more than to make himself agreeable for the few hours which he and this beautiful creature must pass together – in sunshine and with the fair English landscape gliding by them. And, that being so, what need he reck what she called herself or whence she came? It was enough that under her modest bonnet her ears were shells and her eyes pure cornflowers, and that a few pleasant words, a little April dalliance – if only that Frenchman would cease to peep behind him and grin – could harm neither one nor the other.

But opportunities let slip do not always recur. As he turned to address her they rose the ascent of Maidenhead Bridge, had on either hand a peep of the river framed in pale green willows, and halted with sweating horses before the King's Arms. The boots advanced, amid a group of gazers, and reared a ladder against the coach. 'Half an hour for breakfast, gentlemen!' he cried. And through the windows of the inn the travellers had a view of a long table whereat the passengers on the up night-coach were already feasting.

Our friends hastened to descend, but not so fast that Vaughan failed to note the girl's look of uncertainty, almost of distress. He guessed that she was not at ease in a scene so bustling and so new to her. And the thought gave him the courage that he needed.

'Will you allow me to find you a place at the table?' he said. 'I know this inn, and they know me. Guard, the ladder here!' And he took her hand – oh, such a little, little hand! – and aided her in her descent.

'Will you follow me?' he said. And he made way for her through the knot of starers who cumbered the doorway. But once in the coffee-room he had, cunning fellow, an inspiration. 'Find this lady a seat!' he commanded one of the attendant damsels. And when he had seen her seated and coffee set before her, he took himself deliberately to the other end of the room. But whether he did so of pure respect for her feelings, or because he thought – and hugged himself on the thought – that he would be missed, he did not know. Nor was he so much a captive, though he counted how many rolls she ate, and looked a dozen times to see if she looked at him, as to be unable to make an excellent breakfast.

The cheery, noisy throng at the tables, the brisk coming and going of the servants, the smell of hot coffee, the open windows, and the sunshine outside – where the fresh team of the up night-coach were already tossing their impatient heads – he wondered how it all struck her, new to such scenes and to this side of life. And then while he wondered he saw that she had risen from the table and was going out with one of the waiting-maids. To reach the door she had to pass near him; and, oh bliss, her eyes found his – and she blushed. She blushed, ye heavens! He saw it clearly, and he sat thinking about it until, though the coach was not due to start for another five minutes and he might count on the guard summoning him, he was taken with fear lest someone should steal his seat. And he hurried out.

She was alone on the top of the coach, and a youthful waterman, one of the crowd of loiterers below, was making eyes at her to the delight of his companions. When Vaughan came forth, 'I'd like to be him,' the wag said, winking with vulgar gusto. And the bystanders grinned at the good-looking young man who stood in the doorway buttoning up his box-coat. The position might soon have become embarrassing to her, if not to him; but in the nick of time a thing happened. The eye of an inside passenger, who had followed him through the doorway, alighted on a huge placard which hung behind the coach.

'That must be removed!' the stranger cried pompously. And in a moment all eyes were upon him. He prodded with his umbrella at the offending bill. 'Do you hear me? Take it down, sir,' he continued, turning to the guard. He was a portly man, reddish about the gills. 'Take it down, sir, or I will! It is disgraceful! I shall report this conduct to your employers.'

The guard hesitated. 'It don't harm you, sir,' he pleaded, anxious, it was clear, to propitiate a man who would presently be good for half a crown.

'Don't harm me?' the choleric gentleman retorted. 'Don't harm me? What's that to do with it? What right – what right have you, man, to put Party filth like that on a public vehicle in which I pay to ride? "The Bill, the whole Bill, and nothing but the Bill!" Damn the Bill, sir!' with violence. 'Take it down! Take it down at once!' he repeated, as if his order closed the matter.

The guard frowned at the placard, which bore, largely

printed, the legend which the gentleman found so little to his taste. He rubbed his head. 'Well, I don't know, sir,' he said. And then – the crowd about the coach was growing – he looked at the coachman. 'What do you say, Sammy?' he asked.

'Let it be,' growled the coachman, without deigning to turn his head.

'You see, sir, it is this way,' the guard ventured civilly. 'Mr Palmer has a Whig meeting at Reading today. The town will be full. And if we don't want rotten eggs and broken windows – we'll carry that!'

'I'll not travel with it!' the stout gentleman answered positively. 'Do you hear me, man? If you don't take it down I will!'

'Best not!' cried a voice from the little crowd about the coach. And when the angry gentleman turned to see who spoke, 'Best not!' cried another behind him. And he wheeled about again, so quickly that the crowd laughed. This raised his wrath to a white heat.

He grew purple. 'I shall have it taken down!' he said. 'Guard, remove it!'

'Don't touch it,' growled the coachman – one of a class noted in that day for independence and surly manners. 'If the gent don't choose to travel with it, let him stop here and be damned!'

'Do you know,' the insulted passenger cried, 'that I am a Member of Parliament?'

'I'm hanged if you are!' coachee retorted. 'Nor won't be again!'

The crowd roared at the repartee. The guard was in despair. 'Anyway, we must go on, sir,' he said. And he seized his horn. 'Take your seats, gents! Take your seats!' he cried. 'All for Reading! I'm sorry, sir, but I've to think of the coach.'

'And the horses!' grumbled the coachman. 'Where's the gent's sense?'

They all scrambled to their seats except the ex-Member. He stood, bursting with rage and chagrin. But at the last moment, when he saw that the coach would really go without him, he swallowed his pride, plucked open the coach door, and amid the loud jeers of the crowd, climbed in. The coachman, with a chuckle, bade the helpers let go, and the coach swung cheerily away through the streets of Maidenhead, the merry notes of the horn and the rattle of the pole-chains drowning the huzzas of the gutter-boys.

The little Frenchman turned round. 'You will have a refolution,' he said solemnly. 'And the gentleman inside he vill lose his head.'

The coachman, who had hitherto looked askance at Froggy, as if he disdained his neighbourhood, now squinted at him; he could not quite make him out.

'Think so?' he said gruffly. 'Why, Mounseer?'

'I have no doubt,' the Frenchman answered glibly. 'The people will have, and the nobles, they vill not give! Or they vill give a leetle – a leetle! And that is the worst of all. I have seen two refolutions!' he continued with energy. 'The first when I was a child – it is forty years! My *bonne* held me up and I saw heads fall into the basket – heads as young and as lofly as the young Mees there! And why? Because the people would have, and the King, he give that which is worst of all – a leetle! And the trouble began. And then the refolution of last year – it was worth to me all that I had! The people would have, and the Polignac, our Minister – who is the friend of your Vellington – he would not give at all! And the trouble began.'

The coachman squinted at him anew. 'D'you mean to say,' he asked, 'that you've seen heads cut off?'

'I have seen the white necks, as white and as small as the Mees there; I have seen the blood spout from them, bah! like what you call pump! Ah, it was ogly, it was very ogly!'

The coachman turned his head slowly, until he commanded a full view of Vaughan's pretty neighbour; at whom he gazed for some seconds as if fascinated. Then he turned to his horses and relieved his feelings by hitting one of the wheelers below the trace; while Vaughan, willing to hear what the Frenchman had to say, took up the talk.

'Perhaps here,' he said, 'those who have will give, and give enough, and all will go well.'

'Nefer! Nefer!' the Frenchman answered positively. 'By example, the Duke whose *château* we pass – what you call it – Jerusalem House?'

'Sion House,' Vaughan answered smiling. 'The Duke of Northumberland.'

'By example he return four Members to your Commons House. Is it not so? And they do what he tell them. He have this for his nefew, and that for his niece, and the other thing for his *maître d'hôtel*! And it is he and the others like him who rule the country! Gives he up all that? To the *bourgeoisie*? Nefer! Nefer!' he continued with emphasis. 'He will be the Polignac! They will all be the Polignacs! And you will have a refolution. And by-and-by, when the *bourgeoisie* is frightened of the *canaille* and tired of the blood-letting, your Vellington he will be the Emperor. It is as plain as the two eyes in the face! So plain for me, I shall not take off my clothes the nights!'

'Well, King Billy for me!' said the coachman. 'But if he's willing, Mounseer, why shouldn't the people manage their own affairs?'

'The people! The people! They cannot! Your horses, will they govern themselves? Will you throw down the reins and leave it to them, up hill, down hill? The people govern themselves? Bah!' And to express his extreme disgust at the proposition, the Frenchman, who had lost his all with Polignac, bent over the side and spat into the road. 'It is no government at all!'

The coachman looked darkly at his horses as if he would like to see them try it on.

'I am afraid,' said Vaughan, 'that you think we are in trouble either way then? Whether the Tories give or withhold?'

'Eizer way! Eizer way!' the Frenchman answered *con amore*. 'It is fate! You are on the edge of the – what you call it – *chute*! And you must go over! We have gone over. We have bumped once, twice! We shall bump once, twice more, *et voilà* – Anarchy! Now it is your turn, sir. The government has to be – shifted – from the one class to the other!'

'But it may be peacefully shifted?'

The little Frenchman shrugged his shoulders impatiently. 'I have nefer seen the government shifted without all that that I have told you. There will be the guillotine, or the barricades. For me, I shall not take off my clothes the nights!'

He spoke with a sincerity so real and a persuasion so clear that even Vaughan was a little shaken, and wondered if those who watched the game from the outside saw more than the players. As for the coachman,

'Dang me,' he said that evening to his cronies in the tap of the White Lion at Bristol, 'if I feel so sure about this here Reform! We want none of that nasty neck-cutting here! And if I thought Froggy was right I'm blest if I wouldn't turn Tory!'

And for certain the Frenchman voiced what the timid and the well-to-do were thinking. For something like a hundred and fifty years a small class, the nobility and the greater gentry, making their advantage of the growing defects in the representation – the rotten boroughs and the close corporations – had ruled the country through the House of Commons. Was it to be expected that the basis of power could be quietly shifted? Or that all these boroughs and corporations, in which the governing class were so deeply interested, could be swept away without a convulsion; without opening the floodgates of change, and admitting forces which no man could measure? On the other side, was it likely that, these defects once seen and the appetite of the middle class for power once whetted, the claims of the people could be refused without a struggle from which the boldest must flinch? No man could say for certain, and hence these fears in the air. The very winds carried them. They were being discussed in that month of April not only on the White Lion coach, not on the Bath road only, but on a hundred coaches, and a hundred roads over the length and breadth of England. Wherever the sway of Macadam and Telford extended, wherever the gigs of 'riders' met, or farmers' carts stayed to parley, at fair and market, sessions and church, men shook their heads or raised their voices in high debate; and the word *Reform* rolled down the wind!

Vaughan soon overcame his qualms; for his opinions were fixed. But he thought that the subject might serve him with his neighbour, and he addressed her. 'You must not let them alarm you,' he said. 'We are still a long way from guillotines or barricades.'

'I hope so,' she answered. 'In any case I am not afraid.'

'Why, if I may ask?'

She glanced at him with a gleam of humour in her eyes. 'Little shrubs feel little wind,' she murmured.

'But also little sun, I fear,' he replied.

'That does not follow,' she said, without raising her eyes again. 'Though it is true that I – I am so seldom free in a morning that a journey such as this, in the sunshine, is like heaven to me.'

'The morning is a delightful time,' he said.

'Oh!' she cried, as if she now knew that he felt with her. 'That is it! The afternoon is different.'

'Well, fortunately, you and I have – much of the morning left.'

She made no reply to that, and he wondered in silence what was the employment which filled her mornings and fitted her to enjoy with so keen a zest this early ride. The Gloucester up-coach was coming to meet them, the guard tootling merrily on his horn, and a blue and yellow flag – the Whig colours – flying on the roof of the coach, which was crowded with smiling passengers. Vaughan saw the girl's eyes sparkle as the two coaches passed amid a volley of badinage; and demure as she was, he was sure that she had a store of fun within. He wished that she would remove her cheap thread gloves, that he might see if her hands were as white as they were small. She was no common person, he was sure of that; her speech was correct though formal, and her manner was quiet and refined. And her eyes – he must make her look at him again!

'You are going to Bristol?' he said. 'To stay there?'

Perhaps he threw too much feeling into his voice. At any rate the tone in which she answered, 'Yes, I am,' was colder.

'I am going as far as Chippenham,' he volunteered.

'Indeed!'

There! He had lost all the ground he had gained. She thought him a libertine, who aimed at putting himself on a footing of intimacy with her. And that was the last thing – confound it, he meant that to do her harm was the last thing he had in his mind.

It annoyed him extremely that she should think a thing of that kind. And he cudgelled his brains for a subject at once safe and sympathetic, without finding one. But either she was not so deeply offended as he fancied, or she thought him sufficiently punished. For presently she addressed him; and he saw that she was ever so little embarrassed.

'Would you please to tell me,' she said, in a low voice, 'how much I ought to give the coachman?'

Oh, bless her! She did not think him a horrid libertine. 'You?' he said audaciously. 'Why, nothing, of course.'

'But – but I thought it was usual?'

'Not on this road,' he answered, lying resolutely. 'Gentlemen are expected to give half a crown, others a shilling. Ladies nothing at all. Sam,' he continued, rising to giddy heights of invention, 'would give it back to you, if you offered it.'

'Indeed!' He fancied a note of relief in her tone, and judged that shillings were not very plentiful. Then, 'Thank you,' she added. 'You must think me very ignorant. But I have never travelled.'

'You must not say that,' he returned. 'Remember the Clapham Stage!'

She laughed at the jest, small as it was; and her laugh gave him the most delicious feeling – a sort of lightness within, half exhilaration, half excitement. And of a sudden, emboldened by it, he was grown so foolhardy that there is no knowing what he might not have said, if the streets of Reading had not begun to open before them, and give warning of what was to come.

For Mr Palmer's procession, with its carriages, riders, and flags, was entering ahead of them; and the train of tipsy rabble that accompanied it blocked King Street, and soon brought the coach to a stand. The candidate, lifting his cocked hat from time to time, rode a hundred paces before them, barely visible through a forest of flags and banners. But a troop of mounted gentry in dusty black, and of smiling dames in carriages – who hardly masked the disgust with which they viewed the grimy hands extended to them to shake – were under the travellers' eyes, and showed in the sunlight both tawdry and false. Our party, however, were not long at ease to enjoy the spectacle. The crowd surrounded the coach, leapt on the steps, and hung on to the boot. And presently the noise scared the horses, which at the entrance to the market-place began to plunge.

'The Bill! The Bill!' cried the rabble. And with truculence called on the passengers to assent. 'You lubbers,' they bawled, 'shout for the Bill. Or we'll have you over!'

'All right! All right!' replied Sammy, controlling his horses as well as he could. 'We're all for the Bill here! Hurrah!'

'Hurrah! Palmer for ever, Tories in the river!' cried the mob. 'Hurrah!'

'Hurrah!' echoed the guard, willing to echo anything. 'The Bill for ever! But let us pass, lads! Let us pass! We're for the Bear, and we've no votes.'

'Britons never will be slaves!' shrieked a drunken butcher as the market-place opened before them. The space was alive with streamers and gay with cockades, and thronged by a multitude, through which the candidate's procession clove its way slowly. 'We'll have votes now! Three cheers for Lord John!'

'Hurrah! Hurrah!'

'And down with Orange Peel!' squeaked a small tailor in a high falsetto.

The roar of laughter which greeted the sally startled the horses afresh. But the guard had dropped down by this time and fought his way to the head of one of the leaders, and two or three good-humoured fellows seconded his efforts. Between them the coach was piloted slowly but safely through the press; which, to do it justice, meant only to exercise the privileges which the election season brought with it.

CHAPTER V

Rosy-fingered Dawn

'Beaucoup de bruit, pas de mal!' Vaughan muttered in his neighbour's ear, and saw with as much surprise as pleasure that she understood.

And all would have gone well but for the imprudence of

the inside passenger who had distinguished himself by his protest against the placard. The coach was within a dozen paces of the Bear, the crowd was falling back from it, the peril, if it had been real, seemed past, the most timid was breathing again, when he thrust out his foolish head, and flung a taunt at the rabble.

Those on the roof could not hear the words, but their effect was disastrous. A bystander caught them up and repeated them, and in a trice half a dozen louts flung themselves on the door, and strove to drag it open, and get at the man; while others, leaning over their shoulders, aimed missiles at the inside passengers.

The guard saw that more than the glass of his windows was at stake; but he could do nothing. He was at the leaders' heads. The passengers on the roof, who had risen to their feet to see the fray, were as helpless. Luckily the coachman kept his head and his reins.

'Turn 'em into the yard!' he yelled. 'Turn 'em in!'

The guard did so, almost too quickly. The frightened horses wheeled round, and, faster than was prudent, dashed under the low arch, dragging the swaying coach after them.

There was a cry of, 'Heads! Heads!' And then, more imperatively, 'Heads! Stoop!'

The warning was needed. The outsiders were on their feet, engrossed in the struggle at the coach door. And so quickly had the coach turned that, though a score of spectators in the street and on the balcony of the inn saw the peril, it was only at the last moment that Vaughan and the two passengers at the back, men used to the road, caught the warning, and dropped down. And it was only at the very last moment that Vaughan felt rather than saw that the girl was still standing. He had just time, by a desperate effort, and amid a cry of horror – for to the spectators she seemed to be already jammed between the arch and the seat – to drag her down. Instinctively he shielded her face with his arm; but the horror was so near that, as they swept under the low brow, he was not sure that she was safe.

He was as white as she was, when they emerged into the light again. But he saw that she was safe, though her bonnet was dragged from her head; and he cried unconsciously,

'Thank God! Thank God!' Then, with that hatred of a scene which is part of the English character, he put her quickly back into her seat, and rose to his feet, as if he wished to separate himself from her.

But a score of eyes had seen the act; and however much he might wish to spare her feelings, concealment was impossible.

'Christ!' cried the coachman, whose copper cheeks were perceptibly paler. 'If your head's on your shoulders, Miss, it is to that young gentleman you owe it. Don't you ever go to sleep on the roof of a coach again! Never! Never!'

'Here, get a drop of brandy!' cried the landlady, who, from one of the doors flanking the archway, had seen all. 'Do you stay where you are, Miss,' she continued, 'and I'll send it up to you.'

On which, amid a babel of exclamations and a chorus of blame and praise, the ladder was brought, and Vaughan made haste to descend. A waiter tripped out with the brown brandy and water on a tray; and the young lady, who had not spoken, but had remained, sitting white and still, where Vaughan had placed her, sipped it obediently. Unfortunately the landlady's eyes were sharp; and as Vaughan passed her to go into the house – for the coach must be driven up the yard and turned before they could set off again – she let fall a cry.

'Lord, sir!' she said, 'your hand is torn dreadful! You've grazed every bit of skin off it!'

He tried to silence her; and failing, hurried into the house. She fussed after him to attend to him; and Sammy, who was not a man of the most delicate perceptions, seized the opportunity to drive home his former lesson.

'There, Miss,' he said solemnly, 'I hope that'll teach you to look out another time! But better his hand than your head. You'd ha' been surely scalped!'

The girl, a shade whiter than before, did not answer. He thought her, for so pretty a wench, 'a right unfeelin' un!'

Not so the Frenchman. 'I count him a very locky man!' he said obscurely. 'A very locky man.'

'Well,' the coachman answered with a grunt, 'if you call that lucky—'

'*Vraiment! Vraiment!* But I – alas!' the Frenchman

answered with an eloquent gesture, 'I have lost my all, and the good fortunes are no longer for me!'

'Fortunes!' the coachman muttered, looking askance at him. 'A fine fortune, to have your hand flayed! But where's' – recollecting himself – 'where's that fool that caused the trouble? Damn me, if he shall go any farther on my coach! I'd like to double-thong him, and it'd serve him right!'

So when the ex-MP presently appeared, Sammy let go his tongue with such vigour that the political gentleman, finding himself in a minority of one, retired into the house and, with many threats of what he would do when he saw the management, declined to go on.

'And a good riddance of a damned Tory!' the coachman muttered. 'Think all the world's made for them! Fifteen minutes he's cost us already! Take your seats, gents, take your seats! I'm off!'

Vaughan, with his hand bandaged, was the last to come out. He climbed as quickly as he could to his place, and, without looking at his neighbour, he said some ordinary word. She did not reply, and they swept under the arch. For a moment the sight of the thronged market-place diverted him. Then he looked at her, and he saw that she was trembling.

If he was not quite so wise as the Frenchman, having had no *bonnes fortunes* to speak of, he had, nevertheless, keen perceptions. And he guessed that the girl, between her maiden constraint and her womanly gratitude, was painfully placed. It could not be otherwise. A girl who had spent her years, since childhood, within the walls of a school at Clapham, first as genteel apprentice, and then as assistant; who had been taught to consider young men as roaring lions with whom her own life could have nothing in common, and from whom it was her duty to guard the more giddy of her flock; who had to struggle at once with the shyness of youth, the modesty of her sex, and her inexperience – above all, perhaps, with that dread of insult which becomes the instinct of lowly beauty – how was she to carry herself in circumstances so different from any which she had ever imagined? How was she to express a tithe of the feelings with which her heart was bursting, and which overwhelmed her as often as she thought of the hideous death from which he had snatched her?

She could not; and with inborn good taste she refrained from the commonplace word, the bald acknowledgement, in which a shallow nature might have taken refuge. For him, he guessed some part of this, and discerned that if he would relieve her he must speak himself. Accordingly, when they had left the streets behind them and were swinging merrily along the Newbury Road, he leant towards her.

'May I beg,' he said in a low voice, 'that you won't think of what has happened? The coachman would have done as much, and scolded you! I happened to be next you. That was all.'

In a strangled voice, 'But your hand,' she faltered. 'I fear–I—' She shuddered, unable to go on.

'It is nothing!' he protested. 'Nothing! In three days it will be well!'

She turned her eyes on him, eyes which possessed an eloquence of which their owner was unconscious.

'I will pray for you,' she murmured. 'I can do no more.'

The pathos of her simple gratitude was such that Vaughan could not laugh it off.

'Thank you,' he said quietly. 'We shall then be more than quits.' And having given her a few moments in which to recover herself, 'We are nearly at Speenhamland,' he resumed cheerfully. 'There is the George and Pelican, a great baiting-house for coaches. I am afraid to say how much corn and hay they give out in a day. They have a man who does nothing but weigh it out.' And so he chattered on, doing his utmost to talk of indifferent matters in an indifferent tone.

She could not repulse him after what had passed. And now and then, by a timid word, she gave him leave to talk. Presently he began to speak of things other than those under their eyes, and when he thought that he had put her at her ease.

'You understand French?' he said, looking at her suddenly.

'I spoke it as a child,' she answered. 'I was born abroad. I did not come to England until I was nine.'

'To Clapham?'

'Yes. I have been employed in a school there.'

Prudently he hastened to bring the talk back to the road again. And she took courage to steal a look at him when his eyes were elsewhere. He seemed so strong and gentle and courteous; this unknown creature which she had been taught to fear. And he was so thoughtful of her! He could throw so tender a note into his voice. Beside d'Orsay or Alvanley – but she had never heard of them – he might have passed muster but tolerably; but to her he seemed a very fine gentleman. She had a woman's eye for the fineness of his linen, and the smartness of his waistcoat – had not Sir James Graham, with his chest of Palermo stuffs, set the seal of Cabinet approval on fancy waistcoats? Nor was she blind to the easy carriage of his head, and his air of command.

And there she caught herself up, reflecting with a blush that it was by the easy path of thoughts such as these that the precipice was approached; that so it was the poor and pretty let themselves be led from the right road. Whither was she travelling? In what was this to end? She trembled. And if they had not at that moment swung out of Savernake Forest and sighted the red roofs of Marlborough, lying warm and snug at the foot of the steep London Hill, she did not know what she should have done, since she could not repulse him.

They rattled in merry style through the town, the leaders cantering, the bars swinging, the guard tootling, the sun shining; past a score of inn signs before which the heavy stages were baiting; past the two churches, while all the brisk pleasantness of this new, this living world, appealed to her to go its way. Ta-ra-ra! Ta-ra-ra! Swerving to the right they pulled up bravely, with steaming horses, before the door of the far-famed Castle Inn. Ta-ra-ra! Ta-ra-ra!

'Half an hour for dinner, gentlemen!'

'Now,' said Vaughan, thinking that all was well, or rather declining to think of anything but her shy glances and the delightful present, 'you must cut my meat for me!'

She did not reply, and he saw that her eyes went to the basket at her feet. He guessed that she wished to avoid the expense of dining.

'Or perhaps you are not coming in?' he said.

'I did not intend to do so,' she replied. 'I suppose,' she continued timidly, 'that I may stay here?'

'Certainly. You have something with you?'

'Yes.'

He nodded pleasantly and left her; and she remained in her seat. As she ate, the target for many a sly glance of admiration, she was divided between gratitude and self-reproach; now thinking of him with a quickened heart, now taking herself to task for her weakness.The result was that when he strode out, confident and at ease, and looked up at her with laughing eyes, she blushed furiously – to her own unspeakable mortification.

Vaughan was no Lothario, and for a moment the tell-tale colour took him aback. Then he told himself that at Chippenham, less than twenty miles down the road, he must leave her. It was absurd to suppose that, in the short space which remained, either could be harmed. So he mounted gaily, and masking his knowledge of her emotion with a skill which surprised himself, he chatted pleasantly, unaware that with every word he was stamping the impression of her face, her long eyelashes, her graceful head, her trick of this and that, more deeply upon his memory. While she, reassured by the same thought that they would part in an hour – and in an hour what harm could happen? – closed her eyes and drank the sweet draught, the sweeter for its novelty, and for the bitter which lurked at the bottom of the cup. Meantime Sammy winked sagely at his horses, and the Frenchman cast envious glances over his shoulder, and Silbury Hill, Fyfield, and the soft folds of the downs swept by, and on warm commons the early bees hummed above the gorse.

Here was Chippenham at last; and the end was come. He must descend. A hasty touch, a murmured word, a pang half-felt; she veiled her eyes. If her colour fluttered, and she trembled, why not? She had cause to be grateful to him. And if he felt, as his foot touched the ground, that the world was cold, and the prospect cheerless, why not, when he had to face Sir Robert, and when his political embarrassments, forgotten for a time, rose nearer and larger?

It had often fallen to him to alight at the Angel at Chippenham. From boyhood he had known the wide street, in which the fairs were held, the solid Georgian houses, and the stone bridge of many arches over the Avon. But he had never seen these things, he had never alighted there, with less satisfaction than on this day.

Still this was the end. He raised his hat, saluted silently, and turned to speak to the guard. In the act he jostled a person who was approaching to accost him. Vaughan stared.

'Hallo, White!' he said, 'I was coming to see you.'

White's hat was in his hand. 'Your servant, sir,' he said. 'Your servant, sir. I am glad to be here to meet you, Mr Vaughan.'

'But you didn't expect me?'

'No, sir, no. I came to meet Mr Cooke, who was to arrive by this coach. But I do not see him.'

A light broke in upon Vaughan. 'Gad! he must be the man we left behind at Reading,' he said. 'Is he a peppery chap?'

'He might be so called, sir,' the agent answered with a smile. 'I fancied that you knew him.'

'No. Serjeant Wathen I know; not Mr Cooke. Anyway, he's not come, White.'

'All the better, sir, if I can get a message to him by the up-coach. For he's not needed. I am glad to say that the trouble is over. My lord Lansdowne has given up the idea of contesting the borough, and I came to tell Mr Cooke, thinking that he might prefer to go on to Bristol. He has a house in Bristol.'

'Do you mean,' Vaughan said, 'that there will be no contest?'

'No, sir, no. Not now. And a good thing, too. Upset the town for nothing! My lord has no chance, and Pybus, who is his lordship's man here, told me himself—'

He paused with his mouth open, and his eyes on a tall lady wearing a veil, who, after standing a couple of minutes on the farther side of the street, was approaching the coach. To enter it she had to pass by him, and he stared, as if he saw a ghost. 'By Gosh!' he muttered under his breath. And when, with the aid of the guard, she had taken her seat inside, 'By Gosh!' he muttered again, 'if that's not my lady – though I've not seen her for ten years – I've the horrors!'

He turned to Vaughan to see if he had noticed anything. But Vaughan, without waiting for the end of his sentence, had stepped aside to tell a helper to replace his valise on the coach. In the bustle he had noted neither White's emotion nor the lady.

At this moment he returned. 'I shall go on to Bristol for the night, White,' he said. 'Sir Robert is quite well?'

'Quite well, sir, and I shall be happy to tell him of your promptness in coming.'

'Don't tell him anything,' the young man said, with a flash of peremptoriness. 'I don't want to be kept here. Do you understand, White? I shall probably return to town tomorrow. Anyway, say nothing.'

'Very good, sir,' White answered. 'But I am sure Sir Robert would be pleased to know that you had come down so promptly.'

'Ah, well, you can let him know later. Goodbye, White.'

The agent with one eye on the young squire and one on the lady whose figure was visible through the small coach window, seemed to be about to refer to her. But he checked himself.

'Goodbye, sir,' he said. 'And a pleasant journey! I'm glad to have been of service, Mr Vaughan.'

'Thank you, White, thank you,' the young man answered. And he swung himself up, as the coach moved. A good-natured nod, and Tantivy! Tantivy! Tantivy! The helpers sprang aside, and away they went down the hill, and over the long stone bridge, and so along the Bristol road; but now with the shades of evening beginning to spread on the pastures about them, and the cawing rooks, that had been abroad all day on the uplands, streaming across the pale sky to the elms beside the river.

But *varium et mutabile femina.* When he turned, eager to take up the fallen thread, Clotho could not have been more cold than his neighbour, nor Atropos with her shears more decisive.

'I've had good news,' he said as he settled his coat about him. 'I came down with a very unpleasant task before me. And it is lifted from me.'

'Indeed!'

'So I am going on to Bristol instead of staying at Chippenham.'

No answer.

'It is a great relief to me,' he continued cheerfully.

'Indeed!' She spoke in the distant of voices.

He raised his eyebrows in perplexity. What had happened

to her? She had been so grateful, so much moved, a few minutes before. The colour had fluttered in her cheek, the tear had been visible in her eyes, she had left her hand the fifth of a second in his. And now!

Now she was determined that she would blush and smile and be kind no more. She was grateful – God knew she was grateful, let him think what he would. But there were limits. Her weakness, as long as she believed that Chippenham must part them, had been pardonable. But if he had it in his mind to attend her to Bristol, to follow her or haunt her – as she had known foolish young cits at Clapham to haunt the more giddy of her flock – then her mistake was clear; and his conduct, now merely suspicious, would appear in its black reality. She hoped that he was innocent. She hoped that his change of plan at Chippenham had been no subterfuge; that he was not a roaring lion. But appearances were deceitful and her own course was plain.

It was the plainer, as she had not been blind to the respect with which all at the Angel had greeted her companion: even White, a man of substance, with a gold chain and seal hanging from his fob, had stood bareheaded while he talked to him. It was plain that he was a fine gentleman; one of those whom young persons in her rank of life must shun.

So he drew scarcely five words out of her in as many miles. At last, thrice rebuffed, 'I am afraid you are tired,' he said. Was it for this that he had chosen to go on to Bristol?

'Yes,' she answered. 'I am rather tired. If you please I would prefer not to talk.'

He was a little huffed then, and let her be; nor did he guess, though he was full of conjectures about her, how she hated her seeming ingratitude. But there was nought else for it; better seem thankless now than be worse hereafter. For she was growing frightened. She was beginning to have more than an inkling of the road by which young things were led to be foolish. Her ear retained the sound of his voice though he was silent. The fashion in which he had stooped to her – though he was looking another way now – clung to her memory. His laugh, though he was grave now, rang for her, full of glee and good-fellowship. She could have burst into tears.

They stayed at Marshfield to take on the last team. And she tried to divert her mind by watching a woman in a veil who walked up and down beside the coach, and seemed to return her curiosity. But she tried to little purpose, for she felt strained and weary, and more than ever inclined to cry. Doubtless the peril through which she had passed had shaken her.

So that she was thankful when, after descending perilous Tog Hill, they saw from Kingswood heights the lights of Bristol shining through the dusk; and she knew that she was at her journey's end. To arrive in a strange place on the edge of night is trying to anyone. But to alight friendless and alone, amid the bustle of a city, and to know that new relations must be created and a new life built up – this may well raise in the most humble and contented bosom a feeling of loneliness and depression. And doubtless that was why Mary Smith, after evading Vaughan with a success beyond her hopes, felt as she followed her modest trunk through the streets that – but she bent her head to hide the unaccustomed tears.

CHAPTER VI

The Patron of Chippinge

MUCH ABOUT the time when the *Spectator* was painting in Sir Roger the most lovable picture of an old English squire which our gallery contains, Cornelius Vermuyden, of a younger branch of the Vermuydens who drained the fens, was making a fortune in the Jamaica trade. Having made it in a dark office in Bristol, and being, like all Dutchmen, of a sedentary turn, he proceeded to found a family, purchase a borough, and, by steady support of Whig principles and the Protestant succession, to earn a baronetcy in the neighbouring county of Wilts.

Doubtless the first Vermuyden had things to contend with, and at assize ball and sessions got but two fingers from the De

Coverleys and their long-descenced dames. But he went his way stolidly, married his son into a family of like origin – the Beckfords – and, having seen little George II firmly on the throne, made way for his son.

This second Sir Cornelius rebuilt Stapylton, the house which his father had bought from the decayed family of that name, and after living for some ten years into the reign of Farmer George, vanished in his turn, leaving Cornelius Robert to succeed him, Cornelius George, the elder son, having died in his father's lifetime.

Sir Cornelius Robert was something after the pattern of the famous Mr Onslow –

What can Tommy Onslow do?
He can drive a chaise and two.
What can Tommy Onslow more?
He can drive a chaise and four.

Yet he fitted the time, and, improving his father's pack of trencher-fed hounds by a strain of Mr Warde's blood, he hunted the country so conscientiously that at his death a Dutch bottle might have been set upon his table without giving rise to the slightest reflection. He came to an end, much lamented, with the century, and Sir Robert, fourth and present baronet, took over the estates.

By that time, rid of the foreign prenomen, well allied by three good marriages, and since the American War of true blue Tory leanings and thorough Church and King principles, the family was able to hold up its head among the best in the South of England. There might be some who still remembered that –

Saltash was a borough town
When Plymouth was a breezy down.

But the property was good, the borough safe, and any time these twenty years their owner night have franked his letters 'Chippinge' had he willed it. As it was, he passed, almost as much as Mr Western in the East or Sir Thomas Acland in the

West, for the type of a country gentleman. The most powerful Minister gave him his whole hand; and at county meetings, at Salisbury or Devizes, no voice was held more powerful, nor any man's hint more quickly taken, than Sir Robert Vermuyden's.

He was a tall and very thin man, of almost noble aspect, with a nose after the fashion of the Duke's, and a slight stoop. In early days he had been something of a beau, though never of the Prince's following, and he still dressed finely and with taste. With a smaller sense of personal dignity, or with wider sympathies, he might have been a happier man. But he had married too late – at forty-five; and the four years which had followed, and their sequel, had darkened the rest of his life, drawn crow's-feet about his eyes and peevish lines about his mouth. Henceforth he had lived alone, nursing his pride; and the solitude of this life – which was not without its dignity, since no word of scandal touched it – had left him narrow and vindictive, a man just but not over-generous, and pompous without complacency.

The neighbourhood knew that he and Lady Sybil – he had married the beautiful daughter of the last Earl of Portrush – had parted under circumstances which came near to justifying divorce. Some held that he had divorced her; but in those days an Act of Parliament was necessary, and no such Act stood on the Statute Book. Many thought that he ought to have divorced her. And while the people who knew that she still lived and still plagued him were numerous, few save Isaac White were aware that it was because his marriage had been made and marred at Bowood – and not purely out of principle – that Sir Robert opposed the very name of Lansdowne, and would have wasted a half of his fortune to wreck his great neighbour's political power.

Not that his Tory principles were not strong. During five Parliaments he had filled one of his own seats, and had spoken from time to time after a dignified fashion, with formal gestures and a copious sprinkling of classical allusions. The Liberal Toryism of Canning had fallen below his ideal, but he had continued to sit until the betrayal of the Party by Peel and the Duke – on the Catholic Claims – drove him from the House in disgust, and thenceforth Warren's Hotel, his residence when in town, saw him but seldom. He had fancied then that nothing worse could happen; that the depths were plumbed, and that he and those who thought with him might punish the traitor and take no harm. With the Duke of Cumberland, the best-hated man in England – which was never tired of ridiculing his moustachios – with Eldon, Wetherell, and the ultra-Tories, he had not rested until he had seen the hated pair flung from office; nor was any man more surprised and confounded when the result of the move began to show itself. The Whigs, admitted to power by this factious movement, and after an exile so long that Byron could write of them –

Naught's permanent among the human race
Except the Whigs not *getting into place*

– brought in no mild and harmless measure of reform, promising little and giving nothing, such as foe and friend had alike expected; but a measure so radical that O'Connell blessed it and Cobbett might have fathered it: a measure which, if it passed, would sweep away Sir Robert's power and the power of his class, destroy his borough, and relegate him to the common order of country squires.

He was at first incredulous, then furious, then aghast. To him the Bill was not only the doom of his own influence but the knell of the Constitution. Behind it he saw red revolution and the crash of things. Lord Grey was to him Mirabeau, Lord John was Lafayette, Brougham was Danton; and of them and of their kind, when they had roused the many-headed, he was sure that the end would be as the end of the Gironde.

He was not the less furious, not the less aghast, when the moderates of his Party pointed out that he had himself to thank for the catastrophe. From the refusal to grant the smallest reform, from the refusal to transfer the franchise of the rotten borough of Retford to the unrepresented city of Birmingham – a refusal which he had urged his Members to support – the chain was complete; for in consequence of that refusal Mr Huskisson had left the Duke's Cabinet. The appointment of Mr Fitzgerald to fill Huskisson's seat had rendered the Clare election necessary. O'Connell's victory at the Clare election had converted Peel and the Duke to the necessity of granting the Catholic Claims. That conversion had alienated the ultra-Tories, and among these Sir Robert. The opposition of the ultra-Tories had expelled Peel and the Duke from power – which had brought in the Whigs – who had brought in the Reform Bill.

Hinc illae lacrimae! For, in place of the transfer of the franchise of one rotten borough to one large city – a reform which to the most bigoted seemed absurdly reasonable now – here were sixty boroughs to be swept away, and nearly fifty more to be shorn of half their strength, a Constitution to be altered, an aristocracy to be dethroned!

And Calne, Lord Lansdowne's pocket borough, was spared!

Sir Robert firmly believed that the limit had been fixed with an eye to Calne. They who framed the Bill, sitting in wicked, detestable confabulation, had fixed the limit of Schedule B so as to spare Calne and Tavistock – *Arcades ambo*, Whig boroughs both. Or why did they just escape? In the whole matter it was this which troubled him most sorely. For the loss of his own borough – if the worst came to the worst – he could put up with it. He had no children, he had no one to come after him except Arthur Vaughan, the great-grandson of his grandmother. But the escape of Calne, this clear proof of the hypocrisy of the righteous Grey, the blatant Durham, the whey-faced Lord John, the demagogue Brougham – this injustice kept him in a state of continual irritation.

He was thinking of this as he paced up and down the broad walk beside the Garden Pool at Stapylton – a solitary figure dwarfed by the great elms. The placid surface of the pool, which mirrored the shaven lawns and the hoary church set amidst the lawns, the silence about him, broken only by the notes of song-birds or a yelp from the distant kennels, the view over the green undulations of park and covert, all vainly appealed to him today, though on summer evenings his heart took sad and frequent leave of them. For now that which threatened him every day jostled aside that which must happen one day. The home of his fathers might be his for some years, but shorn of its chief dignity, of its pride, its mastery; while Calne – Calne would survive, to lift still higher the fortunes of those who had sold their king and country, and betrayed their order.

Daily a man and horse awaited the mail-coach at Chippenham, that he might have the latest news; and by-and-by seeing a footman hurrying towards him from the house, he supposed that the mail was in. But when the man, after crossing the long wooden bridge which spanned the pool, approached, he remembered that it was too early for the post; and hating to be disturbed in his solitary reverie, he awaited the servant with impatience.

'What is it?' he asked.

'If you please, Sir Robert, Lady Lansdowne's carriage is at the door.'

Only Sir Robert's darkening colour betrayed his astonishment. He had made his feelings so well known that none but the most formal civilities now passed between Stapylton and Bowood.

'Who is it?'

'Lady Lansdowne, Sir Robert. Her ladyship bade me say that she wishes urgently to see you, sir.'

The man, as well as the master, knew that the visit was unusual.

The Baronet was a proud man, and he bethought him that the drawing-rooms, seldom used and somewhat neglected, were not in the state in which he would wish his enemy's wife to see them.

'Where have you put her ladyship?' he asked.

'In the hall, Sir Robert.'

'Very good. I will come.'

The man hastened away over the bridge, and Sir Robert followed, more at leisure. When he had passed the angle of the church, which stood in a line with the three blocks of building, connected with porticoes, which formed the house, and which, placed on a gentle eminence, looked handsomely over the park, he saw that a carriage with four greys, ridden by postillions and attended by two outriders, stood before the main door. In the carriage, her face shaded by the large Tuscan hat of the period, sat a young lady reading. She heard Sir Robert's footsteps, looked up, and in some embarrassment met his eyes.

He removed his hat. 'It is Lady Louisa, is it not?' he said, looking gravely at her.

'Yes,' she answered; and she smiled prettily at him.

'Will you not go into the house?'

'Thank you,' she replied, with a faint blush; 'I think my mother wishes to see you alone, Sir Robert.'

'Very good.' And with a bow, cold but perfectly courteous, he turned and passed up the broad, shallow steps, which were of the same time-tinted, lichen-covered stone as the rest of the building. Mapp, the butler, who had been looking out for him, opened the door, and he entered the hall.

In his heart, which was secretly perturbed, was room for the wish that he had been found in other than the high-buttoned gaiters and breeches of his country life. But he suffered no sign of that or of his more serious misgivings to appear, as he advanced to greet the still beautiful woman who sat daintily warming one sandalled foot at the red embers on the hearth. She was far from being at ease herself. Warnings which her husband had addressed to her at parting recurred and disturbed her. But it is seldom that a woman of the world betrays her feelings, and her manner was perfect as he bent low over her hand.

'It is longer,' she said gently, 'much longer than I like to remember, Sir Robert, since we met.'

'It is a long time,' he answered gravely; and when she had reseated herself, he sat down opposite her.

'It is an age,' she said slowly; and she looked round the hall, with its panelled walls, its deep window-seats, and its panoply of fox-masks and antlers, as if she recalled the past. 'It is an age,' she repeated. 'Politics are sad dividers of friends.'

'I fear,' he replied, in a tone as cold as courtesy permitted, 'they are about to be greater dividers.'

She looked at him with an appeal in her eyes. 'And yet,' she said, 'we saw more of you once.'

'Yes.'

He was wondering much, behind the mask of his civility, what had drawn her hither. He knew that it could be no light, no passing matter which had brought her over thirteen miles of Wiltshire roads to call upon a man with whom her intercourse had been limited, for years past, to a few annual words, a formal invitation as formally declined, a measured salutation at race or ball. She must have a motive, and a strong one. Was it possible – it was only the day before that he had learned that Lord Lansdowne meant to drop his foolish opposition at Chippinge – was it possible that she was here to make a favour of that? And perhaps a bargain? If that were her errand, and my lord had sent her, thinking to make refusal less easy, Sir Robert felt that he would know how to answer. He waited.

CHAPTER VII

The Winds of Autumn

LADY LANSDOWNE looked pensively at the tapering sandal which she held forward to catch the heat.

'Time passes so very, very quickly,' she said with a sigh.

'With some,' Sir Robert answered. 'With others,' he bowed, 'it stands still.'

His gallantry did not deceive her. She knew it for the salute which duellists exchange before the fray, and she saw that if she would do anything she must place herself within his guard. She looked at him with sudden directness.

'I want you to bear with me for a few minutes, Sir Robert,' she said in a tone of appeal. 'I want you to remember that we were once friends, and, for the sake of old days, to believe that I am here to play a friend's part. You won't answer me? Very well. I do not ask you to answer me.' She pointed to the space above the mantel. 'The portrait which used to hang there?' she asked. 'Where is it? What have you done with it? But there, I said I would not ask, and I am asking!'

'And I will answer!' he replied. This was the last, the very last thing for which he had looked; but he would show her that he was not to be overridden. 'I will tell you,' he repeated. 'Lady Lansdowne, I have destroyed it.'

'I do not blame you,' she rejoined. 'It was yours to do with as you would. But the original – no, Sir Robert,' she continued, staying him intrepidly – she had taken the water now, and must swim – 'you shall not frighten me! She was, she is your wife. But not yours, not your property to do with as you will, in the sense in which that picture – but there, I am blaming where I should entreat. I—'

He stayed her by a peremptory gesture. 'Are you here – from her?' he asked, huskily.

'I am not.'

'She knows?'

'No, Sir Robert, she does not.'

'Then why,' – there was pain mingled with the indignation in his tone – 'why, in God's name, madam, have you come?'

She looked at him with pitying eyes. 'Because,' she said, 'so many years have passed, and if I do not say a word now I shall never say it. And because – there is still time, but no more than time.'

He looked at her fixedly. 'You have another reason,' he said. 'What is it?'

'I saw her yesterday. I was in Chippenham when the Bristol coach passed, and I saw her face at the window.'

He breathed more quickly; it was evident that the news touched him home. But he would not blench nor lower his eyes.

'Well?' he said.

'I saw her face for a few seconds only, and she did not see me. And of course – I did not speak to her. But I knew her face though she was changed.'

'And because' – his voice was harsh – 'you saw her for a few minutes at a window, you come to me?'

'No, but because her face called up the old times. And because we are all growing older. And because she was – not guilty.'

He started. This was getting within his guard with a vengeance.

'Not guilty?' he cried in a tone of extreme anger. And he rose. But as she did not move he sat down again.

'No,' she replied firmly. 'She was not guilty.'

His face was deeply red. For a moment he looked at her as if he would not answer her, or, if he answered, would bid her leave his house. Then –

'If she had been,' he said grimly, 'guilty, madam, in the sense in which you use the word, guilty of the worst, she had ceased to be my wife these fifteen years, she had ceased to bear my name, ceased to be the curse of my life!'

'Oh no, no!'

'It is yes, yes!' And his face was dark. 'But as it was, she was guilty of enough! For years' – he spoke more rapidly as his passion grew – 'she made her name a byword and dragged mine in the dirt. She made me a laughing stock and herself a scandal. She disobeyed me – but what was her whole life with me, Lady Lansdowne, but one long disobedience? When she published that light, that foolish book, dedicated it to – to that person – a book which no modest wife should have written, was not her main motive to harass and degrade me? Me, her husband? While we were together was not her conduct, from the first, one long defiance, one long harassment of me? Did a day pass in which she did not humiliate me by a hundred tricks, belittle me by a hundred slights, ape me before those whom she should not have stooped to know, invite in a thousand ways the applause of the fops she drew round her? And when' – he rose, and paced the room – 'when, tried beyond patience by what I heard, I sent to her at Florence and bade her return to me, and cease to make herself a scandal with that person, or my house should no longer be her home, she disobeyed me flagrantly, wilfully, and at a price she knew! She went out of her way to follow him to Rome, she flaunted herself in his company, ay, and flaunted herself in such guise as no Englishwoman had been known to wear before! And after that – after that—'

He stopped, proud as he was, mastered by his feelings; she had got within his guard indeed. For a while he could not go on. And Lady Lansdowne, picturing the old days which his passionate words brought back, days when her children had been infants, saw, as it had been yesterday, the young bride, beautiful as a rosebud and wild and skittish as an Irish colt – and the husband staid, dignified, middle-aged, as little in sympathy with his captive's random acts and flighty words as if he had spoken another tongue.

Thus yoked, and resisting the lightest rein, the young wife had shown herself capable of an infinity of folly. Egged on by the plaudits of a circle of admirers, she had now made her husband ridiculous by childish familiarities: and again, when he found fault with these, by airs of public offence, which covered him with derision. But beauty's sins are soon forgiven; and fretting and fuming, and leading a wretched life, he had yet borne with her, until something which she chose to call a passion took possession of her. *The Giaour* and *The Corsain* were the rage that year; and with the publicity with which she did everything she flung herself at the head of her soul's affinity; a famous person, half poet, half dandy, who was staying at Bowood.

The world, which knew her, decided that the affair was more worthy of laughter than of censure, and laughed immoderately. But to the husband – the humour of husbands is underdeveloped – it was terrible. She wrote verses to the gentleman, and he to her; and she published, with ingenuous pride, the one and the other. Possibly this or the laughter determined the admirer. He fled, playing the innocent Aeneas; and her lamentations, crystallizing in the shape of a silly romance which made shopgirls weep and great ladies laugh, caused a separation between the husband and wife. Before this had lasted many months the illness of their only child brought them together again; and when, a little later, the doctors advised a southern climate, Sir Robert reluctantly entrusted the girl to her. She went abroad with the child, and the parents never met again.

Lady Lansdowne, recalling the story, could have laughed with her mind and wept with her heart; scenes so absurd under the leafy shades of Bowood or Lacock jostled the tragedy; and the ludicrous – with the husband an unwilling actor in it – so completely relieved the pathetic! But her bent towards laughter was short. Sir Robert, unable to bear her eyes, had turned away; and she must say something.

'Think,' she said gently, 'how young she was!'

'I have thought of it a thousand times!' he retorted. 'Do you suppose,' turning on her with harshness, 'that there is a day on which I do not think of it?'

'So young!'

'She had been three years a mother!'

'For the dead child's sake, then,' she pleaded with him, 'if not for hers.'

'Lady Lansdowne!' There were both anger and pain in his voice as he halted and stood before her. 'Why do you come to me? Why do you trouble me? Why? Is it because you feel yourself – responsible? Because you know, because you feel that but for you my home had not been left to me desolate? Nor a foolish life been ruined?'

'God forbid!' she said solemnly. And in her turn she rose in agitation, moved for once out of the gracious ease and self-possession of her life; so that in the contrast there was something unexpected and touching. 'God forbid!' she repeated. 'But because I feel that I might have done more. Because I feel that a word from me might have checked her, and it was not spoken. True, I was young, and it might have made things worse – I do not know. But when I saw her face at the window yesterday – and she was changed, Sir Robert – I felt that I might have been in her place, and she in mine!' Her voice trembled. 'I might have been lonely, childless, growing old; and alone! Or again, if I had done something, if I had spoken as I would have another speak, were the case my girl's, she might have been as I am! Now,' she added tremulously, 'you know why I came. Why I plead for her! In our world we grow hard, very hard; but there are things which touch us still, and her face touched me yesterday – I remembered what she was.' She paused a moment, and then, 'After long years,' she continued softly, 'it cannot be hard to forgive; and there is still time. She did nothing that need close your door, and what she did is forgotten. Grant that she was foolish, grant that she was wild, indiscreet, what you will – she is alone now, alone and growing old, Sir Robert, and if not for her sake, for the sake of your dead child—'

He stopped her by a peremptory gesture, but for the moment he seemed to be voiceless. At length –

'You touch the wrong chord,' he said hoarsely. 'It is for the sake of my dead child that I shall never, never forgive her! She knew that I loved it. She knew that it was all to me. It grew worse! Did she tell me? It was in danger! Did she warn me? No! But when, having heard of her disobedience, of her folly, of things which made her a byword, I bade her return, or my house should no longer be her home, then, then she flung the news of the child's death at me, and rejoiced that she had it to fling. Had I gone out then and found her in the midst of her wicked gaiety, God knows what I should have done! I did try to go, but the Hundred Days had begun, I had to return. But I say again, had I gone, and learned that in her infatuation she had neglected the child, left it to servants, let it fade, I think – I think, madam, that I should have killed her!'

Lady Lansdowne raised her hands. 'Hush! Hush!' she cried.

'I loved the child. Therefore she was glad when it died, glad that she had the power to wound me. Its death was no more to her than a weapon with which to punish me! There was a tone in her letter – I have it still – which betrayed that. And therefore – therefore, for the child's sake, I will never forgive her!'

'I am sorry,' she murmured in a voice which acknowledged defeat. 'I am very sorry.'

He stood for a moment gazing at the blank space above the fireplace; his head sunk, his shoulders brought forward. He looked years older than the man who had walked under the elms. At length he made an effort to speak in his usual tone.

'Yes,' he said, 'it is a sorry business.'

'And I,' she said slowly, 'can do nothing?'

'Nothing,' he replied. 'Time will cure this, and all things.'

'You are sure that there is no mistake?' she pleaded. 'That you are not judging her harshly?'

'There is no mistake.'

Then she saw the hopelessness of argument and held out her hand.

'Forgive me,' she said. 'I have given you pain, and for nothing. But the old days were so strong upon me – after I saw her – that I could not but come. Think of me, at least, as a friend – and forgive me.'

He bowed low over her hand, but he gave her no assurance. And seeing that he was mastering his agitation, and fearing that if he had leisure to think he might resent her action, she wasted no time in adieux. She glanced round the well-remembered hall – the hall once smart, now shabby – in which she had seen the flighty girl play many a mad prank. Then she turned sorrowfully to the door, more than suspecting that she would never pass through it again.

He had rung the bell, and Mapp, the butler, and the two men were in attendance. But he handed her to the carriage himself, and placed her in it with old-fashioned courtesy, and with the same scrupulous observance stood bareheaded until it moved away. None the less, his face by its set expression betrayed the nature of the interview; and the carriage had scarcely left the grounds and entered the park when Lady Louisa turned to her mother.

'Was he very angry?' she asked, eager to be instructed in the mysteries of that life which she was entering.

Lady Lansdowne essayed to snub her. 'My dear,' she said, 'it is not a fit subject for you.'

'Still, Mother dear, you might tell me. You told me something, and it is not fair to turn yourself into Mrs Fairchild in a moment. Besides, while you were with him I came on a passage so beautiful, and so pat, it almost made me cry.'

'My dear, don't say "pat", say "apposite".'

'Then apposite, Mother,' Lady Louisa answered. 'Do you read it. There it is.'

Lady Lansdowne sniffed, but suffered the book to be put into her hand. Lady Louisa pointed with enthusiasm to a line. 'Is it a case like that, Mother?' she asked eagerly –

'But never either found another
To free the hollow heart from paining.
They stood aloof, the scars remaining,
Like cliffs which had been rent asunder.
A dreary sea now flows between,
But neither heat, nor frost, nor thunder,
Shall wholly do away, I ween,
The marks of that which once hath been.'

The mother handed the book back to the daughter without looking at her.

'No,' she said; 'I don't think it is a case like that.'

But a moment later she wiped her eyes furtively, and then she told her daughter more, it is to be feared, than Mrs Fairchild would have approved.

Sir Robert, when they were gone, went heavily to the library, a panelled room looking to the back, in which it was his custom to sit. For many years he had passed some hours of every day, when he was at home, in that room; and until now it had never occurred to his mind that it was dull or time-worn. But it was old Mapp's habit to lower the blinds for his master's after-luncheon nap, and they were still down; and the light which filtered in was like the sheet which rather accentuates than hides the sharp features of the dead. The faded engravings and the calf-bound books which masked the walls, the escritoire, handsome and massive, but stained with ink and strewn with dog-eared accounts, the leather-covered chair long worn out of shape by his weight, the table beside it with yesterday's *Standard*, two or three volumes of the *Anti-Jacobin*, and the *Quarterly*, a month old and dusty – all to his opened eyes wore a changed aspect. They spoke of the slow decay of years, unchecked by a woman's eye, a woman's hand. They told of the slow degradation of his lonely life. They indicated a like change in himself.

He stood a few moments on the hearth, looking about him with a shocked, pained face. The months and the years had passed irrevocably, while he sat in that chair, poring in a kind of lethargy over those books, working industriously at those accounts. Asked, he had answered that he was growing old, and grown old. But he had never for a moment comprehended, as he comprehended now, that he was old. He had never measured the difference between this and that; between those days troubled by a hundred annoyances, cares, humiliations, when in spite of all he had lived, and these days of sullen stagnancy and mere vegetation.

He found the room, he found the reflection intolerable. And he went out, took with an unsteady hand his garden hat, and returned past the church to that broad walk under the elms which was his favourite lounge. Perhaps he fancied that the wonted scene would deaden the pain of memory and restore him to his accustomed placidity. But his thoughts had been too violently broken. His hands shook, his lip trembled with the tearless passion of later life. And when his agitation began to die down and something like calmness supervened, this did but enable him to feel more keenly the pangs, not of remorse, but of regret; of bitter unavailing regret for all the things of which the woman who had lain on his bosom had robbed his life.

Stapylton lies in a side valley projected among the low rich hills which fringe the vale of the Wiltshire Avon. From where he stood all within sight, the low downs above the house, the arable land which fringed them, the rich pastures lowest of all – all, mill and smithy and inn, snug farm and thatched cottage, called him owner. Nay, from the south end of the pool, where a wicket gave entrance to the park and to a foot-road across it – and whence a side view of the treble front of the house could be obtained – the spire of Chippinge church was visible, rising from its ridge in the Avon valley; and to the base of that spire all was his, all had been his father's and his grandfather's. But not an acre, not a rood, would be his child's.

That was no new thought. It was a thought that had saddened him on many and many a summer evening when the shadow of the elms lay far across the sward, and the silence of the stately house, the pale water, the far-stretching farms whispered of the passing of the generations, of the passage of time, of the inevitable end. Where he walked his father had walked; and soon he would go whither his father had gone. And the heir would walk where he walked, listen to the same twilight carollings, hear the first hoot of the distant owl.

Cedes coemptis saltibus, et domo,
Villaque, flavus quam Tiberis lavit,
Cedes, et exstructis in altum
Divitiis potietur heres.

But no heir of his blood. No son of his. No man of the Vermuyden name. And for that he had to thank her.

It was this which today gave the old thought new poignancy. For that he had to thank her. Truly, in the words wrung from him by the bitterness of his feelings, she had left his house unto him desolate. If even the little girl had lived, the child would have succeeded; and that had been something, that had been much. But the child was dead; and in his heart he laid her death at his wife's door. And a stranger, or one in essentials a stranger, the descendant by a second marriage of his grandmother, Katherine Beckford, was the heir.

Presently the young man would succeed, and the old chattels would be swept away to cottage or lumber room. The old horses would be shot, the old dogs would be hanged, the old servants discharged, perhaps the very trees under which he walked and which he loved would be cut down. The house, the stables, the kennels, all but the cellars would be refurnished; and in the bustle and glitter of the new *régime*, begun in the sunshine, the twilight of his own latter days would be forgotten in a month.

We die and are forgotten, 'tis Heaven's decree,
And thus the lot of others will be the lot of me!

Sunday by Sunday he had read those lines on the grave of a kinsman, a man whom he had known. He had often repeated them; they were as familiar as the prayers he had learned at his mother's knee. Today the old memories and the old times, which Lady Lansdowne had made to rise from the dead, gave them a new meaning and a new bitterness.

CHAPTER VIII

A Sad Misadventure

ARTHUR VAUGHAN was much and honestly relieved by the tidings which Isaac White had conveyed to him at Chippenham. The news freed him from a duty which did not appear the less distasteful because it was no longer inevitable. To cast against Sir Robert the vote which he owed to Sir Robert must, whatever the matter at stake, have exposed him to odium. But at this election, at which the issue was, aye or no, was the borough to be swept away or not, to vote 'aye' was an act from which the least sensitive must have shrunk, and which the most honest must have performed with reluctance. Add the extreme exasperation of public feeling, of which every day and every hour brought to light the most glaring proofs, and he had been fortunate indeed if he had not incurred some general blame as well as the utmost weight of Sir Robert's displeasure.

He was spared all this, and he was thankful. Yet, when he rose on the morning after his arrival at Bristol, his heart was not as light as a feather. On the contrary, as he looked from the window of the White Lion into the bustle of Broad Street, he yawned; admitting that life, and particularly the prospect before him, of an immediate return to London, was dull. Why go back? Why stay here? Why do anything? The Woolsack? Bah! The Cabinet? Pooh! They were but gaudy baits for the shallow and the hard-hearted. Moreover they were so distant, so unattainable, that pursuit of them seemed the merest moonshine; more especially on this fine April morning, made for nothing but a coach ride through an enchanted country, by the side of the sweetest face, the brightest eyes, the most ravishing figure, the prettiest bonnet that ever tamed the gruffest of coachmen.

Heigh-ho! If it were all to do over again how happy would he be! How happy had he been, and not known it, the previous morning! It was pitiful to think of his ignorance while he had that day, that blissful day, before him.

Well, it was over, and he must return to Town. For he would play no foolish tricks. The girl was not in his rank in life, and he could not follow her without injury to her. He was no preacher, and he had lived for years among men whose lives, if not worse than the lives of their descendants, wore no disguise; who, if they did not sin more, sinned more openly. But he had a heart, and to mar an innocent life for his pleasure had shocked him; even if the girl's modesty and self-respect, disclosed by a hundred small things, had not made the notion of wronging her abhorrent. None the less he took his breakfast in a kind of dream, whispered 'Mary!' three times in different tones, and, being suddenly accosted by the waiter, was irritable.

With all this he was wise enough to know his own weakness, and that the sooner he was out of Bristol the better. He sent to the Bush office to book a place by the midday coach to Town; and then only, when he had taken the irrevocable step, he put on his hat to kill the intervening time in Bristol.

Unfortunately, as he crossed the hall, intending to walk towards Clifton, he heard himself named; and turning, he saw that the speaker was the lady in black, whom he had remarked walking up and down beside the coach, while the horses were changing at Marshfield.

'Mr Vaughan?' she said. She still wore her veil.

He raised his hat, much surprised. 'Yes,' he said. He fancied that she was inspecting him very closely through her veil. 'I am Mr Vaughan.'

'Pardon me,' she continued – her voice was refined and low – 'but they gave me your name at the office. I have something which belongs to the lady who travelled with you yesterday, and I am anxious to restore it.'

He blushed. He could not have repressed that blush if his life had hung upon it. 'Indeed?' he murmured. His confusion did not permit him to add another word.

'Doubtless it was left in the coach,' the lady explained, 'and was taken to my room with my luggage. Unfortunately I am leaving Bristol in a few minutes, and I cannot myself return it. I shall be much obliged if you see that she has it.'

She spoke as if the thing were a matter of course. But Vaughan had now recovered himself.

'I would with pleasure,' he said; 'but I am myself leaving Bristol at midday, and I do not know how – how I can do it.'

'Then perhaps you will arrange the matter,' the lady replied in a tone of displeasure. 'I have sent the parcel to your room, and I have not time to regain it. I must go now. There is my maid. Good morning!' And with a distant bow she glided from him, and disappeared through the nearest doorway.

He stood where she had left him, looking after her in bewilderment. For one thing he was sure that she was a stranger, and yet she had addressed him in the tone of one who had a right to be obeyed. Then how odd the thing was! What a coincidence! He had made up his mind to end the matter, to go and walk the Hot Wells like a good boy; and this happened and tempted him.

Yes, tempted him.

He would— But he could not tell what he would do until he had seen if the parcel were really in his room. The parcel! The mere thought that it was her parcel sent a foolish thrill through him. He would go and see, and then—

But he was interrupted. There were people standing or sitting round the hall, a low-ceiled, dark-wainscoted room, with sheaves of way-bills hung against the square pillars, and theatre notices flanking the bar window. As he turned a hand gripped his arm and twirled him round, and he met the grinning face of a man in his old regiment, Bob Flixton, commonly called the Honourable Bob.

'So I've caught you, my lad,' said he. 'This is mighty fine. Veiled ladies, eh? Oh, fie! fie!'

Vaughan, innocent as he was, was a little put out. But he answered good-humouredly –

'What brought you here, Flixton?'

'Ay, just so! Very unlucky, ain't it?' grinning. 'Fear I'll cut you out, eh? You're a neat artist, I must say.'

'I do not know the good lady from Eve!'

'Tell that to— But here, let me make you known to Brereton,' hauling him towards a gentleman who was seated in one of the window recesses. 'Old West Indian man, in charge of the recruiting district, and a good fellow, but a bit of a saint! Colonel,' he rattled on, as they joined the gentleman, 'here's Vaughan, once of ours, became a counsellor, and going to be Lord Chancellor. As to the veiled lady, mum, sir, mum!' with an exaggerated wink.

Vaughan laughed. It was impossible to resist Bob's impudent good-humour. He was a fair young man, short, stout, and inclining to baldness, with a loud, hearty voice, and a manner which made those who did not know him for a peer's son, think of a domestic fowl with a high opinion of itself. He was for ever damning this and praising that with unflagging decision; a man with whom it was impossible to be displeased, and in whom it was next to impossible not to believe. Yet at the mess table it was whispered that he did not play his best when the pool was large; nor had he ever seen Service, save in the lists of love, where his reputation stood high.

His companion, Vaughan saw, was of a different stamp. He

was tall and lean, with the air and carriage of a soldier, but with features of a refined and melancholy cast, and with a brooding sadness in his eyes which could not escape the most casual observer. He was somewhat sallow, the result of the West Indian climate, and counted twenty years more than Flixton, for whom his gentle manner formed an admirable foil. He greeted Vaughan courteously, and the Honourable Bob forced our hero into a seat beside them.

'That's snug!' he said. 'And now mum's the word, Vaughan. We'll not ask you what you're doing here among the nigger-nabobs. It's clear enough.'

Vaughan explained that the veiled lady was a stranger who had come down in the same coach with him, and that, for himself, it was election business which had brought him.

'Old Vermuyden?' returned the Honourable Bob. 'To be sure! Man you've expectations from! Good old fellow, too. I know him. Go and see him one of these days. Gad, Colonel, if old Sir Robert heard your views he'd die on the spot! Damn the Bill, he'd say! And I say it too!'

'But afterwards?' Brereton returned, drawing Vaughan into the argument by a courteous gesture. 'Consider the consequences, my dear fellow, if the Bill does not pass.'

'Oh, hang the consequences!'

'You can't,' dryly. 'You can hang men – we've been too fond of hanging them – but not consequences! Look at the state of the country; everywhere you find excitement, and dangerous excitement. Cobbett's writings have roused the South; the papers are full of rioters and special commissions to try them! Not a farmer can sleep for thinking of his stacks, nor a farmer's wife for thinking of her husband. Then for the North; look at Birmingham and Manchester and Glasgow, with their Political Unions preaching no taxation without representation. Or, nearer home, look at Bristol here, ready to drown the Corporation, and Wetherell in particular, in the Float! Then, if that is the state of things while they still expect the Bill to pass, what will be the position if they learn it is not to pass? No! You may shrug your shoulders, but the three days in Paris will be nothing to it.'

'What I say is, shoot!' Flixton answered hotly. 'Shoot! Shoot! Put 'em down! Put an end to it! Show 'em their places! What do a lot of damned shopkeepers and peasants know about the Bill? Ride 'em down! Give 'em a taste of the Float themselves! I'll answer for it a troop of the 14th would soon bring the Bristol rabble to their senses!'

'I should be sorry to see it tried,' Brereton answered, shaking his head. 'They took that line in France last July, and you know the result. You'll agree with me, Mr Vaughan, that where Marmont failed we are not likely to succeed. The more as his failure is known. The three days of July are known.'

'Ay, by the Lord,' the Honourable Bob cried. 'The revolution in France bred the whole of this trouble!'

'The mob there won, and the mob here know it. In my opinion,' Brereton continued, 'conciliation is our only card, if we do not want to see a revolution.'

'Hang your conciliation! Shoot, I say!'

'What do you think, Mr Vaughan?'

'I think with you, Colonel Brereton,' Vaughan answered, 'that the only way to avoid such a crisis as has befallen France is to pass the Bill, and to set the Constitution on a wider basis by enlisting as large a number as possible in its defence.'

'Oh Lord! Oh Lord!' from Flixton.

'On the other hand,' Vaughan continued, 'I would put down the beginnings of disorder with a strong hand. I would allow no intimidation, no violence. The Bill should be passed by argument.'

'Argument? Why, damn me, intimidation is your argument!' the right Honourable Bob struck in, with more acuteness than he commonly evinced. 'Pass the Bill, or we'll loose the dog! At 'em, Mob, good dog! At 'em! That's your argument!' triumphantly. 'But I'll be back in a minute.' And he left them.

Vaughan laughed. Brereton, however, seemed to be unable to take the matter lightly.

'Do you really mean, Mr Vaughan,' he said, 'that if there were trouble, here for instance, you would not hesitate to give the order to fire?'

'Certainly, sir, if it could not be put down with the cold steel.'

The Colonel shook his head despondently. 'I don't think I

could,' he said. 'I don't think I could. You have not seen war, and I have. It is a fearful thing. Bad abroad, infinitely worse here. The first shot – think, Mr Vaughan, of what it might be the beginning! What hundreds and thousands of lives might hang upon it! How many scores of innocent men shot down, of daughters made fatherless!' He shuddered. 'And to give such an order, when that volley might be the signal for a civil war, and twenty-four hours might see a dozen counties in a blaze! It is horrible to think of it! Too horrible! It's too much for one man's shoulders! Flixton would do it – he sees no farther than his nose! But you and I, Mr Vaughan – and on one's own judgement, which might be utterly, fatally wrong! My God, no!'

'Yes there must be a point,' Vaughan replied, 'at which such an order becomes necessary; becomes mercy!'

'Ay,' Brereton answered eagerly; 'but who is to say when that point is reached, when peaceful methods can do no more? Or, granted that they can do no more, that, provocation given, your force is sufficient to prevent a massacre! A massacre in such a place as this!'

Vaughan saw that the idea had taken possession of the other's mind, and, aware that he had distinguished himself on foreign Service, he wondered. It was not his affair, however; and 'Let us hope that the occasion may not arise,' he said politely.

'God grant it!' Brereton replied. And then again, to himself and more fervently, 'God grant it!' he muttered. The shadow lay darker on his face.

Vaughan might have wondered more, if Flixton had not returned at that moment, and overwhelmed him with importunities to dine with him the next evening.

'Gage and Congreve of the 14th are coming from Gloucester,' he said, 'and Codrington and two or three yeomanry chaps. You must come. If you don't, I'll quarrel with you and call you out! It'll do you good after the musty, fusty, goody-goody life you've been leading. Brereton's coming, and we'll drink King Billy till we're blind!'

Vaughan hesitated. He had taken his place on the coach, but – but after all there was that parcel. He must do something about it. It seemed to be his fate to be tempted, yet –

what nonsense that was! Why should he not stay in Bristol if he pleased?

'You're very good,' he said at last. 'I'll stay.'

Yet on his way to his room he paused, half minded to go. But he was ashamed to change his mind again, and he strode on, opened his door, and saw the parcel, a neat little affair, laid on the table.

It bore in a clear handwriting the address which he had seen on the basket at Mary Smith's feet. But, possibly because an hour of the Honourable Bob's company had brushed the bloom from his fancy, it moved him little. He looked at it with something like indifference, felt no inclination to kiss it, and smiled at his past folly as he took it up and set off to return it to its owner. He had exaggerated the affair and his feelings. He had made much out of little, and a romance out of a chance encounter. He could smile now at that which had moved him yesterday. Certainly:

Man's love is of man's life a thing apart,
'Tis woman's whole existence; man may range
The Court, camp, Church, the vessel and the mart,
Sword, gown, gain, glory, offer in exchange
Pride, fame, ambition to fill up his heart.

And the Honourable Bob, with his breezy self-assertion, had brought this home to him, and, with a puff of everyday life, had blown the fantasy away.

He was still under this impression when he reached Queen's Square, once the pride of Bristol, and still, in 1831, a place handsome and well inhabited. Uniformly and substantially built, on a site surrounded on three sides by deep water, it lay, indeed, over-near the quays, of which, and of the basins, it enjoyed a view through several openings. But in the reign of William IV merchants were less averse from living beside their work than they are now. The master's eye was still in repute, and though many of the richest citizens had migrated to Clifton, and the neighbouring Assembly Rooms in Prince's Street had been turned into a theatre, the spacious Square, with its wide lawn, its lofty and umbrageous elms, its colony of rooks, and, last of all, its fine statue of the Glorious and

Immortal Memory, was still the abode of many respectable people. In one corner stood the Mansion House; a little farther along the same side the Custom House; and a third public department, the Excise, also had offices here.

The Cathedral, and the Bishop's Palace on College Green, stood, as the crow flies, scarce a bowshot from the Square; on which they looked down from the westward, as the heights of Redcliffe looked down on it from the east. But marsh as well as water divided the Square from these respectable neighbours; nor, it must be owned, was this the only drawback. The centre of the city's life, but isolated on three sides by water, the Square was as easily reached from the worse as from the better quarters, and owing to the proximity of the Welsh Back, a coasting quay frequented by the roughest class, it was liable in times of excitement to abrupt and boisterous inroads.

Vaughan entered the Square by Queen Charlotte Street, and had not traversed one half of its width before he made a discovery. Under the elms, in the corner which he was approaching, were a dozen children. They were at play, and overlooking them were two young persons, seated on a bench, with their backs to him, the one in that mid-stage between childhood and womanhood when the eyes are at their sharpest and the waist at its thickest; the other, Mary Smith.

The colour rose to his brow, and on a sudden he knew that he was not indifferent. Nor was the discovery that the back of her head and an inch of the nape of her neck had this effect upon him the worst. He had to ask himself what, if he was not indifferent, he was doing there, sneaking on the skirts of a ladies' school. What were his intentions, and what his aim? For to healthy minds there is something distasteful in the notion of an intrigue connected, ever so remotely, with a girls' school. Nor are conquests gained on that scene laurels of which even a Lothario is over-proud. If Flixton saw him, or some others of the gallant Fourteenth?

And yet, in the teeth of all this, and under the eyes of all Queen's Square, he must do his errand. And sheepish within, brazen without, he advanced and stood beside her. She heard his step, and, unsuspicious as the youngest of her flock, looked round to see who came – looked, and saw him standing within a yard of her, with the sunshine falling through the leaves on his wavy, fair hair. For the twentieth part of a second he fancied a glint of glad surprise in her eyes. Then, if anything could have punished him, it was the sight of her confusion; it was the blush of distress which covered her face as she rose to her feet.

Oh, cruel! He had pursued her, when to pursue was an insult! He had followed her when he should have known that in her position a breath of scandal was ruin! And oh, the round eyes of the round-faced child beside her!

'I must apologize,' he murmured humbly, 'but I am not trespassing upon you without cause. I – I think that this is yours.' And rather lamely, for the distress in her face troubled him, he held out the parcel.

She put her hand behind her, and as stiffly as Miss Sibson – of the Queen's Square Academy for Young Ladies of the Genteel and Professional Classes – could have desired, 'I do not understand, sir,' she said. She was pale and red by turns, as the round eyes saw.

'You left this in the coach.'

'I beg your pardon?'

'You left this in the coach,' he repeated, turning very red himself. Was it possible that she meant to repudiate her own property because he brought it? 'It is yours, is it not?'

'No.'

'It is not!' in incredulous astonishment.

'No.'

'But I am sure it is,' he persisted. Confound it, this was overdoing modesty! He had no desire to eat the girl! 'You left it inside the coach, and it has your address upon it. See!' And he tried to place it in her hands.

But she drew back, with a look of reprobation of which he would not have believed her eyes capable.

'It is not mine, sir,' she said. 'Be good enough to leave us!' And then, drawing herself up, mild creature as she was, 'You are intruding, sir,' she said.

Now, if Vaughan had really been guilty of approaching her upon a feigned pretext, he had certainly retired on that with his tail between his legs. But being innocent, and both incredulous and angry, he stood his ground, and his eyes gave back some of the reproach which hers darted.

'I am either mad or it is yours,' he said stubbornly, heedless of the ring of staring children who, ceasing to play, had gathered round them. 'It bears your name and address, and it was left in the coach by which you travelled yesterday. I think, Miss Smith, you will be sorry afterwards if you do not take it.'

She fancied that his words imported a bribe; and in despair of ridding herself of him, or in terror of the tale which the children would tell, she took her courage in both hands.

'You say that it is mine?' she said, trembling visibly.

'Certainly I do,' he answered. And again he held it out to her.

But she did not take it. Instead, 'Then be good enough to follow me,' she replied, with something of the prim dignity of the schoolmistress. 'Miss Cooke, will you collect the children and bring them into the house?'

And, avoiding his eyes, she led the way across the road to the door of one of the houses. He followed, but reluctantly, and after a moment of hesitation. He detested the scene which he foresaw, and bitterly regretted that he had ever set foot inside Queen's Square. To be suspected of thrusting an intrigue upon a little schoolmistress, to be dragged, with a pack of staring, chattering children in his train, before some grim-faced duenna – he, a man of years and affairs, with whom the Chancellor of England did not scorn to speak on equal terms! It was hateful; it was intolerable. Yet to turn back, to say that he would not go, was to acknowledge himself guilty. He wished – he wished to heaven that he had never seen the girl. Or at least that he had had the courage, when she first denied the thing, to throw the parcel on the seat and go.

It was not an heroic frame of mind; but neither was the position heroic. And something may be forgiven him in the circumstances.

Fortunately the trial was short. She opened the door of the house, and on the threshold he found himself face to face with a tall, bulky woman, with a double chin and an absurdly powdered nose, who wore a cameo of the late Queen Charlotte on her ample bosom. Miss Sibson had viewed the encounter from an upper window, and her face was a picture of displeasure, slightly tempered by powder.

'What is this?' she asked, in an intimidating voice. 'Miss Smith, what is this, if you please?'

Perhaps Mary, aware that her place was at stake, was desperate. At any rate she behaved with a dignity which astonished Vaughan.

'This gentleman, madam,' she explained, speaking with firmness though her face was on fire, 'travelled with me on the coach yesterday. A few minutes ago he appeared and addressed me, and insisted that the – the parcel he carries is mine, and that I left it in the coach. It is not mine, and I have not seen it before.'

Miss Sibson folded her arms upon her ample person. The position was not altogether new to her.

'Sir,' she said, eyeing the offender majestically, 'have you any explanation to offer – of this extraordinary conduct?'

He had, indeed. As clearly as his temper permitted he told his tale, his tone half ironical, half furious.

When he paused, 'Who do you say gave it to you?' Miss Sibson asked in a deep voice.

'I do not know her name. A lady who travelled in the coach.'

Miss Sibson's frown grew even deeper. 'Thank you,' she replied, 'that will do. I have heard enough, and I understand. I understand, sir. Be good enough to leave the house.'

'But, madam—'

'Be good enough to leave the house,' she repeated. 'That is the door,' pointing to it. 'That is the door, sir! Any apology you may wish to make you can make by letter to me. To me, you understand! I think one were not ill-fitting!'

He wholly lost his temper at that, and he flung the parcel with a violent word on a chair.

'Then at any rate I shall not take that, for it's not mine,' he cried. 'You may keep it, madam!'

And he flung out, his retreat hampered and made humiliating by the entrance of the pupils, who, marshalled by the round-eyed one, and all round-eyed themselves, blocked the doorway at that unlucky moment. He broke through them, however, without ceremony, though they represented the most respectable families in Bristol, and with his head bent he strode wrathfully across the Square.

To be turned out of a girls' boarding-school! To be shown the door like some wretched philandering schoolboy, or a subaltern in his first folly! He, the man of the world, of experience, of ambition! The man with a career! He was furious.

'The little cat!' he cried as he went. 'I wish I had never seen her face! What a fool, what a fool I was to come!'

Unheroic words and an unheroic mood. But though there were heroes before Agamemnon, it is not certain that there were any after George IV. At any rate, any who, like that great man, were heroic always and in all circumstances.

And yet Vaughan might have forgiven the little cat had he known that she was at that moment weeping very bitterly, with her face plunged into the pillow of her not over-luxurious bed. For she was young, and a woman. And because, in her position, the name of love was taboo; because to her the admiring look, which to a more fortunate sister was homage, was an insult; because the *petits soins*, the flower, the note, the trifle that to another were more precious than jewels, were not for her, it did not follow that she was not flesh and blood, that she had not feeling, affection, passion. True, the pang was soon deadened, for habit is strong. True, the bitter tears were soon dried, for employers like not gloomy looks. True, she soon cried shame on her own discontent, for she was good as gold. And yet to be debarred, in the tender springtime, from the sweet scents, the budding blooms, the gay carols, to have but one April coach ride in a desert of days, is hard – is very hard. Mary Smith, weeping on her hopeless pillow – not without thought of the cruel arch stooping to crush her, the cruel fate from which he had snatched her, not without thought of her own ingratitude, her black ingratitude – felt that it was hard, very hard.

CHAPTER IX

The Bill for Giving Everybody Everything

IT IS difficult to describe and impossible to exaggerate the heat of public feeling which preceded the elections of '31. Four-fifths of the people of this country believed that the Bill – from which they expected so much that a satirist gave it the title at the head of this chapter – had been defeated in the late House by a trick. For that trick the King, God bless him, had punished the House by dissolving it. It remained for the people to show their sense of the trick by returning a very different House; such a House as would not only pass the Bill, but pass it by a majority so decisive that the Lords and particularly the Bench of Bishops, whose hostility was known, would not dare to oppose the public will.

But as no more than a small proportion of these four-fifths had votes, they were forced to act, if they would have their will obeyed, indirectly; in one place by the legitimate pressure of public opinion, in another by bribery, in a third by intimidation, in a fourth, and a fifth, and a sixth by open violence; everywhere by the unspoken threat of revolution. And hence arose the one good, sound, and firm argument against the Bill which the Tory Party enjoyed.

One or two of their other arguments are not without interest, if only as the defence set up for a system so anomalous as to seem to us incredible – a system under which Gatton, with no inhabitants, returned two Members, and Sheffield, with something like a hundred thousand inhabitants, returned none; under which Dunwich, long drowned under the North Sea, returned two Members, and Birmingham returned none; under which the City of London returned four, and Lord Lonsdale returned nine; under which Cornwall, with one-fourth of the population of Lancashire, returned thrice as many representatives; under which the South vastly outweighed the North, and land mightily outweighed all other property.

Moreover, in no two boroughs was the franchise the same.

Nor was this the worst. One man lived in a hovel and had a vote; his neighbour lived in a mansion and had no vote. And often the whole of the well-to-do townsfolk were voteless. Then, while any man with five thousand pounds might buy a seat, nor see the face of a single elector, on the other hand, the poll might be kept open for fifteen days, and a county election might cost two hundred thousand pounds. Bribery, forbidden in theory, was permitted in practice. The very Government bribed under the rose, and it was said that all that a man's constituents required was to be satisfied of the *impurity* of his intentions!

An anomalous system; yet its defenders had something to say for it.

First, that narrow as the franchise seemed, every class found somewhere in England its mouthpiece. At Preston, where all could vote who slept in the borough the previous night, the poorest, ay, the tramps; in the potwalloping boroughs where a fireplace gave a vote, the next class; in a city like Westminster, the ratepayers; in the counties, the freeholders; in the universities, the clergy. And so on, the argument being that the very anomalies of the system provided a mixed representation without giving the masses a preponderant voice.

Secondly, they said that it insured a House of ability, by enabling young men of parts, but small means, to obtain seats. Those who upheld this flourished a long list of statesmen who had come in for nomination boroughs. It began with Pitt and ended with Macaulay – a feather plucked from the enemy's wing; and Burke stood for much in it. It became one of the commonplaces of the struggle.

The third contention was of greater weight. It was that with all its abuses, the old system had worked well. This argument, too, had its commonplace. The maxim, *stare super antiquas vias*, was thundered from a thousand platforms, coupled with copius references to the French wars, and to the pilot who had weathered the storm. This was the argument of the old, and the rich, and the timid – of those who clung to top-boots in the daytime and to pantaloons in the evening. But as the struggle progressed it came to be merged in the one sound argument to which reference has been made.

'If you do not pass the Bill,' said the Whigs, 'there will be a revolution.'

'Possibly,' the Tories rejoined. 'And whom have we to thank for that? Who, using the French Revolution of last July as a fulcrum, have unsettled the whole country? And now, having disturbed everything, tell us that we must grant to force what is not due to reason! You! But if the Bill is to pass, not because it is a good Bill, but because the mob desire it, where will this end? Pass Bills out of fear, and where will you end? Presently there will arise a ranting adventurer, more violent than Brougham, a hoary schemer more unscrupulous than Grey, an angry boy, outscolding Durham, a pedant more bloodless than Lord John, an honest fanatic blinder than Althorp! And when *they* threaten *you* with the terrors of the mob, what will you say?'

To which the Whigs could only reply that the people must be trusted; and – and that the Bill must pass, or not only coronets but crowns would be flying.

Dry arguments nowadays; but in those days alive, and to the Party on its defence – the Party which found itself thrust against the wall, that its pockets might be emptied – of vital interest. From scores of platforms candidates, leaning forward, bland and smiling, with one hand under the coat-tails and the other gently pumping, pumping, pumping, enunciated them – old hands these; or, red in the face, thundered them, striking fist into palm and overawing opposition; or, hopeless amid the rain of dead cats and stale eggs, muttered them in a reporter's ear, since the hootings of the crowd made other utterance impossible. But ever as the contest went on, the smiling candidate grew rarer; for day-by-day the Tories, seeing their cause hopeless, seeing even Whigs, such as Sir Thomas Acland in Devonshire and Mr Wilson Patten in Lancashire, cast out if they were lukewarm, grew more desperate, cried more loudly on high heaven, asserted more frantically that justice was dead on the earth. All this, while those who believed that the Bill was going to give everything to everybody pushed their advantage without mercy. Many a borough which had not known a contest for a generation, many a county, was fought and captured. No Tory felt safe; no bargain, though signed and sealed, held good; no patron, though he had deemed his income from his borough as secure as any part of his property, could say that his voters would dare go to the poll.

This it was which pressed on the mind of Isaac White, Sir Robert Vermuyden's agent, as on the day after Lady Lansdowne's visit he drove his gig and fast-trotting cob up the avenue. The treble front of the house looked down on him from its gentle eminence; its windows blinking in the afternoon sunshine, and the mellow tints of the stone harmonizing with the russet bloom which in April garbs the poplar and the late-bursting trees. Tradition said that the second baronet had built a wing for each of his two sons. In the result the elder son had died and the east wing had been devoted to kitchens and offices and the west to a splendid hospitality. Nowadays the latter wing was so seldom used that it had almost fallen into decay. Laurels grew up the side windows and darkened them, and bats lived in the damp chimneys. The rooms above stairs were packed with the lumber of the last century, the old wig-boxes, the old travelling-trunks, the old harpsichords, even an old sedan chair; while the lower rooms, swept and bare, and hung with flat, hard portraits, enjoyed an evil reputation in the servants' quarters, where many a one could tell of skirts that rustled unseen, and dead feet that trod the polished floors.

To Isaac White all this was nought. He had seen the house in every aspect; and his mind was filled with other things – with votes and voters, with some anxiety on his own account and more on his patron's. What would Sir Robert say if aught went wrong at Chippinge? True, the loss of the borough seemed impossible; it had been held securely for many years. But the times were so stormy, public feeling ran so high, the mob was so rough that nothing seemed impossible, in view of the stress to which the soundest candidates were exposed. If Mr Bankes stood to fail in Dorset, if Mr Duncombe had small chance in Yorkshire, if Sir Edward Knatchbull was a lost man in Kent, if Mr Hart Davies was no better in Bristol, if no man but an out-and-out Reformer could count on success, who was safe?

His grandfather, his father, he himself had lived and thrived by the system which he saw tottering to its fall. He belonged to it, he was part of it; he marked his allegiance to it by wearing top-boots in the daytime and shorts in full dress. And he was prepared – were it only out of gratitude to the ladder by which he had risen – to stand by it and by his patron to the last. But, strange anomaly, White was at heart a Cobbett man. His sneaking sympathies were, in his own despite, with the class from which he sprang. He saw commons filched from the poor, while the labourers fell on the rates; he saw large taxes wrung from the country to be spent in the town; he saw the severity of the laws, and especially the game laws; he saw absentee rectors and starving curates; he saw the dumb impotence of nine-tenths of the people; and he felt that the system under which these things had grown up was wrong. But, wrong or right, he was part of it, he was pledged to it; and all the theories in the world, and all the *Political Registers* which he digested of an evening, would not induce him to betray it.

Notwithstanding, White feared that in the matter of the borough he had not been quite so wide-awake as became him; or Pybus, the Bowood man, would not have stolen a march upon him. His misgivings grew as he came in sight of the door, and saw Sir Robert on the flight of steps which led to it. Apparently the baronet had seen him, for as White drove up a servant appeared to lead the mare to the stables.

Sir Robert looked her over as she was led away. 'The grey looks well, White,' he said. She was of his breeding.

'Yes, Sir Robert. Give me a good horse and they may have the new-fangled railroads that like them. But I am afraid, sir—'

'One moment!' The servant was out of hearing, and the baronet's tone, as he caught White up, betrayed agitation. 'Who is that looking over the Lower Wicket, White?' he continued. 'She has been there a quarter of an hour, and – and I can't make her out.'

His tone surprised White, who looked and saw at a distance of a hundred paces the figure of a woman leaning on the wicket gate nearest the stables. She was motionless, and he had not looked many seconds before he caught the thought in Sir Robert's mind.

He's heard, he reflected, that her ladyship is in the neighbourhood, and it has alarmed him.

'I cannot see at this distance, sir,' he answered prudently, 'who it is.'

'Then go and ask her her business,' Sir Robert replied, as indifferently as he could. 'She has been there a long time.'

White went, a little excited himself; but halfway to the woman, who continued to gaze at the house as if unconscious of his approach, he discovered that, whoever it was, it was not Lady Sybil. The stranger was stout, middle-aged, plain; and he took a curt tone with her when he came within ear-shot.

'What are you doing here?' he said. 'That's the way to the servants' hall.'

The woman looked at him. 'You don't know me, Mr White,' she said.

He looked hard in return. 'No,' he answered bluntly, 'I don't.'

'Ah, well, I know you,' she replied. 'More by token—'

He cut her short. 'Have you any message?' he asked.

'If I have, I'll give it myself,' she retorted dryly. 'Truth is, I'm in two minds about it. What you have, you have, d'you see, Mr White; but what you've given ain't yours any more. Anyway—'

'Anyway,' he retorted, 'you can't stay here!'

'Very good,' she replied, 'very good. As you are so kind, I'll take a day to think of it.' And with an impudent nod she turned her back on the puzzled White, and went off down the park towards the town.

He went back to Sir Robert. 'She's a stranger, sir,' he said; 'and, I think, a bit gone in the head. I could make nothing of her.'

Sir Robert drew a deep breath. 'You're sure she was a stranger?' he said.

'She's no one I know, sir. After one of the men, perhaps.'

Sir Robert straightened himself. He had spent a bad ten minutes gazing at the distant figure.

'Just so,' he said. 'Very likely. And now what is it, White?'

'I've bad news, sir, I'm afraid,' the agent said, in an altered tone.

'What is it?'

'It's that damned Pybus, sir! I'm afraid that, after all—'

'They're going to fight?'

'I'm afraid, Sir Robert, they are.'

The old gentleman's eyes gleamed. 'Afraid, sir, afraid?' he cried. 'On the contrary, so much the better. It will cost me money, but I can spare it; and it will cost them more, and nothing for it. Afraid? I don't understand you.'

The agent, standing on the step below him, coughed dubiously.

'Well, sir,' he said, 'what you say is reasonable. But—'

'But? But what?'

'There is so much excitement in the country at this time—'

'So much greediness in the country,' Sir Robert retorted, striking his stick upon the stone steps. 'So much unscrupulousness, sir; so many liars promising, and so many fools listening; so much to get, and so many who would like it! There's all that, if you please; but for excitement, I don't know' – with a severe look – 'what you mean, or what it has to do with us.'

'I am afraid, sir, there is bad news from Cornwall, where it is said Sir Richard Vyvyan stands no chance.'

'A good man, and a Vyvyan; I'll not believe it!'

'And from Dorset, sir, where they say Mr Bankes will be beaten.'

'I'll not believe it,' Sir Robert repeated positively. 'I'll never believe it. Mr Bankes beaten in Dorset! Absurd! Why do you listen to such tales? Why do you listen? By God, White, what is the matter with you? Or how does it touch us if Mr Bankes is beaten? We can poll nine votes to four! Nine will still be nine, and four four, if he be beaten. When you can make four to be more than nine you may come whining to me!'

White coughed. 'Dyas, the butcher—'

'What of him?'

'Well, Sir Robert, I am afraid he has been getting some queer notions into his head.'

'Notions?' the baronet echoed in astonishment. And he stared.

'He has been listening to someone, and – and thinks he has views on the Bill.'

Sir Robert exploded. 'Views!' he cried. 'Views! The butcher

with views! Why, damme, White, you must be mad! Mad! Since when have butchers taken to politics, or had views?'

'I don't know anything about that, sir,' White mumbled.

Sir Robert struck his stick fiercely on a step. 'But I do! And I know this,' he cried, 'that for twenty years he's had thirty pounds a year to vote as I tell him. By gad, I never heard such a thing in my life! Never! You don't mean to tell me that the man thinks the vote's his own to do what he likes with?'

'I am afraid,' the agent admitted reluctantly, 'that that is what he's saying, sir.'

Sir Robert's thin face turned a dull red. 'I never heard of such impudence in all my life,' he said, 'never. A butcher with views! And going to vote for them! Why, damme,' he continued, with angry sarcasm, 'we'll have the tailors, the bakers, and the candlestick-makers voting their own way next. Good God! What does the man think he's had thirty pounds a year for all these years, if not to do as he is bid?'

'He's behaving very ill, sir,' White said severely, 'very ill.'

'Ill!' Sir Robert cried. 'I should think he is, the scoundrel!' And he foamed over afresh, though we need not follow him. When he had cooled somewhat, 'Well,' he said, 'I can turn him out, and that I'll do, neck and crop! By God, I will! I'll ruin him. But there, it's the big rats set the fashion and the little ones follow it. This is Spinning Jenny's work. I wish I had cut off my hand before I voted for him. Well, well, well!' And he stood a moment in bitter contemplation of Sir Robert Peel's depravity. It was nothing that the late leader in the Commons was sound on reform. By adopting the Catholic side on the claims he – he, whose very nickname was Orange Peel – had rent the Party. And all these evils were the result!

The agent coughed.

Sir Robert, who was no fool, looked sharply at him. 'What!' he said grimly. 'Not another renegade?'

'No, sir,' White answered timidly. 'But Thrush, the pig-killer – he's one of the old lot, the Cripples, that your father put into the Corporation—'

'Ay, and I wish I had kept them cripples,' Sir Robert growled. 'All cripples! My father was right, and I was a fool to think that better men would do as well, and do us credit. In his time there were but two of the thirteen could read and write; but they did as they were bid. They did as they were bid. And now – well, man, what of Thrush?'

'He was goaled yesterday by Mr Forward, of Steynsham, for assault.'

'For how long?'

'For a fortnight, sir.'

Sir Robert nearly had a fit. He reared himself to his full height, and glared at White.

'The infernal rascal!' he cried. 'He did it on purpose!'

'I've no doubt, sir, that it determined them to fight,' the agent answered. 'With Dyas they are five. And five to seven is not such – such odds that they may not have some hope of winning.'

'Five to seven!' Sir Robert repeated; and at an end of words, at an end of oaths, could only stare aghast. 'Five to seven!' he muttered. 'You're not going to tell me – there's something more.'

'No, sir, no; that's the worst,' White answered, relieved that his tale was told. 'That's the worst, and may be bettered. I've thought it well to postpone the nomination until Wednesday the 4th, to give Serjeant Wathen a chance of dealing with Dyas.'

'Well, well!' Sir Robert grumbled. It had come to that. It had come to dealing with such men as butchers, to treating them as if they had minds to alter and views to change. 'Well, well!'

And that was all Sir Robert could say. And so it was settled; the Vermuyden dinner for the 2nd, the nomination and polling for the 4th.

'You'll let Mr Vaughan know,' Sir Robert concluded. 'It's well we can count on somebody.'

CHAPTER X

The Queen's Square Academy for Young Ladies

MISS SIBSON sat in state in her parlour in Queen's Square. Rather more dignified of mien than usual, and more highly powdered of nose, she was dividing her attention between the culprit in the corner, the elms outside – between which fledgling rooks were making adventurous voyages – and the longcloth which she was preparing for the young ladies' plain sewing; for in those days plain sewing was still taught in the most select academies. Nor, while the schoolmistress was thus engaged in providing for the domestic training of her charges, was she without assurance that their minds were under care. The double doors which separated the schoolroom from the parlour were ajar, and through the aperture one shrill voice after another could be heard, raised in monotonous perusal of Mrs Chapone's *Letters to a Young Lady upon the Improvement of the Mind.*

Miss Sibson wore her best dress, of black silk, secured halfway down the bodice by the large cameo brooch. But neither this nor the reading in the next room could avert her attention from her duties.

'The tongue,' she enunciated with great clearness, as she raised the longcloth in both hands and carefully inspected it over her glasses, 'is an unruly member. Ill-nature,' she continued, slowly meting off a portion, and measuring a second portion against it, 'is the fruit of a bad heart. Our opinions of others' – this with a stern look at Miss Hilhouse, fourteen years old, and in disgrace – 'are the reflections of ourselves.'

The young lady, who was paying with the backboard for a too ready wit, put out the unruly member, and, narrowly escaping detection, looked inconceivably sullen.

'The face is the mirror to the mind,' Miss Sibson continued thoughtfully, as she threaded a needle against the light. 'I hope, Miss Hilhouse, that you are now sorry for your fault.'

Miss Hilhouse maintained a stolid silence. Her shoulders ached, but she was proud.

'Very good,' said Miss Sibson, placidly; 'very good! With time comes reflection.'

Time, a mere minute, brought more than reflection. A gentleman walked quickly across the forecourt to the door, the knocker fell sharply, and Miss Hilhouse's sullenness dropped from her. She looked first uncomfortable, then alarmed.

'Please, may I go now?' she muttered.

Wise Miss Sibson paid no heed. 'A gentleman?' she said to the maid who had entered. 'Will I see him? Procure his name.'

'Oh, Miss Sibson,' came from the corner in an agonized whisper, 'please may I go?' Fourteen standing on a stool with a backboard could not bear to be seen by the other sex.

Miss Sibson looked grave. 'Are you sincerely sorry for your fault?' she asked.

'Yes.'

'And will you apologize to Miss Smith for your – your gross rudeness?'

'Ye-es.'

'Then go and do so,' Miss Sibson replied; 'and close the doors after you.'

The girl fled. Simultaneously Miss Sibson rose, with a mixture of dignity and blandness, to receive Arthur Vaughan. The schoolmistress of that day who had not manner at command had nothing; for deportment ranked among the essentials. And she was quite at her ease. The same could not be said of her visitor. But that his pride still smarted, but that the outrage of yesterday was fresh, but that he drew a savage satisfaction from the prospect of the apologies he was here to receive, he had not come. As it was, he had told himself more than once that he was a fool to come; a fool to set foot in the house. He was almost sure that he would have done more wisely had he burned the letter in which the schoolmistress informed him that she had an explanation to offer – and so had made an end.

Now, if in place of meeting him with humble apologies, the woman was going to bear herself as if no amends were due, he had indeed made a mistake.

Yet her manner said almost as much as that. 'Pray be seated, sir,' she said; and she indicated a chair.

He sat down stiffly, and glowered at her. 'I received your note,' he said.

She smoothed her ample lap, and looked at him more graciously.

'Yes,' she said, 'I was relieved to find that the unfortunate occurrence of yesterday was open to another explanation.'

'I have yet,' he said grimly, 'to hear the explanation.' Confound the woman's impudence!

'Exactly,' she said slowly. 'Exactly. Well, it turns out that the parcel you left behind you when you' – for an instant a smile broke the rubicund placidity of her face – 'when you retired so hurriedly contained a pelisse.'

'Indeed?' he said dryly.

'A pelisse and a letter.'

'Oh?'

'A letter from a lady who for some years has taken an interest in Miss Smith. The pelisse proved to be a gift from her.'

'Then I fail to see—'

'Exactly,' Miss Sibson interposed blandly, indeed too blandly. 'You fail to see why you came to be selected as the bearer? So do I. Perhaps you can explain that.'

'No,' he answered curtly. 'Nor is that my affair. What I fail to see, madam, is why Miss Smith did not at once suspect that the present came from the lady in question.'

'Because,' Miss Sibson replied, 'the lady was not known to be in this part of England. And because you, sir, maintained that Miss Smith had left the parcel in the coach.'

'I maintained what I was told.'

'But it was not the fact. However, let that pass.'

'No,' Vaughan retorted, with some warmth. 'For it seems to me, madam, extraordinary that in a matter which was capable of so simple an explanation you should elect to insult a stranger – a stranger who—'

'Who was performing no more than an office of civility, you would say?'

'Precisely.'

'Well – yes.' Miss Sibson spoke slowly, and was silent for a moment after she had spoken. Then, somewhat abruptly,

'You are an usher, I think,' she said, 'at Mr Bengough's Academy?'

Vaughan almost jumped in his chair. 'I, madam?' he cried. 'Certainly not!'

'Not at Mr Bengough's?'

'Certainly not!' he repeated, with indignation. Was the woman mad? An usher? Good heavens!

'I know your name,' she said slowly. 'But—'

'I came from London the day before yesterday. I am staying at the White Lion, and I am late of the 14th Dragoons.'

She raised her eyebrows. 'Oh, indeed,' she said. 'Is that so? Well,' rubbing a little of the powder from her nose with a needlecase, and looking at him shrewdly, 'I think,' she continued, 'that that is the answer to your question.'

Vaughan stared. 'I do not understand you,' he said.

'Then I will speak more plainly. Were you an usher at Mr Bengough's, your civility – civility I think you called it? – to my assistant had passed very well, Mr Vaughan. But the civility of a gentleman, late of the 14th Dragoons, fresh from London, and staying at the White Lion, to a young person in Miss Smith's position, is apt, as in this case – eh? – to lead to misconstruction.'

'You do me an injustice!' he said, reddening to the roots of his hair.

'Possibly, possibly,' Miss Sibson replied. And then, without warning, she gave way to a fit of silent laughter, which caused her portly form to shake like a jelly. This was a habit with her, attributed by some to her private view of Mrs Chapone's famous letters on the improvement of the mind; by others, to that knowledge of the tricks and turns of her sex with which thirty years of schoolkeeping had endowed her.

No doubt the face of rueful resentment with which Arthur Vaughan regarded her did not shorten the fit. But at last –

'Young gentleman,' she said, 'you don't deceive me! You did not come here today merely to hear an old woman make an apology.'

He tried to maintain an attitude of dignified surprise. But her jolly laugh, her shrewd red face, were too much for him. His eyes fell.

'Upon my honour,' he said, 'I meant nothing.'

She shook with fresh laughter. 'It is just of that I complain, sir,' she said.

'You can trust me.'

'I can trust Miss Smith,' she retorted, shaking her head. 'Her I know, though our acquaintance is of the shortest. Still, I know her from top to toe. You, young gentleman, I don't know. Mind,' she continued, with good-nature, 'I don't say that you meant any harm when you came today. But I'll wager you thought that you'd see her.'

Vaughan laughed out frankly. Her humour had conquered him.

'Well,' he said audaciously, 'and am I not to see her?'

Miss Sibson looked at him, and rubbed a little more powder from her nose.

'Umph!' she said doubtfully. 'If I knew you I'd know what to say to that. A pretty girl, eh?' she added, with her head on one side.

He smiled.

'And a good one! That I know. And if you were the usher at Mr Bengough's I'd ask no more, but I'd send for her. But—'

She stopped. Vaughan said nothing, but, a little out of countenance, looked at the floor.

There was a pause. Then, 'Just so, just so,' Miss Sibson said, as quietly as if he had answered her. 'Well, I am afraid I must not send for her.'

He looked at the carpet. 'I have seen so little of her,' he said.

'And are perhaps a gentleman of property?'

'I am independent.'

'Well, there it is.' Miss Smith smoothed out the lap of her silk dress.

'Yet,' he said, in some enbarrassment, 'I do not think that five minutes' talk would hurt her.'

'Umph!'

He laughed – a constrained laugh. 'Come, Miss Sibson,' he said. 'Let us have the five minutes, and let us both have the chance.'

She looked out of the window, and rubbed her glasses reflectively.

'Well,' she said at length, as if she had not quite made up her mind, 'I will be candid with you, Mr Vaughan. I did not intend to be so, but you have met me halfway, and I believe you to be a gentleman. The truth is, I should not have gone as far with you as I have unless' – she looked at him suddenly – 'I had had a character of you.'

'Of me?' he cried in astonishment.

'Yes.'

'From Miss Smith?'

Miss Sibson smiled at his simplicity. 'Oh no,' she said; 'you are going to see the character.' And with that she drew from her workbox a small slip of paper, which she unfolded and gave to him. 'It is from the lady,' she said, 'who made use of you yesterday.'

He took it in astonishment. On the inner side of the paper, which was faintly scented, he read a dozen words in a fine handwriting:

'Mary Smith, from her fairy godmother. The bearer may be trusted.'

Vaughan stared at the paper in undiminished surprise. 'I don't understand,' he said. 'Who is the lady, and what does she know of me?'

'I cannot tell you, nor can Miss Smith,' Miss Sibson replied, 'who, indeed, has seen her only twice or thrice at long intervals, and has not heard her name. But Miss Smith's education – she has never known her parents – was defrayed, I believe, by this godmother. And once a year Miss Smith has been in the habit of receiving a gift, of some value to a young person in her position, accompanied by a few words in that handwriting.'

Vaughan stared. 'And,' he said, 'you draw the inference that this godmother—'

'I draw no inference,' Miss Sibson replied dryly, 'save that I have authority from – shall I say her godmother – to trust you further than I should have trusted you. That is the only inference I draw. But I have one thing to add,' she continued. 'Miss Smith did not enter my employment in an ordinary way. My late assistant left me abruptly. While I was at a loss an attorney of standing in this city called on me and said that a client desired to place a young person in safe hands; that she was a trained teacher, and must live by teaching, but that care was necessary, since she was very young, and had more than her share of good looks. He hinted, Mr Vaughan, at the inference which you, I believe, have already drawn. And – that is all.'

Vaughan looked thoughtfully at the carpet.

Miss Sibson waited awhile. At last: 'The point is,' she said shrewdly, 'do you still wish to have the five minutes?'

Arthur Vaughan hesitated. He knew that he ought, that it was his duty, to say 'No'. But something in the woman's humorous eye challenged him, and recklessly – for the gratification of the moment – he said –

'Yes, if you please, I will see her.'

'Very good, very good,' Miss Sibson answered slowly. She had not been blind to the momentary hesitation. 'Then I will send her to you to make her apologies. Only be kind enough to remember that she does not know that you have seen that slip of paper.'

He assented, and with a good-natured nod Miss Sibson rose and went heavily from the room. Not for nothing was she held in Bristol a woman of sagacity beyond the ordinary, whose game of whist it was a pleasure to watch; nor without reason had that attorney of character, of whom we have heard, chosen her *in custodiam puellae*.

Vaughan waited, and, to be frank, his heart beat more quickly than usual. He knew that he was doing a foolish thing, though he had refused to commit himself; and an unworthy thing, though Miss Sibson, for her own reasons, had winked at it. He knew that he had no right to see the girl if he did not mean her well; and how could he mean her well when he had no intention of marrying her? For, for a man with his career in prospect to marry a girl in her position – to say nothing of the stigma which doubtless lay upon her birth – was a folly of which none but boys and old men were capable.

He listened, ill at ease, already repenting, already thinking that he had been a fool. The voices in the next room, reduced to a faint murmur by the closed doors, ceased. She was being told. She was being sent to him. He coloured. Yes, he was ashamed of himself. He rose and went to the window, and wished that he had said 'No'; that he had taken himself off. What was he doing at this time of life – the most sane and best balanced time of life – in this girls' school? It was unworthy of him.

The door opened, and he forgot his unworthiness, he forgot all. The abnormal attraction, allurement, charm, call it what you will, which had overcome him when she turned her eyes on him on the coach overcame him again – and tenfold. He thought that it must lie in her eyes, gentle as a dove's. And yet he did not know. He had not seen her indoors before, and her hair gathered in a knot at the back of her head was a Greek surprise to him; while her blushes, the quivering of her mouth, her figure slender but full of grace, and high-girdled after the mode of the day – all, all were so perfect, so enticing, that he knew not where the magic lay.

But magic there was. And such magic that though he had prepared himself, and though the last thing in his thoughts was to insult her, he forgot himself. As she paused, her hand still resting on the door, her face downcast and distressed, 'Good God,' he cried, 'how beautiful you are!'

And she saw that he meant no insult, that the words burst from him spontaneously. But not the less for that was their effect on her. She turned white, her very heart seeming to stop, she appeared to be about to swoon. While he, forgetting all but her shrinking beauty, devoured her with his eyes.

Until he remembered himself. Then he turned from her to the window.

'Forgive me!' he cried. 'Forgive me! I did not know what I said. You came on me so suddenly, you looked so beautiful—'

He stopped; he could not go on.

And she was trembling from head to foot; but she made an effort to escape back to the commonplace.

'I came,' she murmured – it was clear that she hardly knew what she was saying – 'Miss Sibson told me to come to say that I – I was sorry, sir, that I – I misjudged you yesterday.'

'Yesterday? Yesterday?' he cried, almost angrily. 'Bah, it is an age since yesterday!'

She could make no answer to that, though she knew well what he meant. If she answered him it was only by suffering him to gaze at her in an eloquent silence – a silence in which his eyes cried again and again, 'How beautiful you are!' While her eyes, downcast, under trembling lashes, her heart beaten down, defenceless, cried only for 'Quarter, quarter!'

They were yards apart. The table, and on it Miss Sibson's squat workbox and a pile of longcloth, was between them. Miss Sibson herself could have desired nothing more proper. And yet –

'Farewell, farewell, my faithless shield;
Thy lord at length is forced to yield.
Vain, vain is every outward care;
The foe's within and triumphs there!'

It was all over. In her ears would ring for ever his words of worship – the cry of the man to the woman, 'How beautiful you are?' She would thrill with pleasure when she thought of them, and burn with shame, and never, never, never be the same again! And for him, with that cry forced from him, love had become present, palpable, real, and the idea of marriage real also; an idea to be withstood, to be combated, to be treated as foolish, Byronic, impossible. But an idea which would not leave him any more than the image of her gentle beauty, indelibly stamped on his brain, would leave him. He might spend some days or some weeks in doubt and wretchedness. But from that moment the odds were against him, for he was young, and passion had never had her way with him – as seriously against him as against the army that with spies and traiters in its midst moves against an united foe.

Not a word that was *convenant* had passed between them, though so much had passed, when a heavy footstep crossed the forecourt, and stopped at the door. The knocker fell sharply twice, and recalled them to realities.

'I – I must go,' she faltered, wrestling herself from the spell of his eyes. 'I have said what I – I hope you understand, and – it is time I went.' How her heart was beating!

'Oh no, no!'

'Yes, I must go!'

Too late! A loud voice in the passage, a heavy step, announced a visitor. The door flew open, and there entered, pushing the startled maid aside, the Honourable Bob Flixton, at the height of his glory, loud, impudent, and unabashed.

'Run to earth, my lad!' he cried boisterously. 'Run to earth! Run—'

He broke off, gaping, as his eyes fell upon poor Mary, who, in making way for him, had in part hidden herself behind the door. He whistled in great amazement, and 'Hope I don't intrude,' he continued. And he grinned; while Vaughan, looking blackest thunder at him, could find no words that were adequate. To think that this loud-voiced, confident fool, the Don Giovanni of the regiment, had stumbled on his pearl!

'Well, well, well!' the Honourable Bob resumed, casting down his eyes as if he were shocked. And again: 'I hope I don't intrude,' he continued – it was the parrot cry of that year. 'I didn't know. I'll take myself off again' – he whistled low – 'as fast as I can.'

But Vaughan felt that to let him go thus, to spread the tale with a thousand additions and innuendoes, was worst of all.

'Wait, if you please,' he said, with a note of sternness in his tone. 'I am coming with you, Flixton. Good morning, Miss Smith.'

'See here, won't you introduce me?' cried the irrepressible Bob.

'No!' Vaughan answered curtly, and without staying to reflect. 'You will kindly tell Miss Sibson, Miss Smith, that I am obliged, greatly obliged to her. Now come, Flixton! I have done my business, and we are not wanted here.'

'I come reluctantly,' said Bob, allowing himself to be dragged out, but not until he had cast a last languishing look at the beauty. And on the doorstep, 'Sly dog, sly dog!' he said. 'To think that in Bristol, where pretty girls are as scarce as mushrooms in March, there should be such an angel! Damme, an angel! And you the discoverer. It beats all!'

'Shut up,' Vaughan answered angrily. 'You know nothing about it!' And then, still more sourly, 'See here, Flixton, I take it ill of you following me here. It was too cool, I say.'

But the Honourable Bob was not quick to quarrel. 'I saw you go in, dear chap,' he cried heartily. 'I wanted to tell you that the hour of dinner was changed. See? Did my own errand, and coming back, thought I'd – truth was, I fancied you'd some little game on hand.'

'Nothing of the kind!'

The Honourable Bob stopped. 'Honour bright? Honour bright?' he repeated eagerly. 'Mean to say, Vaughan, you're not on the track of that little filly?'

Vaughan scowled. 'Not in the way you mean,' he answered sternly. 'You make a mistake. She's a good girl.'

Flixton winked. 'Heard that before, my lad,' he said, 'more than once. From my grandmother. I'll take my chance of that.'

Vaughan would have been glad to fall upon him and pommel him. But there were objections to that course. On the other hand, his feelings had cooled in the last few minutes, and he was far from prepared to announce off-hand that he was going to marry the beauty. So, 'No, you will not, Flixton,' he said. 'Let it go! Do you hear? The fact is,' he continued, in some embarrassment, 'I'm in a sort of fiduciary relation to the young lady, and – and I am not going to see her played with. That's the fact.'

'Fiduciary relation?' the Honourable Bob retorted, in perplexity. 'What the deuce is that? Never heard of it! D'you mean, man, that you are – eh? – related to her? Of course, if so—'

'No, I am not related to her.'

'Then—'

'But I'm not going to see her made a fool of, that's flat!'

An idea struck the Honourable Bob. He stared. 'See here,' he said in a tone of misgiving, 'you ain't – you ain't thinking of marrying her?'

Vaughan's cheeks burned. 'Maybe, and maybe not,' he said curtly. 'Either way, it is my business!'

'But surely you're not? Man alive!'

'It is my business, I say!'

'Of course, of course, if it is as bad as that,' Flixton answered with a grin. 'But – hope I don't intrude, Vaughan, but ain't you making a bit of a fool of yourself? What'll old Vermuyden say, eh?'

'That's my business!' Vaughan answered haughtily.

'Just so, just so; and quite enough for me. All I say is, if you are not in earnest yourself, don't play the dog in the manger!'

CHAPTER XI

Don Giovanni Flixton

MANY WERE the surprises with which the last week of April and the first week of May of that year were fraught in the political world. It is probable that they saw more astonished people than are to be found in England in an ordinary twelvemonth. The Party which had monopolized power for half a century, and to that end and the advancement of themselves, their influence, their friends, and their dependants, had spent the public money, strained the law, and supported the mob, were incredibly, nay, were bitterly surprised when they saw all these engines turned against them; when they found dependants falling off and friends growing cold; above all, when they discovered that rabble, which they had so often directed, aiming its brickbats against their windows.

But it is unlikely that any Tory of them all was more surprised by the change in the political aspect than Arthur Vaughan, when he came to think of it, by the position in which he had placed himself in Queen's Square. Certainly he had taken no irrevocable step. He had said nothing positive; his honour was not engaged. But he had said a good deal. On the spur of the moment, moved by the strange attraction which the girl had for him, he had spoken after a fashion which only further speech could justify. And then, not content with that, as if fortune were determined to make sport of his discretion, he had been led by another impulse – call it generosity, call it jealousy, call it what you will – to say more to Bob Flixton than he had said to her.

He had done this, who had hitherto held himself a little above the common run of men. Who had chalked out his career and never doubted that he had the strength to follow it. Who had not been content to wait, idle and dissipated, for a dead man's shoes, but in the pride of a mind which he believed to be the master of his passions had set his face towards the high prizes of the senate and the forum. He, who if he could not be Fox, would be Erskine. Who would be anything, in a word, except the empty-headed man of pleasure, or the plain dullard satisfied to sit in a corner with a little.

He, who had planned such a future, now found himself on the brink – ay, on the very point – of committing as foolish an act as the most thoughtless could commit. He was dreaming of marrying a girl below him in station, still further below him in birth, whom he had only known three days, whom he had only seen three times! And all because she had beautiful eyes, and looked at him – Heavens, how she had looked at him!

He went hot as he pictured her with her melting eyes, hanging towards him a little as the ivy inclines to the oak. And then he turned cold. And cold, he considered what he was going to do!

Of course he was not going to marry her.

No doubt he had said to her more than he should have said. But his honour was not engaged. The girl was not the worse for him; even if that which he had read in her eyes was real, she would get over it as quickly as he would. But marry her, give way to an evanescent feeling, let himself be swayed by a fancy at which he would laugh a year later – no! He was not so weak. He had not only his career to consider, but the family honours which would be his one day. What would old Vermuyden say if he impaled a baton sinister with the family arms, added a Smith to the family alliances, married the nameless, penniless teacher in a girls' school?

No, of course, he was not going to marry her. What he had said to the Honourable Bob, he had said to shield her from a Don Juan. He had not meant it. He would go for a long walk and put the notion and the girl out of his head, and come back cured of his folly, and make a merry night of it with the old set. And tomorrow – no, the morrow was Sunday – on Monday he would return to London and to all the chances which the changing political situation must open to an ambitious man. He regretted that he had not taken the Chancellor's hint and sought a seat in the House.

But a solitary ramble in the valley of the Avon, which was a hundredfold more beautiful in those days than in these, because less spoiled by the hand of man; a ramble by the

Logwood Mills, with their clear-running weedy stream, by King's Weston and Leigh Woods – such a ramble, tuneful with the songs of birds and laden with the scents of spring, may not be the surest cure for that passion, which

> *is not to be reasoned down or lost*
> *In high ambition or a thirst for greatness!*

At any rate he returned uncured, and for the first part of the Honourable Bob's dinner was wildly merry. After that he fell into a moody silence which his host was not the last to note.

Fortunately with the removal of the cloth and the first brisk journey of the decanters came news. A waiter brought it. Hart Davies, the Tory candidate for Bristol, and for twenty years its Member, had withdrawn, seeing his chance hopeless. The retirement was unexpected, and it caused so much surprise that the party could think of nothing else. Nine-tenths of those present were Tories, and Flixton proposed that they should sally forth, and vent their feelings by smashing the windows of the Bush, the Radical headquarters; a feat performed many a time before with no worse consequences than a broken head or two. But Colonel Brereton set his foot on the proposal.

'I'll put you under arrest if you do,' he said. 'I'm senior officer of the district, and I'll not have it, Flixton! Do you think that this is the time, you madmen,' he continued, looking round the table with indignation, 'to provoke the rabble, and get the throats of half Bristol cut?'

'Oh, come, Colonel, it is not as bad as that!' Flixton remonstrated.

'You don't know how bad it is!' Brereton answered, his brooding eyes kindling. And he developed anew his fixed idea that the forces of disorder, if provoked, were irresistible; that the country was at their mercy, and that only by humouring them, a course suggested also by humanity, could the storm be weathered.

The company consisted mainly of reckless young subalterns flushed with wine. They listened out of respect to his rank, but they grinned behind his back; until, half conscious of ridicule, he grew angry. On ordinary occasions Flixton would have been the worst offender. But he had the grace to remember that the Colonel was his guest, and he sought to turn the subject.

'Come, come!' he cried, hammering the table and pushing the bottle. 'Let the Colonel alone. For Heaven's sake shelve the cursed Bill! I'm sick of it! It's the death of all fun and jollity. I'll give you a sentiment. "The Fair when they are Kind, and the Kind when they are Fair." Fill up! Fill up all, and drink it!'

They echoed the toast in various tones, sober or fuddled. For some began to grow excited. A glass was shattered and flung noisily into the fire. A new one was called for, also noisily.

'Now, Bill,' Flixton continued to his right-hand neighbour, 'it's your turn! Give us something spicy!' And he hammered the table. 'Captain Codrington's sentiment.'

'Let's have a minute!' pleaded the gentleman assailed.

'Not a minute,' boisterously. 'See, the table's waiting for you! Captain Codrington's sentiment!'

Men of small genius kept a written list, and committed some lines to memory before dinner. The Captain was one of these. But the call on him was sudden, and he sought, with an agonized mind, for a sentiment which might seem novel. At last, with a sigh of relief, '*Maids and Missuses!*' he cried.

'Ay, ay, Maids and Missuses!' the Honourable Bob echoed, raising his glass. 'And especially,' he whispered, calling his neighbour's attention to Vaughan by a shove, 'School-missuses! School-missuses, my lad! Here, Vaughan,' he continued aloud, 'you must drink this, and no heeltaps!'

Vaughan caught his name and awoke from a reverie. 'Very good,' he said, raising his glass. 'What is it?'

'Maids and Missuses!' the Honourable Bob replied, with a wink at his neighbour. And then, incited by the fumes of the wine he had taken, he rose to his feet and raised his glass. 'Gentlemen,' he said, 'gentlemen!'

'Silence!' they cried. 'Silence for Bob's speech.'

'Gentlemen,' he resumed, a spark of malice in his eyes, 'I've a piece of news to give you! It's news that – that's been mighty slyly kept by a gentleman here present. Devilish close he's kept it, I'll say that for him! But he's a neat hand that can bamboozle Bob Flixton, and I've run him to earth, run him to earth this morning, and got it out of him.'

'Hear! Hear! Bob! Go on, Bob! What is it?' from the company.

'You are going to hear, my Trojans! And no flam! Gentlemen, charge your glasses! I've the honour to inform you that our old friend and tip-topper, Arthur Vaughan, otherwise the Counsellor, has got himself regularly put up, knocked down, and sold to as pretty a piece of the feminine as you'll see in a twelvemonth! Prettiest in Bristol, 'pon honour,' with feeling, 'be the other who she may! Regular case of—' and in irresistibly comic accents, with his head and glass alike tilted, he trolled –

There first for thee my passion grew,
Sweet, sweet Matilda Pottingen;
Thou wast the daughter of my tu-
-tor, law professor at the U-
-niversity of Göttingen!
-niversity of Göttingen!

'Don't laugh, gentlemen! It's so! He's entered on the way-bill, booked through to matrimony, and' – the Honourable Bob was undoubtedly a little tipsy – 'and it only remains for us to give him a good send-off. So charge your glasses, and—'

Brereton laid his hand on his arm. He was sober, and he did not like the look of Vaughan's disgusted face. 'One moment, Flixton,' he said, 'is this true, Mr Vaughan?'

Vaughan's brow was as black as thunder. He had never dreamt that, drunk or sober, Flixton would be guilty of such a breach of confidence. He hesitated. Then, 'No!' he said.

'It's not true?' Codrington struck in. 'You are not going to be married, old chap?'

'No!'

'But, man,' Flixton hiccoughed, 'you told me so – or something like it – only this morning.'

'You either misunderstood me,' Vaughan answered, in a tone so distinct as to be menacing, 'or, if you prefer it, I've changed my mind. In either case it is my business! And I'll trouble you to leave it alone!'

'Oh, if you put it – that way, old chap?'

'I do put it that way!'

'And any way,' Brereton interposed hurriedly, 'this is no time for marrying! I've told you boys before, and I tell you again—'

And he plunged into a fresh argument on the old point. Two or three joined issue, grinning. Vaughan, as soon as attention was diverted from him, slipped away.

He was horribly disgusted, and sunk very low in his own eyes. He loathed what he had done. He had not, indeed, been false to the girl, for he had given her no promise. He had not denied her, for her name had not been mentioned. He had not gone back on his resolution, for he had never formed one seriously. Yet in a degree he had done all these things. He had played a shabby part by himself and by the girl. He had been meanly ashamed of her. And though his conduct had followed the lines which he had marked out, he hoped that he might never again feel so unhappy, or so poor a thing, as he felt as he walked the streets and cursed his discretion.

Discretion! Cowardice was the right name for it. For he knew now that he loved the girl; yet because she, the most beautiful, pure, and gentle creature on whom his eyes had ever rested, was called Mary Smith, and taught in a school, he disavowed her.

He did not know that he was suffering what a man, whose mind has so far governed his heart, must suffer when the latter rebels. In planning his life he had ignored his heart; now he must pay the penalty. He went to bed at last, but not to sleep. Instead he lived the scene over and over again, now wondering what he ought to have done; now brooding on what Flixton must think of him; now on what she, whose nature, he was sure, was as perfect as her face, would think of him, if she knew. How she would despise him!

The next day was Sunday, and he spent it, in accordance with a previous promise, with Brereton at his pleasant home at Newchurch, a mile from the city. Though the most recent of his Bristol acquaintances, Brereton was the most congenial; and a dozen times Vaughan was on the point of confiding his trouble to him. He was deterred by the melancholy cast of Brereton's character, which gave promise of no decisive advice. And early in the evening he took leave of his host and strolled towards the Downs, balancing *I would* against *I will not;* now facing the bleak of a prudent decision, now thrilling with foolish rapture as he pondered another event. Lord Eldon had married young and with as little prudence; it had not impeded his rise, nor Erskine's. Doubtless Sir Robert Vermuyden would say that he had disgraced himself; but he cared little for that. What he had to combat was the more personal pride of the man who, holding himself a little wiser than his fellows, cannot bear to do a thing that in the eyes of the foolish may set him below them!

Of course he came to no decision; though he wandered on Brandon Hill until the Float at his feet ceased to mirror the lights, and Bristol lay dark below him. And Monday found him still hesitating. Thrice he started to take his place on the coach. And thrice he turned back, hating himself for his weakness. If he could not overcome a foolish fancy, how could he hope to scale the heights of the Western Circuit, or hurl Coleridge and Follett from their pride of place? Or, still harder task, how would he dare to confront in the House the cold eye of Croker or of Goulburn? No, he could not hope to do either. He had been wrong in his estimate of himself. He was a poor creature, unable to hold his own among his fellows, impotent to guide his own life!

He was still contesting the matter when, a little before noon, he espied Flixton in the act of threading his way through the busy crowd of Broad Street. The Honourable Bob was wearing hessians, and a high-collared green riding coat, with an orange vest and a soft many-folded cravat. In fine, he was so smart that suspicion entered Vaughan's head, and on its heels – jealousy.

In a twinkling he was on Flixton's track. Broad Street, the heart of Bristol, was thronged, for Hart Davie's withdrawal was in the air and an election crowd was abroad. Newsboys with their sheets, tipsy ward-leaders, and gossiping merchants jostled one another. The beau's green coat, however, shone conspicuous.

Glorious was his course,
And long the track of light he left behind him!

And before Vaughan had asked himself if he were justified in following, pursued and pursuer were over Bristol Bridge, and making, by way of the Welsh Back – a maze of coal-hoys and dangling cranes – for Queen's Square.

Vaughan doubted no longer, weighed the propriety of his course no longer. For a cool-headed man of the world, who asked nothing better than to master a silly fancy, he was foolishly perturbed. He made on with a grim face; but a dray loading at a Newport coal-hulk drew across his path, and Flixton was moving under the pleasant elms and amid the groups that loitered up and down the sunlit Square, before Vaughan came within hail, and called him by name.

Flixton turned then, saw who it was, and grinned – nothing abashed.

'Well,' he said, tipping his hat a little to one side, 'well, old chap! Are you let out of school too?'

Vaughan had discovered Mary Smith and her little troop under the trees in the farthest corner. But he tried to smile – and did so, a little awry.

'This is not fair play, Flixton,' he said.

'That is just what I think it is,' the Honourable Bob answered cheerfully. 'Eh, old chap? Neat trick of yours the other day, but not neat enough! Thought to bamboozle me and win a clear field! Neat! But no go, I found you out, and now it is my turn. That's what I call fair play.'

'Look here, Flixton,' Vaughan replied – he was fast losing his composure – 'I'm not going to have it. That's plain.'

The Honourable Bob stared. 'Oh!' he answered. 'Let's understand one another. Are you going to marry the girl after all?'

'I've told you—'

'Oh, you've told me, yes, and you've told me, no. The question is, which is it?'

Vaughan controlled himself. He could see Mary out of the corner of his eye, and knew that she had not taken the alarm as yet. But the least violence might attract her attention.

'Whichever it be,' he said firmly, 'is no business of yours.'

'If you claim the girl—'

'I do not claim her, Flixton. I have told you that. But—'

'But you mean to play the dog in the manger?'

'I mean to see,' Vaughan replied sternly, 'that you don't do her any harm.'

Flixton hesitated. Secretly he held Vaughan in respect, and he would have postponed his visit to Queen's Square had he foreseen that that gentleman would detect him. But to retreat now was another matter. The duel was still in vogue; barely two years before the Prime Minister had gone out with a brother peer in Battersea Fields; barely twenty years before one Cabinet Minister had shot another on Wimbledon Common. He could not, therefore, afford to show the white feather, and though he hesitated, it was not for long.

'You mean to see to that, do you?' he retorted.

'I do.'

'Then come and see,' he returned flippantly. 'I'm going to have a chat with the young lady now. That's not murder, I suppose?'

And he turned on his heel and strolled across the turf towards the group of which Mary was the centre.

Vaughan followed with black looks: and when Mary Smith, informed of their approach by one of the children, turned a startled face towards them, he was at Flixton's shoulder, and pressing before him.

But the Honourable Bob had the largest share of impudence, and he was the first to speak.

'Miss Smith,' he said, raising his hat with *aplomb*, 'I – you remember me, I am sure?'

Vaughan pushed before him; and before the girl could speak – for jealousy is a fine spoiler of manners –

'This gentleman,' he said, 'wishes to see—'

'To see' – said Flixton, with a lower bow.

'Miss Sibson!' Vaughan exclaimed.

The children stared, gazing up into the men's faces with the undisguised curiosity of childhood. Fortunately, the Mary Smith who had to confront the two was no longer the Mary Smith whom Vaughan's appearance had stricken with panic three days before. For one thing she knew Miss Sibson better, and feared her less. For another, her fairy godmother – the gleam of whose gifts never failed to leave a hope of change, a prospect of something other than the plodding, endless round – had shown a fresh sign. And last, not least, a more potent fairy, a fairy whose wand had power to turn Miss Sibson's house into a Palace Beautiful, and Queen's Square, with its cawing rooks and ordered elms, into an enchanted forest, had visited her. True, Vaughan had left her abruptly, to cool her burning cheeks and still her heart as she best might! But he had said what she would never forget, and though he had left her doubting, he had left her loving. And so the Mary who found herself addressed by two gallants was much less abashed than she who on Friday had had to do with one.

Still she was astonished by the manner in which they accosted her; and she showed this, modestly.

'If you wish to see Miss Sibson,' she said – instinctively she looked at Vaughan's companion – 'I will send for her.'

And she was turning, with comparative ease, to dispatch one of the children on the errand, when the Honourable Bob interposed.

'But we don't want Miss Sibson – now,' he said. 'A man may change his mind as well as a woman! Eh, old chap?' turning to his friend with simulated good-humour. 'I'm sure you will say so, Miss Smith.'

She wondered what their odd manner to one another meant. And, to add to her dignity, she laid her hand on the shoulder of one of her charges and drew her closer.

'Moreover, I'm sure,' Flixton continued – for Vaughan, after that one outburst, stood sulkily silent – 'I'm sure Mr Vaughan will agree with me—'

'I?'

'Oh yes, he will, Miss Smith, because he is the most changeable of men himself! A weathercock, upon my honour!' And he pointed to the tower of St Mary, which, from the high ground of Redcliffe Parade on the farther side of the water, looks down on the Square. 'Never of the same mind two days together!'

Vaughan snubbed him savagely. 'Be good enough to leave me out!' he said.

'There!' the Honourable Bob answered, throwing himself into an attitude, 'he wants to stop my mouth! But I'm not to be stopped. Of all men he's the least right to say that I mustn't change my mind. Why, if you'll believe me, Miss Smith, no further back than Saturday morning he was all for being married! 'Pon honour! Went away from here talking of nothing else! In the evening he was just as dead the other way! Nothing was further from his thoughts. Shuddered at the very idea! Come, old chap, don't look fierce!' And he grinned at Vaughan. 'You can't deny it!'

Vaughan could have struck him; the trick was so neat and so malicious. Fortunately a man who had approached them touched Vaughan's elbow at the critical moment, and diverted his wrath.

'Express for you, sir,' he said. 'Come by chaise, been looking for you everywhere, sir!'

Vaughan smothered the execration which rose to his lips, snatched the letter, and waved the man aside. Then, swelling with rage, he turned upon Flixton. But, before he could speak, the matter was taken out of his hands.

'Children,' Mary Smith said, in a clear, steady voice, 'it is time we went in. The hour is up, collect your hoops. I think,' she continued, looking coldly at the Honourable Bob, 'you have addressed me under a misapprehension, sir, intending to address yourself to Miss Sibson. Good morning! Good morning!' – with a slight and significant bow which included both gentlemen.

And, taking a child by either hand, she turned her back on them, and with her little flock clustering about her, and her pretty head held high, she went slowly across the road to the school. Her lips were quivering, but the men could not see that. And her heart was bursting, but only she knew that.

Without that knowledge Vaughan was furious. It was not only that the other had got the better of him by a sly trick, but he was conscious that he had shown himself at his worst – stupid when tongue-tied, and rude when he spoke. Yet he controlled himself until Mary was out of earshot, then he turned upon Flixton.

'What right – what right,' he snarled, 'had you to say what I would do? And what I would not do? I consider your conduct—'

'Steady, man!' Flixton, who was much the cooler of the two, said. He was a little pale. 'Think before you speak. You would interfere. What did you expect? That I was going to play up to you?'

'I expected at least—'

'Ah, well, you can tell me another time what you expected, I have an engagement now and must be going,' the Honourable Bob said. 'See you again!'

And with a cool nod he turned on his heel, and assured that, whatever came of the affair, he had had the best of that bout, he strode off.

Vaughan was only too well aware of the same fact. And but that he held himself in habitual control, he would have followed and struck his rival. As it was, he stood a moment looking blackly after him. Then, sobered somewhat, though still bitterly chagrined, he took his way towards his hotel, carrying in his oblivious hand the letter which had been given him. Once he halted, half minded to return to Miss Sibson's and to see Mary and explain. He took, indeed, some steps in the backward direction. But he reflected that if he went he must speak, and plainly. And, angry as he was, furiously in love as he was, was he prepared to speak?

He was not prepared. And while he stood doubting between that eternal would and would not, his eyes fell on the letter in his hand.

CHAPTER XII

A Rotten Borough

CHIPPINGE, Sir Robert Vermuyden's borough, was in no worse case than two-thirds of the small boroughs of that day. Still, of its great men, Cowley might have written:

> *Nothing they but dust can show,*
> *Or bones that hasten to be so.*

And of its greatness he might have said the same. The one and the other belonged to the past.

The town occupies a low, green hill, dividing two branches of the Avon, which join their waters a furlong below. Built on the ridge, and clinging to the slopes of this eminence, the stone-tiled houses look pleasantly over the gentle undulations of the Wiltshire pastures – no pastures more green; and at a distance are pleasantly seen from them. But viewed more closely – at the date of which we write – the picturesque in the scene became mean or incongruous. Of the Mitred Abbey that crowned the hill, and had once owned these fertile slopes, there remained but the maimed hulk, patched and botched, and long degraded to the uses of that parish church, its neighbour, of which nothing but the steeple survived. The crown-shaped market-cross, once a dream of beauty in stone, still stood, but, battered and defaced; while the Abbot's gateway, under which sovereigns had walked, was sunk to a vile lock-up, the due corrective of the tavern which stood cheek by jowl with it.

Still, to these relics, grouped as they were upon an open triangular green, the hub of the town, there clung, in spite of all, some shadow of greatness. The stranger whose eye fell on the doorway of the Abbey Church, with its whorls of sculptured images, gazed and gazed again with a sense of wondering awe. But let him turn his back on these buildings, and his eye met, in grass-grown street and sordid alley, a lower depth. Everywhere were things once fine, sunk to base uses; old stone mansions converted into tenements; the solid houses of medieval burghers into crazy taverns; fretted cloisters into pigsties and hovels; a Gothic arch propped the sagging flank of a timbered stable. Or if anything of the beauty of a building survived, it was masked by climbing penthouses; or, like the White Lion, the old inn which had been the Abbot's guest-house, it was altered out of all likeness to its former self. For the England of '31, gross and matter-of-fact, was not awake to the value of those relics of a noble past which generations of intolerance had hurried to decay.

Doubtless in this smouldering, dusty shell was snug, warm living. Georgian comfort had outlived the wig and the laced coat, and though the influence of the Church was at its lowest ebb, and morals were not much higher, inns were plenty and flourished, and in the panelled parlours of the White Lion or the Heart and Hand was much good eating, followed by deep drinking. The London road no longer passed through the town; the great fair had fallen into disuse. But the cloth trade, by which Chippinge had once thriven, had been revived, and the town was not quite fallen. Still, of all its former glories, it retained but one intact. It returned two Members to Parliament. That which Birmingham and Sheffield had not, this little borough of eighteen hundred souls enjoyed. Fallen in all other points, it retained, or rather its High Steward, Sir Robert Vermuyden, retained, the right of returning, by the votes of its Alderman and twelve capital burgesses, two Members to the Commons' House.

And Sir Robert could not by any stretch of fancy bring himself to believe that the town would willingly part with the privilege. Why should it strip itself? he argued. It enjoyed the honour vicariously indeed. But did he not year by year pay the Alderman and eight of the capital burgesses thirty pounds apiece for their interest, a sum which quickly filtered through their pockets and enriched the town, besides taking several of the voters off the rates? Did he not also at election times set the taps running and distribute a moderate largess among the commonalty, and – and in fact do everything which it behoved a liberal and enlightened patron to do? Nay, had he not, since his accession, raised the status of the voters, long and vulgarly known as the 'Cripples', so that they, who in his father's time had been, almost without exception, drunken illiterates, were now, to the extent of at least one half, men of respectable position?

No, Sir Robert declined to believe that Chippinge had any wish for a change so adverse to its interests. The most he would admit was that there might be some slight disaffection in the place, due to that confounded Bowood, which was for ever sapping and mining and seeking to rob its neighbours.

But even he was presently to be convinced that there was an odd spirit abroad in this year '31. The New Police and the new steam railways, and this cholera of which people were beginning to talk, were not the only new things. There were new ideas in the air; and the birds seemed to carry them. They took possession not only of the troublesome and discontented – poachers whom Sir Robert had gaoled, or the sons of men whom his father had pressed – but of the most unlikely people. Backs that had never been aught but pliant grew stiff. Men who had put up with the old system for more years than they could remember grew restive. Others, who had all their lives stood by while their inferiors ruled the roost, discovered that they had rights. Nay – strangest thing of all – some who had thriven by the old management and could not hope to gain by a change revolted, after the fashion of Dyas the butcher, and proved the mastery of mind over matter. Not many, indeed; martyrs for ideas are rare. But their action went for much, and when later the great mass of the voteless began to move, there were rats in plenty of the kind that desert sinking ships. By that time he was a bold man who in tavern or workshop spoke for the rule of the few, to which Sir Robert fondly believed his borough to be loyal.

Fortunately for himself White had never shared that belief or he had had a rude awakening on the first Monday in May. It was customary for the Vermuyden interest to meet the candidates on the Chippenham road, half an hour before the dinner hour, and to attend them in procession through the town to the White Lion. Often this was all that the commonalty saw of an election, and a little horseplay was both expected and allowed. In old days, when the 'Cripples' had been drawn from the lowest class, their grotesque appearance in the van of the gentlemanly interest had given rise to many a home-jest. The crowd would follow them jeering and laughing, and there would be some pushing, and a drunken man or two would fall. But all had passed in good-humour; the taps had been running in one interest, the ale was Sir Robert's, and the crowd envied while they laughed.

White, as he stood on the bridge reviewing the first-comers, wished he might have no worse to expect today. But he did not hope as much. The town was crowded, and the streets down to the bridge were so cumbered with moving groups that it was plain the procession would have to push its way. For certain, too, many of the people did not belong to Chippinge. With the townsfolk White knew he could deal. He did not believe that there was a Chippinge man who, eye to eye with him, would cast a stone. But here were yokels from Calne and Bowood, who knew not Sir Robert; with Bristol lambs and men as dangerous, and not a few Radicals from a distance, rabid with zeal and overflowing with promises. Made up of such elements the crowd hooted from time to time, and there was a threat in the sound that filled White with misgivings.

Nor was this the worst. The cloth factory stood close to the bridge. The procession must pass it. And the hands employed in it, hostile to a man, were gathered before the doorway, in their aprons and paper caps, waiting to give the show a reception. They had much to say already, their jeers and taunts filling the air; but White had a shrewd suspicion that they had worse missiles in their pockets.

Still, he had secured the attendance of a score of sturdy fellows, sons of Sir Robert's farmers, and these, with a proportion of the tagrag and bobtail of the town, gave a fairly solid aspect to his party. Nor was the jeering all on one side, though that deep and unpleasant groaning which now and again rolled down the street was wholly Whiggish.

Alas, it was when the agent came to analyse his men that he had most need of the smile that deceives. True, the Rector was there and the curate of Eastport, and the clerk and the sexton – the two last-named were voters. And there were also four or five squires arrayed in support of the gentlemanly interest, and as many young bucks come to see the fun. Then there were three other voters: the Alderman, who was a small grocer, and Annibal the basket-maker – these two were stalwarts – and Dewell the barber, also staunch, but a timid man. But where was Dyas, Sir Robert's burliest supporter in old days? And where was Thrush the pig-killer? Alas, the jaws of a Radical gaol held him. And where, last and heaviest blow of all – for it had fallen without warning – was Pillinger of the Blue Duck? Pillinger, his wife said, was ill. Worse, he was in the hands of a Radical doctor, capable, the agent believed, of hocussing him until the polling was over. The truth about Pillinger – whether he lay ill or whether he lay shamming, whether he was at the mercy of the apothecary or under the thumb of his wife – White could not learn. He hoped to learn it before it was too late. But for the present Pillinger was not here.

The Alderman, Annibal, Dewell, the clerk, the sexton, and Arthur Vaughan. White totted them up again and again and made them six. The Bowood voters he made five – four stalwarts and Dyas the butcher.

Certainly he might still poll Pilinger. But, on the other hand, Mr Vaughan might arrive too late. White had written to his address in town, and receiving no answer had sent an express to Bristol on the chance that the young gentleman tarried there. Probably he would be in time. But when things are so very close – and when there are alarm and defeat in the air – men grow nervous. White smiled as he chatted with the pompous Rector and the country squires, but he was very anxious. He thought of old Sir Robert at Stapylton, and he sweated at the notion of defeat. Cobbett had reached his mind, but Sir Robert had reached his heart.

'Boo!' moaned the crowd higher up the street. The sound sank and the harsh voice of a speaker came fitfully over the heads of the people.

'Who's that?' asked old Squire Rowley, one of the country gentlemen.

'Some spouter from Bristol, sir, I fancy,' the agent replied, rising on his toes to look. Then with his eye he whipped in a couple of hobbledehoys who seemed inclined to stray towards the enemy.

'I suppose,' the Squire continued, lowering his voice, 'you can depend on your men, White?'

'Oh Lord. yes, sir,' White answered. Like a good election agent, he took no one into his confidence. 'We've enough here to do the trick. Besides, young Mr Vaughan will be here tomorrow, and the landlord of the Blue Duck, who is not well enough to walk today, will poll. He'd break his heart, bless you,' White continued, with a brow of brass, 'if he could not vote for Sir Robert?'

'Seven to five.'

'Seven to four, sir.'

'But Dyas, I hear, the damned rogue, will vote against you?'

White winked. 'Bad,' he said cryptically, 'but not as bad as that.'

'Oh! oh!' quoth the other, nodding. 'I see.' And then, glancing at the gang before the cloth works, whose taunts and cries of 'Flunkies!' and 'Sell your birthright, will you?' were constant and vicious, 'You've no fear there'll be violence, White?' he asked.

'Lord, no, sir,' White answered; 'you know what election rows are – all bark and no bite!'

'Still I hear that at Bath, where I'm told Lord Brecknock stands a poor chance, they are afraid of a riot.'

'Ay, ay, sir,' White answered indifferently, 'this isn't Bath.'

'No, indeed,' the Rector struck in, in pompous tones. 'I should like to see anything of that kind here! They would soon,' he continued with an air, 'find that I am not on the Commission of the Peace for nothing! I shall make, and I am sure you will make,' he went on, turning to his brother justice, 'very short work of them! I should like to see anything of that kind tried here!'

White nodded, and in his heart thought that his reverence was likely to have his wish gratified. However, no more was said, for the approach of the Stapylton carriages, with their postillions, outriders, and favours, was signalled by persons who had been placed to watch for them, and the party on the bridge, falling into violent commotion, raised the flags and banners and hastened to form an escort on either side of the roadway. As the gaily-decked carriages halted on the crest of the bridge, loud greetings were exchanged. The five voters took up a position of honour, seats in the carriages were found for three or four of the more important gentry, and seven or eight others got to horse. Meanwhile, the smaller folk, who thought they had a claim to the recognition of the candidates, were gratified, and stood back blushing, or being disappointed stood back glowering; this amid confusion and cheering on the bridge, and jeers on the part of the cloth hands. Then the flags were waved aloft, the band of five, of which the drummer could truly say *'Pars magna fui'*, struck up 'See the Conquering Hero comes!' and White stood back for a last look.

Then, 'Shout, lads, shout!' he cried, waving his hat. 'Don't let 'em have it all their own way!'

And with a roar of defiance, not quite so loud or full as the gentlemanly interest had raised of old, the procession got under way, and led by a banner bearing 'Our Ancient Constitution!' in blue letters on a red ground, swayed spasmodically up the street. The candidates for the suffrages of the electors of Chippinge had passed the threshold of the borough.

'Hurrah! Yah! Hurrah! Yah! Yah! Yah! Down with the borough-mongers. Our Ancient Constitution! Hurrah! Boo! Boo!'

White had his eye on the clothmen, and under its spell they did not go beyond hooting and an egg or two, spared from the polling day, and flung at long range when the Tories had passed. No one was struck, and the carriages moved onward, more or less triumphantly. Serjeant Wathen, who was in the first, and whose sharp black eyes moved hither and thither in search of friends, rose repeatedly to bow. But Mr Cooke, who did not forget that he was paying two thousand five hundred pounds for his seat, and thought that it should be a soft one, scarcely deigned to move. For as the procession advanced into the town the clamour of the crowd which lined the narrow High Street and continually shouted 'The Bill! The Bill!' drowned the utmost efforts of Sir Robert's friends, and left no doubt of the popular feeling.

There was some good-humoured pushing and thrusting, the drum beating and the church bells jangling bravely above the hubbub. And once or twice the rabble came near to cutting the procession in two. But there was no real attempt at mischief, until the foremost carriage was abreast of the Cross, which stands at the head of the High Street, where the latter debouches into the space before the Abbey.

Then some foolish person gave the word to halt before Dyas the butcher's. And a voice – it was not White's – cried, 'Three groans for the Radical Rat! Rat! Rat!'

The groans were given before the crowd fully understood their meaning or the motive for the stoppage. The drummer beat out something which he meant for the Rogues' March, and an unseen hand raising a large dead rat on a pole, waved it before the butcher's windows.

The effect was surprising – to old-fashioned folk. In a twinkling, with a shout of 'Down with the borough-mongers!' a gang of white-aproned clothmen rushed the rear of the procession, drove it in upon the main body, and amid screams and uproar forced the column out of the narrow street into the space before the Abbey. Fortunately the White Lion, which faced the Abbey, stood only a score of paces to the left of the Cross, and the carriages were able to reach it; but in disorder, pressed on by such a fighting, swaying, shouting crowd as Chippinge had not seen for many a year.

It was no time to stand on dignity. The candidates tumbled out as best they could, their best supporters followed, and while half a dozen single combats proceeded at their elbows, they hastened across the pavement into the house. The Rector alone disdained to flee. On the threshold of the inn he turned and raised his hat above his head.

'Order!' he cried, in his sonorous bass. 'Order! Do you hear me!'

But 'Yah! Borough-monger!' the rabble answered, and before he could wink a young farmer was hurled against him, and a whip, of which a postillion had just been despoiled, whizzed past his head. He, too, turned tail at that, with his face a shade paler than usual; and with his retreat resistance ceased. The carriages were hustled into the yard, and there the greater part of the procession also took refuge. A few, sad to say, sneaked off and got rid of their badges, and a few more escaped through a neighbouring alley. No one was much hurt; a few black eyes were the worst of the mischief, nor could it be said that any vindictive feeling was shown. But the town was swept clear, and the victory of the Radicals was complete. Left in possession of the open space before the Abbey, they paraded for some time under the windows of the White Lion, waving a captured flag, and cheering and groaning by turns.

Meantime, in the hall of the inn the grandees were smoothing their ruffled plumes, in a state of mind in which it was hard to say whether indignation or astonishment had larger place. Oaths flew thick as hail, unrebuked by the Church, the most outspoken, perhaps, being the landlord, who met them with a pale face.

'Good Lord, good Lord, gentlemen!' he said. 'What violence! What violence! What are we coming to next? What's took the people, gentlemen? Isn't Sir Robert here?'

For to this simple person it seemed impossible that people should behave badly in that presence.

'No, he's not!' Mr Cooke answered with choler. 'And I'd like to know why he's not! I wish to Heaven' – only he did not say 'Heaven' – 'that he were here, and he'd see what sort of thing he has let us into!'

'Ah, well! ah, well!' returned the more discreet and philosophic Serjeant, 'shouting breaks no bones. We are all here, I hope? And after all, this shows up the Bill in a pretty strong light, eh, Rector? If it is to be carried by methods such as these—'

'Damned barefaced intimidation!' Squire Rowley growled.

'Or if it is to give votes to such persons as these—'

'Damned Jacobins! Republicans every man of them!' interposed the Squire.

'It will soon be plain to all,' the Serjeant concluded, in his House of Commons manner, 'that it is a most revolutionary, dangerous, and – and unconstitutional measure, gentlemen.'

'By God!' Mr Cooke cried – he was thinking that if this was the kind of thing he was to suffer he might as well have fought Taunton or Preston, or any other open borough, and kept his money in his pocket – 'By God, I wish Lord John were stifled in the mud he's stirred up, and Gaffer Grey with him.'

'You can add Bruffam, if you like,' Wathen answered good-humouredly – he was not paying two thousand five hundred pounds for his seat. 'And rid me of a rival and the country of a pest, Cooke! But come, gentlemen, now we're here and no bones broken, shall we sit down? We are all safe, I trust, Mr White? And especially – my future constituents?' with a glance of his shrewd Jewish-looking eyes.

'Yes, sir, no harm done,' White replied, as cheerfully as he could; which was not over cheerfully, for in all his experience of Chippinge he had known nothing like this; and he was a trifle scared. 'Yes, sir,' he continued, looking round, 'all here, I think! And – and, by Jove,' in a tone of relief, 'one more than I expected! Mr Vaughan! I am glad, sir, very glad, sir,' he added heartily, 'to see you. Very glad!'

The young man who had alighted from his post-chaise a few minutes before did not appear to reciprocate the feeling. He looked sulky and bored. But he shook the outstretched hand; he could do no less. Then, saying scarcely a word, he stood back. He had hastened to Chippinge on receiving White's belated express more because, irritated by the collision with Flixton, he welcomed any change, than because he was sure what he would do. In the chaise he had thought more of Mary than of politics, more of the Honourable Bob than of his cousin. And though, as far as Sir Robert was concerned, he was resolved to be frank and to play the man, his mind had travelled no further.

Now, thrown suddenly among these people, he was, in a churlish way, taken aback. But he told himself that it did not matter. If they did not like the line he was going to take, that was their business. He was not responsible to them. In fine, he was in a savage mood, with half his mind here and the other half dwelling on the events of the morning. For the moment politics seemed to him a poor game, and what he did or did not do of little consequence.

White and the others were not blind to his manner, and might have resented it in another. But Sir Robert's heir had a right to moods if any man had; doubtless he was become a fine gentleman and thought it a nuisance to vote in his own borough. They were all politeness to him, therefore, and while his eyes passed haughtily beyond them, seeking Sir Robert, they presented to him those whom he did not know.

'Very kind of you to come, Mr Vaughan,' said the Serjeant, who, like many browbeaters, could be a sycophant at need. 'Very kind indeed! I don't know whether you know Mr Cooke? He, equally with me, is obliged to you for your attendance.'

'Greatly obliged, sir,' Mr Cooke muttered. 'Certainly, certainly.'

Vaughan bowed coldly. 'Is not Sir Robert here?' he asked. He was still looking beyond those to whom he spoke.

'No, Mr Vaughan.'

And then, 'This way to dinner,' White cried loudly. 'Come, gentlemen! Dinner, gentlemen, dinner!'

And Vaughan, heedless what he did or where he dined, but inclined in a sardonic way to amuse himself, went in with them. What did it matter? He was not going to vote for them. But that was his business, and Sir Robert's. He was not responsible to them.

Certainly he was in a very bad temper.

CHAPTER XIII

The Vermuyden Dinner

VAUGHAN BEGAN to think more soberly of his position when he found himself at the table. He had White, who took one end, on his right; and the Serjeant was opposite him. At the other end the Alderman presided, supported by Mr Cooke and the Rector.

The young man looked down the board, at the vast tureens that smoked on it, and at the faces, smug or jolly, hungry or expectant, which surrounded it; and amid the flood of talk which burst forth as soon as his reverence had uttered a short grace, he began to feel the situation uncomfortable. True, he had a sort of right to be there, as the heir and a Vermuyden. True, too, he owed nothing to anyone there – nothing to the Serjeant, whom he disliked in his heart, nor to Mr Cooke, on whom he looked down (in his tastes he was as exclusive as Sir Robert himself), nor to White, who would one day be his paid dependent. He owed them no explanation. Why, then, expose himself to their anger and surprise? He would be silent, and speak only at a proper time, when he could state his views to Sir Robert with a fair chance of a fair hearing.

Still, he discerned that the position in which he had placed himself was false, and might become ridiculous. And it crossed his mind to feign illness, and to go out and incontinently walk over to Stapylton and see Sir Robert. Or he might tell White quietly that he did not find himself able to support his cousin's nominations; and before the news got abroad he might withdraw and let them think what they could. But he was too proud to do the one, and in too sulky a mood to do the other. And he sat still.

'Where is Sir Robert?' he asked.

'He left home on a sudden call this morning, sir,' White explained, wondering what made the young squire, who was wont to be affable, so distant. 'On unexpected business.'

'It must have been important as well as unexpected,' Wathen said, with a smile, 'to take Sir Robert away today, Mr White.'

'It was both, sir, as I understood,' White answered, 'for Sir Robert did not make me acquainted with it. He seemed somewhat put out – more put out than I have often seen him. But he said that, whatever happened, he would be back before the nomination.' And then, turning to Vaughan, 'You must have passed him, sir?' he added.

'Well, now I think of it,' Vaughan answered, his spoon suspended, 'I met a travelling carriage-and-four with jackets like his. But I thought that it was empty.'

'No, sir, that was Sir Robert. He will not be best pleased,' the agent continued, turning to the Serjeant, 'when he hears what a reception we had!'

'Ah, well; ah, well!' the Serjeant replied – pleasantness was his cue today. 'Things are worse in Bath, I'll be sworn, Mr White.'

'No doubt, sir, no doubt!' White said. 'I think,' he added, forgetting his study of Cobbett, 'the nation has gone mad.'

After that Vaughan's other neighbour, Squire Rowley, who met him annually at Stapylton, claimed his ear. The old fellow, hearty and good-natured, but a bigoted Tory, who would have given Orator Hunt four dozen, and thought Lord Grey's proper reward a block on Tower Hill, was the last person whom Vaughan would have chosen for a confidant; since only to hear of a Vermuyden turned Radical would have gone near to giving him a fit. Still, Vaughan must listen to him and answer him; the younger man could not without rudeness cut the elder man short. But all the time as they talked Vaughan's uneasiness increased. With every minute his eyes wandered more longingly to the door. Improved in temper by the fare and by the politeness of his neighbours, he began to see that he had been foolish to thrust himself among people with whom he did not agree. Still, he was there, and he must see the dinner to an end. After all, a little more or a little less would not add to Sir Robert's anger. He could explain that he thought it more delicate to avoid an open breach.

Meanwhile the collision with the crowd had loosened the guests' tongues, and never had a Vermuyden dinner gone more freely. Even the 'Cripples', whose wont it was to begin the evening with unpleasant obsequiousness and close it with a freedom as odious, found speech early, and were loudest in denunciation of a Bill which threatened to deprive them of their annuities. By the time huge joints had taken the place of the tureens, and bowls of potatoes and mounds of asparagus dotted the table, the noise was incessant. There was claret for those who cared for it, and strong ale for all. And while some discussed the effect which a Bill that disfranchised Chippinge would have on their pockets and interests, others, driving their arguments home with blows on the table, recalled, almost with tears, the sacred name of Pitt, the pilot who weathered the storm; or held up to execration a Cabinet of Whigs dead to every Whig principle, and live only to the chance of power which a revolution might afford.

'But what was to be expected? What was to be expected?' Squire Rowley insisted. 'We've only ourselves to thank! When Peel and the Duke took up the Catholic Claims they stepped into the Whigs' shoes; and devilishly may they pinch them! The Whigs had to find another pair, you see, sir, and stepped into the Radicals'! And the only people left at a loss are the honest part of us, who are likely to end not only barefoot but barebacked. Ay, by God, we are!'

And so on, and so on. Even White, who was vastly relieved by Vaughan's arrival, which made his majority safe, talked freely, giving Dyas and Pillinger of the Blue Duck the rough side of his tongue; while Vaughan, used to a wider outlook, listened to their one-sided arguments, their trite prophecies, their incredible prejudices – such they seemed to him – and now turned up his nose, now pitied them, as an effete, a doomed, a dying race.

While he thought of this the dinner wore on, the joints vanished, and huge steaming puddings made their appearance on the board. Those who cared not for plum puddings could have marrow puddings. Then cheese and spring onions, and some special old ale, light-coloured, heady, and served in tall, spare glasses, went round. At length the Rector, a trifle flushed, rose to say grace, and Vaughan saw that the cloth was about to be removed. Bottles of strong port and tawny Madeira were at hand. Already some called for their favourite punch, or for hot grog.

'Now,' he thought, 'I can escape with a good grace. And I will!'

But, as he made a movement to rise, the Serjeant rose opposite him, lifted his glass, and fixed him with his eye; and Vaughan felt that he could not leave at that moment without rudeness.

'Gentlemen,' the Serjeant cried in his blandest tone, 'on your feet, if you please. The King! the King, God bless him! The King, gentlemen, and may he never suffer for the faults of his servants! May the Grey mare never run away with him. May William the Good ne'er be ruined by a bad Bill! Gentlemen, the King, God bless him, and deliver him from the Whigs!'

They drank the toast amid a roar of laughter and much laudation of the Serjeant's wit. Once more as they sat down Vaughan thought he would escape; but again he was hindered. This time the interruption came from behind.

'Hallo, Vaughan!' someone muttered in his ear. 'You're the last person I expected to see here!'

He turned, and disgust filled him. The speaker, who had entered late, was the son of a clergyman in the neighbourhood, and had gone to the Bar. He was a shifty, flattering fellow, at once a toady and a backbiter, who had wormed himself into society too good for him, and in London was Vaughan's *bête noire*. But had that been all! Alas! he was also a member of the Academic. He had been present at Vaughan's triumph ten days before, and had heard him proclaim himself a reformer of the Reformers.

For a moment Vaughan could find not a word; he could only mutter 'Oh!' in a tone of dismay. He feared that his face betrayed the chagrin he felt.

'I thought you were quite the other way?' Mowatt said; and he grinned.

He was a weedy, pale young man, with thin lips and a false smile.

Vaughan hesitated. 'So I am!' he said curtly.

'But – but I thought—'

'Order, order!' cried the Alderman, a trifle uplifted by wine and his position. 'Silence, if you please, gentlemen, for the senior candidate! And charge your glasses.'

Vaughan turned to the table, a frown on his brow. Wathen was on his feet, holding his wineglass before his breast with one hand, while the other rested on the table. His attitude was that of a man confident of his powers and pleased to exert them. Nevertheless, as he prepared to speak, he lowered his eyes to the table with an affection of modesty.

'Gentlemen,' he said, 'it is my privilege to propose a toast, that at this time and in this place – this time, gentlemen, when to an extent unknown within living memory all is at stake, and this place which has so much to lose – it is my privilege, I say, to propose a toast that must go straight to the heart of every man in this room – ay, of every true-born Englishman, and every lover of his country. It is *our Ancient Constitution, our Chartered Rights, our Vested Interests*!' (Loud and continued applause.) 'Yes, gentlemen, our Ancient Constitution, the security of every man, woman, and child in this realm. And, coupled with it, our Chartered Rights, our Vested Interests, which, unassailed for generations, are today called in question by the weakness of many, by the madness of some, by the wicked ambition of a few.' (Loud cheering.) 'Gentlemen, to one Cromwell this town owes the destruction of your famous abbey, formerly the pride of this county. To another Cromwell it owes the destruction of the walls that in troublous times secured the hearths of your forefathers. It lies with us, but we must be instant and diligent – it lies with us, I say, to see that those civil bulwarks which protect us and ours in the enjoyment of all we have and all we hope for—'

'In this world,' the Rector murmured in a deep bass voice.

'In this world,' the Serjeant continued, accepting the amendment with a complimentary bow, 'are not laid low by a third Cromwell. I care not whether he mask himself under the name of Grey, or of Russell, or of Brougham, or of Lansdowne!'

He paused amid such a roar of applause as shook the room.

'For think not,' the Serjeant resumed when it died down,

'think not, gentlemen, whatever the easily led vulgar may think, that sacrilegious hands can be laid on the ark of the Constitution without injury to other interests; without the shock being felt through the various members of the State down to the lowest; without danger to all those multiform rights and privileges for which the Constitution is our guarantee. Let the advocates of this pernicious, this revolutionary Bill say what they will, they cannot deny that its effect will be to deprive you in Chippinge, who for nearly five centuries have enjoyed the privilege of returning Members to Parliament, of that privilege, with all' – here he glanced at the rich array of bottles that covered the board – 'the amenities which it brings with it. And for whose benefit? For that of men no better qualified – nay, by practice and heredity less qualified – than yourselves. But, gentlemen, mark me, that is not all. That is but the beginning, and it may be the least part. That loss they cannot hide from you; that loss they do not try to hide from you. But they do,' he continued, in his deepest and most tragic tone, 'they hide from you a fact to which the whole course of history is witness – that a policy of robbery once begun is rarely stayed, if it be stayed, until the victim is bare – bare, gentlemen! Gentlemen, the freemen of this borough have of ancient right, conferred by an ancient sovereign—'

'God bless him!' from Annibal, now somewhat drunk. 'God bless him! Here's his health.'

The Serjeant paused an instant and looked round the table. Then more slowly –

'Ay, God bless him!' he said. 'God bless King Canute! But what – what if those grants of land – I care not whether you call them chartered rights, or vested interests, which you freeman enjoy of him – what if they do not endure? You have them,' with a penetrating glance from face to face, 'but for how long, gentlemen, if this Bill pass? You are too clear-sighted to be blind to the peril, too shrewd to think that you can part with one right, as old, as well vested, as perfectly secured, and keep the others undiminished. Gentlemen, if you are so blind, take warning. For wherever this anarchical, this dangerous, this revolutionary Bill—'

'Hear, hear, hear!' from Vaughan's neighbour, the Squire.

'Wherever, I say, this Bill finds supporters – and I can well believe that in Birmingham and Sheffield, where they have all to gain and nothing to lose, it will find supporters – it should find none in Chippinge, where we have all to lose and nothing to gain – where no man but a fool or a rogue can in reason support it! Gentlemen, you are neither fools nor rogues—'

'No, no! No, no!'

'No, gentlemen, and therefore, though a few silly fellows may shout for the Bill in the streets, I am sure that I shall have the whole of this influential company with me when I give you the toast of our Ancient Constitution, our Chartered Rights, our Vested Interests. May the Bill that assails them be defeated by the good sense of a sober and united people! May those who urge it and those who support it – rogues where they are not fools, and fools where they are not rogues – meet with the fate they deserve! And may we be there to see! Gentlemen,' raising his hand for silence, 'in the absence upon pressing business of our beloved High Steward, the model of an English gentleman and the pattern of an English landlord, I beg to couple this toast' – here the Serjeant's sharp black eyes fixed themselves suddenly on his opposite neighbour – 'with the name of his kinsman, Mr Arthur Vaughan!'

'Hurrah! Hurrah! Hurrah!' The room shook with the volume of applause; the tables trembled. And through it all Arthur Vaughan's heart beat hard and he swallowed nervously. He was caught. Whether the Serjeant knew it or not, he was trapped. From the beginning of the speech he had had his misgivings; he had listened with only half his mind, the other half had been busy scanning the prospect feverishly, weighing the chances of escape, growing chill with the fear of what was coming. If he had only withdrawn in time! If he had only—

'Hurrah! Hurrah! Hurrah!' They were pounding the table with fist and glass, and looking towards him – two lines of flushed, excited, tipsy faces. Some were drinking to him, others were scanning him curiously. All were waiting.

He leant forward. 'I don't wish to speak,' he said, addressing the Serjeant in a troubled voice. 'Call on someone else, if you please.'

'Impossible, sir!' White answered, surprised by his evident

nervousness. He had thought Vaughan anything but a shy person. 'Impossible, sir!'

'Get up! Get up!' cried the Squire, laying a jocund hand on him and trying to lift him to his feet.

But Vaughan resisted; his throat was so dry that he could hardly frame his words.

'I don't wish to speak,' he muttered. 'I don't agree—'

'Say what you like, my dear sir!' the Serjeant rejoined, with a gleam of amusement in his eyes. He had had his doubts of Master Vaughan ever since he had caught him on his way to the Chancellor; now he thought that he had him pinned. He did not suppose that the young man would dare to revolt openly.

'Yes, sir, you must get up,' said White, who had no suspicion that his hesitation arose from anything but shyness. 'Anything will do.'

Vaughan rose, slowly, and with a beating heart. For a moment he stood, deafened by his reception. For the smaller men saw in him one of the old family, the future landlord of two-thirds of them, the sometime owner of the very roof under which they were gathered. And he, while they greeted his rising and he stood waiting with an unhappy face, wondered, even at this last moment, what he would say. And Heaven knows what he would have said – so hard was it to disappoint those cheering men, all looking at him with worship in their eyes, so painful was it to break old ties – if he had not caught behind him Mowatt's whisper, 'Eat his words – he'll have to unsay—'

No more than that – a fragment – but enough; enough to show him that he had better, far better seem false to these men, to his blood, to the past, than be false to himself. He straightened his shoulders and lifted his head.

'Gentlemen,' he said (and his voice, though low, was steady), 'I rise unwillingly – unwillingly, because I feel too late that I ought not to be here, that I have no right to be here.' ('No! No!') 'No right to be here, for this reason,' he continued, raising his hand for silence, 'for this reason, that in much of what Serjeant Wathen has said, I cannot go with him.'

There, it was out! But no more than a look of perplexity passed from the more intelligent faces about him to the duller faces lower down the table. They did not understand; it was only clear to them that he could not mean what he seemed to mean. However, he was going on – in a silence so complete that a pin falling to the floor might have been heard.

'I rise unwillingly, I repeat, gentlemen,' he continued, 'and I beg you to remember this, and that I did not come here of set purpose to flaunt my opinions before you. For I, too' – here he betrayed his secret agitation – 'thus far I do go with Serjeant Wathen – I, too, am for our Ancient Constitution, I give place to no man in love of it. And I, too, am against Revolution. I will stand second to none in abhorrence of it.'

'Hear, hear!' cried the Rector, in a tone of unmistakable relief. 'Hear, hear!'

'Ay, go on,' chimed in the Squire. 'Go on, lad, go on! That's all right!' And half aside in his neighbour's ear, 'Gad, he frightened me!' he muttered.

'But – but to be plain,' Vaughan resumed, pronouncing every word clearly, 'I do not regard the Bill which the Serjeant has mentioned, the Bill which is in all your minds, as assailing the one, or as being tantamount to the other! On the contrary, I believe that it restores the ancient balance of the Constitution, and will avert, as nothing else will avert, a revolution.'

As he paused on that word, the Squire, who was of a free habit, tried to rise and speak, but choked. The Rector gasped. Only Mr Cooke found his voice. He sprang to his feet, purple in the face. 'By God!' he roared, 'are we going to listen to this?'

Vaughan sat down, pale but composed. But he found all eyes were on him, that no one spoke, and he rose again.

'It was against my will I said what I have said,' he resumed. 'I did not wish to speak. I do not wish you to listen. I rose only because I was forced to rise. But, being on my feet, I owed it to myself to say enough to clear myself of – of the appearance of duplicity. That is all.'

The Serjeant did not speak, but gazed darkly at him, his mind weighing the effect which this would have on the election. White, too, did not speak; he sat stricken dumb. The Squire swore, and five or six of the more intelligent hissed. But again it was Cooke who found words.

'That all? But that is not all!' he shouted. 'That is not all! What are you, sir?' For still, in common with most of those at the table, he could not believe that he heard aright. He fancied that this was some trope, some nice debating-club distinction, which he had not followed. 'You may be Sir Robert Vermuyden's cousin ten times over,' he continued vehemently, 'but we'll have it clear what we have to expect. Speak like a man, sir! Say what you mean!'

Vaughan had taken his seat, but he rose again, a gleam of anger in his eyes.

'Have I not spoken plainly?' he said. 'I thought I had. If you still doubt, sir, I am for the Constitution, but I think that it has suffered by the wear and tear of time and needs repair. I think that the shifting of population during the last two centuries, through the decay of one place and the rise of another, calls for some change in the representation! I hold that the spread of knowledge, and the creation of a large and wealthy class unconnected with the land, render that change more urgent if we would avoid a revolution. I believe that the more we enlarge the base upon which our institutions rest, the more safely, the more steadily, and the longer will they last!'

They knew now, they understood; and the storm broke. The smaller men, or such of them as were sober, stared. But the greater number burst into a roar of dissent, of reprobation, of anger.

Led by the Squire. 'A Whig, by God,' he cried violently. And he thrust his chair as far as possible from his neighbour. 'A Whig, by God! And here!'

While others cried, 'Renegade!' 'Radical!' and 'What are you doing here?' and hissed him. But, above all, in some degree stilling all, rose Cooke's crucial question, 'Are you for the Bill? Answer me that!' And he extended his hand for silence. 'Are you for the Bill?'

'I am,' Vaughan answered. The storm steadied him.

'You are?'

'Yes.'

'Fool or rogue, then! Which are you?' shrieked a voice from the lower end of the table. 'Fool or rogue? Which are you?'

Vaughan turned sharply in the direction of the voice. 'That reminds me,' he said, with a keenness which seemed to gain him a hearing, for the noise died down. 'That reminds me, Serjeant Wathen is against the Bill. But he has addressed himself solely to your prejudices, gentlemen! I am for the Bill – I am for the Bill,' he repeated, seeing that their attention was wandering, 'I—'

He stopped – surprised, silenced. Some were on their feet, others were rising. The faces of nine out of ten were turned from him? What was it? He turned to see; and he saw.

A few paces within the door, stood Sir Robert himself; his fur-collared travelling cloak hanging loose about him, and showing his tall spare figure at its best. He stooped, but his high-bred face, cynically smiling, was turned full on the speaker; it was certain that he had heard much, if not all. And Vaughan had been resolute indeed, if, taken by surprise and at this disadvantage, he had not shown some discomfiture.

It is easy to smile now. Easy to say that this was but an English gentleman, bound like others by the law, and Vaughan's own kinsman. But few would have smiled then. He, through whose hands passed a quarter of the patronage of a county; who dammed or turned the stream of promotion; who had made many there and could unmake them; whose mere hint could have consigned, a few years back, the troublesome to the press-gang; who belonged almost as definitely, almost as exclusively to a caste, as do white men in the India of today; who seldom showed himself to the vulgar save in his coach-and-four, or riding with belted grooms behind him – about such an one in '31 there was, if no divinity, at least the aegis of real power, that habit which unquestioned authority confers, that part of Jove to which men bow! Scan the pictured faces of the men who steered this country through the long war – the faces of Liverpool and Castlereagh –

Daring pilots in extremity,
Scorning the danger when the waves ran high;

or of those men, heirs to their traditions, who for nearly

twenty years confronted the no less formidable forces of discontent and disaffection – of Peel and Wellington, Croker and Canning – and he is blind who does not find there the reflection of that firm rule, the shadow of that power which still survived, though maimed and weakened, in the early thirties.

Certainly it was not easy to smile at such men then; at their pride or their prejudice, their selfishness or their eccentricity. For behind lay solid power. Small blame to Vaughan, therefore, if in the face of the servile attitude, the obsequious rising of the company, he felt his countenance change, if he could not quite hide his dismay. And though he told himself that his feelings were out of place, that the man did but stand in the shoes which would one day be his, and was but now what he would be, *vox faucibus haesit* – he was dumb. It was Sir Robert who broke the silence.

'I fear, Mr Vaughan,' he said, the gleam in his eyes alone betraying his passion – for he would as soon have walked the country lanes in his dressing-robe as given way to rage in that company – 'I fear you are uttering in haste words which you will repent at leisure. Did I hear aright that – that you are in favour of the Bill?'

'I am,' Vaughan replied huskily. 'I—'

'Just so, just so,' Sir Robert rejoined with a certain lightness, and, raising his walking-cane, he pointed courteously to the door, a pace or two in front of him. 'That is the door, Mr Vaughan,' he said. 'You must be here, I am sure, under an error.'

Vaughan coloured painfully. 'Sir Robert,' he said, 'I owe you, I know—'

'You will owe me little by tomorrow evening,' Sir Robert rejoined, interrupting him suavely. 'Much less than you now suppose. But that is not to the point. Will you be good enough to withdraw?'

'I would like at least to say this – that I came here—'

'Will you kindly withdraw?' Sir Robert persisted. 'That is all.' He pointed again, and still more blandly, to the door. 'Any explanation you may please to offer – and I do not deny that one were not out of place – you can give to my agent tomorrow. He, on his part, will also have something to say.

For the present – Annibal,' turning with kindly condescension, 'be good enough to open the door for this gentleman. Good evening, Mr Vaughan. You will not, I am sure, compel me to remove with my friends to another room?'

And as he continued to point to the door, and would listen to nothing – and the room was certainly his – Vaughan walked out. And Annibal closed the door behind him.

CHAPTER XIV

Miss Sibson's Mistake

It was, perhaps, fortunate for Miss Hilhouse that she did not hazard any remarks on that second encounter in the Square. Whether this amendment in her manners was due to Miss Sibson's apophthegms, or to the general desire of the school to see the new teacher's new pelisse – which could only be gratified by favour – or to a threatening rigidity in Mary Smith's bearing, must remain a question. But children are keen observers. Their senses are as sharp as their tongues are cruel. And it is certain that Miss Smith had not read four lines of the fifth chapter of *The Fairchild Family*, before a certain sternness in her tone was noted – even by those who had not already marked the danger signal in her eyes. For the gentlest eyes can dart lightnings on occasions. Even the sheep will turn in defence of her lamb. Nor ever walked woman who could not fight for her secret and her pride.

So Miss Hilhouse bit her tongue and kept silence, the girls behaved beautifully, and Mary read *The Fairchild Family* to them in a tone of monotony, that perfectly reflected the future as she saw it. She had been very foolish and very weak; but she was not without excuse. He had saved her life, she could plead that. True, brought up as she had been at Clapham, shielded from all dealings with the other sex, taught to regard them as wolves, or at best as a race with which she could have no safe parley, she should have known better. She should have known that, handsome, courteous, masterful-eyed as they were and with a way with them that made poor girls' hearts throb at one moment and stand still at another – she should have known that they meant nothing. That they were still men, and that she must not trust them, must not think of them, must not expect to find them more steadfast to a point than the weathercock on St Mary's at Redcliffe.

The weathercock? Ah!

She had no sooner framed the thought, in the middle of her reading, than she was aware of a sensation; and a child, one of the youngest, raised her hand.

'Please—'

Mary paused. 'Yes?' she asked; it was not in her nature to be harsh. 'What is it?'

'Please, Miss Smith, did the weathercock speak?'

Mary blushed a rosy red. 'Speak? The weathercock speak? What do you mean, child?'

'Please, Miss Smith, you said that the weathercock told Lucy, the truth, the truth, and all the truth.'

'Impossible!' Mary stammered. 'If – if I did, I should have said the coachman.'

And she resumed the story; but with a hot face, a face which blushed more painfully and more intolerably because she was conscious that every eye was upon it, and that a score of small minds were groping for the cause of her confusion.

She remembered – oh, how well she remembered – that the schoolmistress at Clapham had told her that she had every good quality except strength of will. And how thoroughly, how rapidly had she proved the truth of the exception! Freed from control for only twenty-four hours, left for that time to her own devices, she had listened to the first voice that addressed her, believed the first flattering look that fell on her, taken the most ordinary attentions – attentions at which any girl with knowledge of the world or strength of will would have smiled – for gold, real red gold. So that a light look, without a spoken word, had drawn her heart from her. How, that being so, it behoved her to despise herself, loathe herself, discipline herself! How she ought to guard herself in the future! Above all, how thankful should she be for the dull but safe routine that fenced, and henceforth must fence, her life from such perils!

True. Yet how dreary to young eyes seemed that routine stretched before her! How her courage fainted at the prospect of morning added to morning, formal walk to formal walk, lesson to lesson, one generation of pupils to another! For generation would follow generation, one chubby face would give place to another, and still she would be there, plodding through the stale task, listening with an aching head to the tuneless harpsichord, saying the same things, finding the same faults, growing slowly into a correcting, scolding, punishing machine. By-and-by she would know *The Fairchild Family* by heart, she would sicken at the *Letters on the Improvement of the Mind*. The children would still be young, but grey hairs would come to her, she would grow stout and dull; and these slender hands, these dainty fingers still white and fine, still meet for love, would be seared by a million needle-pricks and roughened by the wear and tear of ten thousand hours of plain sewing.

She was ungrateful – oh, she was ungrateful – to think such thoughts! For in what was her lot worse than the lot of others? Or worse than it had been a week before, when who more humble-minded or contented, more cheerful or helpful than Mary Smith? When her only fault had been a weakness of character, which her old schoolmistress hoped would be cured by time? When, though the shadow of an unknown Miss Sibson loomed formidable before her, she had faced her fate bravely and hopefully, supported not a little by the love and good wishes – won by a thousand kind offices – which went with her into the unknown world?

What had happened in the interval? What had happened to change all this? A little thing, oh, a very little thing. But to think of it under the children's eyes made her face burn anew. She had lost her heart – to a man. To a man! The very word seemed improper in that company, in that place! How much more improper when the man cared nothing for her, but, tossing her a smile for guerdon, had taken her peace of mind, and gone his way, with a laugh. At the best, if he had ever dreamt seriously of her, ever done more than deem her a simpleton lightly flattered, and as lightly to be won, he had changed his mind as quickly as a weathercock shifts in April. And he had talked – that hurt her most! He had talked of her freely, boasted of her silliness, told his companions what he would do, or what he would not do; made her common to them.

She got away for a few minutes at tea time. But twenty pairs of eyes followed her from the room, and seized on her as she returned. And 'Miss Smith, ain't you well?' piped a tiny treble.

She was controlling her voice to answer – that she was quite well – when Miss Sibson intervened.

'Miss Fripp,' she said sombrely, 'write "Are you not" twenty times on your slate after tea! Miss Hilhouse, if you stare in that fashion, you will be goggle-eyed. Young ladies, elbows, elbows! Have I not told you a score of times that the art of deportment consists in the right use of the elbow? Now, Miss Claxton, in what does the art of deportment consist?'

'In the right use of the elbow, ma'am.'

'And what is the right use of the elbow?'

'To efface it, ma'am.'

'That is better,' Miss Sibson replied, somewhat mollified. 'Understood is half done. Miss Smith,' looking about her with benevolence, 'had you occasion to commend any young lady's needle this afternoon?'

Miss Smith looked unhappy; conscious that she had not been as attentive to her duties as became her. 'I had no occasion to find fault, ma'am,' she said timidly.

'Very good. Then every fourth young lady, beginning at my right hand, may take a piece of currant cake. I see that Miss Burges is wearing the silver medal for good conduct. She may take a piece, and give a piece to a friend. When you have eaten your cake you can go to the schoolroom and play for half an hour at blind-man's-buff. But – elbows! Elbows, young ladies,' she added austerely, gazing at them over her glasses. 'In all your frolics let deportment be your first consideration.'

The girls trooped out, and Mary Smith rose to go with them. But Miss Sibson bade her remain.

'I wish to speak to you,' she said.

Poor Mary trembled. Miss Sibson was still in some measure

an unknown quantity to her; a perplexing mixture of severity and benevolence, sound sense and Mrs Chapone.

'I wish to speak to you,' Miss Sibson continued when they were alone. And then, after a pause, during which she poured herself out a third cup of tea, 'My dear,' she said soberly, 'the sooner a false step is retraced the better, I took a false step a few days ago – I blame myself for it – when I allowed you, in spite of my rule to the contrary, to see a gentleman. I made that exception, partly out of respect to the note which the parcel contained; the affair was out of the ordinary. And partly – because I liked the gentleman. I thought him a gentleman, he told me that he had an independence, I had no reason to think him more. But I have heard today, that he is a person of great expectations who will one day be very rich and a man of standing in the country. That alters the position,' Miss Sibson continued gravely. 'Had I known it' – she rubbed her nose thoughtfully with the handle of her teaspoon – 'I should not have permitted the interview.' And then, after a few seconds of silence, 'You understand me, I think, my dear?' she asked.

'Yes,' Mary said in a low voice. She spoke with perfect composure.

'Just so, just so,' Miss Sibson answered, pleased to see that the girl was too proud to give way before her – though she was sure that she would cry by-and-by. 'I am glad to think that there is no harm done. As I have said, the sooner a false step is retraced, the better; and therefore, if he calls again, I shall not permit him to see you.'

'I do not wish to see him,' Mary said with dignity.

'Very good. Then that is understood.'

But, strangely enough, the words had barely fallen from the schoolmistress's lips when a visitor's knock was heard. The same thought leapt to the mind of each; and to Mary's cheek a sudden blush, that, fading as quickly as it came, left her paler than before. Miss Sibson saw the girl's distress, and she was about to suggest, in words equivalent to a command, that she should retire to her room, when the door opened and the maidservant, with thinly veiled excitement, announced that a gentleman wished to see Miss Smith.

Miss Sibson frowned. 'Where is he?' she asked with

majesty; as if she already scented the fray.

'In the parlour, ma'am.'

'Very good. Very good. I will see him.' But not until the maid had retired did the schoolmistress rise to her feet. 'You had better stay here,' she said, looking at her companion, 'until my return. It is of course your wish that I should dismiss him?'

Poor Mary! Those dreams of something brighter, something fuller, something higher than the daily round, those dreams of a life in the sunshine, of eyes that would look into hers – this was their ending! She shivered, but she answered bravely, 'Yes.'

'Good girl,' said Miss Sibson, feeling, kind, honest creature, more than she showed. 'I will do so.' And she swam forth.

And Mary? The door was barely shut before her heart whispered that she had only to cross the hall and she would see him; that, on the other hand, if she did not cross the hall she would never, never, never see him again! She would stay here – always; bound hand and foot to the unchanging round of petty duties, a blind slave in the mill, no longer a woman, though her woman's heart hungered for love, but a dull, formal, old maid, growing more stiff, more peevish with every year. At a glance she seemed to see the whole long vista. And on the other side of the hall were love and change and freedom. And she dared not, she dared not open the door!

And then she bethought her that after all he could not be a weathercock, for he had come again. He had come! And it must be for something. For what? For what?

She heard the door open, on the parlour side of the hall, and she knew that he was going. And she stood listening, waiting, with blanched cheeks.

Then the door of the room in which she stood opened, and Miss Sibson came in, met her look, and started perceptibly.

'Oh!' the schoolmistress exclaimed; and for a moment she was silent, gazing strangely at the girl as if she did not know what to say to her. At last, 'We were mistaken,' she said, with a serious face. 'It is not the gentleman you – we thought it was, my dear. On the contrary, it's – it's a stranger who wishes to see you – on business.'

Mary tried to gain command of herself.

'On business?' she said faintly. 'I – I had rather not, I don't think I can.'

'I fear – you must,' Miss Sibson rejoined, with unusual gravity. 'Still, there is no hurry. He can wait a few minutes. He can await your leisure. Do you sit down and compose yourself. You have no reason to be disturbed.' She paused a moment, and then, 'The gentleman,' she added, with an odd inflection in her voice, 'is old enough to be your father.'

CHAPTER XV

Mr Pybus's Offer

'A NOTE for you, sir.'

Vaughan moodily took it. It was the morning after the Vermuyden dinner, and he had slept ill, had risen late, and was still sitting before his breakfast, toying with it rather than eating it. His first feeling on leaving the dining-room had been bitter chagrin at the ease with which Sir Robert had dealt with him. Later, this feeling had given place to amusement, for he had a sense of humour. And he had laughed, though sorely, at the figure he had cut as he beat his retreat. Still later, as he lay, excited and wakeful, he had fallen a prey to doubt; that horrible three-o'clock-in-the-morning doubt, which defies reason, which sees the *cons* in the strongest light and reduces the *pros* to shadows. One thing, however, was certain; he had crossed the Rubicon. He had divorced himself from the Party to which his forebears – for the Vaughans as well as the Vermuydens had been Tories – had belonged. He had joined the Whigs; nay, he had joined the Reformers. But though he had done this deliberately and from conviction, though his reason approved the step, and his brain teemed with arguments in its favour, the chance that he might be wrong haunted him.

That governing class from which he was separating himself, from which his policy would snatch power, which henceforth would dub him deserter, what had it not done for England? With how firm a hand had it guided the country through storm and stress, with what success shielded it, not only from foreign foes, but from disruption and revolution? He scanned the last hundred and fifty years and saw the country, always under the steady rule of that class which had the greatest stake in its prosperity, advancing in strength and riches and comfort; ay, and – though slowly in these – in knowledge also, and the humanities and decencies. And the question forced itself upon him – would that great middle class, into whose hands the sway must fall, use it better? Would they produce statesmen more able than Walpole or than Chatham, generals braver than Wolfe or than Moore, a higher heart than Nelson's? Nay, would the matter end there? Would not power slip into the hands of a wider and yet a wider circle? Would Orator Hunt's dream of Manhood Suffrage, Annual Parliaments, the Ballot, become a reality? Would government by the majority, government by tale of heads – as if three chawbacons must perforce be wiser than one squire – government by the ill-taught, untrained mass, with the least to lose and the most to gain – would that, in the long run, plunge the country in fatal misfortunes?

It was just possible that those who considered the balance of power, established a hundred and fifty years before, to be the one perfect mean between despotism and anarchy – it was just possible that they were right, and that he was a fool.

Then, to divert his mind from this unpleasant speculation, he had allowed himself to think of Mary Smith. And he had tossed and tumbled, in disgust with his conduct. He was brave in the wrong place, he told himself. He had the courage to break with old associations, to defy opinion, to disregard Sir Robert, where no more than a point of pride was concerned; for it was absurd to fancy that the fate of England hung on his voice. But in a matter which went to the root of his happiness – since he was sure that he loved Mary Smith, and would love no other – he had not the spirit to defy a little talk, a few smiles, the contempt of the worldly. He flushed from head to foot at the thought of a life which, however modest – and modesty was not imcompatible with ambition – was shared by her, and would be pervaded by her. And yet he dared not purchase that life at so trifling a cost! No, he was weak where he should be strong, and strong where he should be weak. And so he had tossed and turned, and now, after two or three hours' feverish sleep, he sat glooming over his teacup.

Presently he broke open the note which the waiter had handed to him. He read it, and –

'Who brought this?' he asked, with a perplexed face.

'Don't know, sir,' Sam replied glibly, beginning to collect the breakfast dishes.

'Will you inquire?'

'Found it on the hall table, sir,' the man answered, in the same tone. 'Fancy it's a runaway knock, sir. Known a man find a cabbage at the door, and a whole year's wages under it – at election time, sir! Yes, sir,' he continued, carrying the tray to the sideboard, 'find funny things in funny places – election time, sir.'

Vaughan made no reply, but after reflecting for some minutes he took his hat, and descending the stairs, strolled with an easy air into the street. He paused, as if to admire the old Abbey Church, beautiful even in its disfigurement. Then he turned, apparently careless which way he went, to the right.

The High Street, with its whitened doorsteps and gleaming knockers, lay languid in the sunshine, enervated perhaps by the dissipation of the previous evening. The candidates who would presently pay formal visits to the voters were not yet afoot; and though taverns, where the tap was running, already gave forth maudlin laughter or the refrain of some tipsy song, no other sign of the coming event declared itself. A few tradesmen stood at their doors, a few dogs lay stretched in the sun; and only Vaughan's common sense told him that he was watched.

From the High Street he presently turned into a narrow alley on the right, which descended between garden walls to the lower level of the town. A man who was lounging in the mouth of the alley muttered 'Second door on the left' as he passed, and, without appearing to heed him, Vaughan moved on, counting the doors. At the one indicated he paused, and after making certain that he was not observed he knocked. The door opened a little way.

'For whom are you?' asked someone, who kept himself out of sight.

'Buff and blue,' Vaughan answered.

'Right, sir,' the voice rejoined briskly. The door opened wide and Vaughan passed in. He found himself in a small walled garden smothered in lilac and laburnum, and shaded by two great chestnut trees already so fully in leaf as to hide the house to which the garden belonged.

The person who had admitted him, a very small, very neat gentleman in a high-collared blue coat and nankeen trousers, with a redundant soft cravat wound about his thin neck, bowed low.

'Happy to see you, Mr Vaughan,' he chirped. 'I am Mr Pybus, his lordship's man of business. Happy to be the intermediary in so pleasant a matter, sir.'

'I hope it may turn out so,' Vaughan replied dryly. 'You wrote me a very mysterious note, Mr Pybus.'

'Can't be too careful, sir,' the little man answered, with an important frown. He was said to model himself upon Lord John Russell. 'Can't be too careful in these matters. You're watched and I am watched, sir.'

'I dare say,' Vaughan replied.

'And the responsibility is great, very great, very great. May I?' he continued, pulling out his box. 'But I dare say you don't take snuff?'

'No, I don't.'

'No? The younger generation! Just so. Many of the younger gentry smoke, I'm told. Other days, other manners! Well, to business. We know of course what happened last night, sir. And I'm bound to say, I honour you, Mr Vaughan! I honour you, sir.'

'You can let that pass,' Vaughan replied coldly.

'Very good! Very good! Of course,' he continued, 'the news was brought to me at once, and his lordship knew it before he slept.'

'Oh!'

'Yes, indeed. Yes. And he wrote to me this morning – in his dressing-gown, I don't doubt. He commanded me to tell you—'

But here Vaughan stopped him, with some abruptness. 'One minute, Mr Pybus,' he said. 'I don't wish to know what Lord Lansdowne said, or did, because it will not affect my conduct. I am here because you asked me to grant you an interview. But if your purpose be merely to convey to me Lord Lansdowne's approval or disapproval, he continued, in a tone a little more contemptuous than was necessary, 'be good enough to understand that they are equally indifferent to me. I have done what I have done without regard to Sir Robert Vermuyden's feelings. You may take it for certain' – loftily – 'that I shall not be led beyond my own judgement by any regard for his lordship's.'

'But hear me out! Hear me out!' the little man cried, dancing to and fro in his eagerness, so that, in the shifting lights, under the great chestnut tree, he looked like a pert, bright-coloured bird hopping about. 'Hear me out, and you'll not say that!'

'I shall still say, Mr Pybus—'

'I beg you to hear me out!'

Vaughan shrugged his shoulders. 'Go on!' he said. 'I have said my say, and I suppose you understand me.'

'I shall hold it unsaid,' Mr Pybus rejoined, 'until I have spoken!' And he waved an agitated finger in the air. 'Observe, Mr Vaughan! His lordship bade me take you entirely into confidence, and I do so. We've only one candidate – Mr Wrench. Colonel Petty is sure of his election in Ireland, and we've no mind to stand a second contest to fill his seat; in fact, we are not going to nominate him. Lord Kerry, my lord's eldest son, thought of it, but it is not a certainty, and my lord wishes him to wait a year or two and sit for Calne. I say it's not a certainty. But it's next door to a certainty since you have declared yourself. And my lord's view, Mr Vaughan, is that he who hits the buck should have the haunch. You take me?'

'Indeed, I don't.'

'Then I'll be downright, sir. To the point, sir. Will you be our candidate?'

'What?' Vaughan said. He turned very red. 'What do you mean?'

'What I say, sir – I am a man of my word. Will you be our

candidate? For the Bill, the whole Bill, and nothing but the Bill? If so, we shall not breathe a word until tomorrow, and then we shall nominate you with Mr Wrench, and take 'em by surprise. There, do you see? They'll have their speeches ready, full of my lord's interference and my lord's dictation; and they will point to Colonel Petty, my lord's cousin, for proof! And then' – Mr Pybus winked, much after the fashion of a mischievous parakeet – 'we'll knock the stool from under 'em by nominating you! And, mind you, Mr Vaughan, we are going to win. We were hopeful before, for we've one of their men in gaol, and another – Pillinger of the Blue Duck – is tied by the leg. His wife owes a bit of money, and thinks more of fifty guineas in her own pocket than of thirty pounds a year in her husband's. Anyway, she and the doctor have got him in bed, and will see that he's not well enough to vote! Ha! Ha! Amusing, isn't it? So there it is, Mr Vaughan! There it is! My lord's offer, not mine. I believe he'd word from London what you'd be likely to do, only he felt a delicacy about moving, until you declared yourself.'

'I see,' Vaughan replied. And, indeed, he did see more than he liked.

'Just so, sir. My lord's a gentleman, if ever there was one!'

And Mr Pybus, pulling down his waistcoat, looked as if he suspected that he had imbibed much of his lordship's gentility.

Vaughan stood in thought, his eyes penetrating the shimmering depths of green, where the branches of the chestnut tree, under which he stood, swept the sun-kissed turf. And as he thought, he tried to still the turmoil in his brain. Here, within reach of his hand, to take or leave, was that which had for some time been his ambition! No longer to play at the game, no longer to make believe, while he addressed the Forum or the Academic, that he was addressing the Commons of England! But verily and really to be one of that august body, and to have all within reach. Had not the offer of Cabinet honours fallen to Lord Palmerston at twenty-five? And what Lord Palmerston had done at twenty-five he might do at thirty-five! And more easily, much more easily, if he gained a footing before the crowd of new Members, whom the Bill must bring in, took the floor. The thought set his pulse galloping. The chance was his! His, but if he let it slip now it might not be his again for long years. For it is poor work, waiting for dead men's shoes.

It was not wonderful that he was tempted. It was not wonderful that such an offer, made without price or preface, by a man who had power to push him, by the man who even now was pushing Mr Macaulay at Calne, tempted him sorely. And not the less because he remembered with bitterness that Sir Robert, with two seats in his hands, had never given him a thought, and now never would! So that, if he refused this offer, he could look for no second offer from either side!

And yet he could not forget that Sir Robert was his kinsman, of his blood, was the head of his family, was the donor of his vote. In the night watches he had decided that, his mind delivered, his independence declared, he would not vote. Neither for Sir Robert, for conscience' sake; nor against Sir Robert, for his name's sake! And now he was invited not only to take an active part against him, but to raise his fortunes on his fall!

He drew a deep breath, and he put the temptation from him.

'I am much obliged to his lordship,' he said, quietly, 'but I cannot accept his offer.'

'Not accept it?' Mr Pybus cried, in astonishment. 'Mr Vaughan, you don't mean it, sir! You don't mean it! It's a safe seat! It's in your own hands, I tell you! And after last night! It's not as if you had not declared yourself.'

'I cannot accept it,' Vaughan repeated coldly. 'I am obliged to Lord Lansdowne for his flattering thought of me, and I beg you to convey my thanks to him. But I cannot, in the position I occupy, accept the offer.'

Mr Pybus stared. Was it possible that the scene at the Vermuyden dinner had been a ruse, a stratagem, a piece of play-acting to gain his secrets? To turn his flank? If so, he was undone!

'But,' he quavered, with an unhappy eye, 'you are in favour of the Bill, Mr Vaughan?'

'I am.'

'And of Reform generally, I understand?'

'Certainly.'

'And you've declared yourself?'

'Yes.'

'Then – then I don't understand. Flatly, I don't understand. Why do you refuse?'

Vaughan raised his head and looked at him with a gesture which would have reminded Isaac White of Sir Robert.

'That is my business, Mr Pybus,' he said.

'But you see,' Mr Pybus remonstrated anxiously – he was rather a crestfallen bird by this time, and far past hopping – 'how you place me! I was never more surprised in my life. Never! You see, I've told you all our secrets.'

'I shall keep them.'

'Oh dear, oh dear! This is most disconcerting.'

'You need be under no alarm.'

'Yes, but – oh dear! oh dear!' Poor Pybus was thinking of what he had said about Mrs Pillinger of the Blue Duck. 'I – I don't know what to say. I am afraid I have been too hasty, very hasty! Very precipitate! Of course, Mr Vaughan,' he continued humbly, 'the offer would not have been made if we had not thought you were certain to accept it!'

'Then,' Vaughan replied with dignity, 'you can consider that it has not been made. You may be sure that I shall not name it!'

'Well! Well!'

'I can say no more,' Vaughan continued, beginning to lose patience. 'Indeed, there is nothing more to be said, Mr Pybus.'

'No,' the agent replied, with all his feathers drooping, 'I suppose not, if you really won't change your mind, sir.'

'I shall not do that,' the young man answered.

And a minute later, with Mr Pybus's twittering appeals still sounding in his ears, he was on the other side of the garden door, and striding down the alley, towards the King's Wall and the meadows beside the Avon, whence, after making a prudent detour, he returned to the High Street.

CHAPTER XVI

Less than a Hero

IT WAS the evening of the day on which the meeting between Arthur Vaughan and Mr Pybus had taken place, and from the thirty-six windows in the front of Stapylton lights shone on the darkening glades of the park: here, twinkling fairy-like over the long slope of sward which shimmered pale-green as with the ghostly reflection of dead daylight; there, shining boldly upon the clump of beeches that topped an eminence with blackness. Vaughan sat beside Isaac White in the carriage which Sir Robert had sent for him; and looking curiously forth on the demesne which would be his if he lived, he could scarcely believe his eyes. Was the old Tory so sure of victory that he already illuminated his windows? Or was the house, long sparely inhabited, and opened only at rare intervals and to dull and formal parties, full from attic to hall? Election or no election, that seemed an unlikely thing. Yet every window, yes, every window had its light!

He was too proud to question the agent, who, his errand done and his message delivered, showed no desire to talk. More than once, indeed, in the course of their short companionship Vaughan had caught White looking at him with something like pity in his eyes. And though the young man was far from letting this distress him – he thought it likely that White, with his inborn reverence for Sir Robert, despaired of all who fell under his displeasure – it closed his lips, and hardened his heart. He was no paid servant, but a kinsman and the heir. And he would have Sir Robert remember this. For his part, he was not going to forget that a Chancellor had stooped to flatter him, and a Cabinet Minister had offered him a seat. After that, and when he had refused, for a point of honour, a bait that few would have rejected, he was not going to be browbeaten by an old gentleman whom the world had outpaced; whose beliefs, whose prejudices, whose views were of yesterday, and who, in his profound ignorance of present conditions, would plunge England into civil war rather than resign a privilege as obsolete as ship-money, and as illegal as the Dispensing Power.

While he thought of this the carriage stopped at the door. He alighted and ascended the steps.

The hall more than made good the outside promise. It was brilliantly lighted, and behind Mapp and the servant who received him Vaughan had a glimpse of three or four servants in full-dress livery. From the dining-room on his left issued peals of laughter, and voices so clear that, though he had not the smallest reason to suspect his presence, he was sure that he caught among them Bob Flixton's tones. The discovery was not pleasing; but Mapp, turning the other way and giving him no time to think, went before him to the suite of state rooms on the right of the hall, which he had not seen in use more than thrice in his life. It must be so, then – he thought. The place must be full! For the gilt mirrors which graced the walls of the drawing-rooms reflected the soft light of a multitude of candles, wood fires burned and crackled on the hearths, the *Morning Chronicle*, the *Quarterly*, and other signs of life lay on the round tables, and an air of cheerful *bienséance* pervaded all. What did it mean?

'Sir Robert has finished dinner, sir,' Mapp said; even he seemed to wear an unusual air of solemnity. 'He will be with you, sir, immediately. Hope you are well, sir?' he continued, unbending a little.

'Quite well, Mapp, thank you.'

Then he was left alone, to wonder if a second surprise awaited him. Pybus had supplied him with one that day. If a second were in store for him, what was its nature? Could Sir Robert, on his side, be going to offer him a seat – if he would recant? He hoped not. But he had not time to give more than a thought to this before he heard footsteps and voices crossing the hall. The next moment there entered the outer room – at such a distance from the hearth on which he stood that he had a leisurely view of all before they reached him – three persons. First came a tall burly man in slovenly evening clothes, with an ungainly rolling walk. After him came Sir Robert himself, and after him again, Isaac White.

Vaughan advanced a step or two, and Sir Robert passed by the burly man, who had a pendulous under lip, and a face at once flabby and melancholy. The baronet held out his hand.

'We have not quarrelled yet, Mr Vaughan,' he said, with a cordiality which took Vaughan by surprise. 'I trust and believe that we are not going to quarrel. I bid you welcome. This,' he continued, with a gesture of deference, 'is Sir Charles Wetherell, whom you know by reputation, and whom, for a reason which you will understand by-and-by, I have asked to be present at our interview.'

The stout man eyed Vaughan from under his bushy eyebrows.

'We have met before,' he said in a deep voice. 'At Westminster, Mr Vaughan, on the 22nd of last month.' He had a habit of blinking as he talked. 'I was beholden to you on that occasion.'

Vaughan had already recalled him, and the incident in Palace Yard. He bowed in silent sympathy. But he wondered all the more. The presence of the late Attorney-General, a man of mark in the political world, whose defeat at Norwich was in that morning's paper – what did it mean? Did they think to browbeat him? Or – yes, it must be that they too had an offer to make to him? He had raised himself, it seemed, into a personage by his independence. Sought by the one side, sought by the other! A *résumé* of the answer he would give flashed before him.

'Will you sit down?' said Sir Robert. To Vaughan's surprise, the great man's manner was more friendly than he had ever known it. Indeed, in comparison of the lion of last evening he was but a mouse. 'First,' he continued suavely, 'I am obliged to you for your compliance with my wishes.'

Vaughan murmured that he had come at no inconvenience to himself.

'I hope not,' Sir Robert replied. 'In the next place, let me say that we have to speak to you on a matter of the first importance; a matter, also, on which we have the advantage of knowledge which you have not. It is my desire, therefore, Mr Vaughan, to admit you to a parity with us in that respect, before you express yourself on any subject on which we are likely to differ.'

Vaughan looked keenly at him; and an observer would

have noticed that there was a closer likeness between the two men than the slender tie of blood warranted.

'If it is a question, Sir Robert,' he said slowly, 'of the subject on which we differed last evening, I would prefer, I would certainly prefer, to say at once—'

'Don't!' Wetherell, who was seated within a long reach of him, grunted. 'Don't!' And he laid an elephantine and not over-clean hand on Vaughan's knee. 'You can spill words as easy as water,' he continued, 'and they are as hard to pick up again. Hear what Vermuyden has to say, and what I've to say – 'tisn't much – and then blow your trumpet. If you've any breath left!' he added *sotto voce*, as he threw himself back.

Vaughan hesitated a moment. Then, 'Very good,' he said, 'if you will hear me afterwards. But—'

'But and If are two wenches always raising trouble!' Wetherell cried in his coarse fashion. 'Do you listen, Mr Vaughan. Do you listen. Now, Vermuyden, go on.'

But Sir Robert did not seem to have words at command. He took a pinch of snuff from the gold box he held; and he opened his mouth to resume; but he hesitated. At length, 'What I have to tell you, Mr Vaughan,' he said, in a voice more diffident than usual, 'had perhaps been more properly told by my attorney to yours. I admit that,' dusting the snuff from his frill. 'And it would have been so told, but for – but for exigencies not immediately connected with it, which are nevertheless so pressing as to – as to induce me to take the one step immediately possible. Less regular, but immediately possible! All the same, you will believe, I am sure, that I do not wish to take any advantage of you other than' – he paused with a look at Wetherell – 'other than that which my position gives me. For the rest I' – he looked again at his snuff box and hesitated – 'I think – I—'

'You'd better come to the point!' Wetherell growled impatiently, jerking his ungainly person back in his chair. 'To the point, man! Or shall I tell him?'

Sir Robert straightened himself with a sigh of relief. 'If you please,' he said. 'I think you had better. It – it may come better from you, as you are not interested.'

Vaughan looked from one to the other, and wondered what on earth they would be at. His cordial reception, followed by this strange exordium; the festive preparations; the presence of the three men seated about him, and plainly ill at ease – these things begot misgivings, which it was not in the power of reason to hold futile. What were they meditating? What argument, what threat, what inducement? And what meant this strange illumination of the house? It could be nothing to him. And yet – but Wetherell was speaking.

'Mr Vaughan,' he said gruffly – and he swayed his heavy body to and fro in his seat, 'my friend here, and your kinsman, has made a discovery of – of the utmost possible importance to him; and, speaking candidly, of scarcely less importance to you. I don't know whether you read the trash they call novels nowadays, *The Disowned*,' he snorted with contempt, 'and *Tremayne* and the rest? I hope not! I don't! But it's something devilish like the stuff they put in them that I've to tell you. You'll believe it or not, as you please. You think yourself heir to the Stapylton estates? Of course, you do. Sir Robert has no more than a life interest, and if he has no children, the reversion is yours. Just so. But if he has children, son or daughter, you are ousted, Mr Vaughan.'

Vaughan's face grew suddenly rigid. 'Are you going to tell me,' he said, 'that he has children?'

His heart was beating furiously under his waistcoat, but, taken aback as he was, he maintained outward composure.

'That's it,' Wetherell answered bluntly.

'Then—'

'He has a daughter.'

'It will have to be proved!' Vaughan said slowly and in the tone of a man who chose his words. And he rose to his feet. He felt, perhaps he was justified in feeling, that they had taken him at a disadvantage; that they had treated him unfairly in trapping him thither, one to three, that they might see, perhaps, how he took it. Not – his thoughts travelled rapidly over the facts – that the thing could be true! The punishment for last night's revolt fell too pat, too *à propos*; he did not believe it! And besides, it could not be true. For Lady Vermuyden lived, and there could be no question of a concealed marriage, or a low-born family! 'It will have to be proved!' he repeated firmly. 'And is matter rather for my lawyers than for me!'

Sir Robert, too, had risen to his feet. But it was Wetherell who answered him.

'Perhaps so!' he said. 'Indeed I admit it, young sir! It will have to be proved. But—'

'It should have been told to them rather than to me!' Vaughan repeated with a sparkling eye. And he turned as if he were determined to treat them as hostile and to have nothing further to say to them.

But Wetherell stopped him. 'Stay, young man!' he said. 'And be ashamed of yourself! You forget yourself!' And before Vaughan, stung and angry, could retort upon him, 'You forget,' he continued, 'that this touches another as closely as it touches you – and more closely! You are a gentleman, sir, and Sir Robert's kinsman. Have you no word, then, for him?' pointing, with a gesture roughly eloquent, to his host. 'You lose, but have you no word for him who gains? You lose, but is it nothing to him that he finds himself childless no longer, heirless no longer? That his house is no longer lonely, his hearth no longer empty! Man alive,' he added, dropping with honest indignation to a lower note, 'you lose, but what does he not gain? And have you no word, no generous thought for him? Bah!' throwing himself back in his seat. 'Poor human nature!'

'Still it must be proved,' Vaughan answered sullenly; though in his heart he acknowledged the truth of the man's reproach.

'Granted!' Wetherell retorted. 'But will you not hear what it is that has to be proved? If so, sit down, sir, sit down, and hear like a man what we have to tell you. Will you do that?' he continued in a tone of exasperation, which did but reflect the slowly hardening expression of Sir Robert's face, 'or are you quite a fool?'

Vaughan hesitated, looking with angry eyes at Wetherell. Then he sat down. 'Am I to understand,' he said coldly, 'that this is news to Sir Robert?'

'It was news to him yesterday.'

Vaughan bowed, and was silent; aware that a more generous demeanour would become him better, but unable to compass it on the spur of the moment. He was ignorant – unfortunately – of the spirit in which he had been summoned; consequently he could not guess that every word he uttered rang churlishly in the ears of his listeners. He was not a churl; but he was taken unfairly, as it seemed to him. And to be called upon in the first moment of chagrin to congratulate Sir Robert on an event which ruined his own prospects and changed his life – was too much. But again Wetherell was speaking.

'You shall know from the beginning what we know,' he said, in his melancholy way. 'You are aware that Sir Robert married – in the year '10, was it not? Yes, in the year '10, and that Lady Vermuyden bore him one child, a daughter, who died in Italy in the year '15. It appears now – we are in a position to prove, I think – that that child did not die in that year, nor in any year; but is now alive, is in this country, and can be identified.'

Vaughan coughed. 'This is strange news,' he said, 'after all these years. And somewhat sudden, is it not?'

Sir Robert's face grew harder, but Wetherell shrugged his shoulders. 'If you will listen,' he replied, 'you will know all that we know. It is no secret, at any rate in this room it is no secret, that in the year '14 Sir Robert fancied that he had reason to be gravely displeased with Lady Vermuyden. It was thought by her friends that a better feeling might be produced by a temporary separation, and the child's health afforded a pretext. Accordingly Sir Robert suffered Lady Vermuyden to take the child abroad, her suite consisting of a courier, a maid, and a nurse. The nurse she sent back to England not long afterwards, on the plea that an Italian woman, from whom the child might learn the language, would be better. In this, I believe, that she acted *bona fide*. But in other respects,' puffing out his cheeks, 'her conduct was such as to alarm her husband; and in terms, perhaps too peremptory, Sir Robert presently bade her return – or cease to consider his house as her home. Her answer was the announcement of the child's death.'

'And that it did not die,' Vaughan murmured, 'as Lady Vermuyden said?'

'We have this evidence. But first let me say that Sir Robert, on the receipt of the news, set out for Italy overland. The Hundred Days stopped him; he could not cross France, and he returned without certifying the child's death. On the other hand he had no suspicion, no reason for suspicion. Well, then, for evidence that it did not die. The courier is dead, and there remains only the maid. She is alive, she is here, she is in this house. And it is from her that we have learned the truth.'

He paused a moment, brooding stolidly on the pattern of the carpet between his feet. Sir Robert, with a face grown very hard, sat upright, listening to the tale of his misfortunes – and doubtless suffered torments as he listened.

'Her story,' Wetherell resumed, 'is this. Lady Vermuyden was living at that time a life of the wildest gaiety; she had no affection for the child; if the woman is to be believed, she hated it. To part with it was nothing to her, one way or the other; and on receipt of Sir Robert's order to return, her ladyship conceived the idea of punishing him, by abducting the child and telling him it was dead. She set out from Florence for Rome; on the way she left it at Orvieto in charge of the Italian nurse, and, arriving in Rome, she put about the story of its death. Shortly afterwards she had it conveyed to England and bred up in an establishment near London – always with the aid and connivance of her maid.'

'The maid's name?' Vaughan asked.

Herapath – Martha Herapath. But to proceed. By-and-by Lady Vermuyden returned to England, and settled at Brighton, and the maid left her and married, but continued to draw a pension from her. Lady Vermuyden persisted, in the company of Lady Conyng – but I need name no names – in the same course of giddiness, if no worse, which she had pursued abroad; and gave little heed, if any, to the child. But this woman Herapath never forgot that the pension she enjoyed was dependent on her power to prove the truth; and when a short time back the girl, now fully grown, was withdrawn from her knowledge, she grew restive. She sought Lady Vermuyden, always a creature of impulse; and when her ladyship, foolish in this as in all things, refused to meet her views, she came to us,' lifting his head abruptly and looking at Vaughan, 'and told us the story.'

'It will have to be proved,' Vaughan said stubbornly.

'No doubt,' Wetherell replied, 'strictly proved. In the meantime, if you would like to peruse the facts in greater detail, they are here, as taken down from the woman's mouth.' He drew from his capacious breast pocket a manuscript consisting of several sheets. He unfolded it and flattened it on his knee. He handed it to Vaughan.

The young man took it, mechanically; and, with his thoughts in a whirl, read it line after line without taking in a single word. For all the time his brain was at work measuring the change. His modest competence would be left to him. He would have enough to live on as he was now living, and to pursue his career; or, in the alternative, he might settle down as a poor squire in his paternal home in South Wales. But the great inheritance which had loomed in the background of his life, and had been more to him than he had admitted, the future dignities which he had undervalued while he thought them certain, the position more enviable than many a peer's, and higher by its traditions than any to which he could attain by his own exertions though he reached the Woolsack – these were gone, if Wetherell's tale was true. Gone in a moment, at a word! And though he might have lost more, though many a man had lost his all by such a stroke and smiled, he could not on the instant smile. He could not in a moment oust all bitterness. He knew that he was taking the news unworthily; that he was playing a poor part. But he could not force himself to play a better – on the instant. When he had read with unseeing eyes to the bottom of the first page, and had turned it, he let the papers fall upon his knee.

'You do not wish me,' he said slowly, 'to express an opinion now – I suppose?'

'No,' Wetherell answered. 'Certainly not. But I have not quite done. I have not quite done,' he repeated. 'I should tell you that, for opening the matter to you now – we have two reasons, Mr Vaughan. Two. First, we think it due to you, as one of the family. Secondly, Vermuyden desires that from the beginning his intentions shall be clear and – be understood.'

'I thoroughly understand them,' Vaughan replied dryly. No one was more conscious than he that he was behaving ill.

'That is just what you do not!' Wetherell retorted. 'You spill words, young man, and by-and-by you will wish to pick them up. You cannot anticipate, at any rate you have no right to anticipate Sir Robert's intentions, of which he has asked me to be the mouthpiece. The estate, of course, and the settled funds must go to his daughter. But there is a large sum arising from the economical management of the property, which is at his disposal. He feels,' Wetherell continued sombrely, an elbow on each knee and his eyes on the floor, 'that some injustice has been done to you, and he desires to compensate you for that injustice. He proposes, therefore, to secure to you the succession to two-thirds of this sum; which amounts – which amounts, in the whole, I believe' – he looked at White – 'to little short of eighty thousand pounds.'

Vaughan, who had been more than once on the point of interrupting him, did so now.

'I could not accept it!' he exclaimed impulsively. And he rose, with a hot face, from his seat. 'I could not accept it.'

'As a legacy?' Wetherell, who was said to be fond of money, returned with a queer look. 'As a legacy, eh? Why not?' While Sir Robert, with compressed lips, repented of his generosity. He had looked for some show of feeling, some word of sympathy, some felicitation from the young man, who after all was his blood relation. But if his return was to be of this sort, if his advances were to be met with suspicion, his benevolence with churlishness, then all, all in this young man was of a piece – and detestable!

And certainly Vaughan was not showing himself in the best light. But he could not change his attitude in a moment. Under no circumstances is it easy to take a gift with grace: to take one with grace under these circumstances, and when he had already misbehaved, was beyond him. As it would have been beyond most men.

For a moment, drawn this way by his temper, that way by his better feelings, he did not know how to answer Wetherell's last words. At length and lamely –

'May I ask,' he said, 'why Sir Robert makes me this offer – while the matter lies open?'

'Sir Robert will prove his case,' Wetherell answered gruffly, 'if that is what you mean.'

'I mean—'

'He does not ask you to surrender anything.'

Vaughan melted.

'I am bound to say, then,' he replied, speaking with

warmth, 'that the offer is very generous, most generous! But—'

'He asks you to surrender nothing,' Wetherell repeated stolidly, his face between his knees.

'But I still think it premature,' Vaughan persisted. 'And handsome as it is, more than handsome as it is, I think that it would come with greater force, were my position first made clear!'

'Maybe,' Wetherell said, his face still hidden. 'I don't deny that.'

'As it is,' Vaughan continued, with a deep breath, 'I am taken by surprise. I do not know what to say. I find it hard to say anything – in the first flush of the matter.' And he looked from one to the other. 'So, for the present, with Sir Robert's permission, and without any slight to his generosity, I will take leave. If he is good enough to repeat in the future this very handsome – this uncalled-for and generous offer which he has outlined, I shall know, I hope, what is due to him, without forgetting what is due to myself. In the meantime I can only acknowledge it, and—'

But the belated congratulation, which was on his lips and which might have altered many things, was never uttered.

'One moment!' Sir Robert struck in, 'one moment!' He spoke with a hardness born of long-suppressed irritation. 'You have taken your stand, Mr Vaughan, strictly on the defensive—'

'But I think you understand—'

'Strictly on the defensive,' the baronet repeated, requiring silence by a gesture. 'You must not be surprised, therefore, if I also say a word on a point which touches me.'

'I wouldn't!' Wetherell growled in his deep voice. And for an instant he raised his huge face, and looked stolidly at the wall before him.

But Sir Robert was not to be bidden. 'I think otherwise,' he said. 'Mr Vaughan, the election tomorrow touches me very nearly – in more ways than one. The vote you have, you received at my hands, and hold only as my heir. I take it for granted, therefore, that under the present circumstances you will use it as I desire.'

'Oh!' Vaughan said. And he removed his eyes from the one

to the other with a singular smile. 'Oh!' he repeated – and there was a world of meaning in his tone. 'Am I to understand—'

'I have made myself quite clear,' Sir Robert cried, his manner betraying his agitation.

'Am I to understand,' Vaughan repeated, 'that the offer which you made a few minutes back, the generous and handsome offer,' he continued, with a faint note of irony in his voice, 'was dependent on my conduct tomorrow? Am I to understand that?'

'If you please to put it so,' Sir Robert replied, his voice quivering with the resentment he had long suppressed. 'And if your own sense of honour does not dictate to you how to act.'

'But do you put it so!'

'Do you mean—'

'I mean,' Vaughan said, 'does the offer depend on the use I make of my vote tomorrow? That is the point, Sir Robert!'

'No,' Wetherell muttered indistinctly.

But again Sir Robert would not be bidden. 'I will be frank,' he said. 'And my answer is, yes! Yes! For I do not conceive, I cannot conceive, sir, that a gentleman would take so great a benefit, and refuse so slight a service! A service, too, which, apart from this offer, most men—'

'Thank you,' Vaughan replied. 'That is clear enough.' He glanced from the one to the other with the look of a man reinstated in his own opinion, and once more master of his company. 'Now I understand,' he continued. 'I see now why the offer which a few minutes ago seemed so premature, so strangely premature, was made this evening. Tomorrow it had been made too late! My vote had been cast, and I could no longer be – bribed!'

'Bribed, sir?' Sir Robert cried, red with anger.

'Yes, bribed, sir. But let me tell you,' Vaughan went on, allowing the bitterness which he had been feeling to appear, 'let me tell you, Sir Robert, that if not only my future but my present, if my all were at stake – I should resent such an offer as an insult.'

Sir Robert took a step towards the bell and stopped.

'An insult!' Vaughan repeated firmly. 'As great an insult as

I should inflict upon you were I unwise enough to do the errand I was asked to do a week ago – by a Cabinet Minister. And offered you, Sir Robert, here in your own house, a peerage conditional on your support of the Bill!'

'A peerage?' Sir Robert's eyes seemed to be starting from his head. 'A peerage! Conditional on my—'

'Yes, sir, conditional on your renunciation of those opinions which you honestly hold as I honestly hold mine!' Vaughan repeated. 'I will make the offer if you wish it.'

Wetherell rose ponderously. 'See here!' he said. 'Listen to me, will you, you two! You, Vermuyden, as well as the young man. You will both be sorry for what you are saying now! Damned sorry! Listen to me! Listen to me, man!'

But the baronet was already tugging at the bell-rope. He was white with rage, and not without reason. This whipper-snapper, this pettifogging lad, just out of his teens, to talk to him of peerages, to patronize him, to offer him – to – to—

For a moment he stammered and could not speak. At last –

'Enough! Enough, sir, leave my house!' he cried, shaking from head to foot with passion, and losing, for the first time in many years, his self-control. 'Leave my house,' he repeated, 'and never set foot in it again! Not a pound and not a penny will you have of mine! Never! Never! Never!'

Vaughan smiled. 'Very good, Sir Robert,' he said, shrugging his shoulders. 'You fortune is your own. But—'

'Begone, sir! Not another word, but go!'

Vaughan raised his eyebrows, bowed in a ceremonious fashion to Wetherell, and nodded to White, who stood petrified and gaping. Then he walked slowly through that room and the next, and with one backward smile – vanished.

And this time, as he passed through the hall, narrowly missing Flixton, who was leaving the dining-room, there could be no doubt that the breach was complete, that the small cordiality which had existed between the kinsmen was at an end. The Bill, which had played so many mischievous tricks, severed so many friends, broken the ties of so many years, had dealt no one a more spiteful blow that it had dealt Arthur Vaughan.

CHAPTER XVII

The Chippinge Election

THE GREAT day was come. Before night the borough of Chippinge must give its vote for Reform or no Reform, the rule of the few or the rule of the many; and in the large room on the first floor of the White Lion were assembled a score of those who on the Tory side were most interested in the issue. The greater number having places at the three windows enjoyed a view of what was going forward in the space below; but it was noticeable that while the two or three who remained in the background talked and joked, these were silent; possibly because the uproar without made hearing difficult. The hour was early, the business of the day was to come; but already the hubbub was indescribable. Nor was this all. Every minute some missile, a much-enduring cabbage stalk, or a dead cat in Tory colours, rose to a level with the windows, hovered, and sank – amid a storm of groans or cheers. For the most part, these missiles fell harmless. But that the places of honour at the windows were not wholly places of safety was proved by a couple of shattered panes, as well as by the sickly hue of some of the spectators' faces.

Nearly all who had attended the Vermuyden dinner were in the room. But things which had worn one aspect across the mahogany wore another now. At the table old and young had made light of the shoving and mauling and drubbing through which they had forced their way to the good things before them; they had even made a jest of the bit of a rub they were likely to have on the polling day. Now the sight of the noisy crowd which filled the open space, from the head of the High Street to the wall of the Abbey, and from the Vineyard east of it, almost to the West Port, made their bones ache. They looked, even the boldest, at one another. The heart of Dewell, the barber, was in his shoes; the Rector stared aghast; and Mowatt, the barrister, Arthur Vaughan's ill-found friend, wished for once that he was on the vulgar side.

True, the doors of the White Lion were guarded by a sturdy

phalanx of Vermuyden lads; mustered with what difficulty, and kept together by what arguments, White best knew. But what were two or three score, however faithful and however strong, against the hundreds and thousands who swayed and cheered and groaned before the inn; who swarmed upon the old town cross until they hid every inch of the crumbling stonework; who clung to every niche and buttress of the Abbey, and from whose mass as from a sea the solitary church spire rose as rises some lighthouse cut off by the breakers; who now, forgetful of their Wiltshire birth, cheered the Birmingham tub-thumper to the echo, and now roared stern assent to the wildest statements of the Political Union?

True, a dozen banners and thrice as many flags gave some show of festivity to the scene. But the timid, who set out to draw solace from these, retreated, appalled by the daring 'Death or Freedom!' inscribed on one banner, or the scarcely less bold 'The Sovereign People' which bellied above the clothiers. Granted, the majority of the placards bore nothing worse than the watchword of the party, 'The Bill, the whole Bill, and nothing but the Bill!' or 'Retrenchment and Reform!' or – in reference to the King – 'God bless the two Bills!' But for all that, Dewell the barber – and some more who would not have confessed it – wished the day well over and no bones broken. A great day for Chippinge; but a day on which many an old score was like to be paid, many a justice to hear the commonalty's opinion of him, many a man who had thriven under the old rule to read the writing on the wall!

Certainly nothing like the spectacle visible from the White Lion windows had been seen in Chippinge within living memory. The Abbey – which had seen the last of the mitred abbots pass out, shorn of his strength and with weeping townsfolk in his train in lieu of belted knights – that pile, stately in its ruin, which had witnessed a revolution more tragic than this which impended – might have viewed its pair, might have seen its precincts seethe as they seethed now. But no living man. Nor did those who scanned the crowd find aught in its detail to lessen its terrors. There were indeed plenty of decent, respectable people in the throng who, though they were set on gaining their rights, had no notion of violence. But wood burns when it is kindled; and here at the corner of the Heart and Hand, the Whig headquarters, was a spark like to light the fire – Boston, the bruiser, and a dozen of his kidney from Bristol, men, who in those days were the idols of the populace. Pybus, who had brought them hither, was not to be seen; he was weaving his spells in the Heart and Hand. But Mr Williams, 'White-Hat Williams', the richest man in Chippinge, who, long voteless, had thirsted to see this day – he was here at the head of his clothmen, and as fierce as the poorest. And half a dozen lesser men of the same kind were present: sallow Blackford the Methodist, the fugleman of every dissenter within ten miles; with two or three small lawyers whom the landlords did not employ, and two or three apothecaries who were in the same class. These, with a couple of famished curates, who had Sydney Smith for their warranty, and a sprinkling of spouters from the big towns – men who had the glories of Orator Hunt and William Cobbett before their eyes – led the party. But everywhere, working in the mass like yeast, moved a score of bitter malcontents, whom the old system had bruised under foot: poachers whom the gentry had gaoled, or the lovers of maids as frail as fair, or labourers whom the Poor Laws had crushed – a score of rogues whose grievances, long muttered in pothouses, now flared to light and cried for vengeance. In a word, there were the elements of mischief in the crowd, and under the surface an ugly spirit. Even the most peaceable were grim, knowing that it was now or never. So that the faces at the White Lion windows grew longer as their owners gazed and listened.

'I don't know what's come to the people!' the Rector bawled, turning about to make himself heard by his daughter. 'Eh, what?'

'I'd like to see Lord Grey hanged!' answered Squire Rowley, his face purple. 'And Lord Lansdowne with him! What do you say, sir?' to Serjeant Wathen.

'Fortunate a show of hands don't carry it!' the Serjeant cried, shrugging his shoulders with an assumption of easiness.

'Carry it? Of course we'll carry it!' the Squire replied wrathfully. 'I suppose two and two still makes four!'

Isaac White, who was whispering with a man in a corner of the room, wished he was sure of that; or, rather, that three and two made six. But the Squire was continuing.

'Bah!' he cried in disgust. 'Give these people votes? Look at 'em! Look at 'em, sir! Votes, indeed! Votes, indeed! Give 'em oakum, I say!'

He forgot that nine-tenths of those below were as good as the voters at his elbow, who were presently to return two Members for Chippinge. Or rather, it did not occur to him, old Tory as he was, and convinced,

'Twas the Jacobins brought every mischief about,

that Dewell's vote was Dewell's, or Annibal's Annibal's.

Meanwhile, 'I wish we were safe at the hustings!' young Mowatt shouted in the ear of the man who stood in front of him.

The man chanced to be Cooke, the second candidate. He turned.

'At the hustings?' he said irascibly. 'Do you mean, sir, that we are expected to fight our way through this rabble?'

'I am afraid we must,' Mowatt answered.

'Then it – it has been damned badly arranged!' retorted the outraged Cooke, who never forgot that as he paid well for his seat it ought to be a soft one. 'Go through this mob, and have our heads broken?'

The faces of those who could hear him grew long. 'And it wants only five minutes to ten,' complained a third. 'We ought to be going now.'

'Damn me, but suppose they don't let us go!' Cooke cried. 'Badly arranged! I should think it is, sir! Damned badly arranged! The hustings should have been on this side.'

But as the hustings at Chippinge had been hitherto a matter of form, it had not occurred to any one to alter their position – cheek by jowl with the Whig headquarters, but divided by fifty yards of seething mob from the White Lion. However, White, on an appeal being made to him, put a better face on the matter.

'It's all right, gentlemen,' he said, 'it's all right! If they have the hustings, we have the returning officer, and they can do nothing without us. I've seen Mr Pybus, and I have his safe conduct for our party to go to the hustings.'

But it is hard to satisfy everybody, and at this there was a fresh outcry.

'A safe conduct?' cried old Squire Rowley, redder about the gills than before. 'For shame, sir! Are we to be indebted to the other side for a safe conduct? Good God! I never heard of such a thing!'

'I quite agree with you,' cried the Rector. 'Quite! I protest, Mr White, against anything of the kind.'

But White was unmoved. 'We've got to get our voters there,' he said. 'Sir Robert will be displeased, I know; but—'

'Never was such a thing heard of!'

'No, sir; but never was such an election,' White retorted with spirit.

'Where is Sir Robert?'

'He'll be here presently,' White replied. 'He'll be here presently. Anyway, gentlemen,' he continued, 'we had better be going down to the hall. In a body, gentlemen, if you please, and voters in the middle. And keep together, if you please. A little shouting,' he added cheerfully, 'breaks no bones. We can shout too!'

The thing was unsatisfactory, without precedent, nay, humiliating. But there seemed to be nothing else for it. As White said, this election was not as other elections. Bath was lost, it was known, and Bristol, too, it was whispered; the country was gone mad. And so, frowning and ill-content, the magnates trooped out, and led by White, began to descend the stairs. There was much confusion, one asking if the Alderman was there, another demanding to see Sir Robert, here a man grumbling about White's arrangements, there a man silent over the discovery, made for the first time, that here was like to be an end of old Toryism and the loaves and the fishes it had dispensed.

In the hall, where the party was reinforced by a crowd of their smaller supporters, a man plucked White's sleeve and drew him aside.

'She's out now!' he whispered. 'Pybus has left two with him, and they won't leave him for me. But if you went and ordered them out there's a chance they'd go, and—'

'The doctor's not there?'

'No, and Pillinger's well enough to come, if you put it strong.

He's afraid of his wife, and they've got him body and soul; but—'

White cast a despairing eye on the confusion about him. 'How can I come?' he muttered. 'I must get these to the poll first.'

'Then you'll never do it,' the man retorted. 'There'll be no coming and going today, Mr White, you take it from me. Now's the time, while they're waiting for you in front. You can slip out at the back, and bring him in and take him with you. It's the only way, so help me! They're in that temper we'll be lucky if we're all alive tomorrow.'

The man was right, and White knew it, yet he hesitated. If he had had an aide fit for the task, the thing might be done. But to go himself, on whom everything fell! He reflected. Possibly Arthur Vaughan might not vote for the enemy after all. But if he did, Sir Robert would poll five to six, and be beaten, unless he polled Pillinger; when the returning officer's vote, of which he was sure, would give him the election. Pillinger's vote, therefore, was vital; everything turned upon it; and White determined to go. His absence would only cause a little delay, and he must risk that. He slipped away.

He was missed at once, and the discovery redoubled the confusion. One asked where he was, and another where Sir Robert was; while Cooke, in tones louder and more irritable than was prudent, found fresh fault, and wished to Heaven that he had never seen the place. Accustomed to one-sided contests of which both Parties knew the issue, the Tory managers were helpless; they were aware that the hour had struck, and that they were expected, but without White they were uncertain how to act. Some cried that the agent had gone on, and that they should follow; some that Sir Robert was to meet them at the hustings, others that they might as well be at home as waiting there; while the babel without deafened and distracted them, and at last, without order given, they found themselves moving out.

Their reception did not clear their brains. Such a roar as greeted them had never been heard in Chippinge. The hair on Dewell the barber's head stood up, the Alderman's cheek grew pale, even Cooke dropped his cane, the stoutest flinched. Changed indeed were the times from those not distant ones, when their exit had been greeted by sycophantic cheers, or, at the worst, by a little good-humoured jesting! Now the whole multitude in the open, not in one part, but in every part, knew as by instinct of their setting forth, brandished on the instant a thousand arms, deafened them with a thousand voices, demanding monotonously 'The Bill! The Bill!' Nor had the demonstration stopped there, but for the intervention of a body of Whig stalwarts, who, posting themselves on the flanks of the derided procession, conferred on its slow march an ignoble safety.

No wonder that many a one who found himself guarded thus, rubbed his eyes. The times were changed indeed. No more despotism of Squire and Parson, no more monopoly of places, no more nominated Members, no more elections that did but mock men who had no share in them, no more 'Cripples', no more snug jobs! The Tories might agree with Mr Fudge,

That this passion for roaring had come in of late
Since the rabble all tried for a voice in the State,

and foretell the ruinous outcome of it. But the thing was; the many-headed, the many-handed had them in its grip. They must go meekly, or not at all; with visions of fish-fags and guillotines before their eyes, and wondering, most of them – as they tried to show a bold front, tried to wave their banners and give some answering shout to the sea which beat upon them – how they would regain their homes with whole skins!

Perhaps there was only one who did not stoop to that thought; he who, alone of them all, was unaware of the precaution taken for his safety. That was Sir Robert himself, the master of all. Attended by Bob Flixton, who had come from Bristol to see the fun – and whose voice, it will be remembered, Vaughan had overheard at Stapylton the evening before – and by two or three other guests, he had entered the White Lion from the rear, arriving in time to fall in, somewhat surprised at his supporters' precipitation, at the tail of the procession. The moment he was recognized by the crowd he was greeted with a roar of 'Down with the borough-monger!' that appalled his companions. But he faced it calmly and imperturbably; a little paler, a little prouder, and a little sterner than before, but with a gleam in his eyes that had not been seen in them for years. For answer, he smiled; and it is probable that, as much as any hour in his life, he enjoyed this hour, which put him to the test before those over whom he had ruled so long. His caste might be passing, the days of his power might be numbered, the waves of democracy might be rising about the system in which he believed the safety of England to lie; but no man should see him falter. No veteran of the old *noblesse* in days which Sir Robert could remember had gone to his fate more proudly than the English patrician was prepared to go to his, though worse than the guillotine awaited him.

His contemptuous attitude, his fearless bearing, impressed even the crowd; appreciative, at bottom, of courage. And presently, where he turned his disdainful eyes, they gaped instead of hissing; and one here and there, under the magic of his look, doffed hat or carried hand to forehead, and henceforth was mute. And so great is the sympathy of all parts of a mob that this silence spread quickly, mysteriously, at last wholly. When he, the last of his party, stepped on the hustings, there was for a moment a complete stillness: a stillness of expectation, while he looked round, a stillness such as startled the leaders of the opposition. It could not be – it could not be that, after all, the old lion would prove too much for them!

White-Hat Williams roared aloud in his rage. 'Up hats and shout, lads,' he yelled, 'or by God the damned Tories will do us after all! Are you afraid of them, you lubbers! Shout, lads, shout!'

CHAPTER XVIII

The Chippinge Election (continued)

THE BEAST that was in the crowd answered to the spur. 'Ye've robbed us enough, ye old rascal!' a harsh Midland voice shrieked over the heads of the throng. 'We'll have our rights now, you blood-sucker!' And 'Boo! Boo!' the lower elements of the mob broke forth. And then in stern cadence, 'The Bill! The Bill! The Bill!'

'Out of Egypt, and out of the House of Bondage!' shrieked a Methodist above the hubbub.

'Ay, ay!'

'Slaves no longer!'

'No! No! No!'

'Hear that, ye hoary tyrant!' in a woman's shrill tones. 'Who gaoled my man for a hare?'

A roar of laughter which somewhat cleared the air followed this. Sir Robert smiled grimly.

The hustings, a strong wooden platform raised four feet above the ground, rested against the Abbey gateway. In front it was closed only by a stout railing, and so public was it, and so exposed its dangerous eminence, that the more timid of the unpopular Party were no sooner upon it than they yearned for the safe obscurity of the common level. Of the three booths into which the interior was divided, the midmost was reserved for the returning officer and his staff.

Bob Flixton, who kept close to Sir Robert's elbow, looked down on the sea of jeering faces.

'I tell you what it is,' he muttered. 'We're going to have a confounded row!'

Mowatt, at some distance from him, was of the same opinion, but regarded the outlook differently.

'It's my belief,' he said, 'that we shall all be murdered.'

'And damn the Bill!' old Squire Rowley ejaculated. 'The people are off their heads! Jack is as good as his master, and better too!'

These four, with the candidates, were in the front row. The

Rector, the Alderman, and one or two of the neighbouring gentry, supported them, and faced as well as they could the hooting and yelling, and the occasional missile. In the front of the other booth were White-Hat Williams and Blackford the minister, Mr Wrench the candidate, wreathed in smiles, a couple of Whig gentry from the Bowood side, a curate of the same colour, Pybus – and Arthur Vaughan!

A thrill ran through Sir Robert's supporters when they saw his kinsman on the other side; actually and publicly arrayed against them. Their hearts, already low, sank a peg lower. Of evil omens this seemed the worst; sunk is the cause the young desert! And many were the curious eyes which searched the renegade's features and strove to read his thoughts.

But in vain. His head high, his face composed, Vaughan looked stonily before him. Nor was it possible to say whether he was really unmoved, or merely masked agitation. Sir Robert on his side never looked at him, nor betrayed the least sense of his presence. But he knew. He knew! And with the first presage of defeat – for he was not a man to be intimidated by noise – he repeated his vow. 'Not a pound, nor a penny! Never! Never!' This public renunciation, this wanton defiance – he would never forgive it! Henceforth, it must be war to the knife between them! No thousands, no compensation, no compromise! As the young man was sowing, so he should reap! He, who, in his darkest hour, insulted and abandoned his family, what punishment was too severe for him?

Vaughan could make a good guess at the old autocrat's feelings: and he was careful to avert his eyes. The proceedings were opened, and he listened languidly, until, midway in the reading of some document which no one heeded – the crowd jeering and flouting merrily – he caught a new note in the turmoil. Immediately he was conscious of a swirling movement among those below him, there was a rush of the throng to his right, and he turned his head to see what it meant.

A man, one of a group of three or four who appeared to be trying to push a way through the crowd, was being hustled and flung to and fro, amid jeers and taunts. The man was striving to gain the hustings, but was still some way from it, and his chance of reaching it with his clothes on his back seemed small. Vaughan saw so much, and saw the man lose his temper, and strike a blow. It was returned – and then, not till then, Vaughan saw that the man was Isaac White. He cried 'Shame!' and had passed one leg over the barrier, to go to the rescue, when he saw that another was before him. Sir Robert's tall spare figure appeared below, among the crowd. His eyes, his air, still had power; the press opened instinctively before his sharp command. He had reached White, had extricated him, and had turned to make good his retreat, when it struck the more brutal element in the crowd – for the most part strangers to him – that he was the prime enemy of the cause, on foot among them, at their mercy! A rush was made at his back. He faced about undaunted, White and two more at his side; the rabble recoiled. But when he turned his face again to the hustings a second rush was made, and they were upon him, and hustled him before he could turn. A man with a long stick struck off his hat, another – a lout with a cockade of amber and blue, the Whig colours – tried to trip him up. He stumbled. At that moment a third man knocked White down.

'Yah! Down with him!' roared the roughs with delight. 'Down with the borough-monger!'

But Vaughan, who had anticipated rather than seen the stumble, was over the rail by this time, and at Sir Robert's side. He reached him a little in front of Bob Flixton, who had descended to the rescue from the other end of the booth. Vaughan hurled back the man who had tripped Sir Robert, and who was still trying to throw him down; and the sight of the amber and blue which the new champion wore checked the assailants, and gave White time to rise.

Vaughan was furious. 'Back, you cowards!' he cried. 'Would you murder an old man? Shame on you!'

'Ay, you bullies!' cried Flixton, neatly hitting one on the jaw, and completely disposing of that one for the day. 'Back with you!'

On which half a dozen of the Tories, taking advantage of the check, surrounded the baronet, and bore him out of danger. Though Sir Robert was undaunted, he was shaken; and breathing quickly, he let his hand rest for support on the nearest shoulder. It was Vaughan's – and the next instant he saw that it was. He withdrew the hand as if he had let it rest on a hot iron.

'Mr Flixton,' he said – the words reached a dozen ears at least – 'your arm, if you please. I would rather be without this gentleman's assistance.'

Neither the action nor the words were lost upon Vaughan, whose face flamed hotly. He stepped back with dignity, slightly touched his hat, and returned to his side of the hustings.

But he was wounded and very angry. Alone of his Party he had intervened; and this was his reward. When Pybus pushed his way to his side and stooped to his ear, talking quickly and earnestly, he did not repel him.

Such an episode was not uncommon, but it appalled the Vermuyden party; White, in particular, took it very seriously. If violence of this sort was to rule, if even Sir Robert's person was not to be respected, he saw that he would not be able to bring his voters to the poll. They would run the risk of losing their lives; and one or two for certain would not vote. The thing must be stopped, and stopped at once. With this in view he forced his way to the passage at the rear of the hustings, which was common to all three booths; and heated and angry – his cheek was cut by the blow he had received – he called for Pybus. But the press at the back of the hustings was great, and one of White-Hat Williams's foremen, who blocked the gangway, laughed in his face.

'I want to speak to Pybus,' said White, glaring at the man, who on ordinary days would have touched his hat to him.

'Then want 'll be your master,' the other retorted. And when White tried to push by him, the man gave him the shoulder.

'Let me pass,' White foamed. No thought of Cobbett now, had the agent. These miserable upstarts, their insolence, their certainty of triumph fired his blood. 'Let me pass!' he repeated.

'See you damned first!' the other answered bluntly. 'Your game's up, old cock! Your master has held the pit long enough, but his time's come.'

'If you don't—'

'If you put your nose in here, we'll pitch you over the rail!' the other declared.

White almost had a fit. Fortunately White-Hat Williams himself appeared at this moment, and White appealed to him.

'Mr Williams,' he said, 'is this your safe conduct?'

'I gave none,' with a grin.

'Pybus did.'

'Ay, for your Party! But if you choose to straggle in one by one, we can't be answerable for every single voter,' with a wink. 'Nor for any of you getting back again! No, no, White.

Beneath the wings of Ministers, and it's the truth I tell,
You've bought us very cheap, good White, and you've sold us very well!

Ha! ha! That's been the ticket! But it's the ticket no longer. There's an end of that! But – what's that?'

That was Sir Robert stepping forward to propose his candidates; or rather, it was the roar, mocking and defiant, which greeted his attempt to do so. It was a roar which made speech impossible. No doubt, among the crowd which filled the space through which he had driven so often with his four horses, the great man, the patron, the master of all, there were some who still respected, and more who feared him; many who would not have insulted him. For if he had used his power stiffly, he had not used it ill. But there were also in the crowd men whose hearts were hot against the exclusiveness which had long effaced them; who believed that freedom or slavery hung on the issue of this day; who saw the prize of a long and bitter effort at stake, and who were set on using intimidation, ay, and violence, if victory could not be had without them. These swept the rest off their feet, and infected them with their own recklessness; these gave that stern note to the roar which continued and thwarted all Sir Robert's efforts to make himself heard.

He stood long, facing them, waiting, and never blenching. But after a while his lip curled, and his eyes looked disdain on the mob below him: such disdain as the old Duke in after days hurled at the London rabble, when, for answer to their fulsome cheers, he pointed to the iron shutters of Apsley

House. Sir Robert Vermuyden had done something, and thought that he had done more, for the men who yelped and snarled and snapped at him. According to his lights, acting on his maxim, all for the people and nothing by the people, he had treated them generously, granted all he thought good for them, planned for them, wrought for them. He had been master, but no taskmaster. He had indeed illustrated the better side of that government of the many by the few, of the unfit by the fit, with which he believed that the safety and the greatness of his country were bound up.

And this was their return! No wonder that, seeing things as he saw them, he felt a bitter contempt for them? Freedom? Such freedom as was good for them, such freedom as was permanently possible – they had. And slavery? Was it slavery to be ruled, wisely and firmly, by a class into which they themselves might rise, a class which education and habit had qualified to rule? In his mind's eye, as he looked down on this fretting, seething mass, he saw that which they craved granted, and he saw, too, the outcome: that most cruel of all tyrannies, the tyranny of the many over the few of the many who have neither a heart to feel nor a body to harm.

Once, twice, thrice one of his supporters thrust himself forward, and, leaning on the rail, appealed with frantic gestures for silence for a hearing, for respect. But each in turn retired baffled. Not a word in that tempest of sound was audible. And no one on the other side intervened. They in the old days had suffered the same thing; it was their turn now. Even Vaughan stood with folded arms and a stern face, feeling the last contempt for the howling rabble before him, but firmly determined to expose himself to no second snub. At last Sir Robert saw that it was hopeless. He shrugged his shoulders in scorn, and, shouting the names of his candidates in a clerk's ear, put on his hat and stood back.

The old Squire seconded him in dumb show.

Then the Serjeant stood forward to state his views. He grasped the rail with both hands and waited with smiling suavity. But he might have waited an hour, he might have waited until night. The leaders for the Bill were determined to make their power felt. They were resolved that not a word on the Tory side should be heard. The Serjeant waited and, after a time, still smiling blandly, bowed and stood back.

It was Mr Cooke's turn. He advanced. 'Shout, and be damned to you!' he cried, apoplectic in the face. An egg flew within a yard of him, and, openly shaking his fist at the crowd, he retired amid laughter.

Then White-Hat Williams, who had looked forward to this as to the golden moment of his life, and had conned his oration until he knew its sounding periods by heart, stepped forward to nominate the Whig candidates. He took off his hat; and, as if that had been the signal for silence, such a stillness fell on all that his voice rang above the multitude like a trumpet.

'Gentlemen,' he said, and smiling looked first to the one side and then to the other. 'Gentlemen—'

Alas, he smiled too soon! The Tories grasped the situation, and furious at the reception which had fallen to the lot of their leaders, were determined that if they were not heard, no one should be heard. Before he could utter another word they broke into rapid bellowings, and what their shouts lacked in volume they made up in ill-will. In a twinkling they drowned White-Hat Williams's voice; and now who so indignant as the Radicals? In thirty seconds half a dozen single combats were proceeding in front of the Tory booth, blood flowed from as many noses, and, amid a terrific turmoil, respectable men and justices of the peace leant across the barriers and shook their fists and flung frenzied challenges broadcast.

All to no purpose. The Tories, though so much the weaker Party, though but one to eight, could not be silenced. After making three or four attempts to gain a hearing, White-Hat Williams saw that he must reserve his oration; and with a bitter scowl he shouted his names into the ear of the clerk.

'Who? Who did he say?' growled the Squire, panting with rage and hoarse with shouting. His face was crimson, his cravat was awry, he had lost his hat. 'Who? Who?'

'Wrench and – one moment, sir!'

'Eh? Who do you say?'

'I couldn't hear! One moment, sir! Oh yes! yes! Wrench and Vaughan!'

'Vaughan?' old Rowley exclaimed with a profane oath. 'Impossible!'

But it was not impossible. Though so great was the surprise, so striking the effect upon Sir Robert's supporters, that for a few seconds something like silence supervened. The serpent! The serpent! Here was a blow indeed – in the back.

Then as Blackford, the Methodist, rose to second the nomination, the storm broke out anew and more vehemently. 'What?' foamed the Squire, 'be ruled by a rabble of grinning, yelling monkeys? By gad, I'll leave the country first! I – I hope someone will shoot that young man! I wish I'd never shaken his hand! By God, I'm glad my father is in his grave! He'd never ha' believed this. Never! Never!'

And from that time until the poll was, in dumb show, declared open not a word was audible.

Then at last the shouting of the rival bands sank to a confused babel of jeers, abuse, and laughter. Exhausted men mopped their faces, voiceless men loosened their neck-cloths, the farthest from the hustings went off to drink, and there was a lull until the sound of a drum and fife announced a new event, and forth from the Heart and Hand advanced a procession of five, led by the accursed Dyas.

They were the Whig voters, and they marched proudly to the front of the polling booth, the mob falling back on either side to give them place.

Dyas flung his hat into the booth. 'Wrench and Vaughan!' he cried in a voice which could be heard in the White Lion. 'And I care not who knows it!'

They put to him the bribery oath. 'I can take it,' he answered. 'Swallow it yourselves, if you can!'

'You should know the taste, Jack,' cried a sly friend. And for a moment the laugh was against him.

One by one they voted; the process was slow in those days, the qualifications of each voter being examined on the spot. 'Five for Wrench and Vaughan.' Wrench rose and bowed to each as he retired. Arthur Vaughan took no notice.

Sir Robert's voters looked at one another uneasily. They had the day before them, but— And none moved until Sir Robert himself became aware of the difficulty. Immediately, putting White and his remonstrances on one side, he joined them, bade them to follow him, and descended before them. He would ask no man to do what he would not do himself.

The moment his action was understood, the moment the men were seen following him, there was a yell so fierce and a movement so threatening that on the lowest step of the hustings he stood bareheaded, raised his hand for silence, and for a wonder was obeyed. In a clear loud voice –

'Do you expect to terrify me?' he cried. 'Either by threats or violence? Let any man look in my face and see if it change colour. Let him come and lay his hand on my heart and feel if it beats the quicker! Keep my voters from the poll and you stultify your own, for there will be no election. Make way, then, and let them pass to their duty!'

And the crowd made way; and Arthur Vaughan felt a reluctant pang of admiration. The five were polled; the result, so far, five for each of the candidates.

There remained to poll only Arthur Vaughan and Pillinger of the Blue Duck, if he could be brought up by the Tories. If neither of these voted the returning officer would certainly give the casting vote for Sir Robert's candidates – if he dared.

Isaac White believed that he would not dare. For some time past the agent had been in covert talk with Pybus at the back of the hustings, two or three of the friends of each masking the conference. Now he drew aside his employer, who had returned in safety to his place, and he conferred with him. But for a time it was clear that Sir Robert would not listen to what he had to say. He looked pale and angry, and returned but curt answers. But White persisted, holding him by the sleeve.

'Mr Vaughan – bah, what a noise they make – has refused to vote,' he explained. 'But in the end he may, sir. If he does that will give it to them unless we can bring up Pillinger, which is impossible. Even if we can bring him up it will be a tie—'

'Well,' Sir Robert struck in, eyeing him sternly, 'what more do we want? The returning officer—'

'He will not dare,' White whispered, 'and if he does, sir, it is my belief he will be murdered. More, if we win they will rush the booth and destroy the books. They have as good as told me that they will stick at nothing. Believe me, sir,' he continued earnestly, 'better than one and one we can't look for now. And better one than none!'

But it was long before Sir Robert could be persuaded. No! defeat or victory, he would fight to the last. He would be beholden to the other side for nothing. White, however, was an honest man, and less afraid of his master than usual; and he held to his point. At length the reflection that the bargain would at least shut out his kinsman prevailed with Sir Robert, and he consented.

He was too chivalrous to return on his own side the man whose success would fill his pockets. He elected for Wathen, and never doubted that the Bowood interest would return their first love, Wrench. But when the landlord of the Blue Duck was brought up by agreement to vote for a candidate on either side, Pillinger voted by order for Wathen and Vaughan!

'There's some damned mistake!' shrieked Squire Rowley as the names reached his ears. Sir Robert said nothing. Probably his feelings were beyond words.

But there was no mistake, and, to the silent disgust of the Tories and amid the frantic cheering of the Whigs, the return was made in favour of Serjeant John Wathen and Arthur Vermuyden Vaughan, Esq. Loud and long was the cheering; the air was black with caps. But when the crowd sought for the two, to chair them according to immemorial custom, only the Serjeant could be found. And he, with great prudence, declined the honour.

CHAPTER XIX

The Fruits of Victory

ARTHUR VAUGHAN could write himself Member of Parliament. The plaudits of the Academic and the mimic contests of the Debating Club were no longer for him. Fortune had placed within his grasp the prize of which he had dreamt; and henceforth all lay open to him. But, as a contemporary in a letter written on a like occasion says, he had gone through innumerable horrors to reach the goal. And the moment the result was known and certain he slipped away from his place, and from the oppressive good wishes of his new and uncongenial friends – the Williamses and the Blackfords; and shutting himself up in his rooms at the White Lion, where his entrance was regarded with suspicion, he set himself to look the future in the face.

He had done nothing of which he was ashamed. Circumstances had put him in a false position, but he had freed himself frankly and boldly; and every candid man must acknowledge that he could not have done otherwise than he had. Yet he was aware that the thing might be misconstrued. There were some, even on his own side, who would say that he had gone to Chippinge prepared to support his kinsman; and that then, tempted by the opportunity of gaining the seat, he had faced about. Few would believe the truth – that twenty-four hours before the election he had declined to stand. Still fewer would believe that in withdrawing his 'No', he had been wholly moved by the unworthy manner in which Sir Robert had treated him.

Yet that was the truth; and so entirely the truth that but for that offer he would have resigned the seat even now. For he had no mind to enter the House under a cloud; he knew that to do so was to endanger the boat in which his fortunes were embarked. But in face of that offer he could not withdraw. Sir Robert, Wetherell, White, all would think that he had resigned, not on the point of honour, but for a bribe, and because the bribe, refused at first, grew larger the longer he eyed it.

So, for good or evil, he stood where he was. And for a few minutes, while the roar of the applauding mob rose to his windows, he enjoyed his triumph. He was a Member of the Commons' House. He stood on that threshold, on which Harley and St John, Walpole the Wise, and the inspired Cornet, Pitt and Fox, spoiled children of fortune, Castlereagh the illogical, and Canning,

Born with an ancient name of little worth,
And disinherited before his birth

and many another had stood; knowing no more than he

knew what fortune had in womb for them, what of hushed silence would one day mark their rising, what homage of loyal hearts and thundering feet would hang upon their words. As their fortunes his might be; to sway to tears or laughter, to a nation's weal of woe, the men who ruled; to know his words were fateful, yet to speak with no uncertain voice; to give the thing he did not deign to wear, and make the man whom he must follow after, ay,

To fall as Walpole and to fail as Pitt!

This, all this might be his, if he were worthy. If the dust of that arena knew no better man.

His heart rose on the wave of exaltation, and he felt himself fit for all, equipped for all. He owned no task too hard, no enterprise too high. Nor was it until he remembered the stupendous change, in his fortunes, and bethought him that henceforth he must depend upon himself, that he fell from the clouds. The story would be sifted of course; its truth or falsehood would be made clear. But, to whatever use Sir Robert might have deigned to turn it, Vaughan did not believe that he would have stooped to invent it. And if it were true, all the importance which had attached to himself as the heir to a great property, all the privileges, all the sanctity of coming wealth were gone.

Ay, but with them the responsibilities of the position were gone also! The change might depress his head and cloud his heart. He had lost much which he could hardly hope to win for himself. Yet there were compensations.

He had passed through many things in the last twenty-four hours; and, perhaps for that reason, he was easily swayed by emotion. At any rate, in the thought that he might now seek a companion where he pleased, in the remembrance that he had no longer any tastes to consult but his own, any prejudices to respect save those which he chose to adopt, he found a comfort at which he clutched eagerly. The world which shook him off – he would no longer be guided by its dictates. The race, strenuous and to the swift, ay, to the draining of heart and brain, he would not run it alone, and uncheered; merely because, while things were different, he had walked by a certain standard of conduct. If he was now a poor man, he was at least free. Free to take the one he loved into the boat in which his fortunes floated, nor ask too closely who were her forebears. Free to pursue his ambition hand in hand with one who would sweeten failure and share success; with one who, in that life of scant enjoyment and high emprise to which he must give himself, would be a guardian angel, saving him from the spells of folly and pleasure!

He might please himself now, and he would. Flixton might laugh, the men of the 14th might laugh. And in Bury Street he might have winced. But in Mecklenburgh Square, where he and she would set up their modest tent, he would not care.

He could not go to Bristol until the morrow, for he had to see Pybus. But he would write and tell her of his fortunes and he would ask her to share them. The step was no sooner conceived than attempted! He took pen and paper, and with a glow about his heart, he prepared to write.

But he had never written to her, he had never called her by her name. And the difficulty of addressing her overwhelmed him. In the end, after sitting appalled by the bold and shameless look of 'Dear Mary,' 'Dearest Mary,' and of addresses warmer than these, he solved the difficulty, after a tame fashion, by writing to Miss Sibson. The letter ran as follows –

DEAR MADAM,

At the interview which I had with you on Saturday last, you were good enough to intimate that, if I were prepared to give an affirmative answer to a question which you did not put into words, you would permit me to see Miss Smith. I am now in a position to give the assurance as to my intentions which you desired, and trust that I may see Miss Smith on my arrival in Bristol tomorrow.

Believe me to remain, madam, truly yours,

ARTHUR V. VAUGHAN

And he told himself that all his life he would remember the use to which he had put his first frank!

That night the toasting and singing, drunkenness and revelry of which the borough was the scene, kept him long waking. But eleven o'clock on the following morning saw him alight-ing from a chaise at Bristol, and before noon he was in Queen's Square.

For the time he had put the world behind him, and it was in the joyous anticipation of what was to come that he approached the house. He came, a visitor from the fight; nor, he reflected, was it every suitor who had it in his power to lay such offerings at the feet of his mistress. In the eye of the world, indeed, he was no longer what he had been; for the match-making mother he had lost his value. But he had still so much to give which Mary had not, he could still so alter the tenor of her life, he could still so lift her in the social scale, those hopes which she was to share still flew on pinions so ambitious – to the scattering of garters and red ribbons – that his heart was full of the joy of giving. He must not be blamed if he felt as King Cophetua when he stooped to the beggar-maiden, or as the Lord of Burleigh when he wooed the farmer's daughter. After all he did but rejoice that she had so little and he had so much; that he could give and she could grace.

When he stood before the house he paused a moment, in wonder that when so much was altered, its face rose unchanged. But the time for hesitation was past; he knocked boldly and asked for Miss Smith. He thought it likely that he would have to wait until the school rose at noon. The maid, however, received him as if she expected him, and ushered him at once into a room on the left of the entrance. There he stood, with a beating heart, holding his hat; but not for long. The door had scarcely closed on the girl before it opened, and Mary Smith came in. She met his eyes, and started – as if she had not expected to see him. She blushed rosy-red, and stood wide-eyed and uncertain, with her hand on the door.

'Did you not know it was I?' he asked, taken aback on his side. For this was not the Mary Smith with whom he had travelled on the coach, with whom he had talked in the Square. This was a Mary Smith, not less beautiful; but gay and fresh as the morning, in dainty white with a broad blue sash, and with something new, something of a prouder bearing in her air. 'Did you not expect me?' he repeated, advancing a step towards her.

'No,' she murmured, and she stood before him, blushing

more deeply with every second. For his eyes were beginning to talk, and to tell the old tale, whether she would or no.

'Did not Miss Sibson get my letter?' he asked.

'I think not,' she murmured.

'Then I have all to do,' he said. And it was – it was certainly a harder thing to do than he had foreseen. 'Will you not sit down, if you please?' he pleaded. 'I want you to listen to me.'

For a moment she looked as if she would run away. Then she let him lead her to a seat.

He sat down within reach of her. 'And you did not know that it was I?' he said, feeling the difficulty increase with every second.

'No.'

'I hope,' he said, 'that you are glad that it is?'

She looked down, and seemed to consider. Then, 'I am glad to see you again for one thing,' she answered. 'That I may thank you again for what you did for me on the coach.'

With the words he could find no fault. Nay, her downcast eyes seemed propitious. But there was a something, some change in her which oppressed him, and which he did not understand. One thing he did understand, however: that she was more beautiful, more desirable, more intoxicating than he had pictured her. And his apprehensions grew upon him, as he paused tongue-tied, worshipping her with his eyes. If, after all, she would not? What if she said, No? For what, now he came to measure them beside her, were those things which he brought her, those things which he came to offer, that career which he was going to ask her to share? What were they beside her adorable beauty and her modesty, the candour of her maiden eyes, the perfection of her form? He saw their worthlessness: and the bold phrase with which he had meant to open his suit, the confident, 'Mary I am come for you,' which he had repeated so often to the rhythm of the chaise wheels that he was sure he would never forget it, died on his lips.

At last, 'You speak of thanks – it is to gain your thanks I am come,' he said nervously. 'But I don't ask for words. I want you to think as highly as you can of what I did for you, if you please! I want you to believe that I saved your life on the coach. I want you to imagine that I did it at great risk to myself. I want you,' he continued hurriedly, 'to exaggerate a hundredfold – everything I did for you. And then I want you to suppose that you owe all to a miser who will be content with nothing short of – of immense interest, of an extortionate return.'

'I don't think that I understand,' she answered in a low tone, and her cheeks glowed. But beyond that he could not tell aught of her feelings; she kept her eyes lowered, so that he could not read them; and there was, even in the midst of her confusion, a distance in her manner, which was new to him and which frightened him. He remembered how quickly she had once before put him in his place: how coldly she had asserted herself; and he began to think that perhaps she had no feeling for him. Perhaps, apart from the incident on the coach, she disliked him!

'You do not understand,' he said unsteadily, 'what is the return I want?'

'No,' she answered.

He stood up abruptly, and took a pace or two from her. 'And I hardly dare tell you,' he said. 'I hardly dare tell you. I came to you, I came here as brave as a lion. And now – I don't know why – I am afraid. You are changed.'

On that she – astonishing thing! – leapt the gulf for him. Possibly the greater distance at which he stood gave her courage.

'Changed!' she murmured, moving her fingers upon her lap and watching them. 'And am I alone not to change?'

'You alone?' he ejaculated, not for the moment understanding her. So much had happened since his collision with Flixton in the Square.

'That gentleman said that you were much in the habit of changing.'

'Oh! Ungenerous!'

'It was not true, then?'

'True?' he exclaimed hotly. 'True that I—'

'Changed your mind?' she repeated, suddenly looking at him. 'And not only did that, sir? Not only did that?'

'But what?' he asked bitterly, 'what else?'

'Talked of me – among your friends!'

'A lie! A miserable lie!' he cried on impulse, finding his tongue again. 'But there, I will tell you all. He saw you – that first morning, you remember, and never having seen anyone so lovely, he intended to make you the object of attentions that were unworthy of you. And to shield you from them, I told him that I was going – to make you my wife.'

She did not speak for a moment. Then, 'Is that what you mean today!' she asked.

'Yes.'

'But you did not mean it then?' she returned. 'It was to protect me you said it?'

He looked at her, astonished at her insight and her boldness. How different, how very different, was this from that to which he had looked forward!

At last, 'I think I meant it,' he said gloomily. 'God knows I mean it now! But that evening,' he continued, seeing that she waited inexorably for the rest of his explanation, 'he challenged me at dinner before them all, and I,' he added jerkily, 'I was not quite sure what I meant – I had no mind that you should be made the talk of the – of my friends—'

'And so you denied it?' she said.

He looked darkly before him. 'Yes,' he said.

She was silent for a moment, and then, 'I think I understand,' she answered. 'What I do not understand is, why you are here today. Why you have changed your mind again? Why you are now willing that I should be the talk of your friends, sir?'

He stood before her, the picture of abasement. Must he acknowledge his doubts and his hesitation, allow that he had been ashamed of her, admit that he had deemed the marriage he now sought, a *mésalliance*? Must he open to her eyes those hours of cowardly vacillation during which he had walked the Clifton Woods weighing *I would* against *I dare not?* And do it in face of that new firmness, almost hardness, which he recognized in her, and which made him doubt if he had an ally in her heart.

More, if he told her, would she understand? Why should she, bred so differently, understand how heavily the old name with its burden of responsibilities, how heavily the past with its obligations to duty and sacrifice, had weighed upon him!

And if he told her and she did not understand, what mercy had he to expect from her!

Still, for a moment he was on the point of telling her: of telling her all; why he was now free to please himself, and why, rid of the burden with the inheritance, he could follow his heart. But the tale was long and roundabout, she knew nothing of the Vermuydens, of their importance, or his expectations, or what he had lost or what he had gained. It seemed simpler to throw himself on her mercy.

'Because I love you!' he said humbly. 'I have nothing else to say.'

'And you are sure – that you will not change your mind again?'

He could not see her face as she spoke, but there was a new note in her voice which brought him across two squares of the carpet as if she had jerked him with a string. In a second he was on his knees beside her, he had laid a feverish hand on hers.

'Mary!' he cried, 'Mary!' and he sought to read her face. 'You will forgive me? You will let me take you? You will let me take you from here? I can no longer offer you what I once thought I could, but I have enough, and you will?' There was a desperate supplication in his voice; for close to her, so close that his breath was on her cheek, she seemed so dainty, so delicate and rare, that he could hardly believe that she could ever be his, that he could be so lucky as to possess her, that he could ever take her beauty in his arms. 'You will? You will?' he repeated, empty of all other words – but his eyes spoke for him.

She did not answer, she could not answer. But she bent her head lower. She had struggled, resentment giving her arms; but he had subdued her.

'You will?'

She turned her eyes on him at last; eyes so tender that they seemed to draw his heart, his being, his strength out of him.

'Yes,' she whispered shyly. 'If you are quite sure now? And if I am allowed.'

'Allowed? Allowed?' he cried in the voice of a giant. How in a moment was all changed for him! 'I would like to see—' And then breaking off – perhaps it was her fault for leaning a little towards him – he did that which he thought a moment before that he would never dare to do. He put his arm round her and drew her gently and reverently to him until – for she did not resist – her head touched his shoulder. 'Mine!' he murmured. 'Mine! Mine! Mine! I can hardly believe it. I can hardly think I am so blessed.'

'And you will not change?' she whispered.

'Never! Never!'

They were silent, blissfully silent. Was she thinking of the dark night, when she had walked lonely and despondent to her new and unknown home. Or of many an hour of solitary depression, spent in cold and dreary schoolrooms, while others made holiday? Or of what she would be to him? Was he thinking of his doubts and fears, his cowardly hesitation? Or only of his present monstrous happiness? No matter; but this was certain. They had forgotten the existence of anything outside the room, they had forgotten the world and Miss Sibson's, they were in a Paradise of their own, such as is given to no man and to no woman more than once, they were a million miles from Bristol City, when the sound made by the opening door surprised them in that posture. Vaughan turned with an exclamation to see who it was; to see who dared to trespass on their Eden. He looked – only looked, and he sprang to his feet amazed. He thought for a moment that he was dreaming, or that he was mad.

For on the threshold, gazing at them with a face of indescribable astonishment, rage, incredulity, was Sir Robert Vermuyden. Ay, Sir Robert Vermuyden! The last man in all the world whom Arthur Vaughan had looked to see there!

CHAPTER XX

A Plot Unmasked

FOR A FEW moments the old man and the young man gazed at one another, alike in this only, that neither found words equal to his feelings. While Mary, covered with confusion, blushing for the situation in which she had been found, could not hold up her head. It was Sir Robert who broke the silence in a voice which trembled with passion.

'You viper!' he said. 'You viper! You would sting me – here also!'

Vaughan stared at him. The intrusion was outrageous; but astonishment rather than anger was the young man's first feeling.

'Here also?' he repeated, as if he thought that he must have heard amiss. '*I* sting you? What do you mean? Why have you followed me?' And then more warmly, 'How dare you, sir, spy on me?'

The old man, every nerve and vein in his high forehead swollen, raised his cane and shook it at him.

'Dare? Dare?' he cried, and then for very rage his voice failed.

Vaughan closed his eyes and opened them again. 'I am dreaming,' he said. 'I must be dreaming. Are you Sir Robert Vermuyden? Is this house Miss Sibson's school? Are we in Bristol? Or is it all – but first, sir,' recalling with indignation the situation in which he had been surprised, 'how come you here? I have a right to know that!'

'How come I here?'

'Yes! How come you here, sir?'

'You ask me! You ask me!' Sir Robert repeated, as if he could not believe his ears. 'How I come here! You scoundrel!'

Vaughan started under the lash of the word. The insult was gratuitous, intolerable! No relationship, no family tie could excuse it. No wonder that the surprise and irritation which had been his first feelings gave way to pure anger. Sir Robert might have, or might have had, certain rights. But now all that was over. And to suppose that he was still to suffer the old gentleman's interference, to put up with his insults, to permit him in the presence of a young girl, his promised wife, to use such language as he was using, was out of the question. Vaughan's face grew dark.

'Sir Robert,' he said, 'you are too old to be called to account. You may say, therefore, what you please. But not, if you are a gentleman, until this young lady has left the room.'

'This – young – lady!' Sir Robert gasped in an indescribable tone. And with the cane quivering in his grasp he looked from Vaughan to the girl.

'Yes,' Vaughan answered sternly. 'That young lady! And do not let me hear you call her anything else, sir, for she has promised to be my wife.'

'You lie!' the baronet cried. The words leapt from his lips.

'Sir Robert!

'My daughter – promised to be your wife! My—'

'Your daughter!' Vaughan's mouth fell open.

'Hypocrite!' Sir Robert retorted. 'You knew it! You knew it!'

'Your daughter?'

'Ay, that she was my daughter! You knew it!'

'Your daughter!'

This time the words fell from the younger man in a whisper. And he stood, turned to stone. His daughter? Sir Robert's daughter? The girl – he tried desperately to clear his mind – of whom Wetherell had told the story; the girl whom her mother had hidden away, while in Italy; the girl whose reappearance in life ousted him from his inheritance? Mary Smith – was that girl his daughter?

But no! The blood leapt back to his heart. It was impossible, it was incredible! The coincidence was too great, too amazing. His reason revolted against it. And –

'Impossible!' he cried, in a bolder tone – though fear underlay its confidence. 'You are playing with me!' he added angrily.

But the elder man, though his hand trembled on his cane and his face was sallow with rage, had by this time regained some control of himself. Instead of retorting on Vaughan – save by one glance of withering contempt – he turned to Mary.

'You had better go to your room,' he said, coldly but not ungently. For how, he was thinking, could he blame her, bred amid such surroundings, for conduct that in other circumstances had irritated him indeed? For conduct that had been unseemly, unmaidenly, improper. 'You had better go to your room,' he repeated. 'This is no fit place for you, and no fit discussion. I am not – the fault is not with you, but it will be better if you leave us.'

She was rising, too completely overwhelmed to dream of resistance, when Vaughan interposed.

'No,' he said, with a gleam of defiance in his eyes. 'By your leave, sir, no! This young lady is my affianced wife. If it be her wish to retire, be it so. But if not, there is no one who has the right to bid her go. You' – stopping Sir Robert's wrathful rejoinder by a gesture – 'may be her father, but before you can exercise a father's rights you must make good your case.'

'Make good my case?' Sir Robert ejaculated.

'And when you have made it good, it will still be for her to choose between us,' Vaughan continued, with growing determination. 'You, who have never played a father's part, who have never guided or guarded, fostered or cherished her – do not think, sir, that you can in a moment arrogate a father's authority.'

Sir Robert gasped. But the next moment he took up the glove. He pointed to the door, and with less courtesy than the occasion demanded.

'Leave the room, girl,' he said.

'Do as you please, Mary,' Vaughan said.

'Go!' cried the baronet, stung by the use of her name.

'Stay!' said Vaughan.

Infinitely distressed, painfully distracted by this appeal from the one, from the other, Mary turned her swimming eyes on her lover.

'Oh, what,' she cried, 'what am I to do?'

He did not speak, but he looked at her, not doubting what she would do, nor conceiving it possible that she could prefer to him, whose professions were still honey in her ears, whose arm was still warm from the pressure of her form – that she could prefer to him a father who was no more than the shadow of a name.

But he did not yet know Mary either in her strength or her weakness. Nor did he consider that her father was already more than a name to her. She hung a moment undecided and wretched; drooping, as the white rose that hangs its head in the first shower. Then she turned to the elder man, and throwing her arms about his neck cried passionately –

'You will be good to him, sir! Forgive him! Oh, forgive him!'

'My dear—'

'Oh, forgive him!'

Sir Robert smoothed her hair with a caressing hand, and with pinched lips and bright eyes, looked at his adversary over her head.

'I would forgive him,' he said, 'I could forgive him – all but this! All but this, my dear! I would forgive him, if he had not deceived you into this! Into the belief that he loves you, while he loves only your inheritance! Or that part,' he added bitterly, 'of which he has not already robbed you!'

'Sir Robert,' Vaughan said, 'you have stooped very low. But it will not avail you.'

'It has availed me so far,' the baronet retorted triumphantly.

Vaughan winced. In proportion as the other recovered his temper, he lost his.

'It will avail me still further,' Sir Robert continued, 'when my daughter understands, that when you came here today, when you stole a march on me, as you thought, and proposed marriage to her behind my back, you knew all that I knew! Knew that she was my daughter, knew that she was my heiress, knew that she ousted you, knew that by a marriage with her, and by that only, you could regain what you had lost!'

'It is a lie!' Vaughan cried, stung beyond endurance. He was pale with anger.

'Then refute it!' Sir Robert said, clasping the girl – who had involuntarily winced at the word – more closely to him. 'Refute it, sir!'

'It is incredible,' Vaughan cried. 'It needs no refutation!'

'Why?' Sir Robert retorted. 'I state it. I am prepared to prove it.'

'To prove—'

'That you knew,' Sir Robert replied. 'Knew this lady to be my daughter when you came here this morning! Knew it as well as I knew it myself.'

Vaughan returned his look in speechless indignation. Did the man really believe in the charge? It was not possible!

And, 'Sir Robert,' he answered, speaking slowly and with dignity, 'I never did you harm by word or deed until a day or two ago. And then, God knows, reluctantly. How, then, can you lower yourself to such a charge?'

'Do you deny, then,' the baronet replied with contemptuous force, 'that you knew?'

Vaughan stared. 'You will say presently,' he replied, 'that I knew her to be your daughter when I made her acquaintance on the coach a week back, at a time when you knew nothing yourself?'

'As to that I cannot say,' Sir Robert rejoined. 'I do not know how nor where you made her acquaintance. But I do know that an acquaintance so convenient, could hardly be the work of chance!'

'Good God!' Vaughan cried. 'Then you will say also that I knew who she was when I called on her the day after, and again two days after that – while you were in ignorance?'

'I have said,' the baronet answered coldly, 'that I do not know how you made your acquaintance with her. But I have, I cannot but have, my suspicions.'

'Suspicions? Suspicions?' Vaughan cried bitterly. 'And on suspicion, the base issue of prejudice and dislike—'

'No, sir!' Sir Robert struck in. 'Though it may be, that if I knew who introduced you to her, and who opened this house to you, I might find ground for more than suspicion! The schoolmistress might tell me somewhat, and – you wince, sir! Ay,' he continued in a sterner tone, 'I see that there is something to be learned! But it is not upon suspicion that I charge you. It is upon evidence. Did you not, before my eyes and before two other witnesses, read in the drawing-room at Stapylton the whole story of my daughter's movements up to her departure from London? With the name of the school to which she was consigned? Did you not?'

'Never! Never!'

'What!' The astonishment in Sir Robert's voice was so unfeigned, that it must have carried conviction to any listener.

Vaughan pressed his hand across his brow; and Mary, who had hitherto kept her face hidden, shivering under the lash of each harsh word, raised her head to listen. What would he answer? For, ah, she alone knew how her heart beat, how sick she was with fear, how she shrank from that which the next minute might unfold.

And yet she listened.

'I – I remember now,' Vaughan said, and the consternation he felt made itself plain in his voice. 'I remember that I looked at a paper—'

'At a paper?' Sir Robert cried, in a tone of contempt. 'At a detailed account, sir, of my daughter's movements down to her arrival at Bristol. Do you deny that?' he continued. 'Do you deny that you perused that account?'

Vaughan stood for a moment with his hand pressed to his brow. He hesitated.

'I remember taking a paper in my hands,' he said, his face flushing as the inference from his words occurred to him. 'But I was thinking so much of the disclosure you had made to me, and of the change it involved, that—'

'That you took no interest in the writing?' Sir Robert cried with bitter irony.

'I did not.'

'You did not read a word, I suppose?'

'I did not.'

Before the baronet could utter the sneer which was on his lips Mary interposed.

'I would rather go,' she murmured. 'I feel – faint!'

She left her father's arm as she spoke, and, with her face averted from her lover, moved uncertainly towards the door. She had no wish to meet his eyes. But something, either the feeling that she she would never see him again, or the hope that even now he might explain his admission – as well as those facts, 'confirmation strong as hell' which she knew, but which Sir Robert did not know – one or other of these feelings made her falter on the threshold, made her turn. Their eyes met.

He stepped forward, white with pain. For what pain is stronger than the pang of innocence accused?

'One moment,' he said, in an unsteady voice. 'If we part so, Mary, we part indeed! We part for ever! I said awhile ago that you must choose between us. And you have chosen – it seems. Yet think! Give yourself, give me a chance. Will you not believe my word?' And he held out his arms to her. 'Will you not believe that when I came to you this morning I thought you penniless? I thought you the unknown schoolmistress you thought yourself a week ago? Will you not trust me when I say that I never connected you with the missing daughter! Never dreamed of a connexion. Why should I?' he added, in growing agitation as the words of his appeal wrought on himself. 'Or why do you in a moment think me guilty of the meanest, and the most mercenary of acts?'

He would have taken her hand, but Sir Robert stepped between them, grim as fate and as vindictive.

'No!' he said. 'No more! You have given her pain enough, sir! Take your dismissal and go! She has chosen – you have said it yourself!'

He cast one look at Sir Robert, and then, 'Mary,' he asked, 'am I to go?'

She was leaning, almost beside herself, against the door. And ah, how much of joy and sorrow she had known since she crossed the threshold. A man's embrace, and a man's treachery. The sweetness of love and the bitterness of – reality!

'Mary!' Vaughan said.

But the father could not suffer this. 'By God, no!' he cried, infuriated by the other's persistence, and perhaps by fear that the girl would give way. 'You shall not soil her name with your lips, sir! You shall torture her no longer. You have your dismissal. Take it and go!'

'When she tells me with her own lips to go,' Vaughan answered doggedly, 'I will go. Not before!' For never had she seemed more desirable to him. Never, though contempt of her weakness wrestled with his love, had he wanted her more. Except that seat in the House which had cost him so dearly, she was all that was left to him. And it did not seem possible that she whom he had held in his arms, she who had allowed her love for him, with whom he had vowed to share his life – it did not seem possible that she could believe this miserable, this incredible, this impossible thing! Or, if she could, he was indeed mistaken in her.

And Mary had not believed it of him, had she known him longer or better; had she known him as girls in the world know their lovers. But his wooing had been short; and we know the distrust of men in which she had been trained. He had taken her heart by storm, stooping to her from the height of his position, having on his side her poverty and loneliness, her inexperience and youth. Now all these things, and her ignorance of his world, weighed against him. Could it be credited, that he, who had come to her bearing her mother's commendation – ah, deadly fact! – knew nothing, though he was her kinsman? That he, who, after plain hesitation and avowed doubt, laid all at her feet as soon as her father was prepared to acknowledge her – was it to be believed that he still sought her in ignorance? That he, who had read her story in black and white, still knew nothing?

No, she could not believe it. But it was a bitter thing to know that he had not loved her! That he had come to her for gain! She must speak if it were only to escape, only to save herself from collapse. She yearned for nothing so much as to be alone.

'Goodbye,' she muttered, with averted eyes and pallid lips. 'I forgive you. Goodbye.'

And she opened the door with groping fingers; and still looking away from him, lest she should give way, she went out.

He drew a deep breath as she passed the threshold; his eyes did not leave her. But he did not speak. Nor did Sir Robert Vermuyden until his daughter's step, light as thistledown that morning, and now slow and heavy, passed out of hearing, and – and at last a door closed on the floor above.

Then the elder man looked at the other. 'Are you not going?' he asked, with grim meaning. 'You have robbed me of my borough – I give you joy of your cleverness. But you shall not rob me of my daughter!'

'I wonder which you love the better!' Vaughan snarled. And with that gibe he took his hat and went.

CHAPTER XXI

A Meeting of Old Friends

IT WAS September. The House elected in those first days of May was four months old, and already it had fulfilled the hopes of the country. Without a division it had decreed the first reading, and by a majority of one hundred and thirty-six the second reading of the People's Bill; that Bill by which the preceding House, slaying, had been slain. New Members were beginning to lose the first gloss of their enthusiasm; the youngest no longer ogled the MP on their letters, nor franked for the mere joy of franking. But the Ministry still rode the flood tide of favour, Lord Grey was still his country's pride, and Brougham a hero. It only remained to frighten the House of Lords, and in particular those plaguy out-of-date fellows, the Bishops, into passing the Bill; and the battle would be won.

The streets be paved with mutton pies,
Potatoes eat like pine!

And, in fine, everyone would live happily ever afterwards.

To old Tories of the stamp of Sir Robert Vermuyden the outlook was wholly dark. But it is not often that public care clouds private joy; and had Eldon been Prime Minister, with Wetherell for his Chancellor, the grounds of Stapylton could not have worn a more smiling aspect than they presented on the fine day in early September, which Sir Robert had chosen for his daughter's first party. The abrupt addition of a well-grown girl to a family of one is a delicate process. It is apt to open the door to scandal. And a little out of respect to Mrs Grundy, and more that she who was now the apple of his eye might not wear her wealth with a difference, nor lack anything of the mode, he had not hastened the occasion. A word had been dropped here and there – with care; the truth had been told to some, the prepossessions of others had been consulted. But at length the day was come on which she must stand by his side and receive the world of Wiltshire.

And she had so stood for more than an hour of this autumn afternoon; with such pride on his side as was fitting, and such blushes on hers as were fitting also. Now, the prime duty of reception over, and his company dispersed through the gardens, Sir Robert lingered with one or two of his intimates on the lawn before the house. In the hollow of the park hard by stood the ample marquee in which his poorer neighbours were presently to feast; gossip had it that Sir Robert was already at work rebuilding his political influence. Near the tent 'hunt-the-slipper' and 'kiss-in-the-ring' were in progress, and 'Monymusk' was being danced to the strains of the Chippinge church band; the shrill voices of the rustic youth proving that their shyness was wearing off. Within the gardens a famous band from Bath played the new-fashioned quadrilles, turn about with Moore's *Irish Melodies*; and a score of the fair, gorgeous as the dragonflies which darted above the water, sauntered delicately up and down the sward, or, under the escort of gentlemen in tightly strapped white trousers and blue coats – or in Wellington frocks, the latest mode – appeared and again disappeared among the elms beside the Garden Pool. In the background the house, adorned and refurnished, winked with all its windows at the sunshine, gave forth from all its doors the sweet scent of flowers, throbbed to the very recesses of the haunted wing, with small talk and light laughter, the tap of sandalled feet and the flirt of fans.

Sir Robert thanked his God as he looked upon it all. And five years younger in face, and more like the Duke than ever, he listened, almost purring with pleasure, to the praises of his new-found darling. The odds had been great that, with such a breeding, she had been coarse or sly, common or skittish. And she was none of these things; but fair as a flower, slender as Psyche, sweet-eyed as a woman, dainty and virginal as the buds of May. And withal gentle and kind and obedient – above all, obedient. He could not thank God enough, as he read in the eyes of young men and old women what they thought of her. And he was thanking Him, though in outward seeming he was attentive to an old friend's prattle, when his eyes fell on a carriage-and-four which, followed by two outriders, was sweeping past the marquee and breasting the gentle ascent to the house. All who were likely to arrive in such state, the Beauforts, Suffolks, Methuens, were come; the old Duke of Beaufort, indeed, and his daughter-in-law were gone again. So Sir Robert stared at the approaching carriage, wondering whom it might contain.

'They are the Bowood liveries,' a friend, who had longer sight, informed him. 'I thought they had gone to town for the Coronation.'

Sir Robert also had been under that impression. Indeed, though he had invited the Lansdownes upon the principle – which even the heats attending the Reform Bill did not wholly abrogate – that family friendships were above Party, he had been glad to think that he would not see the spoliators. The trespass was too recent, the robbery too gross. Ay, and the times too serious.

Here they were, however, Lady Lansdowne, her daughter, and a small gentleman with a merry eye and curling locks. Sir Robert repressed a sigh and advanced four or five paces to meet them. But, though he sighed, no one knew better what became a host; and his greeting was perfect. One of his bitterest flings at Bowood painted it as the common haunt of fiddlers and poets, actors and the like. But he received her ladyship's escort – who was no other than Mr Moore of Sloperton, and of the *Irish Melodies* – with the courtesy which he would have extended to an equal; nor when Lady Lansdowne dismissed her girl to tea under the poet's care did he let any sign of his reprobation appear. Those with whom he had been talking had withdrawn to leave him at liberty, and he found himself alone with Lady Lansdowne.

'We leave for Berkeley Square tomorrow, for the Coronation on the 8th,' she said, playing with her fan in a way which would have betrayed to her intimates that she was not quite at ease. 'I had many things to do this morning in view of our departure, and I could not start early. You must accept our apologies, Sir Robert.'

'It was gracious of your ladyship to come at all,' he said.

'It was brave,' she replied, with a gleam of laughter in her eyes. 'In fact, though I bear my lord's warmest felicitations on this happy event, and wreathe them with my own, Sir Robert—'

'I thank your ladyship and Lord Lansdowne,' he said formally.

'I do not think I should have ventured,' she continued, with another glint of laughter, 'did I not bear also an olive branch.'

He bowed, but waited in silence for her explanation.

'One of a – a rather delicate nature,' she said. 'Am I permitted, Sir Robert, to speak in confidence?'

He did not understand, and he sought refuge in compliments.

'Permitted?' he said, with the gallant bow of an old beau. 'All things are permitted to so much—'

'Hush!' she said. 'But there! I will take you at your word. You know that the Bill – there is but one Bill nowadays – is in Committee?'

He frowned, disliking the subject. 'I don't think,' he said, 'that any good can come of discussing it, Lady Lansdowne.'

'I think it may,' she replied, with a confidence which she did not feel, 'if you will hear me. It is whispered that there is a question in Committee of one of the doomed boroughs. One, I am told, Sir Robert, hangs between Schedule A and Schedule B; and that borough is Chippinge. Those who know whisper Lord Lansdowne that ultimately it will be plucked from the burning, and will be found in Schedule B. Consequently it will retain one Member.'

Sir Robert's thin face turned a dull red. So the wicked Whigs, who had drawn the line of disfranchisement at such a point as to spare their pet preserves, their Calne and Bedford and the like, had not been able, with all their craft, to net every fish. One had evaded the mesh, and, by Heaven, it was Chippinge! Chippinge, though shorn of its full glory, would still return one Member. He had not hoped, he had not expected that. Now

'Non omnis moriar, multaque pars mei
Vitabit Libitinam!'

he thought. And then – another thought darted through his mind and changed his joy to chagrin. A seat had been left to Chippinge. But why? That Arthur Vaughan, the renegade, might continue to fill it, might continue to hold it, under his nose and to his daily, hourly, his constant mortification! It was too much! They had said well who said that an enemy's gift was to be dreaded. But he would fight the seat, at the next election and at every election, rather than suffer that miserable person, miserable on so many accounts, to fill it at his will. And after all the seat was saved; and no one could tell the future. The lasting gain might outlive the temporary vexation.

So, after frowning a moment, he tried to smooth his brow. 'And your mission, Lady Lansdowne,' he said politely, 'is to tell me this?'

'In part,' she answered, with a hesitation which she did not try to hide, for the course of his feelings had been visible in his countenance. 'But also—'

'But also, and in the main,' he suggested with a smile, 'to make a proposition, perhaps?'

'Yes.'

He thought of the most obvious proposition, and he spoke in pursuance of his thought.

'Then forgive me if I speak at once and plainly,' he said. 'Whether the borough lose one Member or both, whether it figure in Schedule B or Schedule A, cannot affect my opposition to the Bill. If you have it in commission to make any proposition based on a contrary notion, I cannot listen even to your ladyship.'

'I have not,' she answered, with a smile. 'Sir Robert Vermuyden's malignancy is too well known. Yet I am the bearer of a proposition. Suppose the Bill to become law – and I am told that it will become law – can we not avoid future conflict, and – I will not say future ill-will, for God knows there is none on our side, Sir Robert – but future friction, by an agreement? Of course it will not be possible to nominate Members as in the past. But, for some time to come, whoever is returned for Chippinge must be returned by your influence, or by my lord's.'

He coughed dryly. 'Possibly,' he said.

'In view of that,' she continued, flirting her fan, as she watched his face – his manner was not encouraging – 'and for the sake of peace between families, Sir Robert, and a little, may be, because I do not wish Kerry to be beggared by contested elections, can we not now, while the Bill is on the lap of the gods—'

'In Committee,' Sir Robert corrected with a grave bow.

She laughed pleasantly. 'Well,' she allowed, 'perhaps that is not the same thing. But no matter. Whoever the Fates in charge, can we not' – with her head on one side and a charming smile – 'make a treaty of peace?'

'But if we do,' Sir Robert asked, with urbane sarcasm, 'what becomes of the rights of the people, Lady Lansdowne? And of the purity of elections? And of the new and independent electors whom my lord has brought into being? Must we not think of them?'

She looked for an instant rather foolish. Then she rallied, and with a slightly heightened colour –

'In good time, we must,' she replied. 'But at first it is plain that they will not be able to walk without assistance.'

'What?' it was on the tip of his tongue to answer. 'The new and independent electors? Not walk without assistance? Oh, what a change is here!' But he forbore. He said instead, with the faintest shade of irony, 'Without *our* assistance, I think you mean, Lady Lansdowne?'

'Yes. And that being so, why should we not agree, his lordship and you – to save Kerry's pocket, shall I say? – to bring forward a candidate alternately?'

Sir Robert shook his head. He would fight.

'Allowing to you, Sir Robert, as the owner of the influence hitherto dominant in the borough, the first return.'

'The first return – after the Bill passes?'

'Yes.'

That was a different thing. That was another thing altogether. A gleam of satisfaction shone for an instant under the baronet's grizzled eyebrows. The object which he had most at heart was to oust his treacherous cousin. And here was a method, more safe by far than any contest under the new Bill.

'Well, I – I cannot say anything at this moment,' he answered at last, trying to hide his satisfaction. 'These heats once over, I do not see – your ladyship will pardon me – why my influence should not still predominate.'

It was Lady Lansdowne's turn. 'And things be as before?'

she answered. 'No, Sir Robert, no. You forget those rights of the people which you were so kind as to support a moment ago. Things will not be as before. But perhaps I shall hear from you? Of course it is not a matter that can be settled, as in old days, by our people.'

'You shall certainly hear from me,' he rejoined with more than courtesy. 'In the meantime—'

'I am dying to see your daughter,' she said. 'I am told that she is as lovely as a picture. Where is she?'

'A few minutes ago she was in the Elm Walk,' Sir Robert answered, a faint flush betraying his gratification. 'I will send for her.'

But her ladyship would not hear of that; nor would she suffer him to leave his post to escort her.

'Here's *la belle* Suffolk coming to take leave of you,' she said. 'And I know my way.'

'But you will not know her,' Sir Robert answered eagerly.

Lady Lansdowne let her parasol sink over her shoulder. 'I think I shall,' she replied, with a glance of meaning. 'If she is like her mother.'

And without waiting to see the effect of her words she moved away.

It was said in old time of Juno that she walked a goddess confessed. And of Lady Lansdowne, as she moved slowly across the sunny lawn before the church, her dainty skirts trailing and her parasol inclined, it might with equal justice have been said that she walked a great lady, of that day when great ladies still were,

Nor mill nor mart had mocked the guinea's stamp.

Whether she smiled on this person or bowed to that, or with a slighter movement acknowledged the courtesy of those who, without claiming recognition, made respectful way for her, grace and nonchalant ease were in all her actions. The deeper emotions seemed as far from her as were Hodge and Joan playing kiss-in-the-ring. But her last words to Sir Robert had reacted on herself; and as she crossed the rustic bridge she paused a moment to gaze on the water. The band was playing the air of *She is far from the Land,* and tears rose to her eyes as she recalled the past, and pictured scene after scene, absurd or pathetic, in the career of the proud beauty who had once queened it here, whose mad pranks and madder sayings had once filled these shrubberies with mirth or chagrin, and whose child she was about to see.

She sighed, as she resumed her course, unable even now to blame Lady Sybil as her conduct to her child deserved. But where was the child? Not in the walk under the elms, which was deserted in favour of the more lively attractions of the park. Lady Lansdowne paused, looking this way and that; at length, availing herself of the solitude, she paced the walk to its end, whence a short path which she well remembered led to the kennels. Rather to indulge her sentiment and recall the days when she was young, and had been intimate here, than because she expected to meet Mary, she took this path. She had not followed it a dozen steps, she was hesitating whether to go on or return, the strains of Moore's melody were scarcely blurred by the intervening laurels, when a tall, dark-robed figure stepped with startling abruptness from the shrubs and stood before her.

'Louisa,' said the stranger. And she raised her veil. 'Don't you know me?'

Lady Lansdowne caught her breath. 'Sybil!' she cried.

'Yes, Sybil!' the other answered curtly. And then, as if something in Lady Lansdowne's tone had wounded her, 'Why not?' she continued, raising her head proudly. 'My name came easily enough to your ladyship's lips once! And I have yet to learn that I have done anything to deprive me of the right to call my friends by their names, be they who they may.'

'No! no! But—'

'But you meant it, Louisa!' the other retorted with energy. 'Or is it that you find me so changed, so old, so worn, so altered from her you once knew, that it astonishes you to trace in this face the features of Sybil Matching?'

'You are changed,' Lady Lansdowne answered, unable to remove her eyes. 'I fear that you have been ill.'

'I am ill,' she replied. 'I am more than ill, I am dying. Not here, nor today, nor tomorrow—'

Lady Lansdowne interrupted her. 'In that sense,' she said

gently, 'we are all dying.' But, though she said it, the change in Lady Sybil's appearance shocked her, almost as much as her presence in that place amazed her.

'I have but three months to live,' Lady Sybil answered feverishly; and her sunken cheeks and bright eyes, which told of some hidden disease, confirmed her words. 'I am dying in that sense! In that sense, do you hear? But I dare say,' with a flash of her old levity, 'it is my presence here that alarms you? You are thinking what Vermuyden would say if he turned the corner behind you, and found us together!' And as Lady Lansdowne, with a nervous start, looked over her shoulder, she laughed with the old recklessness. 'I'd like to see his face, my dear, and yours, too, if he found us. But there,' she continued, with an abrupt change to earnestness, 'it's not to see you that I came today! Don't think it! It's not to see you that I've been waiting for two hours past. I want to see my girl! I must see her, do you hear? I am going to see her. You must bring her to me!'

'Sybil!'

'Don't contradict me, Louisa,' she cried peremptorily. 'Haven't I told you that I am dying? Don't you hear what I say? Am I to die and not see my child? Cruel woman! Heartless creature! But you were always that! Cruel and cold as an icicle!'

'Indeed, I am not! And I think you should see her,' Lady Lansdowne replied in no small distress. How, indeed, could she fail to be distressed by the contrast between this woman, plainly dressed, and with illness stamped on her face, and the brilliant harum-scarum Lady Sybil, with whom her thoughts had been busy a few minutes before? 'I think you ought to see her,' she repeated, in a soothing tone. 'But you should take the proper steps to do so. You—'

'You think – yes, you do,' Lady Sybil retorted with vehemence, 'you think that I have treated her so ill that I have no right to see her, that I cannot care to see her! But you do not know how I was tried, how I was watched. What wrongs I suffered, what misconstructions! And I never meant to hide her for good. When I died she would have come home. I had a plan, too, to right her without Vermuyden's knowledge. I saw her on a coach one day along with— What is it?'

'There is someone coming,' Lady Lansdowne said hurriedly. She was very nervous. She knew that at any moment she might be followed by Sir Robert, and the thought of the scene which would follow, aware as she was of the exasperation of his feelings, appalled her. She tried to temporize. 'Another time,' she said. 'I think someone is coming now. See me another time, and I will do what I can.'

'No!' the other broke in, her face flushing with anger. 'See you, Louisa? What do I care for seeing you? It is my girl I wish to see, that I'm going to see! I'm her mother! I have a right to see her, and I will see her! I demand her, fetch her to me! If you do not go for her—'

'Sybil! Sybil!' Lady Lansdowne cried, thoroughly alarmed by her friend's violence, 'for Heaven's sake be calm!'

'Calm?' Lady Sybil answered. 'Do you cease to dictate to me, and do as I bid you! Go and fetch her, or I will go myself, and claim her before all his friends. He has no heart; he never had a heart! It's sawdust,' with a hysterical laugh. 'But he has pride, and I will trample on it! I will tread it in the mud, if you don't fetch her! Are you going, Miss Gravity? We used to call you that, remember. You were always,' with a sneer, 'a bit of a prude, my dear!'

Miss Gravity! What long-forgotten trifles, what thoughts of youth, the nickname brought back to Lady Lansdowne's recollection. What wars of maidens' wits, and half-owned jealousies, and light resentments, and sunny days of pique and pleasure! Her heart, never anything but soft, waxed sore and pitiful. Yet – how was she to do the other's bidding? How could she betray Sir Robert's confidence? How venture to interfere?

Someone was coming, really coming this time. She looked round.

'I give you five minutes,' Lady Sybil whispered. 'Five minutes, Louisa! Remember!'

And when Lady Lansdowne turned to remonstrate with her, she had vanished among the laurels.

CHAPTER XXII

Women's Hearts

LADY LANSDOWNE left the shrubbery in a state of perplexity, from which the monotonous lilt of the band, which was playing a favourite quadrille, did nothing to relieve her. Whether Sybil Vermuyden were dying or not, it was certain that she was ill. Disease had laid its hand beyond mistaking on that once beautiful face; the levity and wit which had formerly dazzled beholders now gleamed but fitfully and with such a ghastly light as the corpse-candle gives forth. Since Lady Lansdowne had seen her in the coach at Chippenham the change was great; and it might well be that, if words of forgiveness were to be spoken, no time must be lost. Old associations, pity, a mother's feelings for a mother, all urged Lady Lansdowne to compliance with her request; nor did the knowledge that she had once queened it so brilliantly in this place was now lurking on the fringe of the gay crowd, athirst for a sight of her child, fail to move a heart which all the jealousies of a Whig coterie had not hardened or embittered.

Unluckily, the owner of that heart felt that she was the last person who ought to interfere. It behoved her, more than it behoved anyone, to avoid fresh ground for quarrel with her husband's neighbour. Courteously as Sir Robert had borne himself on her arrival, civilly as he had veiled the surprise which her presence caused him, she knew that he was sore hurt by his defeat in the borough. And if those who had thwarted him publicly were to intervene in his private concerns, if those who had suborned his kinsman were now to tamper with his daughter – ay, or were to incur a suspicion of tampering – she knew that his ire would know no bounds. She felt that resentment would be justified.

She had to think, too, of her husband, who had sent her with the olive branch. He was a politic, prudent man; who, content with the solid advantage he had gained, had no mind to push to extremity a struggle which must take place at his own door. He would be displeased, seriously displeased, if her mission, in place of closing, widened the breach.

And yet her heart ached for the friend who had never wholly lost a place in her affections. And there was this to be said on that side. If Lady Sybil were thwarted, no woman was more capable of carrying out her threat and of taking some violent step, which must make matters a hundred times worse, alike for Sir Robert and his daughter.

While she weighed the matter, Lady Lansdowne found herself back at the rustic bridge. She was in the act of stepping upon it, still deep in thought, when her eyes encountered those of a young couple who were waiting at the farther end to give her passage. She looked a second time; and she stood. Then, smiling, she beckoned to the girl to come to her. Meanwhile, a side-thought, born of the conjunction of the two young people, took form in her mind. 'I hope that may come to nothing,' she reflected.

Possibly this was why she made it clear, when the man would have come also, that the smile was not for him.

'No, Mr Flixton,' she said, the faintest possible distance in her tone. 'I do not want you. I will relieve you of your charge.'

And when Mary, timid and blushing, had advanced to her, 'My dear,' she said, holding out both her hands, and looking at her, 'I should have known you anywhere.' And she drew her to her and kissed her. 'I am Lady Lansdowne. I knew your mother, and I hope that you and my daughter will be friends.'

The mention of her mother increased Mary's shyness. 'Your ladyship is very kind,' she murmured.

She did not know that her embarrassment was so far from hurting her that the appeal in her eyes went to the elder woman's heart.

'I mean to be kind, at any rate,' Lady Lansdowne answered, smiling on the lovely face before her. And then, 'My dear,' she said, 'have they told you that you are very beautiful? More beautiful, I think, than your mother was. I hope' – and she did not try to hide the depth of her feelings – 'that you may be more happy.'

The girl's colour faded at this second reference to her mother. For she could not doubt that it was made with intention. Her father, even while he had overwhelmed her with benefits, even while he had opened this new life to her with a hand full of gifts, had taught her – tacitly or by a single word – that that name was the key to a Bluebeard's chamber; that it must not be used. She knew that her mother lived; she guessed that she had sinned against her husband; she understood that she had wronged her child. But she knew no more; and with this, since this at least she must know, Sir Robert would have had her content.

And yet, to speak correctly, she did know more. She knew that the veiled lady who had intervened at long intervals in her life must be her mother. But she felt no impulse of affection towards that woman – whom she had seen. Her heart went out to a shadowy unknown mother who walked the silent house at sunset; whose silken skirts trailed in the lonely passages, and of whose career of wild and reckless gaiety she had vague hints here and there. It was to this mother, radiant and young, with the sheen of pearls in her hair, and the haunting smile, that she yearned. She had learned in some subtle way that the vacant place over the hall mantel, which her own portrait by Maclise was to fill, had been occupied by her mother's picture. And dreaming of the past, as what young girl alone in that stately house would not, she had seen her come and go in the half lights, a beautiful, spoilt child of fashion. She had traced her up and down the wide, polished stairway, heard the tap of her slender sandal on the shining floors, perceived in long-closed chambers the fading odours of her favourite scent. And in a timid, frightened way she had longed to know her and to love her, to feel her touch on her hair, and to give her pity in return.

It is possible that she might have dwelt more intimately on Lady Sybil's fate, possible that she might have ventured on some line in regard to her, if her new life had been free from preoccupation; if there had not been with her a regret, which clouded the sunniest prospects. But love, man's love, woman's love, is the most cruel of monopolists: it tramples on the claims of the present, much more of the absent. And if the novelty of Mary's new life, the many marvels to which she must accustom herself, the new pleasures, the new duties, the strange new feeling of wealth – if, in fine, the necessity of orientating herself afresh in relation to every person and everything did not avail to put thoughts of her lover from her mind, the claims of an unknown mother had an infinitely smaller chance of asserting themselves.

But now at that word, twice pronounced by Lady Lansdowne, the girl stood conscience-stricken.

'You knew my mother?' she asked.

'Yes, my dear,' the elder woman answered soberly. 'I knew her very well.'

The gravity of her tone presented a new idea to Mary's mind. 'She is not happy?' she said.

'No.'

As she uttered the word, Lady Lansdowne glanced over her shoulder; conscience makes cowards. Naturally her nervousness communicated itself to Mary. A possibility, at which the girl had never glanced, presented itself; and, improbable as it seemed, drove the colour from her face.

'She is not here?' she faltered.

'Yes, she is here,' Lady Lansdowne made answer. 'And – don't be frightened, my dear!' she continued. 'But listen to me! A moment ago I thought of throwing you in her way without your knowledge. Since I have seen you, however, I have your welfare at heart as well as hers. And I must tell you, that I do not think your father would wish you to see her. I think that you should know this; and that you should decide for yourself whether you will see her. Indeed you must decide for yourself,' she repeated, her eyes fixed on the girl's face. 'I cannot take the responsibility.'

'She is unhappy?'

'She is unhappy, and she is ill.'

'I ought to go to her? Please' – Mary looked piteously at her companion – 'your ladyship will advise me?'

Lady Lansdowne hesitated. 'I cannot,' she said.

'But – there is no reason,' Mary asked faintly, 'why I should not go to her?'

'There is no reason. I honestly believe,' Lady Lansdowne repeated solemnly, 'that there is no reason – except your father's wish. It is for you to say how far that, which should weigh with you in all other things, shall weigh with you in this.'

Suddenly a burning blush flooded Mary's face. 'I will go to her,' she cried impulsively. She had been weak once, she had been weak! And how she had suffered for that weakness! But she would be strong now. 'Where is she, if you please?' she continued bravely. 'Can I see her at once?'

'She is in the path leading to the kennels. You know it? No, you need not take leave of me, child! Go! And,' Lady Lansdowne added with feeling, 'God forgive me, if I have done wrong in sending you!'

'You have not done wrong!' Mary cried, an unwonted spirit in her tone. And without taking other leave she turned and went, though her limbs trembled under her. She was going to her mother! To her mother! Oh, strange, oh, impossible thought!

Yet, engrossing as was that thought, it could not quite oust fear; fear of her father and of his anger. And the blush soon died; so that the whiteness of her cheeks when she reached the Kennel Path formed a poor set-off for the ribbons that decked her muslin robe. What she expected, what she wished or feared or hoped, she could never remember. What she saw, that which awaited her was a woman, ill, and plainly clad, with the remains of beauty, indeed, in her wasted features; but a woman, cynical of face and hard-eyed, and far, very far from the mother of her daydreams.

Such as she was, the unknown scanned Mary with a kind of amusement.

'Oh!' she said scornfully. 'So this is what they have made of Miss Vermuyden? Let me look at you, girl?' And laying her hands on Mary's shoulders, she looked long into the tearful, agitated face. 'Why, you are like a sheet of paper!' she continued, raising the girl's chin with her finger. 'I wonder you dared to come with Sir Robert saying no! And, you little fool,' she continued in a spirit of irritation, 'as soon not come at all, as look at me like that! You've my chin and my nose and more of me than I thought, but – but God knows where you got your hare's eyes! Are you always frightened?'

'No, ma'am, no!' she stammered.

'No, ma'am? No, goose!' Lady Sybil retorted, mimicking her. 'Why, ten kings on ten thrones had never made me shake as you are shaking! Nor twenty Sir Roberts in twenty passions! What is it you are afraid of? Being found with me?'

'No!' Mary cried. And to do her justice, the emotion with which Lady Sybil found fault arose far more from a natural agitation, on seeing her mother, than from fear on her own account.

'Then you are afraid of me?' Lady Sybil rejoined. And again she lifted the girl's face to the light.

Mary was amazed rather than afraid; but she could not say that. And she kept silence.

'Or is it dislike of me?' her mother continued – a grimace, as of pain, distorting her face. 'You hate me, I suppose? You hate me!'

'Oh no, no!' the girl cried in distress.

'You do, miss!' And with some violence Lady Sybil pushed Mary from her. 'You set down all to me, I suppose! I've kept you from your own, that's it! I am the wicked mother, worse than a stepmother, who robbed you of your rights, and made a beggar of you and would have kept you a beggar! I am she who wronged you and robbed you, the unnatural mother? And you never ask,' she went on with fierce, impulsive energy, 'what I suffered? How I was wronged! What I bore! No, nor what I meant to do with you!'

'Indeed, indeed—'

'What I meant to do, I say!' Lady Sybil repeated violently. 'At my death, I tell you – and I am dying, but what is that to you? – all would have been told, girl! And you would have got your own. Do you believe me?' she added passionately, advancing a step in a manner almost menacing. 'Do you believe me?'

'I do,' Mary cried, inexpressibly pained by the other's vehemence. 'Indeed I do.'

'I'll swear it, if you like! But I hoped that Sir Robert would die first and never know! He deserved no better! He deserved nothing of me! And then you'd have stepped into all. Or better still! Do you remember the day you travelled to Bristol? It's not so long ago that you need forget it, Miss Vermuyden? I saw you, and I saw the young man who was with you. I knew him, and I told myself that there was a God after all – though I've often doubted it – or you two would not have been brought together! I saw another way then. But you'd have parted and known nothing, if,' she laughed recklessly, 'I'd not helped Providence, and sent him with a present to your school. Why, you're red enough now, girl! What is it?'

'You told him,' Mary murmured, with an effort, 'who I was, ma'am?' How her heart beat!

'I told him? Not I!' Lady Sybil answered. 'He knew no more than a doll. I told him nothing, or he'd have told again! I know his kind. But that way I'd have got all for you, and thwarted Vermuyden, too! Married his heir to the little schoolmistress! Oh, it was an opera touch, beyond all the Tremaynes and the Vivian Greys in the world! But, when it promised best, that slut of a maid went to my husband, and trumped my trick!'

'And Mr – Mr Vaughan,' Mary stammered, 'had no knowledge – who I was?'

'Mr – Mr Vaughan!' Lady Sybil repeated, mocking her, 'had no knowledge? No! Not a jot, not a tittle! But what?' breaking off with a keen look, and speaking in a tone of derision. 'Sits the wind there, Miss Meek? You're not all milk and water, bread and butter and backboard, then? But have a spice of your mother, have you? Mr – Mr Vaughan!' again she mimicked her. 'Why, if you were fond of the man, didn't you say so?'

Mary, under the fire of those sharp, hard eyes, could not restrain tears. But, overcome as she was, she managed in broken words to explain that her father had forbidden it.

'Oh, your father, was it?' Lady Sybil rejoined. 'He said No, and no it was! And the lord of my heart and the Man of Feeling is dismissed in disgrace! And now,' she ran on in a tone of raillery, assumed, perhaps, to hide a deeper feeling, 'we weep in secret and the worm feeds on our damask cheek! I suppose,' she added shrewdly, 'Sir Robert would have you think that Vaughan knew who you were, and was practising on you?'

'Yes.'

'And you dismissed him at Papa's command, eh? That was it, was it?'

Mary could only confess the fact with tears; her distress in as strange contrast with the gaiety of her dress as with the strains of the neighbouring band, which sang of festivity and pleasure. Perhaps some thought of this kind forced itself upon Lady Sybil's light and evasive mind; for, as she looked, the cynical glint in her eyes gave place to an expression of emotion better fitted to those wasted features, as well as to the relation in which the two stood to one another. She looked down the path, as if for the first time she feared an intrusive eye. Then her glance reverted to her daughter's slender form and bowed head; and again her face changed, it grew soft, it grew pitiful. The laurels shut all in, the path was empty, they were alone. The maternal feeling, long repressed, long denied, long buried under a mountain of pique and resentment, of fancied wrongs and real neglect, broke forth irresistible. In a step she was at the girl's side, and snatching her to her bosom in a fierce embrace, was covering her face, her neck, her hair with hungry kisses.

The action was so sudden, so unexpected, that at first, crushed and even hurt by the other's grasp, and frightened by her vehemence, Mary would have resisted, would have tried to free herself. Then she understood. And a rush of pent-up affection, of love and pity, carried away the barriers of constraint and timidity. She clung to Lady Sybil with tears of joy, murmuring low broken words, calling her, 'Mother, Mother!' burying her face on her shoulder, pressing herself against her. In that moment her being was stirred to its depths. In all her life no one had caressed her after this fashion, no one had embraced her with passion, no one had kissed her with more than the placid affection which gentleness and goodness earn, and which kind offices, kindly performed, warrant. Even Sir Robert, even her father, proud as he was of her, much as he loved her, had awakened in her respect and gratitude, mingled with fear – rather than love.

After a moment, warned by approaching voices, Lady Sybil put her from her; but with a low and exultant laugh.

'You are mine, now!' she said. 'Mine, not his, mine! You will come to me when I want you. And I shall want you soon! Very soon!'

Mary laid hold of her again. 'Let me come now!' she cried,

forgetting in the depth of her feeling all but the mother she had gained, the arms which had cherished her, the kisses that had rained on her. 'You are ill! Let me come to you!'

'No! Not now! Not now!' Lady Sybil answered. 'I will send for you when I want you. I will promise to send for you. In good time, and it will be soon. And you will come!' she added, with the same ring of triumph in her voice. 'You will come, I know!' For even amid the satisfaction of her mother-love it was joy to her to know that she had tricked her husband; to know that though she had taken all from the child and he had given all, the child was hers – hers, and could never be taken from her! 'You will come! For you will not have me long. But' – this in a whisper, as the voices came nearer – 'go now! Go now! And not a word! Not a word, child, as you love me. I will send for you, when my time comes.'

And with a last look, strangely made up of love and pain and malicious triumph, Lady Sybil moved out of sight among the laurels. And Mary, drying her tears and composing her countenance as well as she could, turned to meet the intruders' eyes.

Fortunately – for she was far from being herself – the two persons who had wandered that way did but pause at the end of the Kennel Path, and, murmuring small talk, turn to retrace their steps. She gained a minute or two, in which to collect her thoughts and smooth her hair; but more than a minute or two she dared not linger lest her absence should arouse curiosity. As sedately as she could, she emerged from the shrubbery and made her way – though her breast heaved with a hundred emotions – towards the rustic bridge on which she saw that Lady Lansdowne was keeping Sir Robert in talk.

In talk, indeed, of her. For as she approached he placed the coping-stone on that edifice of her praises which her ladyship had craftily led him to build.

'The most docile,' he said, 'I assure you, the most docile child you can imagine! A beautiful disposition. She is docility itself!'

'I hope she may always remain so,' Lady Lansdowne answered slyly.

'I've no doubt she will,' Sir Robert replied, with fond assurance, his eye on the Honourable Bob, who was approaching the bridge from the lawns.

Lady Lansdowne followed the look with her eyes and smiled. But she said nothing. She turned to Mary, who was now near at hand, and reading in the girl's looks plain traces of trouble and of agitation, she contented herself with sending for Lady Louisa, and asking that her carriage might be called. In this way she cloaked under a little bustle the girl's embarrassment as she came up to them and joined them. Five minutes later Lady Lansdowne was gone.

After that, Mary would have had ample food for thought, had her mother alone filled her mind; had those kisses which had so stirred her being, those clinging arms, and that face which bore the imprint of illness, alone burdened her memory. Years afterwards the beat of the music which played that evening in the gardens, while the party within sat at dinner, haunted her; bringing back, as such things will, the scene and her aching heart, the outward glitter and the inward care, the Honourable Bob's gallantries and her father's stately figure as he drank wine with her; ay, and the hip, hip, hurrah, which shook the glasses when an old squire, a privileged person, rose, before she could leave, and toasted her.

Burdened only with the sacred memories of the afternoon, and the anxiety, the pity, the love which they engendered, she had been far from happy. But in truth, with all her feeling for her mother, Mary bore about her a keener and more bitter regret. The dull pain which had troubled her of late when thoughts of Arthur Vaughan would beset her was grown to a pang of shame, almost intolerable. She had told herself a hundred times before this that it was her weakness, and her fear of her father, which had led her to give him up – rather than a real belief in his baseness. For she had never, she was sure now, she had never believed in his baseness. But now that she *knew* – now that her mother, whose word it never struck her to doubt, had affirmed his innocence, now that a phrase had brought to her mind every incident of that coach drive, the April morning, the sunshine, the budding trees, the birth of love – pain gnawed at her heart. She rolled her face in the pillow to stifle her sobs. She was sick with misery.

For, oh, how thankless, how poor and small a thing he must think her! He would have given her all, and she had robbed him of all. And then when she had robbed him, and he could give her little, she had turned her back on him, abandoned him, believed evil of him, heard him insulted, and joined in the outrage! Over that thought she shed many and many a bitter tear – that night and in after nights. Romance had come to her in her lowliness, and a noble lover, stooping to her, and she had slain the one and denied the other. And now, now there was nothing she could do, nothing she would dare to do.

For that she had for a moment believed in his baseness – if she had so believed – was not the worst. There she had been the sport of circumstances; and the phase had been brief. But she had been weak, she had been swayed, she had given him up at a word, there was the rub.

There was the rub! And, ah, how happy had she been could she have undone the past! Could she have gone back to Miss Sibson's, and the dull schoolroom and the old stuff dress – and heard his step as he came up to the door! Alas, it was too late. For she could never again make him rich, and herself poor.

CHAPTER XXIII

In the House

As a fact, Mary's notion of the opinion which Arthur Vaughan had of her was above, rather than below, the reality. In her most despondent moments she scarcely exaggerated the things he thought of her, the contempt in which he held her; or the resentment which set his blood coursing when he remembered how she had treated him. He had gone to her and laid all that was left to him at her feet; and she, who had already dealt his fortunes so terrible a blow, had paid him for his offer, for his sacrifice of much that was dear to him, with suspicion, with contumely, with mistrust! Instead of clinging to him, to whom she had that moment plighted her troth, she had deserted him at a word. In place of trusting the man who had wooed her in her poverty, she had believed the first whisper against him. She had shown herself heartless, faithless, inconstant as the wind – a very woman! With a bitterness of which the author of the lines had been quite incapable, he might have murmured –

Away, away – your smile's a curse;
Oh, blot me from the race of men,
Kind, pitying Heaven! by death or worse,
Before I love such things again!'

But then Mr Moore, though his poetry and his singing brought tears to the eyes of women of fashion, hardened by many an intrigue, had never lost at a blow a great estate, a high position, and his love.

Certainly Vaughan had, if man ever had, grounds for a quarrel with fate. He had left London heart-whole and happy, the heir to a large fortune. He returned a fortnight later a Member of the Commons' House indeed, but heartsick and soured, beggared of his expectations, and tortured by the thought of what might have been, if his love had proved true as she was fair, and constant as she was sweet. For dreams of her shape, her face, her beauty still tormented him. Visions of the modest home in which he would have found consolation in failure, and smiles in success, rose up to deride him. He hated Sir Robert. He hated, or he tried to hate, the weakest and the most despicable of women. He saw all things and all men with a jaundiced eye; the sound of his voice and the look of his face were altered. Men who knew him, and who passed him in the street, or who saw him eating his chop in solitary churlishness, nudged one another and said that he took his reverses ill; while others, wounded by his curtness or his ill-humour, added that he did not go the right way to make the most of what was left.

For a certainty he was become a man unpleasant to handle. But, under the thorns was a very human soul, wounded, sore, and miserable, seeking every way for an outlet from its pains, and finding hope of escape at one point only. Men were right when they said that he did not go the way to make the most of his chances. For he laid himself out to please no one; it was not in him. But he worked late and early, and with furious energy, to fit himself for a political career; believing that success in that career was all that was left to him, and that by the necessary labour he could best put the past behind him. Love and pleasure, and those sweets of home life of which he had dreamed, were gone from him. But the stern prizes of ambition, the crown of those who live laborious days, might still be his – if the 'Mirror of Parliament' were never out of his hands, and if Mr Hume himself were not more constant to his favourite pillar under the gallery than he to such chance seat as might fall to him on the same side of the House.

Alas, he had not taken the oath an hour – with a sore heart, in a ruck of undistinguished new Members – before he saw that success was not so near, or so clearly within reach, as hope, with her flattering tale had argued. The times were propitious, indeed. The debates were close and fiery, and were scanned out of doors with an interest unknown before. The strife between Corker and Macaulay in the Commons, the duel between Brougham and Lyndhurst in the Lords, were followed in the country with as much attention as a battle between Belcher and Tom Cribb; and by the same classes. Everywhere men talked politics, talked of Reform, and of little else. The clubs, the 'Change, the taverns, nay, the drawing-rooms and the schools rang with the Bill, the whole Bill, and nothing but the Bill; with Schedule A, cruel as Herod, and Schedule B, which spared one of twins. In front of the window in the Haymarket, which weekly displayed H.B.'s political caricatures, the crowds stood gazing all day long, whatever the weather.

These things were in his favour. He remembered, too, the stress which the Chancellor had laid on the advantage of entering the House in advance of the crowd of new men whom the first Reformed Parliament must contain.

Unfortunately it seemed to him that he was one of just such a mob of tyros, as it was. Nearly a fourth of his colleagues were new to St Stephen's; and the greater part of these, owing to the circumstances of the election, were Whigs and sat on his side of the House. To raise his head above the level of a hundred competitors, numbering not a few men of wit and ability, and to do so within the short life of the present Parliament – for he saw no sure prospect of being returned again – was no mean task. Little wonder that he was as regular in his attendance as Mr Speaker, and grew pale of nights over Woodfall's Important Debates.

In the pride of his first return he had dreamed of a reputation to be gained by his maiden speech; of burning periods that would astonish all who heard them, of flights of fancy to live for ever in the mouths of men, of a marshalling of facts so masterly, and an exposition of figures so clear, as to obscure the fame of Single-speech Hamilton, or of that modern phenomenon, Mr Sadler. But whatever the effect of the present Chamber on the minds of novices, there existed that in the old Chamber – mean and dingy as was its wainscoted interior, and cumbered by galleries – there existed a something, were it but the memory that those walls had echoed the diatribes of Chatham and given back the voice of Burke, had heard the laugh of Walpole and the snore of North, which cooled the spirit of a new Member; which shook his knees as effectually as if the panelling of the room had vanished at a touch, and revealed the glories of the Gothic chapel which lay behind it. For behind that panelling and those galleries the ancient chapel, with its sumptuous tracery and graceful statues, its frescoed walls and stained glass, still existed – no unfit image of the stately principles which lie behind the dull, everyday rules of our Constitution.

To Arthur Vaughan, a student of the history of the House, this effect of the Chamber upon a new Member was a commonplace. But he was a practised speaker in the mimic arena; and he thought that he might rise above the feeling. He fancied that he understood the Genius Loci, its hatred of affectation, and almost of eloquence, its dislike to be bored, its preference for the easy, the conversational, and the personal. And when he had waited three weeks – so much he gave to prudence – his time came.

He rose in a moderately thin House in the middle of the dinner hour; and rose, as he thought, fully prepared. Indeed he started well. He brought out two or three sentences with ease and aplomb; and he fancied the difficulty over, the threshold passed. But then – he knew not why, nor could he overcome the feeling – the silence, kindly meant, which greeted him as a maiden speaker, had a terrifying effect upon him. A mist rose before his eyes, his voice sounded strange to him – and distant and shrill. He dropped the thread of what he was saying, he repeated himself, and lost his nerve. For some seconds, standing with all faces turned to him – they seemed numberless seconds to him, though in truth they were few – he could see nothing but the Speaker's wig, grown to an immense white cauliflower, which swelled and swelled and swelled until it filled the whole House. He stammered, repeated himself a second time – and was silent. Then, as, seeing that he was embarrassed, they cheered him, the mist cleared; and he went on – hurriedly and nervously. But he was aware that he had dropped a link in his argument, which he had not now the coolness to supply. And when he had murmured a few sentences, more or less inept and incoherent, he sat down.

In truth, he had made no mark, but he had also incurred no discredit. But he felt that the eyes of all were on him, that they were gloating over his failure. And comparing what he had done with what he had hoped to do, his achievement with those secret hopes, those absurd aspirations, he felt all the shame of open and ludicrous defeat. His face burned. He sat looking before him, not daring for a while to divert his gaze, or to learn in others' eyes how great had been his mishap.

Unfortunately, when he ventured to change his posture, and to put on his hat, which he had been holding in his hand since he sat down, he encountered Serjeant Wathen's eyes; and he read in them a look of amusement, which wounded his pride more than the open ridicule of a crowd. That was the finishing stroke. He walked out soon afterwards, bearing himself as indifferently as he could. But no man ever carried from the House a lower heart or a heavier sense of failure. He had mistaken his talents, he had no aptitude for debate. Success as a speaker was not within his reach.

He thought something better of it next day, but not much.

Nor could he put off a sneaking hang-dog air when he entered the lobby. A number of Members were gossiping inside the double doors, where the stairs from the cloisters came up by a third door; and one or two whom he knew spoke to him – but not of his attempt. He fancied that he read in their looks a knowledge that he had failed, and that he was no longer a man to be reckoned with. He imagined that they used a different tone to him. At length one of them spoke of it.

'Well, Vaughan,' he said pleasantly, 'you got through yesterday. But, if you'll take my advice, you'll wait a bit. It's only one here and there can make much of it to begin.'

'I certainly cannot,' Vaughan said, smiling frankly, the better to hide his mortification.

'Ah, well, you're not alone,' the other answered, shrugging his shoulders. 'You'll pick it up by-and-by, I dare say.' And he turned to speak to another Member.

Vaughan on his side turned to the paper for the day which hung against each of the four pillars of the lobby; and he pretended to be absorbed in it. The employment helped him to keep his countenance, but he was sore wounded. He had held his head so high in imagination. He had given so loose a rein to his ambition. He had dreamt of making such an impression on the House as Mr Macaulay, though new to it, had made in his speech on the second reading of the former Bill – and had deepened by his speech at the like stage of the present Bill. Now he was told that he was no worse than the common run of country Members who twice in three sessions rose and blundered through half a dozen sentences. He was consoled with the reflection that only 'one here and there' succeeded. Only one here and there! When to him it was everything to succeed and to succeed quickly. It was all that he had left.

The stream of Members, entering the House, was large; for the motion to commit the Bill was down for that afternoon, and, if carried, would virtually put an end to opposition in the Commons.

Out of the corner of his eye, Vaughan scanned them, and envied the leaders. Peel, cold, proud, and unapproachable, went by on the arm of Goulburn. Croker, pale and saturnine, casting frowning glances here and there, went in alone. The handsome portly form of Sir James Graham passed, in talk with the Rupert of Debate. After these came a rush of Members; and at the tail of all lumbered in the unwieldy, slovenly form of Sir Charles Wetherell, followed by a couple of his satellites.

Vaughan, glancing on one side of the paper which he appeared to be studying, caught Sir Charles's eye, reddened, and looked away. Seated on opposite sides of the House – and no man on either side was more bitter, virulent, and pugnacious than Wetherell – the two had not encountered one another since that evening at Stapylton, when the existence of Sir Robert's daughter had been disclosed to Vaughan. They had not spoken, much less had there been any friendly passage between them. But now Sir Charles paused and held out his hand.

'How do you do, Mr Vaughan?' he said in his deep bass voice. 'Your maiden essay yesterday?'

Vaughan winced. 'Yes,' he said stiffly, fancying that he read amusement in the other's moist eye.

To his surprise, 'You'll do,' Sir Charles rejoined; and looking at the floor and speaking in a despondent tone, 'It's a deal better to begin in that way than like some damned peacock on a lady's terrace,' he continued. 'Take the opportunity of saying three or four sentences some fine day – and repeat it a week later. And I'll wager you'll do.'

'But little, I am afraid,' Vaughan said. None the less was his heart full of gratitude to the fat ungainly man.

'All, maybe,' Wetherell grunted. 'I shouldn't wonder. I've been told, by one who heard him, that Canning hesitated in his first speech, very much as you did. It was on the Sardinian Subsidy. The men who don't feel the House never know the House. They dazzle it, Mr Vaughan, but they don't guide it. And that's what we've got to do.'

He passed on then, with a melancholy nod and averted eyes, but Vaughan could have blest him for that 'we'. 'There's one man at least believes in me,' he told himself. And when a few hours later, in the midst of a scene as turbulent as any which the House of Commons had ever witnessed – nine times without a pause it divided on the motion that 'this House do now adjourn' – when in the midst of the fray he watched the man who had commended him, riding the storm, and directing the whirlwind, now lashing the Whigs to fury by his sarcasm, and now carrying the whole House away in a hurricane of laughter – if he did not approve, and with his views he could not approve – he learnt, and learnt much. He saw that the untidy man, with the heavy face and that hiatus between his breeches and his waistcoat which had made him famous, was allowed to do things, and to say things, and to look things, for which a less honest man had been hurried to the Clock Tower. And this because the House believed in him; because it knew that he was fighting for a principle really dear to him; because it knew that he honestly put faith in those predictions of woe which he scattered so freely, and in that ruin of the Constitution with which he twitted his opponents.

A week later Vaughan acted upon his advice. He seized an opportunity and, catching the Chairman's eye – the Bill was in Committee – he delivered himself of a dozen sentences with so much spirit and propriety that Sir Robert Peel, speaking an hour later, referred to the 'plausible suggestion made by the Honourable Member for Chippinge'. The reference drew all eyes to Vaughan; and though nothing was said to him, and he took care to bear himself as if he had done no better than before, he left the House with a lighter step and a comfortable warmth about the heart. That evening he was more at ease, if not more happy, than he had felt for weeks past. Love, pleasure, and the rest were gone: and faith in woman. But if he could be sure of gaining a seat in the next Parliament, the way might be longer than he had hoped, it might be more toilsome and more dusty; but in the end he would arrive at the Treasury Bench.

He little thought that the effort on which he hugged himself would prove a fount of misfortunes. But so it turned out. His maiden speech had attracted neither notice nor envy. But these few sentences, short and simple as they were, by drawing an answer from the leader of the Opposition, had gained both for him. Within five minutes a score of Members had asked 'Who is he?' and another score had detailed the circumstances of his election for Chippinge. He had gone down to vote for his cousin, in his cousin's borough – family vote and the rest: so the story ran. Then, finding on the morning of the polling that if he threw over his cousin he might gain the seat for himself, he had turned his coat in a – well, in a very dubious manner, snatched the seat, and – here he was!

In brief, it was the version of the facts which he had once dreaded, and about which he had long ceased to trouble himself.

There were, perhaps, half a dozen men in the House who knew the facts, and knew that the young man had professed from the first the opinions which he was now supporting. But there was just so much truth, just so much vraisemblance in the garbled version, that even those who knew the facts could not wholly contradict it. To Wetherell's ears the story did not come; or he, for certain, would have gainsaid it. But it did come to Wathen's. Now the Serjeant was capable of spite. He had not forgotten the manner after which Vaughan had flouted him at Chippinge; and his defence – if a defence it could be called – was accompanied by so many nods and shrugs that persons less prejudiced than Tories, wounded by personalities and soured by defeat, might have been forgiven if they quitted the Serjeant with a lower opinion of our friend than before.

At any rate from that day Vaughan, though he knew nothing of the matter, and no one spoke to him of it, was a marked man in the eyes of the opposite Party. They regarded him as a renegade; while his own side were not over-anxious to make his cause their own. The May election had been contested with more spirit and less scruple than any election within living memory; and many things had been done and many said of which honourable men were not proud. But though it was acknowledged that such things must be done here and there, and even that the doers must not be repudiated, it was felt that the Party need not grapple them to its breasts with hooks of steel. Rumour had it that Lord Lansdowne felt himself to blame in this case; that the offender had been disinherited by his cousin was whispered. Provided the latter were true, the man would be of no great importance in the future; and if he did not make a second appearance in Parliament, the loss to the Party would be small. Not a few summed up the matter in that way.

Vaughan was not intimate with anyone in the House, or he would have learned what was afoot; and he might have taken steps to set himself right. But until lately he had lived with his regiment; he had but made his bow to Society; and, since his misfortune, he had been too sore to make new friends. Of course he had acquaintances not a few – all men have acquaintances; but no one in political circles knew him well enough to think it worth while to put him on his guard.

Unluckily, the next occasion which brought him to his feet was of a nature to give point to the feeling against him. On a certain Thursday, Serjeant Wathen moved that the borough of Chippinge be removed from Schedule A to Schedule B – his object being to save one Member; and Vaughan, thinking the opening favourable, rose, intending to make a few remarks in a strain to which the House, always fond of a personal explanation, is apt to listen with indulgence. For the motion itself, he had not much hope that it would be carried, since in a dozen other cases a similar motion had failed.

He began well enough.

'It can only be, Mr Bernal,' he said, addressing the Chairman of Committees – and this time the sound of his voice did not perturb him – 'from a strict sense of duty, it cannot be without pain that any Member – and I say this not on my account only, but on behalf of many honourable Members of this House—'

'No! No!' a voice cried. 'Leave us out!'

The words were uttered so loudly and so rudely that he paused in some confusion, and looked in the direction whence they came. At once cries of 'No, no! Divide! No! No!' poured on him from all parts of the House, accompanied by a dropping fire of cat-calls and cock-crows. He lost the thread of his sentence, and for a moment stood confounded. The Chairman of Committees did not interfere, and for an instant it looked as if the young speaker would be compelled to sit down.

But he recovered himself, gaining courage from the very spirit with which he was attacked, and which seemed out of proportion to his importance. The moment a lull in the fire of interruption occurred, he spoke in a louder voice.

'I say, sir,' he proceeded, looking about him courageously, 'that it is only with pain, only under the *force majeure* of a love for his country, that any Member can support the deletion from the Borough Roll of this House of that constituency which has honoured him with its confidence.'

'Divide! Divide!' roared many on both sides of the House. 'Cock-a-doodle-doo! Doo! Doo!'

But this fresh outburst of disapproval found him better prepared. Firmly, though the beads of perspiration stood on his brow, he persisted.

'And if,' he continued, 'in a case which appeals so nearly to himself, an honourable Member sees that the standard which justifies the survival of a representative is reached, with what gratification, sir, with what earnestness, sir, whether he sit on this side of the House or on that—'

'No! Leave us out!' in a roar of sound. In truth the Tories were uncertain on which side he was speaking. And 'Divide! Divide!' they shouted.

'Or on that,' he repeated.

'Divide! 'Vide!'

'Must he not press its claims,' he persisted gallantly, 'and support its interests? Ay, sir, and welcome, in the event of success, a decision at once just, and of so much advantage, I will not say to himself—'

'It never will be to you!' shrieked a voice from the darkest corner under the opposite gallery. 'Never!'

The shaft went home. He faltered, paused, tried to go on. But a roar of laughter drowned his next words, and continued so long that he gave up the struggle and sat down with a burning face; in some confusion, but in greater perplexity. Had he transgressed, he wondered ruefully, some unwritten law of the House? Had he offended in ignorance, and persisted in his offence? Ought he, though Wathen had spoken, to have been silent in his own case? In a matter so nearly touching himself?

He spoke to the Member who chanced to sit next him. 'What was it?' he asked. 'Did I do something wrong?'

The man glanced at him coldly. 'Oh no,' he said. And he shrugged his shoulders.

'But—'

'On the contrary, I fancy you've to congratulate yourself,' his neighbour continued with a sneer so faint that Vaughan did not perceive it. 'I understand that we're to do as we like on this – and they know it on the other side. Yes, there's the division. I think,' with the same sneer, 'you'll save your seat.'

'By jove!' Vaughan exclaimed. 'You don't say so!' He could hardly believe it.

But so it turned out. And so great was the boon – the greater, as no other borough was transferred in Committee – that it swept away for the time the memory of what had happened. The seat saved, it was odd if, with the wider electorate created by the Bill, he was not sure of his return! Odd, if he was not sure of beating Wathen – he, who had opened the borough and been returned by the Whig interest, even while it was closed. He need no longer feel so anxious and despondent when the Dissolution, which must follow the passage of the Bill, was named. No longer need he be in so great a hurry to make his mark, so envious of Mr Macaulay, so jealous of Mr Sadler.

Certainly, as far as his political career was in question, the horizon seemed to be clearing. If only other things had been as favourable. If only there had been someone, were it in a cottage at Hammersmith or in a dull street off Bloomsbury Square, to whom he might take home this piece of news; certain that other eyes would sparkle more brightly than his, and another heart beat quick with joy!

That could not be. There was an end of that. And his face grew gloomy again. Yet he was less unhappy. The certainty of a seat in the next Parliament was a great point gained. A great point to the good.

CHAPTER XXIV

A Right and Left

IF ANYTHING was certain in a political world so changed, it was certain that if the Reform Bill passed the Lords – in the teeth of those plaguy Bishops of whose opposition much was heard – a Dissolution would immediately follow. To not a few of the Members the contingency was a spectre, ever present, seated at bed and board and able to defy the rules even of Almack's and Crockford's. For how could a gentleman, who had just given five thousand pounds for his seat, contemplate with equanimity a notice to quit, so rude and so premature? And worse, a notice to quit which meant extrusion into a world in which seats at five thousand for a Parliament would be few and far between; and fair agreements to pay a thousand a year while the privilege lasted would be unknown!

Many a Member asked loudly and querulously, 'What will happen to the country if the Bill pass?' But more asked themselves in their hearts, and more often and more querulously, 'What will happen to me if the Bill pass? How shall I fare at the hands of these new constituencies, which, unwelcome as a gipsy's brats, I am forced to bring into the world?'

Hitherto few on his own side of the House, and not many on the Tory side, had regarded a Dissolution with more misgiving than Arthur Vaughan. The borough for which he sat lay under doom, and he had no longer influence or prospects, or such a fortune as justified him in an appeal to one of the new and populous constituencies. For the present, it was a pleasant thing to go in and out by the door of the privileged, to take his chop at Bellamy's, to lounge in the dignified seclusion of the library, or to air his new honours in Westminster Hall. It was agreeable to have that sensation of living at the hub of things, to receive whips, to give franks, to feel that the ladder of ambition was open to him. But he knew that an experience of the House counted by months did no man good; and the prospect of losing his plumes and going forth a common biped had been the more painful to him because his all was embarked in the venture. He might, indeed, fall back on the Bar; but with half a heart, and the reputation of a man who had tried to fly before he could walk.

His relief, therefore, when Chippinge – alone of all the boroughs in Schedule A – was removed in Committee to Schedule B, was great. The road was open once more, while the exceptional nature of his luck almost persuaded him that he was reserved for greatness. True, Serjeant Wathen might pride himself on the same fact: but at the thought Vaughan smiled. The Serjeant and Sir Robert would find it a trifle harder to deal with the hundred and odd voters whom the Act enfranchised than with the old 'Cripples'. And very, very ungrateful would those hundred and odd be, if they did not vote for the man who had made their cause his own.

A load, indeed, was lifted from his mind, and for some days his relief could be read in the lightness of his step, and the returning gaiety of his eyes. He knew nothing of the things which were being whispered about him. And though he had cause to fancy that he was not a *persona grata* on his own benches, he thought sufficiently well of himself to set this down to jealousy. There is a stage in the life of a rising man when all hands are against him; and those most cruelly which will presently applaud him most loudly. He flattered himself that he had set a foot on the ladder: and while he waited for an opportunity to raise himself another step, he came as near to a kind of feverish happiness as thoughts of Mary, ever recurring when he was alone, would permit. For the time the loss of his prospects ceased to trouble him – he tried to think of other things. He lived less in his rooms, more among men. He was less crabbed, less moody. And so the weeks wore away in Committee, and a day or two after the Coronation the Bill came on for the third reading.

The House was utterly weary. The leaders on both sides were reserving their strength for the final debate, and Vaughan had some hope that he might find an opportunity of speaking with effect. With this in his mind he was on his way across the Park about three in the afternoon, conning his peroration, when a hand was clapped on his shoulder, and he turned to find himself face to face with Flixton.

So much had happened since they had stood together on the hustings, Vaughan's fortunes had changed so greatly since they had parted in anger in Queen's Square, that he, at any rate, had no thought of bearing malice. To Flixton's 'Well, my hearty, you're a neat artist, ain't you? Going to the House, I take it?' he gave a cordial answer.

'Yes,' he said. 'That's it.'

'Bringing ruination on the country, eh?' And Flixton passed his arm through his, and walked on with him. 'That's the ticket?'

'Some say so, but I hope not.'

'Hope's a cock that won't fight, my boy!' the Honourable Bob rejoined. 'Fact is, you're doing your best, only the House of Lords is in the way, and won't let you! They'll pull you up sweetly, see if they don't!'

'And what will the country say to that?' Vaughan rejoined good-humouredly.

'Country be damned! That's what all you chaps are saying. And I tell you what! That book-in-breeches man – what do you call him – Macaulay? – ought to be pulled up! He ought indeed. I read one of his farragoes the other day and it was full of nothing but "Think long, I beg, before you thwart the public will!" and "The might of an angered people!" and "Let us beware of rousing!" and all that rubbish. Meaning, my boy, only he didn't dare to say it straight out, that if the Lords did not give way to you chaps there'd be a revolution, and the deuce to pay! And I say he ought to be in the dock. He's as bad as old Brereton down in Bristol, predicting fire and flames and all the rest of it.'

'But you cannot deny, Flixton,' Vaughan answered soberly, 'that the country is excited as we have never known it excited before? And that a rising is not impossible!'

'A rising! I wish we could see one! That's just what we want,' the Honourable Bob answered, stopping and bringing his companion to a sudden stand also. 'Eh? Who was that old Roman – Poppaea, or some name like that, who said he wished the people had all one head that he might cut it off?' suiting the action to the word with his cane. 'A rising, begad? The sooner the better! The old Fourteenth would know how to deal with it!'

'I don't think that you would be so confident if you were once face to face with it!' Vaughan answered.

'Oh, come!'

'Well, but the position—'

'Oh, I know all about that! But I say, old chap,' he continued, changing his tone, and descending abruptly from the political to the personal situation, 'you've played your cards badly, haven't you? Eh?'

Vaughan fancied that he referred to Mary; or at best to his quarrel with Sir Robert. And he froze.

'I won't discuss that,' he said in a different tone. And he moved on again.

'But I was there the evening you had the row!'

'At Stapylton?'

'Yes.'

'Well?' Vaughan said stiffly. 'What of that?'

'And, Lord, man, why didn't you sing a bit small? And the old gentleman would have done no end for you!'

Vaughan halted, with anger in his face. 'I won't discuss it!' he said, with a hint of violence in his tone.

'Very well, very well!' Flixton replied, with the superabundant patience of the man whose withers are not wrung. 'But when you did get your seat, why didn't you come to terms with someone?' with a wink. 'As it is, what's the good of being in the House three months, or six months – and out again?'

Vaughan wished most heartily that he had not met the Honourable Bob; who he remembered, had always possessed, hearty and jovial as he seemed, a singular knack of rubbing him the wrong way.

'How do you know?' he asked, with a touch of contempt – was he, a rising Member of Parliament, to be scolded after this fashion? 'How do you know that I shall be out?'

'You'll be out, if it's Chippinge you are looking to.'

'Why so sure, my friend?'

Flixton winked with deeper meaning than before. 'Ah, that's telling,' he said. 'Still – why not? If you don't hear it from me, old chap, you'll soon hear it from someone. Why, you ask? Well, because a little bird whispered to me that Chippinge was – arranged! That Sir Robert and the Lansdownes understood one another; and whichever way it went, it would not come your way!'

Vaughan reddened deeply. 'I don't believe it,' he said bluntly.

'Did you know that Chippinge was going to be spared?'

'No.'

'They didn't tell you?'

'No.'

'Ah!' shrugging his shoulders and preparing to take his departure. 'Well, other people knew, and there it is. I may be wrong, I hope I am, old chap. Hope I am. But anyway I must be going. I turn here. See you soon, I hope!'

And with a wave of the hand the Honourable Bob marched off through Whitehall, his face breaking into a mischievous grin as soon as he was out of Vaughan's sight.

'Return hit for your snub, Miss Mary!' he muttered. 'You prick me, I prick him! And do him good, too! He was always a most confounded prig.'

Meanwhile Vaughan strode on past Downing Street; the old street, long swept away, in which Walpole lived, and to which the dying Chatham was carried. And unconsciously, under the spur of his angry thoughts, he quickened his pace. It was incredible, it was inconceivable that so monstrous an injustice had been planned, or could be perpetrated. He, who had stepped into the breach, in his own despite; he, who had refused, so scrupulous had he been, to stand on a first invitation; he, who had been elected almost against his will – was, for all thanks, to be set aside, and by his friends! By those whose unsolicited act it had been to return him and to put him into this position. It was impossible, he told himself; it was unthinkable! Were it so, the meanness of political life had reached its apogee! The faithlessness of the Whigs, their incredible treachery to their dependants, could need no other exemplar!

'I'll not bear it! By Heaven, I'll not bear it!' he muttered.

And striding along in the hurry of his spirits as if he carried a broom and swept the whole Whig Party before him, he overtook no less a person than Serjeant Wathen, who had been lunching at the Athenaeum.

The Serjeant heard his voice and, turning, saw who it was.

He fancied that Vaughan's words had been addressed to him.
'I beg your pardon,' he said politely. 'I did not catch what you said, Mr Vaughan.'
For a moment Vaughan glowered at him, as if he would sweep him from his path, along with the Whigs. Then out of the fullness of the heart the mouth spoke.
'Mr Serjeant,' he said, in a not very friendly tone, 'do you know anything of an agreement disposing of the future representation of Chippinge?'
The Serjeant, who knew all under the rose, looked shrewdly at his companion to learn, if possible, what he knew. And, to gain time.
'I beg your pardon,' he said. 'I don't think I quite understand you.'
'I am told,' Vaughan said haughtily, 'that an agreement has been made to avoid a contest at Chippinge.'
'Do you mean,' the Serjeant asked suavely, 'at the next election, Mr Vaughan?'
'At future elections!'
The Serjeant shrugged his shoulders. 'As a Member,' he said primly, 'I take care to know nothing of such agreements. And I recommend you, Mr Vaughan, to adopt the same rule. For the rest,' he added, with a candid smile, 'I give you fair warning that I shall contest the seat. May I ask who was your informant?'
'Mr Flixton.'
'Flixton? Flixton? Ah! The gentleman who is to marry Miss Vermuyden! Well, I can only repeat that I, at any rate, am no party to any agreement.'
His sly look, which derided his companion's inexperience, said as plainly as a look could say, 'You find the game of politics less simple than you thought?' And at another time it would have fired the younger man's anger. But as one pellet drives out another, the Serjeant's reference to Mary Vermuyden had in one second driven the prime subject from Vaughan's mind. He did not speak for a moment; and then with his face averted –
'Is Mr Flixton – going to marry Miss Vermuyden?' he asked, in a constrained tone. 'I had not heard of it.'
'I only heard it yesterday,' the Serjeant replied. He was not

unwilling to shelve the other topic. 'But it is rumoured, and I believe it is true. Quite a romance, her story?' he continued airily. 'Quite a nine days' wonder! But' – he checked himself sharply – 'I beg your pardon! I was forgetting how nearly it concerned you. Dear me, dear me! Well, it is a fair wind, indeed, that blows no one any harm!'

Vaughan made no reply. He could not speak, for the hard beating of his heart. Wathen looked at him inquisitively. But the Serjeant had not the clue; he could only suspect that the marriage touched the other, because issue of it would bar his chance of succession. So, though they walked some distance together, no more was said. As they crossed New Palace Yard a Member drew the Serjeant aside, and Vaughan went up alone to the Lobby.

But all thought of speaking was gone from his mind; nor did the thinness of the House when he entered tempt him. There were hardly a hundred present, and these were lolling here and there with their hats on in the dull light of a September afternoon. A dozen more looked sleepily from the galleries, their arms flattened on the rail, their chins on their arms. There were only a couple of Ministers on the Treasury Bench, whence Lord John Russell was moving the third reading. No one seemed to take much interest in the matter; a stranger entering at the moment would have learned with amazement that this was the mother of parliaments, the renowned House of Commons, and with still greater amazement that the small boyish-looking gentleman in the high-collared coat, and with lips moulded on Cupid's bow, who appeared to be making some perfunctory remarks upon the state of the crops – or the weather – was really advancing by an important stage the famous Bill, which had convulsed three kingdoms and was destined to change the political face of the land.

Lord John sat down at length, thrusting his head at once into a packet of papers, which the gloom hardly permitted him to read. A clerk at the table mumbled something; a gentleman on the other side of the House rose and began to speak. He had not uttered many sentences, however, before the Members on the Reform benches awoke, not only to life, but to fury. Stentorian shouts of 'Divide! 'Vide!' rendered the speaker inaudible: and after looking towards the door of the House more than once he sat down, and the House went to a Division. In a few minutes it was known that the Bill had been read a third time, by 113 to 58.

But the foreign gentleman would have made a great mistake had he gone away supposing that Lord John's placid words – and not those spiteful shouts – represented the feelings of the House. In truth the fiercest passions were at work under the surface. Among the fifty-eight who shrugged their shoulders and accepted the verdict in gloomy silence were some primed with the fiercest invectives; and others, tongue-tied men who nevertheless believed that Lord John Russell was a Republican, and Althorp a fool. These were certain that the Whigs, wittingly or unwittingly, were working the destruction of the country. Already they saw her dragged from the pride of place to which a nicely balanced Constitution had raised her, and laid, with her choicest traditions, at the feet of the rabble. Men who believed such things, and saw the deed doing before their eyes, might accept their doom in silence – even as the King of old went silently to the Banqueting Hall hard by. But not with joy or easy hearts.

Vaughan, therefore, was not the only one who walked into the Lobby that evening, brooding darkly on his revenge. Yet he behaved himself as men so bred, so trained, do behave themselves. He held his peace. And no one dreamed, not even Orator Hunt, who sat not far from him under the shadow of his White Hat, that this well-connected young gentleman was revolving thoughts of the Social Order, and of the Party System, and of most things which the Church Catechism commends, beside which that terrible Radical's own opinions were mere Tory prejudices. 'The fickleness of women! The treachery of men! Oh, Aetna, bury them! Oh, Ocean, overwhelm them! Let all cease together and be no more! But give me sweet, oh sweet, oh sweet Revenge!'

CHAPTER XXV

At Stapylton

IT WAS about a week before his encounter with Vaughan in the Park – and on a fine autumn day – that the Honourable Bob, walking with Sir Robert by the Garden Pool, allowed his eyes to travel over the prospect. The smooth-shaven lawns, the stately, lichened house, the far-stretching park, with its beech knolls and slopes of verdure, he found all fair; and when to these, when to the picture on which his bodily eyes rested, he added that portrait of Mary – in white muslin and blue ribbons, bowing her graceful head while Sir Robert read prayers – which he carried in his memory, he told himself that he was an uncommonly happy fellow.

Beauty he might have had, wealth he might have had, family, too. But to alight on all in such perfection, to lose his heart where his head approved the step, was a gift of fortune so rare that, as he strutted and talked by the side of his host, his face beamed with ineffable good-humour.

Nevertheless, for a few moments, silence had fallen between the two; and little by little Sir Robert's face had assumed a grave and downcast look. He sighed more than once, and when he spoke, it was to repeat in different words what he had already announced.

'Certainly, you may speak,' he said, in a tone slightly formal. 'And I can admit little doubt, Mr Flixton, that your overtures will be received as they deserve.'

'Yes? Yes?' Flixton answered with manifest delight. 'You think so? You really think so, Sir Robert?'

'I think so,' his host replied. 'Not only because your suit is in every way eligible, and one which does us honour.' He bowed courteously as he uttered the compliment. 'But because, Mr Flixton, for docility – and I think a husband may congratulate himself on the fact—'

'To be sure! To be sure!' Flixton cried, not permitting him to finish. 'Yes, Sir Robert, capital! You mean that if I am not a happy man—'

'It will not be the fault of your wife,' Sir Robert said; remembering with a faint twinge of conscience that the Honourable Bob's past had not been without its histories.

'No! By gad, Sir Robert, no! You're quite right! By the Lord she's got an ank—' He stopped abruptly, his mouth open, bethinking himself, when it was almost too late, that her father was not the person to whom to detail her personal charms.

But Sir Robert had not divined the end of the sentence. He was a trifle deaf.

'Yes?' he said.

'She's an an – animated manner, I was going to say,' Flixton continued with more readiness than fervour. And he blessed himself for his presence of mind.

'Animated? Yes, certainly animated. But, gentle also,' Sir Robert replied, 'I should say that gentleness, and – and indeed, my dear fellow, goodness, were the – the striking qualities in her. But perhaps I am saying more than I should?'

'Not at all!' Flixton answered with heartiness. 'Not at all! Gad, I could listen to you all day, Sir Robert.'

He had listened, indeed, during a large part of the past week, and with so much effect that those histories to which reference has been made had almost faded from the elder man's mind. Flixton seemed to him a hearty, manly young fellow, a little boastful and self-assertive, but remarkably sound. A soldier, who asked nothing better than to put down the rabble rout which was troubling the country; a Tory, of precisely his, Sir Robert's, opinions; the younger son of a peer, too, and a West Country peer to boot. In fine, he deemed him a staunch, open-air patrician, with good old-fashioned instincts, and none of that intellectual conceit, none of those cranks and fads and follies, which had ruined a man who also might have been Sir Robert's son-in-law.

With that man, Sir Robert, partly because his conscience pricked him at times, by suggesting impossible things and incredible excuses, was still bitterly angry. So angry that, had the baronet been candid, he must have acknowledged that the Honourable Bob's main virtue was his unlikeness to Arthur Vaughan. It was in proportion as he differed from the young fellow who had so meanly intrigued to gain his daughter's affections that Flixton appeared desirable to the father. Even those histories proved that, at any rate, he had blood in his veins; while his loud good-nature, his positiveness, as long as it marched with Sir Robert's positiveness, his short views, all gained by contrast. 'I am glad he is a younger son,' the baronet thought. 'He shall take the old Vermuyden name!' And he lifted his handsome shapely chin a little higher as he pictured the honours that, even in a changed and worsened England, might cluster about his house. After all, and if the Bill passed, he had a seat alternately with the Lansdownes; and in a future which would know nothing of Lord Lansdowne's cat-o'-nine-tails, in which pocket boroughs would be rare, and great peers would have scarce a representative, much might be done with half a seat.

Suddenly, 'Damme, Sir Robert,' Flixton cried, 'there is the little beau – hem! – there she is, I mean. With your permission I'll join her.'

'By all means, by all means,' Sir Robert answered indulgently. 'You need not stand on ceremony with me.'

Flixton waited for no more. Possibly he had no mind to be bored, now that he had gained what he wanted. He hurried after the slim figure with the floating white skirts and the Leghorn hat, which had descended the steps of the house, moved lightly across the lawns – and vanished. He guessed, however, whither she was bound. He knew that she had a liking for walking in the wilderness behind the house; a beech wood which was already beginning to put on its autumn glory. And sure enough, hastening to a point among the smooth grey trunks where the three paths met, he discerned her a hundred paces away, walking slowly from him with her eyes raised.

'Squirrels!' Flixton thought. And he made up his mind to bring the terriers and have a hunt on the following Sunday afternoon. In the meantime he had another quarry in view, and he made after the white-frocked figure.

Mary heard his tread on the carpet of dry beech leaves, and she turned and saw him. She had come out on purpose to be alone, that she might consider at her leisure the fresh and astonishing views which, in this new life, were daily opening before her. Or possibly that was but a pretext; an excuse to herself, and an explanation to others of a love of solitude, which was not natural at her age. For, for certain, amid sombre thoughts of her mother, she continued to think more often and more sombrely of another; of happiness which she had forfeited by her own act; of weakness, and cowardice, and ingratitude; of a man's head that stooped to her adorably, and then again of a man's eyes that burned her with contempt.

Most likely she was not overjoyed when she saw Mr Flixton. But Sir Robert was so far right in his estimate of her nature, that she hated to give pain. It was there, perhaps – yes, it was there, that she was weak. And so, seeing the Honourable Bob, she smiled pleasantly on him.

'You have discovered a favourite haunt of mine,' she said. She did not add that she spent a few minutes of every day there; that the smooth beech trunks knew the touch of her burning cheeks, and the rustle of the falling leaves the whisper of her penitence. Daily she returned by way of the Kennel Path, and there breathed a prayer for her mother, where a mother's arms had first enfolded her, and a mother's kisses won her love. What she did add was, 'I often come here.'

'I know you do,' the Honourable Bob replied, with a look of admiration. 'I assure you, Miss Mary, I could astonish you with the things I know about you!'

'Really?'

'Oh yes – really!'

There was a significant chuckle in his voice which brought the blood to her cheeks. But she was determined to ignore its meaning.

'You are observant?' she said.

'Of those – yes, by Jove, I am of those I admire,' he rejoined eagerly. He had had it on his tongue to say 'those I love', but she turned her eyes on him at the critical moment, and though he was doing a thing which he had often done, and he had impudence enough, his tongue failed him. There are women so naturally modest that, until the one man who awakens the heart appears, it seems an outrage to speak to them of love. Mary Vermuyden, partly by reason of her bringing up, was one of these; and though Flixton had had little to do with women of her kind, he recognized the fact and bowed to it. He was here with her father's leave to speak to her; yet he found himself less at his ease than on many a less legitimate occasion. 'Yes, by Jove,' he repeated. 'I observe them, I can tell you.'

Mary laughed. 'Some are more quick to notice than others,' she said.

'And to notice some than others!' he rejoined. 'That is what I mean. Now, that old girl who is with you—'

'Miss Sibson?' Mary said, setting him right with stiffness.

'To be sure! She isn't young, is she? Anyway, you don't suppose I could say what she wore yesterday! But what you wore, Miss Mary' – he tried to catch her eye and ogle her – 'ah, couldn't I! But then you don't wear powder on your nose, nor need it!'

'I don't wear it,' she answered, laughing in spite of herself. 'But you don't know what I may do some day! And for Miss Sibson, it does not matter, Mr Flixton, what she wears. She has one of the kindest hearts, and was one of the kindest friends I had – or could have had – when things were different with me.'

'Oh yes, good old girl,' he rejoined, 'but snubby! Bitten my nose off two or three times, I know. And come now, not quite an angel, you know, Miss Mary!'

'Well,' she replied smiling, 'she is not, perhaps, an angel to look at. But—'

'She can't be! For she is not like you!' he cried exultantly. 'And you are one! You are the angel for me!' looking at her with impassioned eyes. 'I'll never want another, nor ask to see one!'

His look frightened her; she began to think he meant – something. And she took a new way with him.

'How singular it is,' she said thoughtfully, 'that people say those things! Because they sound so very silly – to one who has not lived in your world.'

'Silly!' Flixton replied, in a tone of mortification; and for a moment he felt the check. He was really in love to a moderate extent, and on the way to be more deeply in love, were he thwarted. Therefore he was, to a moderate extent, afraid of her. And 'Silly?' he repeated. 'Oh, but I mean it, so help me! I do indeed! It's not silly to call you an angel, for I swear you are as beautiful as one. That's true anyway!'

'How many have you seen? And what coloured wings had they?' she asked, ridiculing him. But her cheek was hot. 'Don't say, if you please,' she continued, before he could speak, 'that you've seen me. Because that is only saying again what you've said, Mr Flixton. And that is worse than silly. It is dull.'

'Miss Mary,' he cried pathetically, 'you don't understand me! I want to assure you – I want to make you understand—'

'Hush!' she said, cutting him short, in an earnest whisper. And halting, she extended a hand behind her to stay him. 'Please don't speak!' she continued. 'Do you see the beauties? Flying round and round the tree after one another faster than your eyes can follow them. One, two, three – three squirrels! I never saw one, do you know,' she went on in a tone of hushed rapture, 'until I came here. And until now I never saw them at play. Oh, who could harm them?'

He stood behind her, biting his lip with vexation, and quite untouched by the scene, which, whether her raptures were feigned or not, was warrant for them. Hitherto he had had to do with women who met him halfway; who bridled at a compliment, were alive to an equivoque, and knew how to simulate, if they did not feel, a soft confusion under his gaze. For this reason Mary's backwardness, her easy manner, her apparent belief that they were friends of the same sex, puzzled him, nay, angered him. As she stood now, a hand extended to check his advance, the sunshine which filtered through the beech leaves cast a soft radiance on her figure. She seemed more dainty, more graceful, more virginal than aught that he had ever encountered in the garb of woman. It was in vain that he told himself, with irritation, that she was but a girl after all: that, under her aloofness, she was a woman like the others; as vain, passionate, flighty, as jealous as other women. He knew that he stood in awe of her. He knew that the words which he had many a time uttered so lightly – to those to whom he had no right to address them – stuck in his throat now. He wanted to say, 'I love you!' and he had the right to say it. Yet he dared not. All the boldness which he had exhibited in her presence in Queen's Square – where another had stood tongue-tied – was gone.

He took at last a desperate step. The girl was within arm's reach of him; her delicate waist, the creamy white of her slender neck, invited him. Be she never so innocent, never so maidenly, a kiss, he told himself, would awaken her. It was his experience, it was a scrap drawn from his store of worldly wisdom, that a woman kissed was a woman won.

As he thought of it, his heart began to riot, as it had not rioted from that cause since he had kissed the tobacconist's daughter at Exeter; his first essay in gallantry. Only the bold, he reminded himself, deserve the fair! How often had he boasted that, where women were concerned, lips were made for other things than talking!

And – and in a moment it was done.

Twice! Then she slipped from his grasp, and stood at bay with flaming cheeks and eyes that – that had certainly not ceased to be virginal.

'You! You!' she cried, barely able to articulate. 'Don't touch me!'

She had been taken utterly, wholly by surprise; and the shock was increased by the facts of her bringing-up, and the restraints and traditions of school life. In his grasp, with his hot breath on her cheek, all those notions about ravening wolves and the danger which attached to beauty in low places – notions no longer applicable, had she taken time to reason – returned upon her in force. The man had kissed her.

'How – how dare you?' she continued, trembling with rage and indignation.

'But your father—'

'How dare you?'

'Your father sent me,' he pleaded, crestfallen. 'He gave me leave—'

'To insult me?' she cried.

'No, but – but you won't understand!' he reasoned querulously. He was quite chapfallen. 'You don't listen to me. I want to marry you. I want you to be my wife. Your father said I might come to you, and – and ask you. And – you'll say "Yes", won't you – without any silliness? That's a good girl!'

'Never,' she answered.

He stared at her, and turned very red. 'Oh, nonsense!' he stammered. And he made as if he would go nearer. 'You didn't mean it. My dear girl. Listen to me! I do love you! And I – I tell you what it is, I – never loved any woman—'

But she looked at him in such a way that he could not go on.

'Do not say those things!' she said. And her austerity was terrible to him. 'And go, if you please. My father, if he sent you to me—'

'He did!'

'Then he did not,' she replied with dignity, 'understand my feelings.'

'But – but you must marry someone,' he complained. 'You know you're making a great fuss about nothing!'

'Nothing!' she cried, her eyes sparkling anew. 'You insult me, Mr Flixton, and—'

'If a man may not kiss the girl he wants to marry—'

'If she does not want to marry him?' she retorted with fine contempt. 'What then?'

'But it's not as bad as that,' he pleaded. 'No, by Jove. You'll not be so cruel. Come, miss Mary, listen, listen to me a minute. You must marry someone, you know. You are young, and I'm sure you've the right to choose—'

'I've heard enough,' she struck in, interrupting him with something of Sir Robert's hauteur. 'I understand now what you meant, and I forgive you. I forgive you. But I can never be anything to you, Mr Flixton.'

'You can be everything to me,' he declared. It couldn't, it really couldn't be that she meant to refuse him! Finally and altogether!

'But you can be nothing to me!' she answered cruelly – very cruelly for her, but her cheek was tingling. 'Nothing! Nothing! And that being so, I beg that you will leave me.'

He looked at her with a mixture of supplication, resentment, chagrin. But she showed no sign of relenting.

'You really – you really do mean it!' he muttered with a sickly smile. 'Come, Miss Mary, think of it!'

'Don't! Don't!' she cried, as if his words pained her. And that was all. 'Please go,' she said, 'or I shall go.'

The Honourable Bob's conceit had been so far taken out of him, that he felt that he could make no further fight at this time. He could see no sign of relenting, and feeling that, with all his experience, he had played his cards ill, he gave up the struggle.

'Oh, I will go,' he said. And he longed to add something witty, as he turned away. But he could not add anything. He, Bob Flixton, the hero of so many *bonnes fortunes*, to be refused! He had laid his all, and *pour le bon motif*, at the feet of a girl who but yesterday was a little schoolmistress. And she had refused him! It was impossible! It was incredible! But, alas! it was also a fact.

He returned to the house; and Mary, the moment his back was turned, hurried towards the kennels to hide her hot cheeks and calm her feelings in the depths of the shrubbery. Oddly enough, her first thoughts were less of that which had just happened to her than of that suit which had been paid to her months before. This man might love her or not; she could not tell. But Arthur Vaughan had loved her; the fashion of this love taught her to prize the fashion of that.

He had loved her. And if he had treated her as Mr Flixton had treated her, would she have clung to him – she wondered in a tumult of feeling. She believed that she would. But the mere thought set her knees trembling, made her cheeks flame afresh, filled her with rapture. So that, shamefaced, frightened, glancing this way and that, as one hunted, she longed to be within doors, longed to be safe in her room, there to cry at her ease.

Doubtless it was natural that the incident should turn her thoughts to that other love-making, and presently to her father's dislike of that other lover. She could not understand that dislike; for the Bill, and the Borough, Franchise or No Franchise, were nothing to her. And the grievance, when Sir Robert had essayed to explain it, had been nothing. To her mind Trafalgar and Waterloo and the greatness of England were the work of Nelson and Wellington – at the remotest perhaps, of Mr Pitt and Lord Castlereagh. She could not enter into the reasoning which attributed these and all other blessings of her country to a System! To a System, which her lover, it seemed, was pledged to destroy.

She walked until the heat of her cheeks had somewhat abated, and then, yearning for the security of her own chamber, she made for the house. She saw nothing of Flixton; no one was stirring. Already she thought herself safe; so that it seemed the very spirit of mischief which brought her, at the corner of the church, face to face with her father. Sir Robert's brow was clouded, and the 'My dear, one moment' with which he stayed her, was pitched in a more decisive key than he commonly used to her.

'I wish to speak to you, Mary,' he continued. 'Will you come with me to the library?'

She would fain have postponed any discussion on Mr Flixton; but her father, affectionate and mild, was still unfamiliar, and she had not the courage to make her petition. She followed him, with a sinking heart, to the library. And when he pointed to a seat, she was glad to sit down.

He took up his own position on the hearthrug, whence he looked at her gravely before he spoke. At length –

'My dear,' he said, 'I am sorry for this, though I do not blame you! I think that you do not understand – owing to those drawbacks of your early life which have otherwise, thank God, left so slight a mark upon you – that there are things which at your age you must leave to the decision of your elders.'

She looked at him, and there was not that complete docility in her look which he expected to find.

'I don't think I understand, sir,' she murmured.

'But you can easily understand this, Mary,' he replied, 'that young girls of your age, without experience of life or of – of the darker side of things, cannot be allowed to judge for themselves on all occasions. There are sometimes circumstances to be weighed which it is not possible to detail to them.'

She closed her eyes for an instant to collect her thoughts. 'But – but, sir,' she said, 'you cannot wish me to have no will – no choice – in a matter which affects me so nearly.'

'No,' he said, speaking seriously and almost sternly, 'but that will and that choice must be guided. Your feelings are natural – God forbid that I should think them otherwise! But you must leave the decision to me.'

She looked at him, aghast. She had heard, but had never believed, that in the upper classes matches were arranged after this fashion. But to have no will and no choice in such a thing as marriage! She must be dreaming.

'You cannot,' he continued, looking at her firmly but not unkindly, 'have either the knowledge of the past,' with a slight grimace, as of pain, 'or the experience needful to enable you to measure the result of the step you take. You must, therefore, let your seniors decide for you.'

'But I could never – never,' she answered, with a deep blush, 'marry a man without – liking him, sir.'

'Marry?' Sir Robert repeated. He stared at her.

She returned the look. 'I thought, sir,' she faltered, with a still deeper blush, 'that you were talking of that.'

'My dear,' he said gravely, 'I am referring to the subject on which I – I certainly understood that you requested Miss Sibson to speak to me.'

'My mother!' she whispered, her colour fading suddenly.

He paused a moment. Then, 'You would oblige me,' he said slowly and formally, 'by calling her Lady Sybil Vermuyden!'

'But she is – my mother,' she protested.

He looked at her, his head slightly bowed, his lower lip thrust out.

'Listen,' he said. 'What you propose – to go to her, I mean – is impossible. Impossible, let that be thoroughly understood. There must be an end of any thought of it!' His tone was cold, but not unkind. 'The thing must not be mentioned again, if you please, Mary.'

She was silent for a moment. Then, 'Why, sir?' she asked. She spoke tremulously, and with an effort. But he had not expected her to speak at all.

Yet he merely continued, as he stood on the hearthrug, to look at her askance.

'That is for me,' he said, 'to decide.'

'But—'

'But I will tell you,' he said stiffly. 'Because she has already ruined part of your life!'

'I forgive her, from my heart!'

'And ruined also,' he continued, disregarding the interruption, 'a great part of mine. At your age I do not think fit to tell you all. It is enough that she robbed me of you, and deceived me. Deceived me,' he repeated more bitterly, 'through long years when you, my daughter, might have been my comfort and – my joy.'

The last words were almost inaudible and with them he turned his back on her, and paced the room, his chin sunk on his breast. It was clear to Mary, watching him with pitying eyes, that his thoughts were with the unhappy past; with the short fever, the ignoble contentions of his married life, or with the lonely, soured years which had followed; that he was laying to his wife's charge the wreck of his life, and the slow dry-rot which had sapped hope, and strength, and development.

Mary waited until his step trod the carpet less hurriedly. Then, as he paused to turn, she stepped forward.

'Yet, sir, forgive her!' she cried; and there were warm tears in her voice. 'Forgive her!'

He turned and looked at her. Possibly he was astonished at her temerity.

'Never!' he said in a tone of finality. 'Never! Never! Let that be the end.'

But Mary had been dreaming of this moment for days; and she had resolved that, come what might, though he frown, though his tone grow hard and his eye angry, though he bring to bear on her the sternness of his visage, she would not be found lacking a second time. She would not again give way to her besetting weakness, and spend sleepless nights in futile remorse. Diffidence in the lonely schoolmistress had been pardonable, had been natural. But now, if she were indeed sprung from those who had a right to hold their heads above the crowd, if the doffed hats which greeted her when she went abroad, in the streets of Chippinge as well as in the lanes and roads – if these meant anything, shame on her if she proved craven.

'It cannot be the end, sir,' she said in a low voice. 'For she is – still my mother. And she is alone and ill. And she needs me.'

He had begun to pace the room anew – this time with an impatient, angry step. But at the sound of her voice he stood and faced her, and she needed all her courage to support the gloom of his look.

'How do you know?' he retorted. For Miss Sibson, discharging an ungrateful task, had not entered into details. 'Have you seen her?'

She felt that she must judge for herself. And though her mother had said something to the contrary, and hitherto she had obeyed her, she thought it best to tell all.

'Yes, sir,' she said.

'When?'

'A fortnight ago,' she replied; though she trembled under the growing severity of his look.

'Here?'

'In the grounds, sir.'

'And you never told me!' he cried. 'You never told me!' he repeated, with a strange glance, a glance which strove with shrinking to discern the mother's features in the daughter's face. 'You, too – you, too, have learnt to deceive me!' And he threw up his hands.

'Oh no, no!' she cried, infinitely distressed.

'But you have deceived me!' he rejoined. 'You, too! You have kept this from me.'

'Only, believe me, sir,' she cried, 'until I could find a fitting time.'

'And now you want to go to her!' he continued, unheeding, and with the same gesture of despair. 'She has suborned you! She, who has done the greatest wrong to you, has now done the last wrong to me!' He began again to pace up and down the room.

'Oh no, no!' she sobbed.

'It is so!' he answered, darting an angry glance at her. 'It is so! But I shall not let you go! Do you hear, girl? I shall not let you go! I have suffered enough! No!' he continued with a gesture which called those walls to witness to the humiliations, the sorrows, the loneliness, from which he had sought refuge within them. 'I will not suffer again. I will not! You shall not go!'

She was full of love for him, and of pity. Even that gesture and the past wretchedness to which it bore witness were patent to her; and she yearned to comfort him, and to convince him that nothing that had happened, nothing that could happen, would set her against him. Had he been seated she would have knelt and kissed his hand, or cast herself on his breast, and won him to her. But as he walked she could not approach him, she did not know how to soften him. Her duty, indeed, was clear; it lay beside her dying mother. Yet, if he forbade her to go, if he withstood her, how was she to perform it?

At length: 'But if she is dying, sir,' she murmured. 'Will you not then let me go to her?'

He looked at her from under his eyebrows. 'I tell you I will not let you go!' he said. 'She has forfeited her right to you. When she made you die to me, you died to her! That is my decision. You hear me? That is my decision. And now – now,' he continued, striving to regain his composure, 'let there be an end! I say – let there be an end!'

She stood silenced, but not conquered, knowing him more intimately than she had known him before; loving him not less but more, since pity and sympathy entered into her love; but assured that he was wrong. It could not be her duty to forsake, it must be his duty to forgive. But for the present she saw that in spite of his efforts and his apparent firmness he was cruelly agitated; she felt that she had stirred pangs long lulled to rest, that he had borne as much as he could bear. And she would not press him further for the present.

Meanwhile, he, as he stood fingering his trembling lips, was trying to bring the cunning of age to bear. He was silently forming his plan. She had been too much alone, he reflected; that was it. He had forgotten that she was young, and that change and movement and life and gaiety were needful for her. This notion about – that woman, was an obsession, an unwholesome fancy, which a few days in a new place and amid lively scenes would weaken, and perhaps remove. And by-and-by, when he thought that he could trust his voice, he spoke.

'I said, "Let there be an end!" ' he began. 'But – you are all I have, and I will say instead, "Let this be for a time." I must have space to think. You want – there are many things you want that you ought to have – frocks and laces, and gewgaws,' he continued, with a sickly smile, 'and I know not what, that you cannot get here, nor I choose for you. Lady Worcester has offered to take you to town – she goes the day after tomorrow. I was uncertain this morning whether to send you or not, whether I could spare you or not. Now, I say, go. Go, and when you return, Mary, we will talk again.'

'And then,' she pleaded softly, 'you will let me go?'

'Never!' he cried, forgetting himself, and lifting his head with an uncontrollable recurrence of rage. 'Never! But there, there! There! there! I shall have thought it over – more at leisure. Perhaps; I don't know! I will tell you then. I will think it over!'

She saw with clear eyes that this was but an evasion; that he was deceiving her. But she felt no resentment, only pity. She had no reason to think that her mother needed her on the instant, and much was gained by the discussion of the subject. At least he promised to consider it; and though he meant nothing, though he meant at best to amuse her, perhaps when he was alone he would think of his wife, and more pitifully. She was sure that he would.

'I will go if you wish it,' she said. She would show herself obedient in all things lawful.

'I do wish it,' he answered. 'My daughter must know her way in the world. Go and enjoy yourself, and Lady Worcester will take care of you. And when – when you come back we will talk. We will talk. You will have things to prepare, my dear,' he continued, avoiding her eyes, 'a good deal to prepare, I dare say, since this is sudden. You had better go now. I think that is all.'

CHAPTER XXVI

The Scene in the Hall

ARTHUR VAUGHAN had not been slow to see that he could not step at once into fame; that success in political life could not in these days be attained at a bound. But, had he been less quick, the debate which preceded the passage of the Bill through the Commons must have availed to persuade him.

That their last words of warning to the country, their solemn remonstrances might have more effect, the managers of the Opposition had permitted the third reading to be carried in the manner which has been described. But, that done, they unmasked all their forces, bent on proving that, if in the time to come the Peers threw out the Bill, they did so with a respectable weight, not only of argument, but of public feeling behind them; and that, not only in the country, but in the popular House. All that the bitter invective of Croker, the mingled gibes and predictions of Wetherell, the close and weighty reasoning of Peel, the precedents of Sugden, could do to warn the timid and arouse the prudent, was done. The ancient Chamber which was never again to echo the accents of a debate so great, which stood, indeed, already doomed, as if it could not long survive the order of things of which it had been for generations the centre, had heard, it may be, speeches more lofty, men more eloquent – for whom had it not heard? – but never men more in earnest, or words more keenly barbed by the prejudices of the passing or the aspirations of the coming age. On the one side were those who could see nought but glory in the bygone, nought but peril in change. On the other, those whose strenuous aim it was to make the future redress the wrongs of the past. The former were like children viewing the Armada hangings which tapestried the neighbouring chamber, and seeing only the fair front: the latter resembled the same children picking with soiled fingers at the backing, coarse, dusty, and cobwebbed, which for two hundred years had clung to the roughened masonry.

Vaughan sat through the three nights, brooding darkly on the feats performed before him. If they who fought in the arena were not giants, if the House no longer held a match for Canning and Brougham, the combatants seemed giants to him; for a man's opinion of himself is never far from the opinion which others hold of him. And he soon perceived that a common soldier might as easily step from the ranks and set the battle in order as he, Arthur Vaughan, rise up without further training, and lead the attack or cover the defence. He sat soured and gloomy, a mere spectator; dwelling, even while he admired the flowery periods of Macaulay or the trenchant arguments of Peel, on the wrong done to himself by the disposal of his seat.

It was so like the Whigs, he told himself. On the floor of the House, who so loud as they in defence of the purity of elections, of the people's right to be represented, of the unbiassed vote of the electors? But behind the scenes they were as keenly bent as they had ever been on jobbing a seat here, or neutralizing a seat there – and as careless of the people's rights! It was atrocious, it was shameful! If this were political life, if this were political honesty, he had had enough of it, and too much!

But alas, though he said it in his anger, there was the rub! He had not had, and now he was not likely to have, enough of it. His unpopularity, which he had come to perceive, as a man grows slowly to perceive a frostiness in the air, had sapped his self-confidence and insensibly lowered his claims. He no longer dreamt of rising and outshining the chiefs of his Party. But he still believed that he had it in him to succeed, were time given him. And all through the long hours of the three nights' debate, his thoughts were as often on his wrongs as on the momentous struggle which was passing before his eyes, and for the issue of which the clubs of London were keeping vigil.

But enthusiasm is infectious. When the tellers for the last time walked up to the table, at five o'clock on the morning of September 22nd, with the grey light stealing in to shame the candles and betray the jaded faces – when he and all men knew that for them the end of the great struggle was come – Vaughan waited, breathless, with the rest and strained his ears to catch the result. And when on the announcement peel upon peel of fierce cheering shook the old panels in their frames, and, being taken up by waiting crowds outside, carried the news through the dawn to the very skirts of London – the news that Reform had passed the People's House, and that only the Peers now stood between the country and its desire – he shared the triumph and shouted with the rest, shook hands with the exultant neighbours, and waved his hat, perspiring.

But in his case the feeling of exultation was shortlived; perhaps in the case of many another, who roared himself hoarse and showed a gleeful face to the daylight. Certainly it was something to have taken part in such a scene, the memory of which must survive for generations. He might tell it in days to come to his grandchildren. But for him, personally, it meant that all was over; that here, if the Lords passed the Bill, was the end. A Dissolution must follow, and when the House met again, his place would know him no more. He would be gone, and no man would feel the blank.

Nor were less selfish doubts wanting. As he stood, caught in the press, awaiting his turn to escape from the crowded House, his eyes rested on the scowling faces which dotted the opposite benches, the faces of men who, honestly believing that here, and now, the old Constitution of England had got its death blow, could not hide their chagrin, or their scorn of the foe. He, at any rate, could not view those men without sympathy; without the possibility that they were right weighing on his spirits; without a touch of fear that this might indeed be the beginning of decay, the starting point of that decadence which every generation since Queen Anne's had foreseen. For if many on that side represented no one but themselves, they still represented vast interests, huge incomes, immense taxation. They were those who, if England sank, had most to lose. He, indeed, had given up almost his all that he might stand aloof from them – because he thought them prejudiced, wrong-hearted, unreasonable. But he continued to respect them. And – what if they were right?

Meanwhile the persistent cheering of his friends began to jar on his tired nerves. He seemed to see in it a beginning of disorder, of licence, of revolution, of those evils which the other Party foretold. And then he had small liking for the statistics of the bloodless Hume; and Hume, with his arm about his favourite pillar, was high among the triumphant. Hard by him again was the tall thin form of Orator Hunt, for whom the Bill was too moderate; and the taller, thinner form of Burdett. They, crimson with shouting, were his partners in this; the bedfellows among whom his opinions had cast him.

Thinking such thoughts, he was among the last to leave the House; which he did by way of Westminster Hall. The scene as he descended to the Hall was so striking that he paused on the steps to view it. The nearer half of the great paved space was comparatively bare, but the farther half was occupied by a dense throng of people, held back by a line of the New Police, who were doing all they could to keep a passage for the departing Members. As groups of the latter, after chatting at the upper end, passed, conscious of the greatness of the occasion, down the lane thus formed, bursts of cheering greeted the better-known Reformers. Some of the more forward of those who waited shook hands with them, or patted them on the back; while others cried 'God bless you, sir! Long life to you, sir!' At intervals an angry moan or a volley of hisses marked the passage of a known Tory, or a voice called to these to bid the Lords beware. A few lamps, which had burned through the night, contended pallidly with the growing daylight, and gave to the scene that touch of obscurity, that mingling of light and shadow, under the dusky, far receding roof, which is so necessary to the picturesque.

Vaughan did not suspect that as he paused, looking down upon the Hall, he was himself watched, and by men sore enough at that moment to be glad to wreak their feelings in any direction. As he set his foot on the stone pavement, a group near at hand raised a cry of 'Turncoat! Turncoat!' uplifting their voices so that he could not but hear it. An unrestrained hiss followed; and then, 'Who stole a seat?' cried one of the group.

'And isn't going to keep it?' cried another.

Vaughan turned short at the last words – he had not felt sure that the first were addressed to him. With a hot face, and every fibre in his body tingling with indignation, he stepped up to the group.

'Did you speak to me?' he said.

A man put himself before the others. He was a spendthrift Irish squire, one who had sat for years for a close borough, and for whom the Bill meant duns, bailiffs, a sponging-house, ruin, the loss of all those things which made life tolerable. He was full of spite, and spoiling for a fight with someone, no matter with whom.

'Who are you?' he retorted, confronting our friend with a sneer. 'I have not the pleasure of your acquaintance, sir!'

Vaughan was about to answer him in kind, when he espied

in the middle of the group the pale keen face and grey whiskers of Serjeant Wathen.

'Perhaps you have not,' he replied, 'but that gentleman has!' He pointed to Wathen. 'And, if what was said a moment ago was meant for me, I have the honour to ask for an explanation.'

'Explanation?' a Member in the background cried in a jeering tone. 'Is there need of one?'

Vaughan was no longer red, he was white with anger. 'Who spoke?' he asked, his voice ringing aloud.

The Irishman looked over his shoulder and laughed. 'Right you are, Jerry?' he said. 'I'll not give you up!' And then to Vaughan, 'I did not,' he said rudely. 'For the rest, sir, the Hall is large enough for all. And we don't need heroics here!'

'Your pleasure, however,' Vaughan replied, 'is not my law. Someone of you, I know not which, used words a moment ago which seemed to imply—'

'What, sir?'

'That I obtained my seat by unfair means! And the truth being known to that gentleman' – again he pointed to the Serjeant, in a way which left Wathen anything but comfortable – 'I am sure that he will tell you that the statement—'

'Statement?'

'Statement or imputation, or whatever you please to call it,' Vaughan answered, sticking to his point in spite of interruptions, 'is absolutely unfounded – and false! False sir! And therefore must be retracted.'

'Must, sir?'

'Yes, must,' Vaughan replied – he was no coward. 'Must, if you call yourselves gentlemen. But first, Mr Serjeant,' he continued, fixing Wathen with his eye, 'I will ask you to tell these friends of yours that I did not turn my coat at Chippinge, and that there was nothing in my election which in any degree touched my honour.'

The Serjeant looked flurried. He was of those who love to wound but do not love to fight. And at this moment he wished, from the crown of his head to the soles of his feet, that he had held his tongue. But unluckily, whether the cloud upon Vaughan's reputation were his work or not, he had certainly said more than he liked to remember; worse still, he had said some part of it within the last five minutes in the hearing of those about him. To retract, therefore, was to dub himself a liar; and he sought refuge, the perspiration standing on his brow, in that half-truth which is at once worse than a lie, and safer.

'I must say, Mr Vaughan,' he said, 'that the – the circumstances in which you used the vote given to you by your cousin, and – and the way in which you turned against him after attending a dinner of his supporters—'

'Turned, openly, fairly, and after warning,' Vaughan cried, enraged at the show of justice which the accusation wore. 'And that, sir,' he continued vehemently, 'in pursuance of opinions which I had publicly confessed. More, I allowed myself to be elected only after I had once refused Lord Lansdowne's offer of the seat! And after, only after Sir Robert Vermuyden had so treated me that all ties between us were broken. Serjeant Wathen, I appeal to you, sir! Was that not so?'

'I know nothing of that!' Wathen answered sullenly.

'Nothing? You know nothing of that?' Vaughan cried.

'No,' the Serjeant answered, still more sullenly. 'I know nothing of what passed between you and your cousin. I know only that you were present, as I have said, at a dinner of his supporters on the eve of the election, and that on a sudden, at that dinner, you declared yourself against him – with the result that you were elected by the other side!'

For a moment Vaughan stood glowering at him, struck dumb by his denial, and by the unexpected plausibility, nay, the unexpected strength of the case against him. He was sure that Wathen knew more; he was sure that, if he would, he could say more! He was sure that the man was dishonest. But he did not see how he could prove it, and—

The Irish Member laughed. 'Well, sir,' he said derisively, 'is the explanation, now you've got it, to your mind?'

The taunt stung Vaughan; he took a step forward, The next moment would have seen him commit a foolish action, which could only have led him to Wimbledon Common or Primrose Hill. But in the nick of time a voice stayed him.

'What's this, eh?' it asked, its tone more lugubrious than usual. And Sir Charles Wetherell, who had just descended the stairs from the lobby, turned a dull eye from one disputant to the other. 'Can't you do enough damage with your tongues?' he rumbled. 'Brawl upstairs as much as you like! That's the way to the Woolsack! But you mustn't brawl here!' And the heavy-visaged man, whose humour had again and again conciliated a House which his coarse invective had offended, once more turned from one to the other.

'What is it?' he repeated. 'What's the matter?'

Vaughan hesitated to appeal to him. Then he decided to do so.

'Sir Charles,' he said, 'I will abide by your decision! – though I do not know, indeed, that I ought to take any man's decision on a point which touches my honour!'

'Oh!' Wetherell said, in an inimitable voice. 'Court of Honour, is it?' And he cast a queer look round the circle. 'Court of Honour, eh? Well, I dare say I'm eligible. I dare say I know as much about honour as Brougham about equity! Or the Serjeant there' – Wetherell reddened angrily – 'about law! Or Captain McShane here about his beloved country! Yes,' he continued amid the unconcealed grins of those of the Party whose weak points had escaped, 'you may proceed, I think.'

'You are a friend, Sir Charles,' Vaughan said, in a voice which quivered with anxiety, 'you are a friend of Sir Robert Vermuyden?'

'Well, I won't deny him until I know more!' Wetherell answered quaintly. 'What of it?'

'You know what occurred at Chippinge before the election?'

'None better. I was there.'

'And what passed between Sir Robert Vermuyden and me?' Vaughan continued eagerly. 'Before the election?'

'I think I do,' Wetherell answered. 'In the main, I do.'

'Then I appeal to you. You are opposed to me in politics, sir, but you will do me justice. These gentlemen have thought fit to brand me as a turncoat; and worse, as one who was – who was elected' – he could scarcely speak for passion – 'in opposition to my relative's candidates under circumstances dishonourable to me!'

'Indeed? Indeed? That is serious.'

'And I ask you, sir, is there a word of truth in that charge?'

Wetherell had lowered his eyes to the pavement. He appeared to consider the matter for a moment or two; then he shook his head.

'Not a word,' he said ponderously.

'You bear me out, sir?'

'Quite,' the other answered, as he took out his snuff box. 'To tell you the truth, gentlemen,' he continued in the same melancholy tone, 'Mr Vaughan was fool enough to quarrel with his bread and butter for the sake of the most worthless, damnable, and mistaken convictions any man ever held! That's the truth. He showed himself, I'll swear to it, a very perfect fool; but an honourable and an honest fool – and that's a rare thing. I see none here.'

No one laughed at the gibe, and he turned to Vaughan, who stood relieved, indeed, but stiff and uncomfortable, uncertain what to do next.

'I'll take your arm,' he said. 'I've saved you,' he continued, with cool contempt, 'from the ragged regiment on my side. Do you take me safe,' with a glance towards the lower end of the Hall, 'through your ragged regiment outside, my lad!'

Vaughan understood the generous motive which underlay the invitation. But for a moment he hung back.

'I am your debtor, Sir Charles,' he said, 'as long as I live. But I would like to know before I go,' and he raised his head, with a look worthy of Sir Robert, 'whether these gentlemen are satisfied. If not—'

'Oh, perfectly,' the Serjeant cried hurriedly. 'Perfectly!' And he muttered something about being glad – their explanation – satisfactory.

But the Irish Member stepped up and held out his hand.

'Faith,' he said, 'there's no man whose word I'd take before Sir Charles's. There's no hiatus in his honour, whatever may be said of his breeches. That's one for you,' he added, addressing Wetherell. 'I owed you one, my boy.' And then he continued, turning to Vaughan, 'There's my hand, sir! I apologize. You're a man of honour, and it's mistaken we were.'

'I am obliged to you for your candour,' Vaughan replied.

Half a dozen others raised their hats to him, or shook hands with him frankly. The Serjeant did so at last, less frankly. But Vaughan saw that he was cowed. Wetherell was Sir Robert Vermuyden's friend, the Serjeant was Sir Robert's nominee. So the young man pushed his triumph no further. With a feeling of gratitude, too deep for words, he offered his arm to Sir Charles, and went down the Hall in his company.

By this time the crowd at the lower end had carried their joy and their horse-play elsewhere; and no attempt was made – Vaughan only wished an attempt had been made – to molest Wetherell. They walked side by side across the yard to Parliament Street, as the first sunshine of the day fell on the river. Flocks of gulls were swinging to and fro in the clear air above the water, and dumb barges were floating up with the tide. The hubbub had passed from the neighbourhood of the Hall. Far away a score of coaches were speeding through the suburbs, bearing to market town and busy city – ay, and to village greens, where the news was awaited as eagerly – the tidings that the Bill had passed the Lower House.

Sir Charles walked a short distance in silence. Then, 'I thought some notion of the kind was abroad,' he said. 'It's as well this happened. What are you going to do about your seat if the Bill pass, young man?'

'I am told that it is pre-emptied,' Vaughan answered, in a tone between jest and earnest.

'It is. That's true. But—'

'What ought I to do?'

'You should see your own side about it,' Wetherell answered gruffly. 'I can't say more than that. I can't advise you.'

'I am obliged to you for so much.'

'You should be!' Wetherell retorted in a peculiar tone. And with an oath and a vehement gesture he disengaged his arm. He halted, he wheeled about, he pointed with a shaking hand to the towers of the Abbey, which, two hundred paces from them, rose against the blue, beatified by the morning sunshine. 'If I said,' he cried, '"Batter down those walls, undig the dead, away with every hoary thing of time, the present and the future are enough, and we, the generation that burns the mummies which three thousand years have spared – we are wiser than all our forebears," what would you say? You would call me mad. Yet what are you doing? Ay, you, you among the rest!' he continued in a voice hoarse with emotion. 'The building that our fathers built, patiently through many hundred years, adding a little here and there – the building that Hampden, and Shrewsbury, and Walpole, Chatham and his son, and Canning, and many another tended reverently, repairing in parts as time required, you, you, who think you know more than all who have gone before you – hurry in ruin to the ground. That you may build your own building, built in a day, to suit the day, and to perish with the day! Oh, mad! Mad! Mad! Ay.

> *'Hostis habet muros; ruit alta a culmine Troja*
> *Sat patriae Priamoque datum; si Pergama lingua*
> *Defendi possent, etiam hac defensa fuissent!'*

His voice quavered on the last accent, and his chin sank on his breast. He turned wearily and resumed his course. When Vaughan, who did not venture to address him again, parted from him in silence at the door of his house, the old man's pendulous lip quivered, and a single tear ran down his cheek.

CHAPTER XXVII

Wicked Shifts

IT WAS with a lighter heart that Vaughan walked on to Bury Street. There were still, it seemed, faith and honour in the world, and some men who could be trusted. But if he expected much to come of this, if he expected to be received with an ovation on his next appearance at Westminster, he was doomed to disappointment. Wetherell's defence convinced those who heard it; and in time, no doubt, passing from mouth to mouth, would improve the young Member's relations, not only on the floor of the House, but in the lobbies and at Bellamy's. But the English are not dramatic. They have no love for scenes. And no one of those whose silence or whose cat-calls had wronged him thought fit to take his hand in cold blood, and ask his pardon; nor did any Don Quixote cast down a glove in Westminster Hall, and offer to do battle with his traducers. The manner of one man became a shade more cordial; another spoke where he would have nodded. And if Vaughan had risen at this time to speak on any question which he understood, he would have been heard upon his merits.

But the change, slow though genial, like the breaking-up of an English frost, came too late to do him much service. With the transfer of the Bill to the House of Lords, public interest deserted the Commons. They sat, indeed, through the month of September, to the horror of many a country gentleman, who saw in this the herald of evil days; and they debated after a fashion. But the attendance was sparse, and the thoughts and hopes of all men were in another place. Vaughan saw that, for all the reputation he could now make, the Dissolution might be come already. And with this, and the emptiness of his heart, from which he could no more put the craving for his mistress than he could dismiss her image from the retina of his mind, he was very miserable. The void left by love was rendered worse by the void left unsatisfied by ambition. Mary's haunting face was with him at his rising, and went with him to his pillow; her little hand was often on his sleeve, her eyes often pleaded to his. In his lonely rooms he would pace the floor feverishly, savagely, pestering himself with what might have been; kicking the furniture from his path, and – and hating her. For the idea of marriage, once closely presented to man or woman, leaves neither unchanged, leaves neither as it found them, however quickly it be put aside.

Still it was not possible for one who sprang from the governing classes, and was gifted with political instincts, to witness the excitement which moved the country during those weeks of September and the early days of October without feeling his own blood stirred; without sharing to some extent the exhilaration with which the adventurous view the approach of adventures. What would the Peers do? All England was asking that question. At Crockford's, in the little supper-room, or at the French hazard table, men turned to put it, and to hear the answer. At White's and Boodle's, in the hall of the Athenaeum, as they walked before Apsley House, or under the gas lamps of Pall Mall, men asked that question again and again. It shared with Pasta and the slow-coming cholera – which none the less was coming – the chit-chat of drawing-rooms; and with the next prize fight or with ridicule of the New Police, the wrangling debates of every tavern and post-house. Would the Peers throw out the Bill? Would they – would those doting old Bishops in particular – dare to thwart the People's Will? Would they dare to withhold the franchise from Birmingham and Manchester, Leeds and Sheffield? On this husbands took one side, wives the other, families quarrelled. What Croker thought, what Lord Grey threatened, what the Duke had let drop, what Brougham had boasted, how Lady Lyndhurst had sneered, or her husband retorted, what the Queen wished – scraps such as these were tossed from mouth to mouth, greedily received, carried far into the country, and, changed beyond recognition, were repeated in awe-struck ears, in county ballrooms and at sessions.

One member of the Privy Council who had left his party on the Bill, and whose vote, it was thought, had turned a division, shot himself. And many another, it was whispered, was never the same after the strain of those days.

For far more hung upon the Lord's decision than the mere fate of the Bill. If they threw it out, what would the Ministry do? And, more momentous still, and looming larger in the minds of men, what would the country do? What would Birmingham and Sheffield, Manchester and Leeds do? What would they do?

Lord Grey, strong in the King's support, would persevere, said some. He would bring in the Bill again, and create peers in number sufficient to carry it. And Macaulay's squib was flung from club to club, and meeting to meeting, until it reached the streets:

What, though now opposed I be,
Twenty peers shall carry me!
If twenty won't, thirty will,
For I am his Majesty's bouncing Bill.

Ay, his Majesty's Bill, God bless him! His Majesty's own Bill! Hurrah for Lord Grey! Hurrah for Brougham! Hurrah for Lord John, and down with the Bishops! So the word flew from mouth to mouth in the streets, so errand boys yelled it under the windows of London House in St James's Square – ay, and wherever aproned legs might be supposed to congregate.

But others maintained that Lord Grey would resign, and let the consequences fall on the heads of those who opposed the People's Will. Those consequences, it was whispered, and not by the timid and the rich only, spelled Revolution! Revolution, red and anarchical, was at hand, said many. Was not Scotland ready to rise? Was not the Political Union of Birmingham threatening to pay no taxes? Were not the Political Unions everywhere growling and lashing their sides? The winter was coming, and there would be fires by night and drillings by day, as there had been during the previous autumn. Through the long dark nights there would be fear and trembling, and barring of doors, and waiting for the judgement to come. And then, some morning, the crackling sound of musketry would awaken Pall Mall and Mayfair, the mob would march upon the Tower and Newgate, the streets would run blood, and the guillotine would rise in Leicester Square or Finsbury Fields.

So widely were these fears spread, fostered as they were by both Parties – by the Tories for the purpose of proving whither Reform was leading the country, by the Whigs to show to what the obstinacy of the borough-mongers was driving it – that few were proof against them. So few, that when the Bill was rejected by the Lords in the early morning of Saturday, October the 8th, the Tory peers, from Lord Eldon downwards, though they had not shrunk from doing their duty, could hardly be made to believe that they were at liberty to go to their homes unscathed.

They did so, however. But the first mutterings of the storm soon made themselves heard. Within twenty-four hours the hearts of many failed them for fear. The Funds fell at once. The journals appeared in mourning borders. In many towns the bells were tolled and the shops were shut. The mob of Nottingham rose and burned the Castle, and fired the house of an unpopular squire. The mob of Derby besieged the gaol and released the prisoners. At Darlington, Lord Tankerville narrowly escaped with his life; Lord Londonderry was attacked and left for dead; no bishop dared to wear his apron in public. Everywhere rose the cry of 'No Taxes!' Finally the rabble rose in immense numbers, paraded the West End of London, broke the windows of many peers, assaulted others, and were only driven from Apsley House by the timely arrival of the Life Guards. The country, amazed and shaken from end to end, seemed to be already in the grip of rebellion; with the result that within the week the very Tories hastened to beg Lord Grey to retain office. Even the King, it was supposed, was shaken, and his famous distich, his one contribution to the poetry of his country,

I consider Dissolution
Tantamount to Revolution,

found admirers for its truth, if not for its beauty.

Such a ferment could not but occupy Vaughan's mind and divert his thoughts from his own troubles, even from thoughts of Mary. Every day there was news; every day, in the opinion of many, the sky grew darker. But though the rejection of the Bill promised him a second session in the House, and many who sat for close boroughs chuckled over the respite, he was ill-content with a hand-to-mouth life. He saw that the Bill must pass eventually. He did not believe that there would be a revolution. It was clear that his only chance lay in following Wetherell's advice, and laying his case before one of his chiefs.

Some days after the division he happened on an opportunity. He was walking down Parliament Street when he came on a scene much of a piece with the unrest of the time. A crowd was pouring out of Downing Street, and in the van of the rabble he espied the tall ungainly figure of no less a man than Lord Brougham. Abreast of the Chancellor, but keeping himself to the wall as if he desired to dissociate himself from the demonstration, walked another tall figure, also in black, with shepherd's plaid trousers. A second glance informed Vaughan that this was no other than the Mr Cornelius who had been present at his interview with Brougham; and, accepting the omen, he made up to the Chancellor just as the latter halted to rid himself of the ragged tail, which had perhaps been more pleasing to his vanity in the smaller streets.

'My friends,' Brougham cried, checking with his hand the ragamuffins' shrill attempt at a cheer, 'I am obliged to you for your approval, but I beg leave to bid you good day. Assemblages such as these are in these times of doubt—'

'Disgusting!' Cornelius muttered audibly, wrinkling his nose as he eyed them over his high cravat.

'Are apt to cause disorder,' the Chancellor continued, smiling. 'Rest assured that your friends, of whom, if I am the highest in office, I am not the least in good will, will not desert you.'

'Hurrah! God bless you, my lord! Hurrah!' cried the tatterdemalions in various tones more or less drunken. And some held out their caps. 'Hurrah! If your lordship would have the kindness—'

'Disgusting!' repeated Cornelius, wheeling about.

Vaughan seized the opportunity to intervene. 'May I,' he said, raising his hat and addressing the Chancellor as he turned, 'consult you, my lord, for two minutes as you walk?'

Brougham started on finding a gentleman of his appearance at his elbow, and looked as if he were somewhat ashamed of the guise in which he had been detected.

'Ah!' he said. 'Mr – Mr Vaughan? To be sure! Oh yes – yes, you can speak to me. Certainly. What can I do for you? It is,' he added, with affected humility, 'my business to serve.'

Vaughan looked doubtfully at Mr Cornelius, who raised his hat.

'I have no secrets from Mr Cornelius,' said the Chancellor pleasantly. And then, with a backward nod and a tinge of colour in his cheek, 'Gratifying, but troublesome,' he continued. 'Eh? Very troublesome these demonstrations! Ah, I often long for the old days when I could walk out of Westminster Hall, with my bag and my umbrella, and no one the wiser.'

'Those days are far back, my lord,' Vaughan said politely.

'Ah, well! Ah, well! Perhaps so.' They were walking on by this time. 'I can't say that since the Queen's trial I've known much privacy. However, it is something that those whom one serves are grateful. They—'

'Cry "Hosanna" today,' Cornelius muttered gruffly, with his eyes fixed steadily before him, 'and "Crucify him" tomorrow.'

'Cynic!' said the Chancellor, with unabated good humour. 'But even you cannot deny that they are better employed in cheering their friends than in breaches of the peace? Not that,' cocking his eye at Vaughan, with a whimsical expression of confidence, 'a little disorder here and there? – eh, Mr Vaughan, though to be deplored, and by no one more than by one in my position, has not its uses. Were there no apprehension of mob rule, how many borough-mongers, think you, would vote with us? How many waverers, like my lords Harrowby and Wharncliffe, would waver? And how, if we have no little ebullitions here and there, are we to know that the people are in earnest? That they are not grown lukewarm? That Wetherell is not right in his statement – of which he'll hear more than he will like at Bristol, or I am mistaken – that there is a Tory reaction, and ebb in the tide that so far has carried us bravely? But, of course,' he added, with a faint smile, 'God forbid that we should encourage violence.'

'Amen!' said Mr Cornelius; and sniffed in a very peculiar manner.

'Nevertheless to discern that camomile,' the Chancellor continued gaily, 'though bitter today, makes us better tomorrow, is a different thing from—'

'Administering a dose,' Vaughan laughed, falling into the great man's humour.

'To be sure. But enough of that. Now I think of it, Mr Vaughan,' he continued, looking at his companion, 'I have not had the pleasure of seeing you since – but I need not remind you of the occasion. You've had good cause to remember it. Yes, yes,' he went on, with voluble complacency – he was walking as well as talking very fast – 'I seldom speak without meaning, or interfere without result. I knew well what would come of it. It was not for nothing, Mr Vaughan, that I got down our Borough List and asked you if you had not thought of entering the House. The spark – and tinder! For there you are, in the House!'

'Yes,' Vaughan replied, astonished at the coolness with which the other unveiled, and even took credit for, the petty intrigue of six months back. 'But—'

'But,' Brougham said, taking him up with a laughing glance, 'you are not yet on the Treasury Bench, eh?'

'No, not yet,' Vaughan answered.

'Ah, well, time and patience and Bellamy's chops, Mr Vaughan, will carry you far, I am sure.'

'It is on that subject – the subject of time – I venture to trouble your lordship.'

The Chancellor's lumpish but remarkably mobile features underwent a change. Caught in a complacent, vain humour, he had forgotten a thing which, with Vaughan's last words, recurred to him.

'Yes,' he said slowly, 'yes, Mr Vaughan.' But the timbre of that marvellously flexible voice, with which he boasted that he could whisper so as to be heard to the very door of the House of Commons, was altered. 'Yes, what is it, pray?'

'It is time I require,' Vaughan answered. 'In a word, I have done some service, yeoman service, my lord. And I think that I ought not to be cast aside by the Party in whose interests I was returned, and with whose objects I am in sympathy.'

'Cast aside? Tut, tut! What do you mean?'

'I am told that, though the borough for which I sit will continue to return one Member, I shall not have the support of the Party in retaining my seat.'

'Indeed! Indeed!' Brougham answered in a serious tone. 'Is it so? I am sorry to hear that.'

'But—'

'Very sorry, Mr Vaughan.'

'But, with submission, my lord, it is something more than sorrow I seek,' Vaughan rejoined, too sore to hide his feelings. 'You have owned very candidly that I derived from you the impulse which has carried me so far. Is it unreasonable if I venture to turn to you, when advised to see one of the chiefs of my Party?'

'Who,' Brougham asked, with a quick look, 'gave you that advice, Mr Vaughan?'

'Sir Charles Wetherell.'

'Um!' the exclamation came through pinched lips; and

Brougham stood. They had crossed Piccadilly and Berkeley Square, and had reached the corner of Hill Street, where, at No 5, he lived.

'I repeat, my lord,' Vaughan continued, 'is it unreasonable if I apply to you in these circumstances, rather—'

'Rather than to one of the whips?' Brougham said dryly.

'Yes.'

'But I know nothing of the matter, Mr Vaughan.'

But the young man was in no mood to put up with subterfuges. If the other did not know, he should know. The Chancellor had been all-powerful, it seemed, to bring him in. Was he powerless to keep him in?

'There is a compact, I am told,' he said, 'under which the seat is to be surrendered – for this turn at any rate – to my cousin's nominee. To a Tory.'

Brougham shrugged his shoulders, and looked at Mr Cornelius.

'Dear me, dear me!' he said. 'That's not a thing of which I can approve. Far from it, far from it. But you must see, Mr Vaughan, that I cannot meddle, in my position, with arrangements of that kind. Impossible, my dear sir, clearly impossible!'

Vaughan stared; and with some spirit and more temper found his retort.

'But the spark, my lord? I'm sure you won't forget the spark,' he said.

For an instant a gleam of fun shone in the Chancellor's eyes; then he was funereal again.

'Before the Bill, and after the Bill, are two things,' he said dryly. 'Before the Bill all is, all was, impure; and in an impure medium – you understand me, I am sure? You are scientific. But after the Bill – to ask me, who, in my humble measure, Mr Vaughan, may call myself its prime cause – to ask me to infringe its first principles by interposing between the electors and their rights, to ask me to use an influence which cannot be held legitimate – no, Mr Vaughan, no!' He shook his head solemnly and finally. And then to Mr Cornelius: 'Yes, I am coming, Mr Cornelius,' he said. 'I know I am late.'

'I can wait,' said Mr Cornelius.

'But I cannot. Good day, Mr Vaughan, good day,' Brougham

repeated, refusing to see the young man's ill-humour. 'I am sorry that I cannot help you. Or, stay,' he continued, halting in the act of turning away, 'one minute! I gather that you are a friend of Sir Charles Wetherell's?'

'He has been a friend to me,' Vaughan replied sullenly.

'Ah, well, he is going to Bristol to hold his sessions on the 29th, I think. Go with him. He hates me like poison, but I would not have a hair of his head injured. We have been warned that there will be trouble, and we are taking steps; but an able-bodied young man by his side will be no bad thing. And, upon my honour,' he continued, eyeing Vaughan with impudent frankness, impudent in view of all that had gone before, 'upon my honour, I am beginning to think that we spoiled a good soldier when we— eh!'

'The spark,' Mr Cornelius muttered grimly.

'Good day, my lord,' Vaughan cried.

His blood was boiling, and he turned and strode away, scarcely smothering an execration. The two, who did not appear to be in a hurry after all, remained looking after him; and presently Mr Cornelius smiled.

'What amuses you?' Brougham asked, with a certain petulance; for at bottom, and in cases where no rivalry existed, he was good-natured, and in his heart he was sorry for the young man. But, then, if one began to think of the pawn's feelings, the game he was playing would be spoiled! 'What is it?'

'I was thinking,' Mr Cornelius answered slowly, 'of purity.' He sniffed. 'And the Whigs!'

Meanwhile Arthur Vaughan was striding down Bruton Street with every angry passion up in arms. He was too clever to be tricked twice, and he saw precisely what had happened. Brougham – well, well was he called Wicked Shifts! – reviewing the Borough List before the General Election, had let his eyes fall on Sir Robert's seats at Chippinge, and, looking about with his customary audacity for a means of snatching them, had alighted on him, and used him for a tool. Now he was of no further use; and, as the loss of his expectations rendered it needless to temporize with him, he was tossed aside.

And this was the game of politics which he had yearned to play! This was the party whose zeal for the purity of elections and the improvement of all classes he had shared, and out of loyalty to which he had sacrificed a fortune! He strode along the crowded pavement of Bond Street – it was the fashionable hour of the afternoon, and the political excitement kept London full – his head high, his face flushed; and unconsciously, as he shouldered the people to right and left, he swore aloud.

As he spoke, regardless in his anger of the scene about him, his gaze pierced for an instant the medley of gay bonnets and smiling faces, moving chariots, and waiting footmen, which even in those days filled Bond Street – and met another pair of eyes.

The encounter lasted for a second only. Then half a dozen heads and a parasol intervened; and then – in another second – he was abreast of the carriage in which Mary Vermuyden sat, her face the prettiest and her bonnet the daintiest – Lady Worcester had seen to that – of all the faces and all the bonnets in Bond Street that day. The landau in which she sat was stationary at the edge of the pavement; and on the farther side of her reposed a lady of kind face and ample figure.

For an instant their eyes met again; and Mary's colour, which had fled, returned in a flood of crimson, covering brow and cheeks. She leaned from the carriage and held out her white-gloved hand.

'Mr Vaughan!' she said, and he might have read in her face, had he chosen, the sweetest and tenderest appeal. 'Mr Vaughan!'

But the moment was unlucky; the devil had possession of him. He raised his hat and passed on – passed on wilfully. He fancied – afterwards, that is, he fancied – that she had risen, after he had passed, to her feet, and called him a third time in a voice at which the convenances of Bond Street could only wink. But he went on; he heard, but he went on. He told himself that all was of a piece. Men and women were all alike. He was a fool who trusted any, believed in any, loved any.

CHAPTER XXVIII

Once More, Tantivy!

VAUGHAN HAD been sore at heart before the meeting in Parliament Street. After that meeting he was in a mood to take any step which promised to salve his self-esteem. The Chancellor, Lord Lansdowne, Sir Robert, and – and Mary, all, he told himself, were against him. But they should not crush him. He would prove to them that he was no negligible quantity. Parliament was prorogued; the Long Vacation was far advanced; the world, detained beyond its time, was hurrying out of Town. He, too, would go out of Town; and he would go to Chippinge. There, in defiance alike of his cousin and the Bowood interest, he would throw himself upon the people. He would address himself to those whom the Bill enfranchised, he would appeal to the future electors of Chippinge, he would ask them whether the will of their great neighbours was to prevail, and the claims of service and of gratitude were to go for nothing. Surely at this time of day the answer could not be adverse!

True, this course matched ill with the notions of Party discipline which prevailed; with the family traditions in which he had been reared it was a breach still more complete. But in his present mood Vaughan liked his plan the better for this. Henceforth he would be iron, he would be adamant! And only by a little thing did he betray that under the iron and under the adamant he carried an aching heart. When he came to book his place, deliberately, wilfully, he chose to travel by the Bath road and the White Lion coach, though he could have gone at least as conveniently by another coach and another route. Thus have men ever, since they felt the pangs of love, rejoiced to press the dart more deeply in the wound.

A dark October morning was brooding over the West End when he crossed Piccadilly to take his place outside the White Horse Cellar. Now, as on that distant day in April, when the car of rosy-fingered love had awaited him ignorant, the coaches stood one behind the other in a long line before the low-browed windows of the office. But how different was all else! Today the lamps were lighted and flickered on wet pavements, the streets were windy and desolate, the day had barely broken above the wet roofs, and on all a steady rain was falling. The watermen went to and fro with sacks about their shoulders, and the guards, bustling from the office with their way-bills and the late parcels, were short of temper and curt of tongue. The shivering passengers, cloaked to the eyes in box-coats and wrap-rascals, climbed silently and sullenly to the roof, and there sat shrugging their shoulders to their ears. Vaughan, who had secured a place beside the driver, cast an eye on all, on the long dark vista of the street, on the few shivering passengers; and he found the change fitting. Let it rain, let it blow, let the sun rise niggardly behind a mask of clouds! Let the world wear its true face! He cared not how discordantly the guard's horn sounded, nor how the coachman swore at his cattle, nor how the mud splashed up, as two minutes after time they jolted and rattled and bumped down the slope and through the dingy narrows of Knightsbridge.

Perhaps to please him, the rain fell more heavily as the light broadened and the coach passed through Kensington turnpike. The passengers, crouching inside their wraps, looked miserably from under dripping umbrellas on a wet Hammersmith, and a wetter Brentford. Now the coach ploughed through deep mud, now it rolled silently over a bed of chestnut or sycamore leaves which the first frost of autumn had brought down. Swish, swash, it splashed through a rivulet. It was full daylight now; it had been daylight an hour. And, at last, joyous sight, pleasant even to the misanthrope on the box-seat, not far in front, through a curtain of mist and rain, loomed Maidenhead – and breakfast!

The up night-coach, retarded twenty minutes by the weather, rattled up to the door at the same moment. Vaughan foresaw that there would be a contest for seats at the table, and, without waiting for the ladder, he swung himself to the ground, and entered the house. Hastily doffing his streaming overcoats, he made for the coffee-room, where roaring fires and a plentiful table awaited the travellers. In two minutes he was served, and isolated by his gloomy thoughts and almost unconscious of the crowded room and the clatter of plates, he was eating his breakfast when his next-door neighbour accosted him.

'Beg your pardon, sir,' he said in a meek voice. 'Are you going to Bristol, sir?'

Vaughan looked at the speaker, a decent, clean-shaven person in a black high-collared coat, and a limp white neckcloth. The man's face seemed familiar, and Vaughan asked if he knew him.

'You've seen me in the Lobby, sir,' the other answered, fidgeting in his humility. 'I'm Sir Charles Wetherell's clerk, sir.'

'Ah! To be sure!' Vaughan replied. 'I thought I knew your face. Sir Charles opens the Assizes tomorrow?'

'Yes, sir, if they will let him. Do you think that there is danger, Mr Vaughan?'

'Danger?' Vaughan answered with a smile. 'No serious danger.'

'The Government did not wish him to go, sir.'

'Oh, I don't believe that,' Vaughan said.

'Well, the Corporation didn't, for certain, sir,' the man persisted in a low voice. 'They wanted him to postpone the Assizes. But he doesn't know what fear is. And now the Government's ordered troops to Bristol, and I'm afraid that'll make 'em worse. They're so set against him for saying that Bristol was no longer for the Bill. And they're a desperate rough lot, sir, down by the docks!'

'So I've heard,' Vaughan said. 'But you may be sure that the authorities will see that Sir Charles is well guarded!'

The clerk said nothing to that, although it was clear that he was far from convinced, or easy. And Vaughan returned to his thoughts. But by-and-by it chanced that as he raised his eyes he met those of a girl who was passing his table on her way from the room; and he remembered with a pang how Mary had passed his table and looked at him, and blushed; and how his heart had jumped at the sight. Why, there was the very waiting-maid who had gone out with her. And there, where the April sun had shone on her through the window, she had sat. And there, three places only from his present seat, he had sat himself. Three seats only – and yet how changed was all! The unmanly tears rose very near to his eyes as he thought of it.

He sat so long brooding over this, in that mood in which a man recks little of time, or of what befalls him, that the guard had to summon him. And even then, as he donned his coats, with the 'boots' fussing about him, and the coachman grumbling at the delay, his memory was busy with that morning. There, in the porch, he had stood and heard the young waterman praise her looks! And there Cooke had stood and denounced the Reform placard! And there—

'Let go!' growled the coachman, losing patience at last. 'The gentleman's not coming!'

'I'm coming,' he answered curtly.

And crossing the pavement in two strides, he swung himself up hand-over-hand, as the stablemen released the horses. The coach started as his foot left the box of the wheel. And something else started – furiously.

His heart. For in the place behind the coachman, in the very seat which Mary Smith had occupied on that far-off April morning, sat Mary Vermuyden! For an infinitely small fraction of a second, as he turned himself to drop into his seat, his eyes swept her face. The rain had ceased to fall, the umbrellas were furled; for that infinitely short space his eyes rested on her features. Then his back was turned to her.

Her eyes had been fixed elsewhere, her face had been cold – she had not seen him. So much, in the confused pounding rush of his thoughts, as he sat tingling in every inch of his frame, he could remember; nothing else except that in lieu of the plain Quaker-like dress which Mary Smith had worn – oh, dress to be remembered! – she was wearing rich furs, with a great muff and a small hat of sable, and was Mary Smith no longer.

Probably she had been there from the start, seated behind him under cover of the rain and the umbrellas. If so – and he remembered that that seat had been occupied when he got to his place – she had perceived his coming, had seen him mount, had been aware of him from the first. She could see him now, watch every movement, read his self-consciousness in the stiff pose of his head, perceive the rush of colour which dyed his ears and neck.

And he was planted there, he could not escape. And he

suffered. Asked beforehand, he would have said that his uppermost feeling in such circumstances would be resentment. But, in fact, he could think of nothing except that meeting in Bond Street, and the rudeness with which he had treated her. If he had not refused to speak to her, if he had not passed her by, rejecting her hand with disdain, he might have been his own master now; he would have been free to speak, or free to be silent, as he pleased. And she who had treated him so ill would have been the one to suffer. But, as it was, he was hot all over. The intolerable *gêne* of the situation rested on him and weighed him down.

Until the coachman, calling his attention to a passing waggon, broke the spell and freed his thoughts. After that he began to feel a little of the wonder which the coincidence demanded. How came she in the same seat, on the same coach, that coach on which they had travelled together? He remembered that a manservant shared the hind seat with the clerk who had spoken to him; and probably the middle-aged woman who sat with her was her maid. But he knew Sir Robert well enough to be sure that he would not countenance her journeying, even with this attendance, on a public vehicle; therefore, she must be doing it without her father's knowledge, in pursuance of some whim of her own. Could it be that she, too, wished to revive the bitter-sweet of recollection, the aftermath of that April day! And, to do so, had gone out of her way to travel on this cold wet morning on the same coach, which six months before had brought them together?

If so, she must love him in spite of all. And in that case, what must her feelings have been when she saw him take his place? What, when she knew that she would not taste the bitter-sweet alone, but in his company? What, when she foresaw that through the day she would not pass a single thing of all those well-remembered things, that milestone which he had pointed out to her, that baiting-house of which she had asked the name, that stone bridge with the hundred balustrades which they had crossed in the gloaming – that her eyes would not alight on one of these without another heart answering to every throb of hers, and another breast aching as hers ached.

At that thought a subtle attraction, almost irresistible, drew him to her, and he could have cried to her, under the pain of separation. For it was all true. Before his eyes those things were passing. There was the milestone which he had pointed out to her. And there the ruined inn. And here were the streets of Reading opening before them, and the market-place, and the Bear Inn, where he had saved her from injury, perhaps from death.

They were out of the town, they were clear of the houses, and he had not looked, he had not been able to look at her. Her weakness, her inconstancy deserved their punishment: but for all her fortune, to recover all that he had lost and she had gained, he would not have looked at her there. Yet, while the coach changed horses in the square before the Bear, he had had a glimpse of her – reflected in the window of a shop; and he had marked with greedy eyes each line of her figure and seen that she had wound a veil round her face and hat, so that, whatever her emotions, she might defy curious eyes. And yet, as far as he was concerned, she had done it in vain. The veil could not hide her agitation, could not mask the strained rigidity of her pose, or the convulsive force with which one hand gripped the other in her lap.

Well, that was over, thank God! For he had as soon seen a woman beaten. The town was behind them; Newbury was not far in front. And now with shame he began to enjoy her presence, her nearness to him, the thought that her eyes were on him and her thoughts full of him, and that if he stretched out his hand he could touch her; that there was that between them, that there must always be that between them, which time could not destroy. The coach was loaded, but for him it carried her only: and for Mary he was sure that he filled the landscape were it as wide as that which, west of Newbury, reveals to the admiring traveller the wide vale of the Kennet. He thrilled at the thought; and the coachman asked if he were cold. But he was far from cold, for he knew that she too trembled, she, too, thrilled. And a foolish exultation possessed him. He had hungry thoughts of her nearness, and her beauty; and insane plans of snatching her to his breast when she left the coach, and covering her with kisses though a hundred looked on. He might suffer for it, he would deserve to suffer for it, it would be an intolerable outrage. But he would have kissed her, he would have held her to his heart. Nothing could undo that.

Yet it was only in fancy that he was bold, for he did not dare to look at her even now. And when they came to Marlborough, and drew up at the door of the Castle Inn, where west-bound travellers dined, he descended hurriedly and went into the coffee-room to secure a place in a corner – whence he might see her enter without meeting her eyes.

But she did not enter the house, soon or late. And a vain man might have thought that she was not only bent on doing everything which she had done on the former journey, but that it was not without intention that she remained alone on the coach exposed to his daring – if he chose to dare. Some, indeed, of his fellow-passengers wandered out before the time, and on the pretence of examining the façade of the handsome old house, shot sidelong glances at the young lady who, wrapped in her furs and veiled to the throat, sat motionless in the keen October air. But Vaughan was not one of these; nor was he vain. When he found that she did not come in, he decided that she would not meet him – that she remained on the coach rather than sit in his company; and, forgetting the overture in Bond Street, he remembered only her fickleness and weakness. He fell to the depths. She had never loved him, never, never!

On that he almost made up his mind to stay there, and to go on by the next coach. His presence must be hateful to her, a misery, a torment. It was bad enough to force her to remain exposed to the weather while others dined; it would be monstrous to go on and continue to make her wretched.

But, before the time for leaving came, he changed his mind, and he went out, feeling cowed and looking hard. He could not mount without seeing her out of the corner of his eye; but the veil masked all, and left him no wiser. The sun had burst through the clouds, and the sky above the curving line of the downs was blue. But the October air was still chilly, and he heard the maid fussing about her, and wrapping her up more warmly. Well, it mattered little. At Chippenham, the carriage with its pomp of postillions and outriders – Sir

Robert was particular about such things – would meet her; and he would see her no more.

His pride weakened at that thought. She could never be anything to him now; he had no longer the least notion of kissing her. But at Chippenham, before she passed out of his life, he would speak to her. Yes, he would speak. He did not know what he would say, but he would not part from her in anger. He would tell her that, and bid her goodbye. Later, he would be glad to remember that they had parted in that way, and that he had forgiven!

While he thought of it they fell swiftly from the lip of the downs, and rattling over the narrow bridge and through the stonebuilt streets of Calne, were out again on the Bath road. After that, though they took Black Dog Hill at a slow pace, they seemed to be at Chippenham in a twinkling. Before he could calm his thoughts the coach was rattling between houses, and the wide straggling street was opening before them, and the group assembled in front of the Angel to see the coach arrive was scattered to right and left.

A glance told him that there was no carriage-and-four in waiting. And because his heart was jumping so foolishly he was glad to put off the moment of speaking to her. She would go into the house and wait for a carriage, and when the coach, with its bustle and its many eyes, had gone its way, he would be able to speak to her.

Accordingly, the moment the coach stopped he descended and hastened into the house. He sent out the 'boots' for his valise and betook himself to the bar-parlour, where he called for something and jested with the smiling landlady, who came herself to attend upon him. He kept his back to the door which Mary must pass to ascend the stairs, for well he knew the parlour of honour to which she would be ushered. But though he listened keenly for the rustle of her skirts, a couple of minutes passed and he heard nothing.

'You are not going on, sir?' the landlady asked. She knew too much of the family politics to ask pointblank if he were going to Chippinge.

'No,' he replied; 'no, I' – his attention wandered – 'I am not.'

'I hope we may have the honour of keeping you tonight, sir?' she said.

'Yes, I' – was that the coach starting? – 'I think I shall stay the night.' And then, 'Sir Robert's carriage is not here?' he asked, setting down his glass.

'No, sir. But two gentlemen have just driven in from Sir Robert's in a chaise. They are posting to Bath. One's Colonel Brereton, sir. The other's a young gentleman, short and stout. Quite the gentleman, but that positive, the postboy told me, and talkative, you'd think he was the Emperor of China! That's their chaise coming out of the yard now, sir.'

A thought, keen as a knife-stab, darted through Vaughan's mind. In three strides he was out of the bar-parlour, in three more he was at the door of the Angel.

The coach was in the act of starting, the ostlers were falling back, the guard was swinging himself up; and Mary Vermuyden was where he had left her, in the place behind the coachman. And in the box-seat, the very seat which he had vacated, was Bob Flixton, settling himself in his wraps and turning to talk to her.

Vaughan let fall a word which we will not chronicle. It was true, then, that they were engaged. And Flixton had come to meet her, and all was over. Fan-fa-ra! Fan-fa-ra! The coach was growing small in the distance. It veered a little, a block of houses hid it, Vaughan saw it again. Then in the dusk of the October evening the descent to the bridge swallowed it, and he turned away miserable.

He walked a little distance from the door that his face might not be seen. He did not tell himself that, because the view grew misty before his eyes, he was taking the blow contemptibly; he told himself only that he was very wretched, and that she was gone. It seemed as if so much had gone with her; so much of the hope, and youth, and fortune, and the homage of men, which had been his when he and she first saw the streets of Chippenham together, and he alighted to talk to Isaac White, and mounted again to ride on by her side.

He was standing with his back to the inn, thinking of this – and not bitterly, but in a broken fashion – when he heard his name called, and he turned and saw Colonel Brereton striding after him.

'I thought it was you,' Brereton said. But though he had not met Vaughan for some months, and the two had liked one another, he spoke with little cordiality, and there was a weary look in his face.

'You came with Flixton?' Vaughan said, speaking dully on his side.

'Yes, and meant to go on with him. But there's no counting on men in love,' Brereton continued, with more irritation than the occasion seemed to warrant. 'He saw his charmer on the coach, and a vacant seat – and I may find my way to Bath as I can.'

'They are to be married, I hear?' Vaughan said with his face averted.

'I don't know,' Brereton answered, frowning. 'What I do know is that I'm not best pleased that he has left me. I heard Sir Charles Wetherell was sleeping at your cousin's last evening, and I posted there to see him about the arrangements for his entry. But I missed him – he's at Bath for this evening. I took Flixton with me because I didn't know Sir Robert and he did, and because, too, he's supposed to be playing aide-de-camp to me. But a fine aide-de-camp he's like to prove if this is the way he treats me. You know Wetherell opens the Assizes tomorrow?'

'At Bristol? Yes I saw his clerk on the way down.'

'There'll be trouble, Vaughan!'

'Really?'

'Ay, and bad trouble. I wish it was over.' He looked vaguely into the distance.

'I heard something of it in London,' Vaughan answered.

'Not much, I'll wager,' Brereton rejoined, with a brusqueness which betrayed suppressed irritation. 'They don't know much, or they wouldn't be sending eighty sabres to keep order in a city of a hundred thousand people! Enough to anger, and not enough to intimidate! Why, man, it's madness. But I've made up my mind! I've made up my mind!' he repeated, speaking in a tone which revealed the tenseness of his nerves. 'Not a man will I show if I can help it! And not a shot will I fire, whatever comes of it! I'll be no butcher of innocent folk.'

'I hope nothing will come of it,' Vaughan answered, interested in spite of himself. 'You're in command, sir?'

'Yes, and I wish to Heaven I were not! But there, there!' he continued, pulling himself up as if he kept a watch on himself and feared that he said too much. 'Enough of my business. What are you doing here?'

'Well, I was going to Chippinge.'

'Come to Bath with me! You know Wetherell, and you may be of use to me. There's half the chaise at your service, and I will tell you all about it as we go.'

Vaughan cared little at that moment where he went; and after the briefest hesitation he consented. A few minutes later they started together. It happened that, as they drove in the last of the twilight over the long stone bridge, an open car drawn by four horses and containing a dozen rough-looking men overtook them and raced them for a hundred yards.

'There's another!' Brereton said, rising with an oath and looking after it. 'I was told that two had gone through!'

'Who are they?' Vaughan asked, leaning out on his side to see.

'Midland Union men, come to stir up the Bristol lambs,' Brereton answered. 'They may spare themselves the trouble,' he continued bitterly. 'The fire will need no poking, I'll be sworn!'

And brought back to the subject, he never ceased from that moment of talk of it. It was plain to anyone who knew him that a nervous excitability had taken the place of his wonted melancholy. Long before they reached Bath, Vaughan was sure that, whatever his own troubles, there was one man in the world more unhappy than himself, more troubled, less at ease; and that that man sat beside him in the chaise.

He believed that Brereton exaggerated the peril. But if his fears were well based, then he agreed that the soldiers sent were too few.

'Still a bold front will do much!' he argued.

'A bold front!' Brereton replied feverishly. 'No, but management may! Management may. They gave me eighty swords to control eighty thousand people! Why, it's my belief' – and he dropped his voice and laid his hand on his companion's arm – 'that the Government want a riot! Ay, by God, it is! To give the lie to Wetherell and prove that the country, and Bristol in particular, is firm for the Bill!'

'Oh, but that's absurd!' Vaughan answered; though he recalled what Brougham had said.

'Absurd or not, nine-tenths of Bristol believe it,' Brereton retorted. 'And I believe it! But I'll be no butcher! Besides, do you see how I am placed? If in putting down this riot, which is in the government interests, and is believed to be fostered by them, I exceed my duty by a jot, I am a lost man! A lost man! Now do you see?'

'I can't think it is as bad as that,' said Vaughan.

CHAPTER XXIX

Autumn Leaves

MISS SIBSON paused to listen, but heard nothing. And disappointed, and with a sigh, she spread a clean handkerchief over the lap of her gown and helped herself to part of a round of buttered toast.

'She'll not come,' she muttered. 'I was a fool to think it! An old fool to think of it!' And she bit viciously into the toast.

It was long past her usual tea time, yet she paused a second time to listen, before she raised her first cup of tea to her lips. A covered dish which stood on a brass trivet before the bright coal fire gave forth a savoury smell, and the lamplight, which twinkled on sparkling silver and old Nantgarw, discovered more than the tea-equipage. The red moreen curtains were drawn before the windows, a tabby cat purred sleepily on the hearth; in all Bristol was no more cosy or more cheerful scene. Yet Miss Sibson left the savoury dish untouched, and ate the toast with less than her customary appetite.

'I shall set,' she murmured, ' "The Deceitfulness of Riches" for the first copy when the children return. And for the second, "Fine Feathers make Fine Birds"! And' – she continued with determination, though there was no one to be intimidated – 'for the third, "There's no Fool like an Old Fool"!'

She had barely uttered the words when she set down her

cup. The roll of distant wheels had fallen on her ears. She listened for a few seconds, then she rose and rang the bell.

'Martha,' she said when the maid appeared, 'are the two warming-pans in the bed?'

'To be sure, ma'am'

'And well filled?' Miss Sibson asked suspiciously.

'The sheets are as nigh singeing as you'd like, ma'am,' the maid answered. 'You can smell 'em here! I only hope,' she continued, with a quaver in her voice, 'as we mayn't smell fire before we're two days older!'

'Smell fiddlesticks!' Miss Sibson retorted. Then, 'That will do,' she continued. 'I will open the door myself.'

When she did so the lights of the hackney-coach which had stopped before the house, disclosed first Mary Vermuyden in her furs, standing on the step; secondly, Mr Flixton, who had placed himself as near her as he dared; and thirdly and fourthly, flanking them at a distance of a pace or two, a tall footman and a maid.

'Good gracious!' Miss Sibson exclaimed, dismay in her tone.

'Yes,' Mary answered, almost crying. 'They would come! I said I wished to come alone. Goodnight, Mr Flixton!'

'Oh, but I – I couldn't think of leaving you like this!' the Honourable Bob answered.

He had derived a minimum of satisfaction from his ride on the coach, for Mary had shown herself of the coldest. And if he was to part from her here he might as well have travelled with Brereton. Besides, what the deuce was afoot? What was she doing here?

'And Baxter is as bad,' Mary said plaintively. 'As for Thomas—'

'Beg pardon, ma'am,' the man said, touching his hat, 'but it is as much as my place is worth.'

The maid, a woman of mature years, said nothing, but held her ground, the image of stolid disapproval. She knew Miss Sibson. But Bristol was strange to her; and the dark windy Square, with its flickering lights, its glimpses of gleaming water and skeleton masts, and its unseen but creaking windlasses, seemed to her, fresh from Lady Worcester's, a most unfitting place for her young lady.

Miss Sibson cut the knot after her own fashion. 'Well, I

can't take you in,' she said bluffly. 'This gentleman,' pointing to Mr Flixton, 'will find quarters for you at the White Lion or the Bush. And your mistress will see you tomorrow. Thomas, bring in your young lady's trunk. Goodnight, sir,' she added, addressing the Honourable Bob. 'Miss Vermuyden will be quite safe with me.'

'Oh, but I say, Miss Sibson!' he remonstrated. 'You can't mean to take the moon out of the sky like this, and leave us in the dark? Miss Vermuyden—'

'Goodnight,' Mary said, not a whit placated by the compliment. And she slipped past Miss Sibson into the passage.

'Oh, but it's not safe, you know!' he cried. 'You're not a hundred yards from the Mansion House. And if those beggars make trouble tomorrow – positively there's no knowing what will happen!'

'We can take care of ourselves,' Miss Sibson replied curtly. 'Goodnight, sir!' And she shut the door in his face.

The Honourable Bob glared at it for a time, but it remained closed and dark. There was nothing to be done save to go.

'Damn the woman!' he cried. And he turned about.

It was something of a shock to him to find the two servants still at his elbow, patiently regarding him.

'Where are we to go, sir?' the maid asked, as stolid as before.

'Go?' cried he, staring. 'Go? Eh? What? What do you mean?'

'Where are we to go, sir, for the night? If you'll please to show us, sir. I'm a stranger here.'

'Oh! This is too much!' the Honourable Bob cried, finding himself on a sudden a family man. 'Go? I don't care if you go to—' But there he paused. He put the temptation to tell them to go to blazes from him. After all, they were Mary's servants. 'Oh, very well! Very well!' he resumed, fuming. 'There, get in! Get in!' indicating the hackney-coach. 'And do you,' he continued, turning to Thomas, 'tell him to drive to the White Lion. Was there ever? That old woman's a neat artist, if ever I saw one!'

And a moment later Flixton trundled off, boxed in with the mature maid, and vowing to himself that in all his life he had never been so diddled before.

Meanwhile, within doors – for farce and tragedy are never far apart – Mary, with her furs loosened, but not removed, was resisting all Miss Sibson's efforts to restrain her.

'I must go to her!' she said, with painful persistence. 'I must go to her at once, if you please, Miss Sibson. Where is she?'

'She is not here,' Miss Sibson said, plump and plain.

'Not here!' Mary cried, springing from the chair into which Miss Sibson had compelled her. 'Not here!'

'No. Not in this house.'

'Then why – why did she tell me to come here?' Mary cried dumbfounded.

'Her ladyship is next door. No, my dear!' And Miss Sibson interposed her ample form between Mary and the door. 'You cannot go to her until you have eaten and drunk. She does not expect you, and there is no need of such haste. She may live a fortnight, three weeks, a month even! And she must not, my dear, see you with that sad face.'

Mary gave way at that. She sat down and burst into tears. The schoolmistress knew nothing of the encounter in Bond Street, nothing of the meeting on the coach. But she was a sagacious woman, and she discerned that something more than the fatigue of the journey, something more than grief for her mother, underlay the girl's depression. She said nothing, however, contenting herself with patting her guest on the shoulder and gently removing her wraps and shoes. Then she set a footstool for her in front of the fire and poured out her tea, and placed hot sweetbread before her, and toast, and Sally Lunn. And when Mary, touched by her kindness, flung her arms round her neck and kissed her, she said only, 'That's better, my dear; take your tea, and then I'll tell you all I know.'

'I cannot eat anything.'

'Oh yes, you can! And after that you are going to see your mother, and then you will come back and take a good night's rest. Tomorrow you will do as you like. Her ladyship is with an old servant next door, through whom she first heard of me.'

'Why did she not remain in Bath?'

'I cannot tell you,' Miss Sibson answered. 'She has whims.

If you ask me, I should say that she thought Sir Robert would not find her here, and so could not take you from her.'

'But the servants?' Mary said in dismay. 'They will tell my father. And, indeed—'

'Indeed what, my dear?'

'I do not wish to hide from him.'

'Quite right!' Miss Sibson said. 'Quite right, my dear. But I fancy that that was her ladyship's reason. Perhaps she thought also that when she – that afterwards I should be at hand to take care of you. As a fact,' Miss Sibson continued, rubbing her cheek with the handle of a teaspoon, a sure sign that she was troubled, 'I wish that your mother had chosen another place. You don't ask, my dear, where the children are.'

Mary looked at her hostess. 'Oh, Miss Sibson!' she exclaimed, conscience-stricken. 'You cannot have sent them away for my sake?'

'No, my dear,' Miss Sibson answered, noting with satisfaction that Mary was making a meal. 'No, their parents have removed them. The Recorder is coming tomorrow, and he is so unpopular on account of this nasty Bill – which is setting everyone on horseback whether they can ride or not – and there is so much talk of trouble when he enters, that all the foolish people have taken fright and removed their children for the week. It's pure nonsense, my dear,' Miss Sibson continued comfortably. 'I've seen the windows of the Mansion House broken a score of times at elections, and not another house in the Square a penny the worse! Just an old custom. And so it will be tomorrow. But the noise may disturb her ladyship, and that's why I wish her elsewhere.'

Mary did not answer, and the schoolmistress, noting her spiritless attitude and the dark shadows under her eyes, was confirmed in her notion that here was something beyond grief for the mother she had scarcely known. And Miss Sibson felt a tug at her own heartstrings. She was well-to-do and well considered in Bristol, and she was not conscious that her life was monotonous. But the gay scrap of romance which Mary's coming had wrought into the dull patchwork of days, long toned to the note of Mrs Chapone, was welcome to her. Her little relaxations, her cosy whist parties, her hot suppers to follow, these she had: but here was something brighter and higher. It stirred a long-forgotten youth, old memories, the ashes of romance. She loved Mary for it.

To rouse the girl, she rose from her chair. 'Now, my dear,' she said, 'you can go to your room if you will. And in ten minutes we will step next door.'

Mary looked at her with grateful eyes. 'I am glad now,' she said, 'I am glad that she came here.'

'Ah!' the schoolmistress answered, pursing up her lips. And she looked at the girl uncertainly. 'It's odd,' she said. 'I sometimes think that you are just – Mary Smith.'

'I am!' the other answered warmly. 'Always Mary Smith to you!' And the old woman took the young one to her arms.

A quarter of an hour later Mary came down, and she was Mary Smith in truth. For she had put on the grey Quaker-like dress in which she had followed her trunk from the coach office six months before.

'I thought,' she said, 'that I could nurse her better in this than in my new clothes!'

But she blushed deeply as she spoke: for if she had this thought, she had others, also in her mind. She might not often wear that dress, but she would never part with it. Arthur Vaughan's eyes had worshipped it; his hands had touched it. And in the days to come it would lie, until she died, in some locked coffer, perfumed with lavender, and sweet with the dried rose leaves of her dead romance. And on one day in the year she would visit it, and bury her face in its soft faded folds, and dream the old dreams.

It was but a step to the door of the neighbouring house. But the distance, though short, steadied the girl's mind and enabled her to taste that infinity of the night, that immensity of nature, which, like a fathomless ocean, islands the littleness of our lighted homes. The groaning of strained cordage, the creaking of timbers, the far-off rattle of a boom came off the dark water that lipped the wharves which still fringe three sides of the Square. Here and there a rare gas lamp, lately set up, disclosed the half-bare arms of trees, or some vague opening leading to the Welsh Back. But for all the two could see, as they glided from the one door to the other, the busy city about them, seething with so many passions, pregnant with so much danger, hiding in its entrails the love, the fear, the secrets of a myriad lives, might have been in another planet.

Mary owned the calming influence of the night and the stars, and before the door opened to Miss Sibson's knock, the blush had faded from her cheek. It was with solemn thoughts that she went up the wide oaken staircase, still handsome, though dim and dusty and fallen from its high estate. The task before her, the scene on the threshold of which she trod, brought the purest instincts of her nature into play. But her guide knocked, someone within the room bade them enter, and Mary advanced. She saw lights and a bed – a four-poster, heavily curtained. And half blinded by her tears, she glided towards the bed – or was gliding, when a querulous voice arrested her midway.

'So you are come!' it said. And Lady Sybil, who, robed in a silken dressing-gown, was lying on a small couch in a different part of the room, tossed a book, not too gently to the floor. 'What stuff! What stuff!' she ejaculated wearily. 'A schoolgirl might write as good! Well, you are come,' she continued. 'There,' as Mary, flung back on herself, bent timidly and kissed her, 'that will do! That will do! I can't bear anyone near me! Don't come too near me! Sit on that chair, where I can see you!'

Mary beat back her tears and obeyed with a quivering lip. 'I hope you are better,' she said.

'Better!' her mother retorted in the same peevish tone. 'No, and shall not be!' Then, with a shrill scream, 'Heavens, child, what have you got on?' she continued. 'What have you done to yourself? You look like a *soeur de Charité*!'

'I thought that I could nurse you better in this,' Mary faltered.

'Nurse me!'

'Yes, I—'

'Rubbish!' Lady Sybil exclaimed with petulant impatience. 'You nurse? Don't be silly! Who wants you to nurse me? I want you to amuse me. And you won't do that by dressing yourself like a dingy death's-head moth! There, for Heaven's sake,' with a catch in her own voice which went to Mary's heart, 'don't cry! I'm not strong enough to bear it. Tell me something! Tell me anything to make me laugh. How did you trick Sir Robert, child? How did you cheat him? That will amuse me,' with a mirthless laugh. 'I wish I could see his solemn face when he hears that you are gone!'

Mary explained that the summons had found her in London; that her father was not there, but that she had had to beat down Lady Worcester's resistance before she could have her way and leave.

'I don't know her,' Lady Sybil said shortly.

'She was very kind to me,' Mary answered.

'I dare say,' in the same tone.

'But she would not let me go until I gave her my address.'

Lady Sybil sat up sharply. 'And you did that?' she shrieked. 'You gave it her?'

'I was obliged to give it,' Mary stammered, 'or I could not have left London.'

'Obliged? Obliged?' Lady Sybil retorted, in the same passionate tone. 'Why, you fool, you might have given her fifty addresses! Any address! Any address but this! There!' Lady Sybil continued sullenly, as she sank back and pressed her handkerchief to her lips. 'You've done it now. You've excited me. Give me those drops! Those, those! There! Are you blind? And – and sit farther from me! I can't breathe with you close to me!'

After which, when Mary, almost heartbroken, had given her the medicine, and seated herself in the appointed place, she turned her face to the wall and lay silent and morose, uttering no sound but an occasional sigh of pain.

Meantime, to eyes that could read, the room told its story, and told it eloquently. The table beside the couch was strewn with rose-bound Annuals and Keepsakes, and a dozen volumes bearing the labels of more than one library; books opened only to be cast aside. Costly toys and embroidered nothings, vinaigrettes and scent bottles lay scattered among them; and on other tables, on the mantelpiece, on the floor, a litter of similar trifles elbowed and jostled the gloomy tokens of illness. Near the invalid's hand lay a miniature in a jewelled frame, while a packet of letters tied with a fragment of gold lace, and a buhl desk half closed upon a broken fan, told the same tale of ennui, and of a vanity which survived the charms on which it had rested. The lesson was not lost on the daughter's heart, but it moved her only to pure pity; and presently, wrung by a sigh more painful than usual, she crept to the couch, sank on her knees, and pressed her cool lips to the wasted hand which hung from it. Even then for a time her mother did not move or take notice. But slowly the weary sighs grew more frequent, grew to sobs – how much less poignant! – and her weak arm drew Mary's head to her bosom.

And by-and-by the arm tightened its hold, and gripped her convulsively, the sobs grew deeper and shook the worn form at each respiration; and presently, 'Ah, God, what will become of me?' burst from the depths of the poor quaking heart, too proud until now to make its fear known. 'What will become of me?'

That cry pierced Mary like a knife, but its confession of weakness made mother and daughter one. Her feeble arms could not avert the approach of the dark shadow, whose coming terrified though it could not change. But what human love could do, what patient self-forgetfulness might teach, she vowed that she would do and teach; and what clinging hands might compass to delay the end, her hands should compass. When Miss Sibson's message, informing her that it was time to return, was brought to her, she shook her head, smiling, and locked the door. 'I shall be your nurse after all!' she said. 'I shall not leave you.' And before midnight, with a brave contentment, for which Lady Sybil's following eyes were warrant, she had taken possession of the room and all its litter; she had tidied as much as it was good to tidy, she had knelt to heat the milk or brush the hearth, she had smoothed the pillow, and sworn a score of times that nothing, no Sir Robert, no father, no force should tear her from this her duty, this her joy – until the end.

No thought of her dull childhood, no memory of the days of labour and servitude which she owed to the dying woman, no reflection on the joys of wealth and youth which she had lost through her, rose to mar the sincerity of her love. Much less did such thoughts trouble her on whose flighty mind they should have rested heavily. So far indeed was this from being the case, that when Mary stooped to some office which the mother's fastidiousness deemed beneath her –

'How can you do that?' Lady Sybil cried peevishly. 'I'll not have you do it! Do you hear me, girl? Let some servant see to it! What else are they for!'

'But I used to do it every day at Clapham,' Mary answered cheerfully. She had scarcely spoken before, aware of the reproach which her words conveyed, she could have bitten her tongue.

But Lady Sybil did not wince. 'Then why did you do it?' she retorted. 'Why did you do it? Why were you so foolish as to stoop to such things? I'm sure you didn't get your poor spirit from me! And Vermuyden was as stiff as a poker! But there! I remember the Prince saying once that ladies went out of fashion with hoops, and gentlemen with snuff-boxes. You make me think he was right. Oh, clumsy!' she continued, raising her voice, 'now you are turning the light on my face! Do you wish to see me hideous?'

Mary moved it. 'Is that better, Mother,' she asked.

Lady Sybil cast a resentful glance at her, 'There, there, let it be!' she said. 'You can't help it. You're like your father. He never could do anything right! I suppose I am doomed to have none but helpless people about me.'

And so on, and so on. Like many invalids, she was most lively at night, and she continued to complain through long restless hours; with the candles burning low and lower, and the snuffers coming into more frequent request. Until, with the chill before the dawn, she fell at last into a fitful sleep; and Mary, creeping to the close-curtained windows to cool her weary eyes, peeped out and saw the grey of the morning. Before her the Square was beginning to discover its half-bare trees and long straight rows of houses. Through openings here and there, the water glimmered mistily; and on the height facing her the tall tower of St Mary Redcliffe rose above the roofs and pointed skywards. Little did Mary think what the day would bring forth in the deserted place on which she looked; or in what changed conditions, under what stress of mind and heart, she would, before the sun set twice, view that Square.

CHAPTER XXX

The Mayor's Reception in Queen's Square

THE DAY, of which Mary watched the cloudy opening from her mother's window, was drawing to a close; and from a house in the same Square – but on the north side, whereas Miss Sibson's was on the west – another pair of eyes looked out, while a heart, which a few hours before had been as sore as hers, rose a little at the prospect. Arthur Vaughan, ignorant of her proximity – to love's shame be it said – sat in a window on the first floor of the Mansion House, and, undismayed by the frequent crash of glass, watched the movements of the swaying, shouting crowd, which occupied the middle space of the Square, as well as the roadways, clustered upon the Immortal Memory, overflowed into the side streets, and now joined in one mighty roar of 'Reform! Reform!' and now goaded thunderously at the name of Wetherell. Behind Vaughan in the same room, some twenty or thirty persons argued and gesticulated; at one time approaching a window to settle a debated point, at another scattering with exclamations of anger as a missile fell among them.

'Boo! Boo!' yelled the mob below. 'Throw him out! Reform! Reform!'

Vaughan looked down on the welter of moving faces. He saw that the stone throwers were few; that the dare-devils, who at times adventured to pull up the railings which guarded the forecourt, were fewer. But he saw also that the mass sympathized with them, egged them on, and applauded their exploits. And he wondered what would happen when night fell, and wondered again why the peaceable citizens who wrangled behind him made light of the position. The glass was flying, here and there an iron bar had vanished from the railings, night was approaching. For him it was very well. He had accompanied Brereton to see what would happen, and if the adventure proved to be of the first class, so much the better. But the good pursy citizens behind him, who, when they were not deafening the little Mayor with their counsels, were making a jest of the turmoil, had wives and daughters, goods and houses within reach. And in their place he felt that he would have been far from easy.

By-and-by it appeared that some of them shared his feelings. For in a momentary lull of the babel outside, a voice he knew rose high.

'Nothing? You call it nothing?' Mr Cooke – for his was the voice – cried. 'Nothing, that His Majesty's Judge has been hooted and pelted from Totterdown to the Guildhall? Nothing, that the Recorder of Bristol has been hunted like a criminal from the Guildhall to this place! You call it nothing, sir, that His Majesty's Commission has been flouted for six hours by all the riffraff of the Docks? And with half of decent Bristol applauding?'

'Oh no, no!' the little Mayor remonstrated. 'Not applauding, Mr Cooke!'

'Yes, sir, applauding!' Cooke retorted with vigour.

'And teach Wetherell a lesson!' someone in the background muttered.

The man spoke low, but Cooke heard the words and wheeled about.

'There, sir!' he cried, stuttering in his indignation. 'What do you say to that? In your presence, the King's Judge is insulted. But I warn you,' he continued, 'I warn you all! You are playing with fire! You are laughing in your sleeves, but you'll cry in your shirts! You, Mr Mayor, I call upon you to do your duty! I call upon you to summon the military and clear the streets before worse comes of it.'

'I don't – I really don't think that it is necessary,' the Mayor answered pacifically. 'I have seen as bad as this, Mr Cooke, at half a dozen elections.'

The Town Clerk, a tall, thin man, who wore his gown though he had laid aside his wig, struck in.

'Quite true, Mr Mayor!' he said. 'The fact is, the crowd thinks itself hardly used if it is not allowed to break the windows on these occasions.'

'By God, I'd teach it a lesson then!' Cooke retorted. 'It seems to me it is time someone did!'

Two or three said the same. But the main part smiled at Cooke's heat as at a foolish display of temper.

'I've seen as much many times,' said one, shrugging his shoulders. 'And no harm done!'

'I've seen worse!' another answered. 'And after all,' the speaker added with a wink, 'it is good for the glaziers.'

Fortunately Cooke did not hear this. But Vaughan heard it, and judged that the rioters had their backers within as well as without; and that within, as without, the notion prevailed that the Government would not be pleased if the movement were roughly checked. A proverb about the wisdom of dealing with the beginnings of mischief occurred to him. But he supposed that the authorities knew their business and Bristol, and could gauge the mob and the danger, of which they made so light.

Still he wondered. And he wondered more three minutes later. Two servants brought in lights. Unfortunately these revealed the interior of the room to the mob, and the change was the signal for a fusillade of stones so much more serious and violent than anything which had gone before that a quick *sauve qui peut* took place. Vaughan was dislodged with the others; and in two minutes the room was empty, and the mob were celebrating their victory with peals of Titanic laughter, accompanied by fierce cries of 'Throw him out! Throw out the damned Recorder! Reform!'

Meanwhile the company, with one broken head and two or three pale faces, had taken refuge on the landing behind the drawing-room, the stairs ascending to which were guarded by a reserve of constables. The Mayor and his satellites were beginning to look at one another, and Vaughan noticed that more than one was shaken. Still the little Mayor retained his good humour.

'Oh dear, dear!' he said indulgently. 'This is too bad! Really too bad!'

'We'd better go upstairs,' Serjeant Ludlow, the Town Clerk, suggested. 'We can see what passes as well from that floor as from this, and with less risk!'

'No, but really this is growing serious,' a third said timidly. 'It's too bad, this!'

He had scarcely spoken, and the Mayor was pausing, as if he did not quite like the idea of retreat, when two persons, one with a bandaged head, came quickly up the stairs.

'Where's the Mayor?' cried the first.

And then, 'Mr Mayor, they are pushing us too hard,' said the second, an officer of special constables. 'We must have help, or they will pull the house about our ears.'

'Oh, nonsense!'

'But it's not nonsense, sir!'

'But—'

'You must read the Riot Act,' the other, who was the Under-Sheriff, chimed in. 'And the sooner the better, Mr Mayor. We've half a dozen men badly hurt. In my opinion you should send for the military.'

The persons on the landing looked aghast at one another. What, danger? Really – danger? Half a dozen men badly hurt? Then one made an effort to carry it off.

'Send for the military?' he gasped. 'Oh, but that is absurd!'

The others did not speak, and the Mayor looked upset. Perhaps for the first time he appreciated the responsibility which lay on his shoulders. Meanwhile Vaughan saw all; and Cooke laughed maliciously.

'Perhaps you will listen now,' he said. 'You would not listen to me!'

'Dear, dear,' the Mayor quavered. 'Is it as serious as that, Mr Hare?' He turned to the Town Clerk. 'What do you advise?' he asked.

'I think, with Mr Hare, that you should read the Riot Act, sir.'

'Very well, I'll come down at once,' the Mayor assented with spirit. 'Only,' he continued, looking round him, 'I beg that some gentleman known to be on the side of reform will attend me. Who has the Riot Act?'

'Mr Burges. Where is he?'

'I am here, sir,' replied the gentleman named. 'Quite ready, Mr Mayor. If you will say a word to the crowd, I am sure they will listen.'

Twenty minutes later the same group, but with disordered clothes and sickly faces – and as to Mr Burges, with a broken head – stood again on the landing. In those twenty minutes, despite the magic of the Riot Act, the violence of the mob had grown. They were beginning to talk of burning the Mansion House, were calling for straw, were demanding lights. Darkness had fallen, and there could be no question now that the position was serious. The Mayor, who, below stairs, had shown a good courage, turned to the Town Clerk.

'Ought I to send for the military?' he asked.

'I think we should take Sir Charles Wetherell's opinion,' the thin man answered, shifting the burden from his own shoulders.

'The sooner Sir Charles is gone the better!' cried Cooke. 'If we don't want to have his blood on our heads.'

'I am with Mr Cooke there,' the Under-Sheriff assented. He was responsible for the Judge's safety. 'Sir Charles should be got away. That's the first thing to be done. He cannot hold the Assizes, and I cannot be responsible if he stays.'

'Jonah!' someone muttered with a sneering laugh.

The Mayor turned about. 'That's very improper!' he said.

'It's very improper to send a judge who is a politician!' the voice answered.

'And against the Bill!' a second jeered.

'For shame! For shame!' the Mayor cried.

'I fancy, sir,' the Under-Sheriff struck in, 'the gentlemen who have just spoken – I can guess their names – will be sorry before morning! They will find that it is easier to kindle a fire than to put it out! But – silence, gentlemen! Silence! Here is Sir Charles!'

Wetherell had that moment opened the door of his private room, of which the window looked to the back. He showed no sign of fear, but his face betrayed surprise at the sight of twenty or thirty persons huddled in disorder at the head of the stairs. The lights which had survived the flight from the drawing-room flared in the draught of the shattered windows, and the wavering illumination gave a sinister cast to the scene. The rattle of stones on the floor of the rooms exposed to the Square – varied at times by a roar of voices or a rush of feet in the hall below – suggested that the danger was pressing, and that the assailants might at any moment break into the building.

Sir Charles let his eyes travel over the group. Then, 'How long is this going on, Mr Under-Sheriff?' he asked, plunging his hands deep in his breeches' pockets.

'Well, Sir Charles—'

'They seem' – with a touch of sternness – 'to be carrying the jest rather too far.'

'Mr Cooke,' the Mayor said, 'wishes me to call out the military.'

Wetherell shook his head. 'No, no,' he said. 'You cannot say that life is in danger?'

The Under-Sheriff stepped forward. 'I can say, sir,' he answered firmly, 'that yours is in danger. And in serious danger!'

Wetherell planted his feet farther apart, and thrust his hands lower into his pockets.

'Oh no, no,' he said.

'It is yes, yes, sir,' the Under-Sheriff replied bluntly. 'Unless you leave the house I cannot be responsible! I cannot, indeed, Sir Charles.'

'But—'

'Listen, sir! If you don't wish a very terrible catastrophe to happen, you must go! By God you must!' the Under-Sheriff repeated, forgetting his manners.

The noise below had swollen suddenly. Cries, blows, and shrieks ascended the staircase, and announced that at any moment the party might have to defend their lives. At the prospect thus suddenly presented, respect for dignities took flight; panic seized the majority. Constables, thrusting aldermen and magistrates aside, raced up the stairs, and bundled down again laden with beds with which to block the windows; the picked men who had guarded the foot of the staircase left their posts in charge of two or three wounded comrades, who groaned dismally.

Mr Cooke struck his hand on the balusters. 'By Heavens!' he said, 'this is what comes of your damned Reform! Your damned Reform! We shall all be murdered!'

'For God's sake, Mr Mayor,' a quavering voice cried, 'send for the military.'

'Ay! the soldiers. Send for the soldiers!'

'Certainly,' said the Mayor, who was cooler than most. 'Who will go?'

A man volunteered. On which Vaughan also stepped forward.

'Sir Charles,' he said, 'you must retire. Your duties are at an end, and your presence hampers the defence. Permit me to escort you. I am unknown, and can pass through the streets.'

Wetherell, as brave, stout stolid a man as any man in England, hesitated. But he saw that it would soon be everyone for himself. The din was waxing louder and more menacing; the group on the stairs was melting away. In terror on their own account, the officials were beginning to forget his presence. Several had already gone, seeking to save themselves, this way and that. Others were going. Every moment the confusion increased, and the panic.

'You think I ought to go, Vaughan?' he asked, in a low voice.

'I do, sir,' Vaughan answered.

And, entering the Recorder's room, he brought out Sir Charles's hat and cloak and hastily thrust them on him. As he did this his eye alighted on a constable's staff which lay where its owner had dropped it. Thinking that he might as well possess himself of it, he left Wetherell's side and was going to pick it up, when a roar of sound, as sudden as the explosion of a gun, burst up the staircase. Two or three cried in a frenzied way that the mob were coming; some fled this way, some that, a few to windows at the back, more to the upper storey, while a handful obeyed Vaughan's call to stand and hold the head of the stairs. For a brief space all was disorder and – save in his neighbourhood – panic. Then a voice below shouted that the soldiers were come, and a general 'Thank God! Not a moment too soon!' was heard on all sides. Vaughan made sure that the news was true, then he turned to rejoin Sir Charles.

But Wetherell had vanished, and no one could say in which direction. Vaughan hurried upstairs and along the passages in anxious search; but in vain. One told him that Sir Charles had left by a window at the back; another, that he had been seen with the Under-Sheriff. He could learn nothing certain, and was asking himself what he should do, when the sound of cheering reached his ear. A man who met him told him that the mob was cheering the soldiers.

'That's good news!' Vaughan answered.

'I'd say so, too,' the other rejoined glumly, 'if I was certain on which side the soldiers were! But you're wanted, sir, in the drawing-room. The Mayor asked me to find you.'

'Very good,' Vaughan said, and, following the messenger to the room he had named, found himself in the presence of the Mayor and of four or five officials who looked woefully shaken. With them were Brereton and the Hon Bob, both in uniform. The stone throwing had ceased, for the front of the house was now guarded by a double line of troopers in red cloaks. Lights, too, had been brought, and the danger seemed to be over. But about this council there was none of the easy contempt which had characterized the one held an hour before. The lesson had been learnt in a measure.

The Mayor looked at Vaughan. 'Is this the gentleman?' he asked.

'Yes, that is the gentleman who got us together at the head of the stairs,' a person, a stranger to Vaughan, answered. 'If he,' the man continued, 'were put in charge of the constables, who are at sixes and sevens, we might manage something.'

A voice from the background mentioned that it was Mr Vaughan, the Member for Chippinge.

'I shall be glad to do anything I can,' Vaughan said.

'In support of the military,' the tall, thin Town Clerk interposed. 'That must be understood.'

And he looked at Colonel Brereton, who, to Vaughan's surprise, had not acknowledged his presence.

'Of course, of course,' said the Mayor, pacifically. 'It is understood that Colonel Brereton will use his utmost force to clear the streets and quiet the city.'

'I shall do what I think right,' Brereton replied, standing up straight, with his hand on his sword hilt, and looking, among the flustered citizens, like a Spanish hidalgo among a troop of peasants. 'I shall do what is right,' he repeated, stubbornly; and Vaughan perceived that, quiet as he seemed, he was labouring under strong excitement. 'I shall walk my horses about. The crowd are perfectly good-humoured, and only need to be kept moving.'

The Town Clerk exchanged a glance with a neighbour. 'But do you think, sir,' he said, 'that that will be sufficient? You are aware that great damage has been done already, and that had your troop not arrived many lives might have been sacrificed?'

'That is all I shall do,' Brereton answered. 'Unless the Mayor gives me an express and written order to attack the people.'

The Mayor's face was a picture. 'I?' he gasped.

'Yes, sir.'

'But I could not take that responsibility,' the Mayor cried. 'I couldn't, I really couldn't! I can't judge, Colonel Brereton – I am not a military man – whether it is necessary or not.'

'I should consider it unwise,' Brereton replied.

'Very good! Then you must use your discretion.'

'That's what I supposed,' Brereton returned, not masking his contempt for the vacillation of those about him. 'In that case I shall pursue the line of action I have indicated. I shall walk my horses up and down. The crowd are perfectly good-humoured. Well – what is it?'

A man had entered the room and was whispering in the Town Clerk's ear. The latter straightened himself with a heated face.

'You call them good-humoured, sir?' he said. 'I hear that two of your men, Colonel Brereton, have been brought in severely wounded. I do not know whether you call that good-humour?'

Brereton's face betrayed his annoyance. 'They must have brought it on themselves,' he said, 'by some rashness. Your constables have no discretion.'

'I think,' the Town Clerk persisted, 'you should at least clear the Square and the neighbouring streets.'

'I have indicated what I shall do,' Brereton replied, with a gloomy look. 'And I am prepared to be responsible for the safety of the city. If you wish me to act beyond my judgement, the civil power must give me an express and written order.'

Still the Mayor looked uneasy, though he did not dare to do what Brereton suggested. The howls of the rabble still rang in his ears, and before his eyes he had the black, gaping casements, through which an ominous murmur entered. He had waited long before calling in the military, he had hesitated long; for Peterloo had erased Waterloo from the memory of an ungrateful generation, and men, secure abroad and straining after reform at home, held a redcoat in distaste, if not in suspicion. But having called the redcoats in, the townsfolk looked for something more than this, for some stroke which would cast terror into the hearts of misdoers. The Town Clerk, in particular, had his doubts, and when no one else spoke he put them into words.

'May I ask,' he said, 'if you have any orders, Colonel Brereton, from the Secretary of State or the Horse Guards, which prevent you from obeying the directions of the magistrates?'

Brereton looked at him sternly. 'No,' he said, 'I am prepared to obey your orders, stated in the manner I have laid down. Then the responsibility will not lie with me.'

But the Mayor stepped back. 'I couldn't take it on myself, sir. I – God knows what the consequences might be!' He looked round piteously. 'We don't want another Manchester massacre.'

'I fancy,' Brereton answered, 'that if we have another Manchester business it will go ill with those who sign the order! Times are changed since '19 – and governments! I think we understand that. You leave it to me then, gentlemen?'

No one spoke.

'Very good,' he continued. 'If your constables will do their duty with discretion – and you could not have a better man to command them than Mr Vaughan, but he ought to be going about it now – I will answer for the peace of the city.'

'But – but we shall see you again, Colonel Brereton,' the Mayor cried.

'See me, sir?' Brereton answered contemptuously. 'Oh yes, you can see me! But—' He shrugged his shoulders, and turned away without finishing the sentence.

Vaughan knew then that, cool as Brereton seemed, he was not himself. A moody stubbornness had taken the place of last night's excitement, but that was all. And as the party trooped downstairs – he had requested the Mayor to say a few words, placing the constables under his control – he swallowed his private feelings and approached Flixton.

'Flixton,' he whispered, throwing what friendliness he could into his voice. 'Do you think Brereton's right?'

Flixton turned an ill-humoured face towards him, and dragged at his sword belt.

'Oh, I don't know,' he said irritably. 'It's his business, and I suppose he can judge. There's a deuce of a crowd, I know, and if we go charging into it we shall be swallowed up in a twinkling!'

'But I hear,' Vaughan replied, 'that he has told the people that he's for Reform. And they think that the soldiers may side with them? Is not that unwise?'

'Fine talking,' Flixton answered with a sneer. 'And God knows if we had five hundred men, or three hundred, I'd agree. But what can sixty or eighty men do galloping over slippery pavements in the dark? While if we fire and kill a dozen, the Government will hang us to clear themselves! And these damned nigger-drivers and sugar-boilers behind us will be the first to swear against us!'

Vaughan had his own opinion. But they had to part. Flixton in his blue uniform – there were two troops present, one of the 3rd Dragoon Guards in red, and one of the 14th Dragoons in blue – went out by Brereton's side with his spurs ringing on the stone pavement and his sword clanking. Meanwhile Vaughan, who could not see the old blue uniform without a pang, went with the Mayor to marshal the constables.

Of these no more than eighty remained, with little stomach for the task before them. That task, indeed, was far from easy. The ground floor of the Mansion House looked like a place taken by storm and sacked. The railings which guarded the forecourt were gone, even the wall on which they stood had been demolished to furnish missiles. The doorways and windows, where they were not barricaded, were apertures inviting entrance. In one room lay a pile of straw ready for kindling. In another lay half a dozen wounded men. Everywhere the cold wind, blowing off the water of the Welsh Back, entered by a dozen openings and extinguished the flares as quickly as they could be lighted, casting now one room and now another into shadow.

But if the men had little heart for further exertions, Vaughan's manhood rose to meet the call. Bringing his soldier's training into play, in a few minutes he had his force divided into four companies, each under a leader. Two he held in reserve, bidding them get what rest they could; with the other two he manned the forecourt, and guarded the flank which lay open to the Welsh Back. And as long as the troopers rode up and down within a stone's throw all was well. But when the soldiers passed to the other side of the Square a rush was made on the house – mainly by a gang of the low Irish of the neighbourhood – and many a stout blow was struck before the rabble, who thirsted for the strong ale in the cellars, could be dislodged from the forecourt and driven to a distance. The danger was not great, though the tale of wounded grew steadily; nor could the post of Chief Constable be held to confer much honour on one who so short a time before had dreamt of Cabinets and portfolios, and of a Senate hanging on his words. But the joy of conflict was something to a stout heart, and the sense of success. Something, too, it was to feel that where he stood his men stood; and that where he was not, the Irish, with their brick-bats and iron bars, made a way. There was a big lout, believed by some to be a Brummagem man and a tool of the Political Union, who more than once led on the assailants; and when Vaughan found that this man shunned him and chose the flank where he was not, that too was a joy.

'After all, this is what I am good for,' he told himself as he stood to take breath after a mêlée which was at once the most serious and the last. 'I was a fool to leave the regiment,' he continued, stanching a trickle of blood which ran from a cut on his cheekbone. 'For, after all, better a good blow than a bad speech! Better, perhaps, a good blow than all the speeches, good and bad!' And in the heat of the moment he swung his staff. Then – then he thought of Mary and Flixton, and his heart sank, and his joy was at an end.

'Don't think they'll try us again, sir,' said an old pensioner who had known the neigh of the war horse in the Peninsula, and who had constituted himself his orderly. 'If we had had you at the beginning we'd have had no need of the old Blues, nor the Third either!'

'Oh, that's rubbish!' Vaughan replied.

But he owned the flattery, and his heart warmed to the pensioner; whose prediction proved to be correct. The crowd melted after that. By eleven o'clock there were but a couple of hundred in the Square. By twelve, even these were gone. A half-dozen troopers, and as many tatterdemalions, slinking about the dark corners, were all that remained of the combatants; and the Mayor, with many words, presented Vaughan with the thanks of the city for his services.

'It is gratifying, Mr Vaughan,' he added,' to find that Colonel Brereton was right.'

'Yes,' Vaughan readily agreed. And he took his leave, carrying his staff for a memento.

He was very weary, and it was not the shortest way to the White Lion, yet his feet carried him across the dark Square and past the Immortal Memory to the front of Miss Sibson's house. It showed no lights to the Square, but in a first-floor window of the next house he marked a faint radiance as of a shaded taper, and the outline of a head – doubtless the head of someone looking out to make sure that the disorder was at an end. He saw, but love was at fault. No inner voice told him that the head was Mary's! No thrill revealed to him that at that very moment, with her brow pressed to the cold pane, she was thinking of him! With a sigh, and a further fall from the light-heartedness of an hour before, he went his way.

Broad Street was quiet, but half a dozen persons were gathered before the White Lion. They were listening: and one of them told him that the Blues, in beating back a party from the Council House, had shot a rioter. In the hall he found others debating the act with heat, but they fell silent when they saw him, one nudging another; and he fancied that they paid especial attention to him. As he moved towards the office, a man detached himself from them and approached him with a formal air.

'Mr Vaughan, I think?' he said.

'Yes.'

'Mr Arthur Vaughan?' the man, who was a complete stranger to Vaughan, repeated. 'Member of Parliament for Chippinge, I believe?'

'Yes.'

'Reform Member?'

Vaughan eyed him narrowly. 'If you are one of my constituents,' he said dryly, 'I will answer that question.'

'I am not one,' the man rejoined, with a little less confidence. 'But it's my business to warn you, Mr Vaughan, in your own interests, that the part you have been taking here will not commend you to them! You have been handling the people very roughly, I am told. Very roughly! Now, I am Mr Here—'

'You may be Mr Here or Mr There,' Vaughan said, cutting him short – but very quietly. 'But if you say another word to me, I will throw you through that door for your impudence! That is all. Now – have you any more to say?'

The man tried to carry it off, for there was sniggering behind him. But Vaughan's blood was up, the agitator read it in the young man's eye, and being a man of words, not deeds, he fell back. Vaughan went up to bed.

CHAPTER XXXI

Sunday in Bristol

IT WAS far from Vaughan's humour to play the bully, and before he had even reached his bedroom, which looked to the back, he repented of his vehemence. Between that and the natural turmoil of his feelings he lay long waking; and twice, in a stillness which proclaimed that all was well, he heard the Bristol clocks tell the hour. After all, then, Brereton had been right, and he had been wrong. He, had the command been his, would have adopted more strenuous measures. He would have tried to put fear into the mob before the riot reached its height. And how dire might have been the consequences! How many homes might at this moment be mourning his action, how many innocent persons be suffering pain and misery!

Whereas Brereton, the strong, quiet man, resisting importunity, shunning haste, keeping his head where others wavered, had carried the city through its trouble, with scarce the loss of a single life. Truly he was one whom –

Non civium ardor prava jubentium,
Non vultus instantis tyranni
Mente quatit solida!

Vaughan thought of him with a new respect, and of himself with a new humility. He was forced to acknowledge that even in that field of action which he had quitted, and to which he was now inclined to return, he was not likely to pick up a marshal's baton.

He slept at length, and long and heavily, awaking towards ten o'clock with aching limbs and a cheek so sore that in a twinkling it brought all back to him. He found his hot water at his door, and he dressed slowly and despondently, feeling the reaction and thinking of Mary, and of that sunny morning, six months back, when he had looked into Broad Street from a window of this same house, and dreamed of a modest bonnet and a sweet blushing face. An hour after that, he remembered, he had happened on the Honourable – oh, damn Flixton! All his troubles had started from that unlucky meeting with him.

He found his breakfast laid in the next room, the coffee and bacon in a Japan cat by the fire. He ate and drank in an atmosphere of gloomy retrospect. If he had never met Flixton! If he had not gone to that unlucky dinner at Chippinge! If he had spoken to her in Bond Street! If – if – if! The bells of half a dozen churches were ringing, drumming his regrets into him; he stood awhile irresolute, looking through the window. The inn yard, which was all the prospect the window commanded, was empty; an old liver-and-white pointer, scratching itself in a corner, was the only living thing in it. But while he looked, wondering if the dog had been a good dog in its time, two men came running into the yard with every sign of haste and pressure. The leader, who wore a yellow jacket, flung himself against a stable door and vanished within, leaving the door open. The other pounced on a chaise, one of half a dozen ranged under a shed, and by main force dragged it into the open.

The men's actions impressed Vaughan with a vague uneasiness. He listened. Was it fancy, or did he catch the sound of a distant shot? And there seemed to be an odd murmur in the air. He seized his hat, put on his caped coat – for a cold drizzle was falling – and went downstairs.

The hall was empty, but through the doorway he could see a knot of people, standing outside, looking up the street. He made for the threshold, and asked the rearmost of the starers what it was.

'Eh, what?' the man answered volubly. 'Oh, they're gone! It's true enough! And such a crowd as was never seen, I'm told – stoning them, and shouting "Bloody Blues!" after them. They're gone right away to Keynsham, and glad to be there with whole bones!'

'But what is it?' Vaughan asked impatiently. 'What has happened, my man? Who're gone?'

The man turned for the first time, and saw who it was. 'You've not heard, sir?' he exclaimed.

'Not a word.'

'Not that the people have risen, and most part pulled down the Mansion House? Ay, first thing this morning, sir! They say old Pinney the Mayor, got out at the back just in time or he'd have been murdered! He's had to send away the Blues who killed the lad last night on the Pithay.'

'Impossible!' Vaughan exclaimed, turning red with anger. 'You cannot have heard aright.'

'It's as true as true!' the man replied, rubbing his hands in excitement. 'As for me,' he continued, 'I was always for Reform, and this will teach the Lords a lesson! They'll know our mind now, and that Wetherell's a liar, begging your pardon, sir. And the old Corporation's not much better. A set of Tories mostly! If the Welsh Back drinks their cellars dry it won't hurt me, nor Bristol.'

Vaughan was too sharply surprised to rebuke the man. Could the story be true! And, if it were, what was Brereton doing? He could not have been so foolish as to halve his force in obedience to the people he was sent to check! But the murmur in the air was a fact, and past the end of the street men were running in anything but a Sunday fashion.

He went back to his room and pocketed his staff. Then he descended again and was on his way out, when a person belonging to the house stopped him.

'Mr Vaughan,' she said earnestly, 'don't go, sir. You are

known after last night, and will come to harm. And you can do no good. My father says that nothing can be done until tomorrow.'

'I will take care of myself,' he replied lightly. But his eyes thanked her. He pushed his way through the gazers at the door, and set off towards Queen's Square.

At every door men and women were standing looking out. In the distance he could hear cheering, which waxed louder and more insistent as, avoiding the narrower lanes, he passed down Clare Street to Broad Quay, from which there was an entrance to the northwest corner of the Square. Alongside the quay, which was fringed with warehouses and sheds, lay a line of brigs and schooners, the masts of the more distant tapering to vanishing point in the mist which lay upon the water. At the moment, however, Vaughan had no eye for these. His thoughts were with the rioters, and in a twinkling he was within the Square, and seeing what was to be seen.

He judged that there were not more than fifteen hundred persons present, of whom about one half belonged to the lowest class. These were gathered about the Mansion House, some drinking before it, others bearing up liquor from the cellars, while others again were tearing out the woodwork of the casements, or wantonly flinging the last remnants of furniture from the windows. The second moiety of the crowd, less reckless or of higher position, looked on as at a show; or now and again, at the bidding of some active rioter, raised a cheer for Reform, 'The King and Reform! Reform!'

There was nothing dreadful, nothing awe-inspiring in the sight. Yet it was such a sight, for an English city on a Sunday morning, that Vaughan's gorge rose at it. A hundred resolute men might have put the mob to flight. And meantime, on every point of vantage, on Redcliffe Parade, eastward of the Square, on College Green, and Brandon Hill, to the westward of it, thousands stood, looking in silence on the scene, and by their supineness encouraged the work of destruction.

He thought for a moment of pushing to the front and trying what a few reasonable words would effect. But, as he advanced, his eye caught a gleam of colour, and in the corner of the Square, most remote from the disorder, he discovered a handful of dragoons, seated motionless in their saddles, watching the proceedings.

The folly of this struck him dumb, and he hurried across the Square to remonstrate. He was about to speak to the sergeant in charge, when Flixton, with a civilian cloak masking his uniform, rode up to the men at a footpace. Vaughan turned to him instead.

'Good Heavens, man!' he cried, too hot to mince his words or remember at the moment what there was between him and Flixton, what's the Chief doing? What has happened? It is not true that he has sent the Fourteenth away?'

Flixton looked down at him. 'He's sent 'em to Keynsham,' he said sulkily. 'If he hadn't, the crowd would have been out of hand!'

'But what do you call them now?' Vaughan retorted, with angry sarcasm. 'They are destroying a public building in broad daylight! Ain't they sufficiently out of hand?'

Flixton shrugged his shoulders, but did not answer. He was flushed and his manner was surly.

'And your squad here, looking on and doing nothing? They're worse than useless!' Vaughan continued. 'They encourage the beggars! They'd be better in their quarters than here! Better at Keynsham,' he added bitterly.

'So I've told him,' Flixton answered, taking the last words literally. 'And he sent me to see how things are looking. A damned pleasant way this is of spending a wet Sunday!'

On which, having seen, apparently, what he came to see, he turned his horse to go out of the Square by the Broad Quay.

Vaughan walked a few paces beside the horse. 'But, Flixton, press him,' he said urgently, 'press him, man, to act! To do something!'

'That's all very fine,' the Honourable Bob answered churlishly; 'but Brereton's in command. And you don't catch me interfering. I am not going to take the responsibility off his shoulders.'

'But think what may happen tonight!' Vaughan urged.

Already he saw that the throng was growing denser and its movements less random. Somewhere in the heart of it a man was speaking.

'Think what may happen after dark, if they are as bad as this in daylight?'

Flixton looked askance at him. 'Ten to one, only what happened last night,' he answered. 'You croaked then, but Brereton was right.'

Vaughan saw that he argued to no purpose. For Flixton, forward and positive in small things and on the surface, was discovered by the emergency; all that now remained of his usual self-assertion was a sense of injury. Vaughan inquired, instead, where he would find Brereton, and as by this time the crowd had clearly outgrown the control of a single man, he contented himself with walking round the Square, and learning, by mingling with the fringe, what manner of spirit moved it.

That spirit, though he heard some ugly threats against Wetherell and the Bishops and the Lords, was rather a reckless and mischievous than a bloodthirsty one. To obtain drink, to destroy this or that gaol, and by-and-by to destroy all gaols, seemed to the crowd the first principles of Reform.

Presently a cry of 'To the Bridewell! Come on! To the Bridewell!' was raised, and led by a dozen hobbledehoys, armed with iron bars plucked from the railings, a body of some hundreds trooped off, helter-skelter, in the direction of the prison of that name.

Vaughan saw that someone must be induced to act; and to him the following hours of that wet dismal Sunday were a waking nightmare. He hurried hither and thither, from the Guildhall to the Council House, from Brereton's lodgings to the dragoons' quarters, striving to effect something and always failing; seeking some cohesion, some decision, some action, and finding none. Always there had just been a meeting, or was going to be a meeting, or would be a meeting by-and-by. The civil power would not act without the military; and the military did not think itself strong enough to act, but would act if the civil power would do something which the civil power had made up its mind not to do. And meantime the supineness of the mass of the citizens was marvellous. Vaughan seemed to be moving endlessly between lines of men who lounged at their doors, and joked, or waited for the crowd to pass that way. Nothing, it seemed to him, would rouse these men to a sense of the position. It would be a lesson to Wetherell, they said. It would be a lesson to the Peers. It would be a lesson to the Tories. The Bridewell was sacked and fired, the great gaol across the New Cut was firing, the Gloucester gaol in the north of the city was threatened. And still it did not occur to these householders, as they looked down the wet, misty streets, that presently it would be a lesson to them.

But at half past three, with the dusk on that rainy day scarce an hour off, there was a meeting at the Guildhall. Still no cohesion, no action. On the other hand, much recrimination, many opinions. One was for casting all firearms into the float. Another for arming all, fit or unfit. One was for fetching the Fourteenth back, another for sending the Third to join them at Keynsham. One was for appeasing the people by parading a dummy figure of their own Recorder through the city and burning it on College Green. Another for relying on the Political Union. In vain Vaughan warned them that the mob would proceed to attack private property; in vain he offered, in a few spirited words, to lead the special constables to the rescue of the gaol. The meeting, small to begin and always divided, dwindled fast. The handful who were ready to follow him made the support of the military a condition. Everybody said, 'Tomorrow!' Tomorrow the *posse comitatus* might be called out; tomorrow the yeomanry, summoned by the man in the yellow jacket, would be here! Tomorrow the soldiers might act. And in fine – Tomorrow!

There was over the door of the Council House of those days a statue of Justice, which for some reason lacked the sword and the bandage. Vaughan, passing out in disgust from the meeting, pointed to it.

'There is Bristol, gentlemen,' he said bitterly. 'Your authorities have dropped the sword, and until they regain it we are helpless. I have done my best.'

And, shrugging his shoulders, he started for Brereton's lodgings to try a last appeal.

He might well think it necessary. For a night which Bristol was long to remember was closing down upon the city. Though it was Sunday, the churches were empty; in few was a second service held. The streets, on the contrary, were full, in spite of the cold; full of noise and turmoil and disorder; of bands of men hastening up and down with reckless cries and flaring lights, at the bidding of leaders as unwitting. In Queen's Square the rioters were drinking themselves drunk as at a fair; while amid the falling rain, through which the last stormy gleams of daylight strove to pass, amid the thickening dusk, those who all day long had jested at their doors began to turn doubtful looks on one another. From three points the smoke of fired prisons rose to the clouds and floated in a dense pall over the city; and men whispered that a hundred, two hundred, five hundred criminals had been set free. On Clifton Downs, on Brandon Hill, on College Green, on Redcliffe the thousand gazers of the morning were doubled and redoubled. But they no longer wore the cynical faces of the morning. On the contrary, there were some who, following with their eyes the network of waterways, laden with inflammable shipping, which pierced the city in every direction – who, tracing these and the sinuous alleys and steep lanes about them, predicted that the morning would find Bristol a heap of ruins. And not a few, taking fright at the last moment, removed their families to Clifton, and locked up their houses.

Vaughan, as he walked through the dusk, had those waterways, those lanes, those alleys, the congested heart of the old city, in his mind. He doubted, even he, if the hour for action was not past. And he was not surprised when Brereton met his appeal with a flat *non possumus*. But he was surprised by the change which twenty-four hours had wrought in the man. He looked worn and haggard. The shadows under his eyes were deeper, the eyes shone with a more feverish light. His dress, too, was disordered, and while he was not still for a moment, he repeated what he said over and over again as if to persuade himself of its truth.

Naturally Vaughan laid stress on the damage already done. 'But, I tell you,' Brereton answered angrily, 'we are well clear for that! It's not a tithe of the harm we'd have suffered if I had given way! I've done, thank God, the only thing it was possible to do. A little too much, and if I'd succeeded I'd have been hung – for they're all against me, they're all against me, above and below! And if I'd failed, a thousand lives would have paid the bill! And do you consider,' he continued, striking the table, 'what a massacre in this crowded place would be! Think of the shipyards, the dockyards, the quays! The water pits and the sunk alleys! How could I clear them with ninety swords? How could I clear them? With ninety swords? I tell you they never meant me to clear them.'

'But why not clear the wider streets, sir?' Vaughan persisted, 'and keep a grip on those?'

'No! I say, no!'

'Yet even now, if you were to move your full force to Queen's Square, sir, you might clear it. And driven from their headquarters, and taught that they were not going to have their own way, the more prudent would fall off and go home.'

'I know,' Brereton answered. 'I know the argument. But who's to thank for the whole trouble? Your Blues, who went beyond their orders last night. The Fourteenth, sir! The Fourteenth! But I'll have no more of it. Flixton is of my opinion, too.'

'Flixton is an ass!' Vaughan cried incautiously.

'And you think me one too!' Brereton retorted, with so strange a look that for the first time Vaughan was sure that his mind was off its balance. 'Well, think what you like! Think what you like! But I'll trouble you not to take that tone here.'

CHAPTER XXXII

The Affray at the Palace

A LITTLE before the hour at which Vaughan interviewed Brereton, Sir Robert Vermuyden, the arrival of whose travelling carriage at the White Lion about the middle of the afternoon had caused some excitement, walked back to his inn. He was followed by Thomas, the servant who had attended Mary to Bristol, and by another servant. As he passed through the streets the signs of the times were not lost upon him; far from it. But the pride of caste was strong in him, and he hid his anxiety.

On the threshold of the inn he turned to the servants, 'Are you sure,' he asked for the fourth time, 'that that was the house at which you left her?'

'Certain sure, Sir Robert,' Thomas answered earnestly.

'And sure – but, ah!' The baronet broke off abruptly, his tone one of relief. 'Here's Mr Cooke! Go now, but be within call. Mr Cooke' – he stepped as he spoke, in front of that gentleman, who was about to enter the house – 'well met!'

Cooke was hot with haste and ire, but at the unexpected sight of Sir Robert he stood still.

'God bless my soul!' he cried. 'You here, sir?'

'Yes. And you know Bristol well. You can help me.'

'I wish I could help myself!' Cooke cried, forgetting his manners in his excitement.

'My daughter is in Bristol.'

'Indeed!' the angry merchant replied. 'Then she could not be in a worse place. That is all I can say!'

'I am inclined to agree with you.'

'This is your Reform!' the other cried.

Sir Robert stared. 'Not my Reform, Mr Cooke,' he said in a tone of displeasure.

'I beg your pardon, Sir Robert,' Cooke rejoined, speaking more coolly. 'I beg your pardon. But what I have suffered today is beyong telling. By God, it's my opinion that there's only one man worthy of the name in Bristol! And that's your cousin, the Radical.'

Sir Robert struck his stick on the pavement. 'Mr Vaughan?' he exclaimed. 'He is here, then? I feared so.'

'You feared, by God? I tell you he's the only man, to be called a man, who is here! If it had not been for him and the way he handled the constables last night we should have been burnt out then, instead of tonight! I don't know that the gain's much, but for what it's worth we have him to thank!'

Sir Robert frowned. 'Indeed!' he said. 'I am surprised to hear it. He behaved well?'

'Damned well! Damned well! If there had been half a dozen like him we'd be out of the wood!'

'Where is he staying?' Sir Robert asked after a momentary hesitation. 'I've lost my daughter in the confusion, and I think it possible that he may know where she is.'

'He is staying here at the Lion,' Cooke answered. 'But he's been up and down all day trying to put heart into poltroons.' And he ran over the chief events of the last few hours.

He punctuated the story with oaths and bitter complaints, and perhaps it was for this reason that Sir Robert broke away as soon as he had heard the main facts. The baronet went through the hall to the bar, where the landlord, who knew him, came forward and greeted him respectfully. But to Sir Robert's inquiry as to Mr Vaughan's whereabouts he shook his head.

'I wish he was in the house, your honour,' he said in a low voice. 'For he's a marked man in Bristol since last night. I was in the Square myself, and it was wonderful what spirit he put into his men. But the scum and the riffraff who are uppermost today say he handled them cruelly, and my daughter tried to persuade him from showing himself. But he would go, sir.'

Sir Robert reflected with a gloomy face. 'Where are Mr Flixton's quarters?' he asked at last. He might possibly learn something from him.

The man told him, and Sir Robert summoned his servants and went out. It was dark by this time, but a faint glare shone overhead and there was a murmur in the air, as if, in the gloom beneath, the heart of the city was palpitating, in dread of it knew not what. Sir Robert had not far to go. He had barely passed into College Green when he met Flixton, under a lamp. And two minutes later Vaughan, on his way from Brereton's lodgings in Unity Street, came plump upon the two. He might have gone by in ignorance, but as he passed, the taller man looked up, and Vaughan, with a shock of surprise, recognized Sir Robert Vermuyden.

Flixton caught sight of Vaughan at the same moment, and –

'Here's your man, Sir Robert,' he cried, with a little malice in his tone. 'Here, Vaughan,' he continued, 'here is Sir Robert Vermuyden! He's looking for you. He wants to know—'

Sir Robert stopped him. 'I will speak for myself, Mr Flixton, if you please,' he said, with the dignity which seldom deserted him. 'Mr Vaughan,' he continued, with a piercing glance, 'where is my daughter?'

Vaughan returned the look with interest. Since the parting in Miss Sibson's parlour, the remembrance of which still set his blood in a flame, Sir Robert and he had not met. Now, in the wet gloom of College Green, under a rare gas lamp, with turmoil about them, and the murmur of fresh trouble drawing near through the streets, Sir Robert asked him for his daughter! He could have laughed. As it was –

'I know nothing, sir, of your daughter,' he replied.

'But,' Sir Robert retorted, 'you travelled with her from London!'

'How do you know that I did?'

'The servants, sir, told me that you did.'

'Then they must also have told you,' Vaughan rejoined, 'that I did not take the liberty of speaking to Miss Vermuyden. And that I left the coach at Chippenham. That being so, I can only refer you,' he continued coldly, raising his hat and preparing to move on, 'to Mr Flixton, who went with her the rest of the way to Bristol.'

He turned away. But he had not taken two paces before Sir Robert touched his shoulder.

'Wait, sir,' he said, 'wait, if you please. You do not escape me so easily. You will attend to me one moment. Mr Flixton accompanied Miss Vermuyden, as did her man and maid, to Miss Sibson's house. She gave that address to Lady Worcester, in whose care she was; and I sought her there this afternoon. But she is not there,' Sir Robert continued, striving to read Vaughan's face. 'She is not there. The house is empty. So is the house on either side. I can make no one hear.'

'And you come to me for news of her?' Vaughan asked in the tone he had used throughout. He was very sore.

'I do.'

'You do not think that I am the last person of whom you should ask tidings of your daughter?'

'She came here,' Sir Robert answered sternly, 'to see Lady Sybil.'

Vaughan stared. The answer seemed to be irrelevant. Then he understood.

'Oh,' he said, 'I see. You are still under the impression that your wife and I are in conspiracy to delude you? You think that your daughter is in the plot? And that she gave the schoolmistress's address to deceive you?'

'No!' Sir Robert cried. But, after all, that was what he did think. Had he not told himself, more than once, that she was her mother's daughter? Had he not told himself that it could not have been by chance that Vaughan and she met a second time on the coach? He knew that she had left London and gone to her mother in defiance of him. And though she had entwined herself about his heart, though she had seemed to him all gentleness, goodness, truth – she was still her mother's daughter! Nevertheless, he said 'No!' – and said it angrily.

'Then I do not know what you mean!' Vaughan retorted.

'I believe that you can tell me something.'

Vaughan looked at him. 'I have nothing to tell you,' he said, stubbornly.

'You mean, sir, that you will tell me nothing!'

'That, if you like.'

For nearly half a century the old man had found few to oppose him, and now by good luck he had not time to reply. A man running out of the darkness in the direction of Unity Street – the place was full of moving groups, of alarms and confusion – caught sight of Vaughan's face, checked himself, and addressed him.

'Mr Vaughan!' he said. 'They are coming! They are making for the Palace! The Bishop must be got away, if he's not gone! I am going to the Colonel! The Mayor is following with all he can get together. If you will give warning at the Palace, there will be time for his lordship to escape.'

'Right,' Vermuyden cried, glad to leave his company. And he started without the loss of a moment. Even so, he had not gone twenty paces down the Green before the head of the mob entered it from St Augustine's, and passed, with hoarse shouts, along the south side, towards the ancient Archway which led to the Lower Green. It was a question whether he or they reached the Archway first; but he won the race by a score of yards.

The view from the Lower Green, which embraced the burning gaol, as well as all Queen's Square and the Floating Basin, had drawn together a number of gazers. These impeded

Vaughan's progress, but he got through them at last, and as the mob burst into the Lower Green he entered the paved passage leading to the Precincts, hurried along it, turned the dark elbow near the inner end, and halted before the high gates which shut off the Cloisters. The Palace door was in the innermost or southeast corner of the Cloisters.

It was very dark at the end of the passage; and fortunately. For the gates were fast closed, and before he could, groping, find the knocker, the rabble had entered the passage behind him and cut off his retreat. The high wall which rose on either side made escape impossible. Nor was this all. As he awoke to the trap in which he had placed himself, a voice at his elbow muttered, 'My God, we shall be murdered!' And he learned that Sir Robert had followed him.

He had no time to remonstrate, nor thought of remonstrance. 'Stand flat against the wall!' he muttered, his fingers closing upon the staff in his pocket. 'It is our only chance!'

He had barely spoken before the leaders of the mob swept round the elbow. They had one light, a flare borne above them, which shone on the tarpaulins and white smocks, and on the huge ship hammers they carried. There was a single moment of great peril, and instinctively Vaughan stepped before the older man. He could not have made a happier movement, for it seemed to the crowd who caught a glimpse of the two, as if he advanced against the gates along with their leaders.

The peril indeed, or the worst of it, was over the moment they fell into the ranks. 'Hammers to the front!' was the cry. And Sir Robert and Vaughan were thrust back into the second line, that those who wielded the hammers might have room. Vaughan tipped his hat over his face, and the ruffians who pressed upon the two and jostled them, and whose cries of 'Burn him out! Burn the old devil out!' were dictated by greed rather than hate, were too full of the work to regard their neighbours closely. In three or four minutes – long minutes they seemed to the two enclosed in that unsavoury company – the bars gave way, the gates were thrown open, and Vaughan and Sir Robert, hardly keeping their feet in the rush, were borne into the Cloisters.

The rabble, with cries of triumph, raced across the dark

court to the Palace door and began to use their hammers on that. Vaughan hoped that the Bishop had had warning – in truth he had escaped some hours earlier. At any rate, he saw that he and his companion could do no more, and under cover of the darkness they retreated to the porch of a smaller house which opened on the Cloisters. Here they were safe for the time; and, his heart opened and his tongue loosed by the danger through which they had passed, he turned to his companion and remonstrated with him.

'Sir Robert,' he said, 'this is no place for a man of your years.'

'England will soon be no place for any man of my years,' the baronet answered bitterly. 'I would your leaders, sir, were here to see their work! I would Lord Grey were here to see how well his friends carry out his hints!'

'I doubt if he would be more pleased than you or I!' Vaughan answered. 'In the meantime—'

'The soldiers! Have a care!'

The alarm came from the gate by which they had entered, and Vaughan broke off with an exclamation of joy.

'We have them now!' he said. 'And red-handed! Brereton has only to close the passage, and he must take them all!'

But the rioters took that view also, and the alarm. And they streamed out panic-stricken. When the soldiers rode in, Brereton at their head, not more than twenty or thirty remained in the Precincts. And on that followed the most remarkable of all the scenes that disgraced Bristol that night; the scene which beyond others convinced many of the complicity of the troops, if not of the Government, in the outrage.

Not a man could leave the Palace except with the troops' good will, yet they let the rascals pass. In vain a handful of constables, who had arrived on the heels of the military, exerted themselves to seize such as passed with plunder in their hands. The soldiers discouraged the attempt, and even beat back the constables. 'Let them go! Let them go!' was the cry. And the nimbleness of the scamps in escaping was greeted with laughter.

Vaughan and the companion whom fate had so strangely joined saw these things with indignation. But Vaughan had made up his mind that he would not approach Brereton again; and he controlled himself until a blackguard bolting from the Palace with his arms full of spoil was seized, close to him, by an elderly man, who seemed to be one of the Bishop's servants. The two wrestled fiercely, the servant calling for help, the soldiers looking on and laughing. A moment and the two fell to the ground, the servant undermost. He uttered a cry of pain.

That was too much for Vaughan. He sprang forward, dragged the ruffian from his prey, and drew his staff. He was about to strike his prisoner – for the man continued to struggle desperately – when a voice above them shouted 'Put that up! Put that up!' And a trooper urged his horse almost on the top of them, at the same time threatening him with his naked sword.

Vaughan lost his temper at that. 'You blackguard!' he cried. 'Stand back. The man is my prisoner!'

For answer the soldier struck at him. Fortunately the blade was turned by his hat, and only the flat alighted on his head. But the man, drunk or reckless, repeated the blow, and this time would have cut him down if Sir Robert, with a quickness beyond his years, had not turned aside the stroke with his walking-cane. At the same time, in a tone of command –

'Are you mad?' he shouted. 'Where is your colonel?'

The tone, rather than the words, sobered the trooper. He swore sulkily, reined in his horse, and moved back to his fellows. Sir Robert turned to Vaughan, who, dazed by the blow, was leaning against the porch of the house.

'I hope you are not wounded?' he said.

'It's thanks to you, sir, he's not killed!' the man whom Vaughan had rescued answered; and he hung about him solicitously. 'He'd have cut him to the chin! Ay, to the chin, he would!' – with quavering gusto.

Vaughan was regaining his coolness. He tried to smile. 'I hardly saw what happened,' he said. 'I am only sure I am not hurt. Just – a rap on the head!'

'I am glad that it is no worse,' Sir Robert said gravely. 'Very glad!'

Now it was over he had to bite his lower lip to repress its trembling.

'You feel better, sir, now?' the servant asked, addressing Vaughan.

'Yes, yes,' Vaughan said.

But after that he was silent. And Sir Robert was silent too. The soldiers were withdrawing; the constables, outraged and indignant, were following them, declaring aloud that they were betrayed. And for certain the walls of the Cathedral had looked down on few stranger scenes, even in those troubled days when the crosslets of the Berkeleys first shone from their casements.

Vaughan thought of the thing which had happened; and what was he to say? The position was turned upside down. The obligation was on the wrong person; the boot was on the wrong foot. If he, the young, the strong, and the injured, had saved Sir Robert, that had been well enough. But this? It required some magnanimity to take it gracefully, to bear it with dignity.

'I owe you thanks,' he said at last, but awkwardly and with constraint.

'The blackguard!' Sir Robert cried.

'You saved me, sir, from very serious injury.'

'It was as much threat as blow!' Sir Robert rejoined.

'I don't think so,' Vaughan returned. And then he was silent, finding it hard to say more. But after a pause, 'I can only make you one return,' he said, with an effort. 'Perhaps you will believe me when I say that upon my honour I do not know where your daughter is. I have neither spoken to her nor communicated with her since I saw her in Queen's Square in May. And I know nothing of Lady Sybil.'

'I am obliged to you,' Sir Robert said.

'If you believe me,' Vaughan said. 'Not otherwise!'

'I do believe you, Mr Vaughan.' And Sir Robert said it as if he meant it.

'Then that is something gained,' Vaughan answered, 'besides the soundness of my head.' Try as he might, he felt the position irksome, and was glad to seek refuge in flippancy.

Sir Robert removed his hat, and stood in perplexity. 'But where can she be?' he asked. 'If you know nothing of her.'

Vaughan paused before he answered. Then, 'I think I should look for her in Queen's Square,' he suggested. 'In that neighbourhood neither life nor property will be safe until Bristol comes to its senses. She should be removed if she be there.'

'I will take your advice and try the house again,' Sir Robert rejoined. 'I think you are right, and I am much obliged to you.'

He put his hat on his head, but removed it to salute the other.

'Thank you,' he repeated, 'I am much obliged to you.' And he departed across the court.

Halfway to the entrance, he paused, and fingered his chin. He went on again; again he paused. He took a step or two, turned, hesitated. At last he came slowly back.

'Perhaps you will go with me?' he asked.

'You are very good,' Vaughan answered, his voice shaking a little.

Was it possible that Sir Robert meant more than he said? It did seem possible.

But after all, they did not go out that way. For, as they approached the broken gates, shouts of 'Reform!' and 'Down with the Lords!' warned them that the rioters were returning. And the Bishop's servant, approaching them again, insisted on taking them through the Palace, and by way of the garden and a low wall, conducted them into Trinity Street. Here they were close to the Drawbridge which crossed the water to the foot of Clare Street; and they passed over it, one of them walking with a lighter heart, notwithstanding Mary's possible danger, than he had borne for weeks. Soon they were in Queen's Square, and, avoiding as far as possible the notice of the mob, were knocking doggedly at Miss Sibson's door. But that time the Palace, high above them on College Green, had burst into flames, and, a sign to all the country side, had flung the red banner of Reform to the night.

CHAPTER XXXIII

Fire!

SIR ROBERT and his companions might have knocked longer and more loudly, and still to no purpose. For the schoolmistress, prepared to witness a certain amount of disorder on the Saturday, had been taken aback by the sight which met her eyes when she rose on Sunday morning. And long before noon she had sent her servants to their friends, locked up her house, and gone next door, to dispel by her cheerful face and her comfortable common sense the fears which she knew would prevail there. The sick lady was not in a state to withstand alarm, Mary was a young girl and timid, and neither the landlady nor Lady Sybil's maid were persons of strong mind. Miss Sibson felt that here was an excellent occasion for the display of that sturdy indifference with which firm nerves and a long experience of Bristol elections had endowed her.

'La, my dear,' was her first remark, 'it's all noise and nonsense! They look very fierce, but there's not a man of them all, that if I took him soundly by the ear and said, "John Thomas Gaisford, I know you well and your wife! You live in the Pithay, and if you don't go straight home this minute I'll tell her of your goings on!" – there's not one of them, my dear,' with a jolly laugh, 'wouldn't sneak off with his tail between his legs! Hurt us, my lady? I'd like to see them doing it. Still, it will be no harm if we lock the door downstairs, and answer no knocks. We shall be cosy upstairs, and see all that's to be seen besides!'

These were Miss Sibson's opinions, a little after noon on the Sunday. Nor when the day began to draw in, without abating the turmoil, did she recant them aloud. But when the servant, who found amusement in listening at the locked door to the talk of those who passed, came open-eyed to announce that the people had fired the Bridewell, and were attacking the gaol, Miss Sibson did rub her nose reflectively. And privately she began to wonder whether the prophecies of evil, which both parties had sown broadcast, were to be fulfilled.

'It's that nasty Brougham!' she said. 'Alderman Daniel told me that he was stirring up the devil; and we're going to get the dust. But la, bless your ladyship,' she continued comfortably, 'I know the Bristol lads, and they'll not hurt us. Just a gaol or two, for the sake of the frolic. My dear, your mother'll have her tea, and will feel the better for it. And we'll draw the curtains and light the lamps and take no heed. Maybe there'll be bones broken, but they'll not be ours!'

Lady Sybil, with her face turned away, muttered something about Paris.

'Well, your ladyship knows Paris and I don't,' the schoolmistress replied respectfully. 'I can fancy anything there. But you may depend upon it, my lady, England is different. I know old Alderman Daniel calls Lord John Russell "Lord John Robespierre", and says he's worse than a Jacobin. But I'll never believe he'd cut the King's head off! Never! And don't you believe it, either, my lady. No, English are English! There's none like them, and never will be. All the same,' she concluded, 'I shall set "Honour the King!" for a copy when the young ladies come back.'

Her views might not have convinced by themselves. But taken with tea and buttered toast, a good fire and a singing kettle, they availed. Lady Sybil was a shade easier that afternoon; and, naturally of a high courage, found a certain alleviation in the exciting doings under her windows. She was gracious to Miss Sibson, whose outpourings she received with languid amusement; and when Mary was not looking, she followed her daughter's movements with mournful eyes. Uncertain as the wind, she was this evening in her best mood; as patient as she could be fractious, and as gentle as she was sometimes violent. She scouted the notion of danger with all Miss Sibson's decision; and after tea she insisted that the lights should be shaded, and her couch be wheeled to the window, in order that, propped high with pillows, she might amuse herself with the hurly-burly in the Square below.

'To be sure,' Miss Sibson commented, 'it will do no good to anyone, this; and many a poor chap will suffer for it by-and-by. That's the worst of these Broughams and Besoms, my lady. It's the low down that swallow the dust. It's very fine to cry "King and Reform!" and drink the Corporation wine!

But it will be "Between our sovereign lord the King and the prisoner at the bar!" one of these days! And their throats will be dry enough then!'

'Poor misguided people!' Mary murmured.

'They've all learned the Church catechism,' the schoolmistress replied shrewdly. 'Or they should have; it's lucky for them – ay, you may shout, my lads – that there's many a slip between the neck and the rope – Lord ha' mercy!'

The last words fitted the context well enough; but they fell so abruptly from her lips that Mary, who was bending over her mother, looked up in alarm.

'What is it?' she asked.

'Only,' Miss Sibson answered with composure, 'what I ought to have said long ago that nothing can be worse for her ladyship than the cold air that comes in at the cracks of this window!'

'It's not that,' Lady Sybil replied, smiling. 'They have set fire to the Mansion House, Mary. You can see the flames in the room on the farther side of the door.'

Mary uttered an exclamation of horror, and they all looked out. The Mansion House was the most distant house on the north, or left-hand side of the Square, viewed from the window at which they stood; the house next Miss Sibson's being about the middle of the west side. Nearer them, on the same side as the Mansion House, stood another public building – the Custom House. And nearer again, being the most northerly house on their own side of the Square, stood a third – the Excise Office.

They had thus a fair, though a side view, of the front of the Mansion House, and were able to watch, with what calmness they might, the flames shoot from one window after another; until, presently, meeting in a wavering veil of fire, they hid – save when the wind blew them aside – all the upper part of the house from their eyes.

A great fire in the night, the savage, uncontrollable revolt of man's tamed servant – is at all times a terrible sight. Nor on this occasion was it only the horror of the flames, roaring and crackling and pouring forth a million of sparks, which chained their eyes. For as these rose, they shed an intense light, not only on the heights of Recliffe, visible above the east side of the Square, and on the stately tower which rose from them, but on the multitude below; on the hurrying forms that, monkey-like, played before the flames and seemed to feed them, and on a still stranger sight, the expanse of upturned faces that, in the rear of the active rioters, extended to the farthest limit of the Square.

For it was the quiescence, it was the inertness of the gazing crowd which most appalled the spectators at the window. To see that great house burn and to see no man stretch forth a hand to quench it, this terrified.

'Oh, but it is frightful! It is horrible!' Mary exclaimed.

'I should like to knock their heads together!' Miss Sibson cried sternly. 'What are the soldiers doing? What is anyone doing?'

'They have hounded on the dogs,' Lady Sybil said slowly – she alone seemed to view the sight with a dispassionate eye, 'and they are biting instead of barking! That is all.'

'Dogs?' Miss Sibson echoed.

'Ay, the dogs of Reform!' Lady Sybil replied cynically. 'Brougham's dogs! Grey's dogs! Russell's dogs! I could wish Sir Robert were here, it would so please him to see his words fulfilled!' And then, as in surprise at the thing she had uttered, 'I wonder when I wished to please him before!' she muttered.

'Oh, but it is frightful!' Mary repeated, unable to remove her eyes from the flames.

It was frightful; even while they were all sane people in the room, and, whatever their fears, restrained them. What then was it a moment later, when the woman of the house burst in upon them, with a maid in wild hysterics clinging to her, and another on the threshold screaming 'Fire! Fire!'

'It's all on fire at the back!' the woman panted. 'It's on fire, it's all on fire, my lady, at the back!'

'It's all – what?' Miss Sibson rejoined, in a tone which had been known to quell the protest of seventeen-year-old rebels. 'It is what, woman? On fire at the back? And if it is, is that a ground for forgetting your manner? Where is your deportment? Fire, indeed! Are you aware whose room this is? For shame! And you, silly,' she continued, addressing herself to the maid, 'be silent, and go outside, as becomes you.'

But the maid, though she retreated to the door, continued to scream, and the woman of the house to wring her hands.

'You had better go and see what it is,' Lady Sybil said, turning to the schoolmistress. For, strange to say, she who a few hours before had groaned if a coal fell on the hearth, and complained if her book slid from the couch, was now quite calm.

'They are afraid of their own shadows,' Miss Sibson cried contemptuously. 'It is the reflection they have seen.' But she went. And as it was but a step to a window overlooking the rear, Mary went with her.

They looked. And for a moment something like panic seized them. The back of the house was not immediately upon the quay, but through an opening in the warehouses which fringed the latter it commanded a view of the water and the masts, and of the sloping ground which rose to College Green. And high above, dyeing the Floating Basin crimson, the Palace showed in a glow of fire; fire which seemed to be on the point of attacking the Cathedral, of which every pinnacle and buttress, with every chimney of the old houses clustered about it, stood out in the hot glare. It was clear that the building had been burning for some time, for the roar of the flames could be heard, and almost the hiss of the water as innumerable sparks floated down to it.

Horror-struck, Mary grasped her companion's arm. And 'Good Heavens!' Miss Sibson muttered. 'The whole city will be burned!'

'And we are between the two fires,' Mary faltered. An involuntary shudder might be pardoned her.

'Ay, but far enough from them!' the schoolmistress answered, recovering herself. 'On this side, the water makes us safe.'

'And on the other?'

'La, my dear,' Miss Sibson replied confidently. 'The folks are not going to burn their own houses. They are angry with the Corporation. They hold them all one with Wetherell. And for the Bishop, they've so abused him the last six months that he dare not show his wig in the streets, and it's no wonder the poor ignorants think him fair game. For us, we're just ordinary folk, and they'll no more harm us than fly. But we must go back to your mother.'

They went back, and wisely Miss Sibson made no mystery of the truth; repeating, however, those arguments against giving way to alarm which she had used to Mary.

'The poor dear gentleman has lost his house,' she concluded piously. 'But we should be thankful he has another.'

Lady Sybil took the news with calmness; her eyes, indeed, seemed brighter, as if she enjoyed the excitement. But the frightened woman at the door refused to be comforted, and underlying the courage of the two who stood by Lady Sybil's couch was a secret uneasiness, which every cheer of the crowd below the windows, every 'Huzza' which rose from the revellers, every wild rush from one part of the Square to another tended to strengthen. In her heart Miss Sibson owned that in all her experience she had known nothing like this; no disorder so flagrant, so unbridled, so daring. She could carry her mind back to the days when the cheek of England had paled at the Massacres of September in Paris. The deeds of '98 in Ireland, she had read morning by morning in the journals. The Three Days of July, with their street fighting, were fresh in all men's minds – it was impossible to ignore their bearing on the present conflagration. And if here was not the dawn of Revolution, if here were not signs of the crash of things, appearances deceived her. But she was not to be dismayed. She believed that even in revolutions a comfortable courage, sound sense, and a good appetite went far. And 'I'd like to hear John Thomas Gaisford talk to me of guillotines!' she thought. 'I'd make his ears burn!'

Meanwhile, Mary was thinking that, whatever the emergency, her mother was too ill to be moved. Miss Sibson might be right, the danger might be remote. But it was barely midnight; and long hours of suspense must be lived through before morning came. Meanwhile there were only women in the house, and, bravely as the girl controlled herself, a cry more reckless than usual, an outburst of cheering more savage, a rush below the windows, drove the blood to her heart. And presently, while she gazed with shrinking eyes on the crowd, now blood-red in the glow of the burning timbers, now lost for a moment in darkness, a groan broke from it, and she saw pale flames appear at the windows of the house next to the Mansion House. They shot up rapidly, licking the front of the building.

Miss Sibson saw them at the same moment, and 'The villains!' she exclaimed. 'God grant it be an accident!'

Mary's lips moved, but no sound came from them.

Lady Sybil laughed her shrill laugh. 'The curs are biting bravely!' she said. 'What will Bristol say to this?'

'Show them that they have gone too far!' Miss Sibson answered stoutly. 'The soldiers will act now, and will put them in their places, as they did in Wiltshire in the winter! And high time too!'

But though they watched in tense anxiety for the first sign of action on the part of the troops, for the first movement of the authorities, they gazed in vain. The miscreants, who fed the flames and spread them, were few; and in the Square were thousands who had property to lose, and friends and interests in jeopardy. If a tithe only of those who looked on, quiescent and despairing, had raised their hands, they could have beaten the rabble from the place. But no man moved. The fear of coming trouble, which had been long in the air, paralysed even the courageous, while the ignorant and the timid believed that they saw a revolution in progress, and that henceforth the mob would rule – and woe betide the man who set himself against it! As it had been in Paris, so it would be here. And so the flames spread, before the eyes of the terrified women at the window, before the eyes of the inert multitude, from the house first attacked to its neighbour, and from that to the next and the next. Until the noise of the conflagration, the crash of sinking walls, the crackling of beams were as the roar of falling waters, and the Square in that hideous red light, which every moment deepened, resembled an inferno, in which the devils of hell played pranks, and wherein, most terrible sight of all, thousands who in ordinary times deemed the salvation of property the first of duties, stood with scared eyes, passive and cowed.

It was such a scene – and they were only women, and alone in the house – as the mind cannot imagine and the eye views but once in a generation, nor ever forgets. In quiet Clifton, and on St Michael's Hill, children were snatched from their midnight slumbers and borne into the open, that they might see the city stretched below them in a pit of flame, with the over-arching fog confining and reflecting the glare. Dundry Tower, five miles from the scene, shone a red portent visible for leagues; and in Chepstow and South Monmouth, beyond the wide estuary of the Severn, the light was such that men could see to read. From all the distant Mendips, and from the Forest of Dean, miners and charcoal burners gazed southward with scared faces, and told one another that the Revolution was begun; while Lansdowne Chase sent riders galloping up the London Road with the news that all the West was up. Long before dawn on the Monday horsemen and yellow chaises were carrying the news through the night to Gloucester, to Southampton, to Salisbury, to Exeter, to every place where scanty companies of foot lay, or yeomanry had their headquarters. And where these passed, alarming the sleeping inns and posthouses, panic sprang up upon their heels, and the travellers on the down night-coaches marvelled at the tales which met them with the daylight.

If the sight viewed from a distance was so terrible as to appal a whole countryside, if, on those who gazed at it from vantage spots of safety, and did not guess at the dreadful details, it left an impression of terror never to be effaced, what was it to the three women who, in the Square itself, watched the onward march of the flames towards them, were blinded by the glare, choked by the smoke, deafened by the roar? Whom distance saved from no feature of the scene played under their windows: who could shun neither the savage cries of the drunken rabble, dancing before the doomed houses, nor the sight, scarce less amazing, of the insensibility which watched the march of the flames and stretched forth not a finger to stay them! Who, chained by Lady Sybil's weakness to the place where they stood, saw house after house go up in flames, until all the side of the Square adjoining their own was a wall of fire; and who then were left to guess the progress, swift or slow, which the element was making towards them! For whom the copper-hued fog above them must have seemed, indeed, the roof of a furnace, from which escape grew moment by moment less likely?

CHAPTER XXXIV

Hours of Darkness

THE WOMEN of the house had fled long before, taking Lady Sybil's maid with them. And dreadful as was the situation of those who remained, appalling as were the fears of two of them, they were able to control themselves; the better because they knew that they had no aid but their own to look to, and that their companion was helpless. Fortunately Lady Sybil, who had watched the earlier phases with the detachment which is one of the marks of extreme weakness, had at a certain point turned faint, and demanded to be removed from the window. She was ignorant, therefore, of the approach of the flames and of the imminence of the peril. She had even, in spite of the uproar, dozed off, after a few minutes of trying irritation, into an uneasy sleep.

Mary and Miss Sibson were thus left free. But for what? Compelled to gaze in suspense on the progress of the flames, driven at times to fancy that they could feel the heat of the fire, assailed more than once by gusts of fear, as one or the other imagined that they were already cut off, they could not have held their ground but for their unselfishness – but for their possession of those qualities of love and heroism which raise women to the height of occasion, and nerve them to a pitch of endurance of which men are rarely capable. In the schoolmistress, with her powdered nose and her portly figure, and her dull past of samplers and backboards and Mrs Chapone, there dwelt as sturdy a spirit as in any of the Bristol shipmasters from whom she sprang. She might be fond of a sweetbread, and a glass of port might not come amiss to her. But the heart in her was stout and large, and she had as soon dreamed of forsaking her forlorn companions as those bluff sailormen would have dreamed of striking their flag to a codfish Don, or to a shipload of mutinous slaves.

And Mary? Perchance the gentlest and the mildest are also the bravest, when the stress is real. Or perhaps those who have never known a mother's love cling to the veriest shred and tatter of it, if it fall in their way. Or perhaps – but why try to explain that which all history has proved a hundred times over – that love casts out fear. Mary quailed, deafened by the thunder of the fire, with the walls of the room turning blood-red round her, and the smoke beginning to drift before the window. But she stood; and only once, assailed by every form of fear, did her courage fail her, or sink below the stronger nerve of the elder woman.

That was when Miss Sibson, after watching that latest and most pregnant sign, the eddying of smoke past the window, spoke out.

'I'm going next door,' she cried, in Mary's ear. 'There are papers I must save; they are all I have for my old age. The rest may go, but I can't see them burn when five minutes may save them.'

But Mary clung to her desperately. 'Oh!' she cried, 'don't leave me!'

Miss Sibson patted her shoulder. 'I shall come back,' she said. 'I shall come back, my dear. And then we must move your mother – into the Square if no better can be. Do you come down and let me in when I knock three times.

Lady Sybil was still dozing, with a woollen wrap about her head to deaden the noise; and giving way to the cooler brain Mary went down with the schoolmistress. In the hall the roar of the fire was less, for the only window was shuttered. But the raucous voices of the mob, moving to and fro outside, were more clearly heard.

Miss Sibson remained undaunted. 'Put up the chain the moment I am outside,' she said.

'But are you not afraid?' Mary cried, holding her back.

'Of those scamps?' Miss Sibson replied truculently. 'They had better not touch me!'

And she turned the key and slipped out. Nor did she quit the step until Mary had put up the chain and re-locked the door.

Mary waited – oh, many, many minutes it seemed – in the gloom of the hall, pierced here and there by a lurid ray; with half her mind on her mother upstairs, and the other half on the ribald laughter, the drunken oaths and threats and curses which penetrated from the Square. It was plain that Miss

Sibson had not gone too soon, for twice or thrice the door was struck by some heavy instrument, and harsh voices called on the inmates to open if they did not wish to be burned. Uncertain how the fire advanced, Mary received these warnings with a sick heart. But she held her ground, until, oh, joy! she heard voices raised in altercation, and among them the schoolmistress's. A hand knocked thrice, she turned the key and let down the chain. The door opened upon her, and on the steps, with her hand on a man's shoulder, appeared Miss Sibson. Behind her and her captive, between them and that background of flame and confusion, stood a group of four or five men – dock labourers, in tarpaulins and frocks, who laughed tipsily.

'This lad will help to carry your mother out,' Miss Sibson said, with the utmost coolness. 'Come, my lad, and no nonsense! You don't want to burn a sick lady in her bed!'

'No, I don't, missis,' the man grumbled, sheepishly. 'But I'm none here for that! I'm none here for that, and—'

'You'll do it, all the same,' the schoolmistress replied. 'And I want one more. Here, you,' she continued, addressing a grinning hobbledehoy in a sealskin cap. 'I know your face, and you'll want someone to speak for you at the Assizes. Come in, you two, and the rest must wait until the lady's carried out!'

And thereon, with that strange mixture of humanity and unreasoning fury of which the night left many examples, the men complied. The two whom she had chosen entered, the others suffered her to shut the door in their faces. Only, 'You'll be quick!' one bawled after her. 'She's afire next door!'

That was the warning that went with them upstairs, and it nerved them for the task before them. Over that task it were well to draw a veil. The poor sick woman, roused anew and abruptly to a sense of her surroundings, to the flickering lights, the smell of smoke, the strange faces, to all the horrors of that scene rarely equalled in our modern England, shrieked aloud. The courage which had before upheld her deserted her. She refused to be moved, refused to believe that they were there to save her; she failed even to recognize her daughter, she resisted their efforts, and whatever Mary could say or do, she added to the peril of the moment all the misery which frantic terror and unavailing shrieks could add. They did not know, while they reasoned with her, and tried to lift her, and strove to cloak her against the outer air, the minute at which the house might be entered; nor even that it was not already entered, already in some part on fire. The girl, though her hands were steady, though she never wavered, though she persisted, was white as paper. And even Miss Sibson was almost unnerved, when nature came to their aid, and with a last frantic protest, a last attempt to thrust them from her, the poor woman swooned; and the men who had looked on, as unhappy as those engaged, lifted the couch and bore her down the stairs. Odd are the windings of Chance and Fate. These men, in whom every good instinct was awakened by the sight before them, might, had the schoolmistress's eye alighted on others, have plundered on with their fellows; and with the more luckless of those fellows have stood on the scaffold a month later!

Still, time had been lost, and perforce the men descended slowly, so that as they reached the hall the door gave way, and admitted a dozen rascals, who tumbled over one another in their greed. The moment was critical, the inrush of horrid sounds and sights appalling. But Mary rose to the occasion. With a courage which from this time remained with her to the end, she put herself forward.

'Will you let us pass out?' she said. 'My mother is ill. You do not wish to harm her?'

Now Lady Sybil had made Mary put off the Quaker-like costume in which she had wished to nurse her, and she had had no time to cover the light muslin dress she wore. The men saw before them a beautiful creature, white-robed, bare-headed, bare-armed – even the schoolmistress had not snatched up so much as a cloak – a Una with sweet shining eyes, before whom they fell aside abashed.

'Lord love you, miss!' one cried heartily. 'Take her out! And God bless you!' while the others grinned fatuously.

So down the steps and into the turmoil of the seething Square, walled on two sides by fire, and crowded with a drunken, frenzied rabble – for all decent onlookers had fled, awake at last to the result of their quiescence – the strange procession moved, the girl going first. Tipsy groups, singing and dancing delirious jigs to the music of falling walls, pillagers hurrying in ruthless haste from house to house, or quarrelling over their spoils, householders striving to save a remnant of their goods from dwellings past saving – all made way for it. Men who swayed on their feet, brandishing their arms and shouting obscene refrains, being touched on the shoulder by others, stared, and gave place with mouths agape. Even boys, whom the madness of that night made worse than men, and unsexed women, shrank at sight of it, and were silent – nay, followed with a strange homage the slender white figure, the shining eyes, the pure sweet face.

In the worst horrors of the French Revolution it is said that the devotion of a daughter stayed the hands which were lifted to slay her father. Even so, in this night in Bristol, amid surroundings less bloody, but almost as appalling, the wildest and the most furious made way for the daughter and the mother.

Led by instinct rather than by calculation, Mary did not pause, or look aside, but moved onward, until she reached the middle of the Square; until some sixty or seventy yards divided her charge from the nearest of the burning houses. The heat was less scorching here, the crowd less compact. A fixed seat afforded shelter on one side, and by it she signed to the bearers to set the couch down. The statue stood not far away on the other side, and secured them against the ugly rushes which were caused from time to time by the fall of a roof or a rain of sparks.

Mary gazed round her in stupor. The whole of the north side of the great Square, and a half of the west side – full thirty lofty houses – were in flames, or were sinking in red-hot ruin. The long wall of fire, the canopy of glowing smoke, the ceaseless roar of the element, the random movements of the forms which, pygmy-like, played between her and the conflagration, the doom which threatened the whole city, held her awe-struck, spell-bound, fascinated.

But even the feelings which she experienced, confronted by that sight, were exceeded by the emotions of one who had seen her advance; of one who, at first with horror, then as he recognized her, with incredulity, had watched the white figure which threaded its way through this rout of satyrs, this orgy of recklessness. She had not succeeded in wresting her eyes from the spectacle before a hand fell on her arm, and the last voice she expected to hear called her by name.

'Mary!' Sir Robert cried. 'Mary! My God! What are you doing here?' For, taken up with staring at her, he had seen neither who accompanied her nor what they bore.

A sob of relief and joy broke from her, as she flung herself into his arms and clung to him. 'Oh!' she cried. 'Oh!' She could say no more at that moment. But the joy of it! To have at last a man to turn to, a man to lean upon, a man to look to!

And still he could not grasp the position. And 'My God!' he repeated in wonder. 'What, child, what are you doing here?'

But before she could answer him his eyes sank to the level of the couch, which the figures about it shaded from the scorching light. And he started, and stepped back. In a lower voice and a quavering tone he called upon his Maker. He was beginning to understand.

'We had to bring her out,' she sobbed. 'We had to bring her out. The house is on fire. See!'

She pointed to the house beside Miss Sibson's, from the upper windows of which smoke was beginning to curl and eddy. Men were pouring from the door below, carrying their booty and jostling others who sought to enter.

'You have been here all day?' he asked, passing his hand over his brow.

'Yes.'

'All day? All day?' he repeated.

'Yes.'

He covered his eyes with his hand, while Mary, recalled by a touch from Miss Sibson, knelt beside her mother, to feel her pulse, to rub her hands, to make sure that life still lingered in the inanimate frame. He had not asked, he did not ask who it was over whom his daughter hung with so tender a solicitude. He did not even look at the cloaked figure. But the sidelong glance which at once sought and shunned, the quivering of his mouth, which his shaking fingers did not avail to hide, the agitation which unnerved a frame erect but feeble, all betrayed his knowledge. And what must have been his thoughts, how poignant his reflections as he considered that there, there, enveloped in those shapeless wraps, there lay the bride whom he had wedded with hopes so high a score of years before! The mother of his child, the wife whom he had last seen in the pride of her beauty, the woman from whom he had been parted for sixteen years, and who through all those sixteen years had never been absent from his thoughts for an hour, nor ever been aught in them but an abiding, clinging, embittering memory – she lay there!

What wonder, if the scene about them rolled away and he saw her again in the stately gardens at Stapylton, walking, smiling, talking, flirting, the gayest of the gay, the lightest of the butterflies, the admired of all? Or if his heart bled at the remembrance – at that remembrance and many another? Or again, what wonder if his mind went back to long hours of brooding in his sombre library, hours given up to the rehearsal of grave remonstrances, vain reproofs, bitter complaints, all destined to meet with defiance? And if at this picture of the irrevocable past his head sank lower, his hands trembled more senilely, his breast heaved?

Of all the abnormal things wrought in Bristol that night, of all the strangely begotten brood of riot and fire, and Reform, none were stranger than this meeting, if meeting that could be called where one was ignorant of the other's presence, and he would not look upon her face. For he would not, perhaps he dared not. He stood with bent head, pondering and absorbed, until an uprush of sparks, more fiery than usual, and the movement of the crowd to avoid them, awoke him from his thoughts. Then his eyes fell on Mary's uncovered head and neck, and he took the cloak from his own shoulders and put it on her, with a touch as if he blessed her. She was kneeling beside the couch at the moment, her head bent to her mother's, her hair mingling with her mother's. But he contrived to close his eyes and would not see his wife's face.

After that he moved to the farther side of the couch, where some sneaking hobbledehoys showed a disposition to break in upon them. And old as he was, and shaken and weary, he stood sentry there, a gaunt stooping figure, for long hours, until the prayed-for day began to break above Redcliffe and to discover the grim relics of the night's work.

CHAPTER XXXV

The Morning of Monday

IT HAS been said that midnight of that Sunday saw the alarm speeding along every road by which the forces of order could hope to be recruited; nevertheless in Bristol itself nothing was done to stay the work of havoc. True, a change had come over the feeling in the city; to acquiescence had succeeded the most lively alarm, and to approval, rage and boundless indignation. But the handful of officials who throughout the day had striven, honestly if not very ably, to restore order, were exhausted; and the public without cohesion or leaders were in no condition to make head against the rioters. So great, indeed, was the confusion that a troop of Gloucestershire Yeomanry which rode in after nightfall received neither orders nor billets; and being poorly led, withdrew within the hour. This, with a tumult at Bath, where the quarters of the yeomanry were beset by a mob of Reformers, who would not let them go to the rescue, completed the isolation of the city.

One man only, in the midst of that welter, had power to intervene with effect. And he could not be found. From Queen's Square to Leigh's Bazaar, where the Third Dragoons stood inactive by their horses; from Leigh's to the Recruiting Office on College Green, where a couple of non-commissioned officers stood inactive by their desks; from the Recruiting Office to his lodgings in Unity Street, men, panting and protesting, in terror for their property, hurried in vain nightmare pursuit of that man. For to these persons it seemed impossible that in face of the damage already done, of thirty houses in flames, of a mob which had broken all bounds, of a city disturbed to its entrails, he could still refuse to act.

But to go to Unity Street was one thing, and to gain speech with Brereton was another. He had gone to bed. He was asleep. He was not well. He was worn out and was resting. The seekers, with the roar of the fire in their ears and ruin staring them in the face, heard these incredible things, and went away, swearing profanely. Nor did anyone gain speech with him, until the small hours were well advanced. Then Arthur Vaughan, unable to abide by the vow he had taken not to importune him, arrived, he too furious, at the door, and found a knot of gentlemen clamouring for admission.

Vaughan had parted from Sir Robert Vermuyden some hours earlier, believing that, bad as things were, he might make head against the rioters, if he could rally his constables. But he had found no one willing to act without the soldiery; and he was here in the last resort, determined to compel Colonel Brereton to move, if it were by main force. For Vaughan had the law-keeping instincts of an Englishman and his blood boiled at the sights he had seen in the streets, at the wanton destruction of property, at the jeopardy of life, at the women made homeless, at the men made paupers. Nor was it quite out of his thoughts that if anything could harm the cause of Reform it was these deeds done in its name, these outrages fulfilling to the letter the worst which its enemies had predicted of it!

He spoke a few words to the persons who, angry and nonplussed, were wrangling at the door, then he pushed his way in, deaf to the remonstrances of the woman of the house. He did not believe, he could not believe, the excuse given – that Brereton was in bed. Nero, fiddling while Rome burned, seemed nought beside that! His surprise was great when, opening the sitting-room door, he saw before him only the Honourable Bob; who, standing on the hearthrug, met his indignant look with one of forced and sickly amusement.

'Good Heavens!' Vaughan cried, staring at him. 'What are you doing here? Where's the Chief?'

Flixton shrugged his shoulders. 'There,' he said irritably, 'it's no use blaming me! Man alive, if he won't, he won't! And it's his business, not mine!'

'Then I'd make it mine!' Vaughan retorted. 'Where is he?'

Flixton flicked his thumb in the direction of an inner door. 'He's there,' he said. 'He's there, safe enough! For the rest, it is easy to find fault! Very easy for you, my lad! You're no longer in the Service.'

'There are a good many will leave the Service for this!' Vaughan rejoined; and he saw that the shot told. Flixton's face fell, he opened his mouth to reply. But disdaining to listen to excuses, of which the speaker's manner betrayed the shallowness, Vaughan opened the bedroom door and passed in.

To his boundless astonishment Brereton was really in bed, though he had a light beside him. Asleep he probably was not, for he rose at once to a sitting posture and, with dishevelled hair, confronted the intruder, his looks betraying both anger and discomfiture. His sword and an undress cap, blue with a silver band, lay beside the candle on the table, and Vaughan saw that though in his shirt sleeves he was not otherwise undressed.

'Mr Vaughan!' he cried. 'What, if you please, does this mean?'

'That is what I am here to ask you!' Vaughan answered, his face flushed with indignation. He was too angry to pick his words. 'Are you, can you be aware, sir, what is done while you sleep?'

'Sleep?' Brereton rejoined, with a sombre gleam in his eyes. 'Sleep, man? God knows it is the last thing I do!' He clapped his hand to his brow and for a moment remained silent, holding it there. Then, 'Sleep has been a stranger to me these three nights!' he said.

'Then what do you do here?' Vaughan answered, in astonishment. He looked round the room as if he might find his answer there.

'Ah!' Brereton rejoined, with a look half suspicious, half cunning. 'That is another matter. But never mind! Never mind! I know what I am doing.'

'Know—'

'Yes, well!' the soldier replied, bringing his feet to the floor, but continuing to keep his seat on the bed. 'Very well, sir, I assure you.'

Vaughan looked aghast at him. 'But, Colonel Brereton,' he rejoined, 'do you consider that you are the only person in this city able to act? That without you nothing can be done and nothing can be ventured!'

'That,' Brereton returned, with the same shrewd look, 'is just what I do consider! Without me they cannot act! They cannot venture. And I – go to bed!'

He chuckled at it, as at a jest; and Vaughan, checked by the oddity of his manner, and with a growing suspicion in his mind, knew not what to think. At last, 'I fear that you will not be able to go to bed, Colonel Brereton,' he said gravely, 'when the moment comes to face the consequences.'

'The consequences?'

'You cannot think that a city such as this can be destroyed, and no one be called to account?'

'But the civil power—'

'Is impotent!' Vaughan answered, with returning indignation, 'in the face of the disorder now prevailing! I warn you! A little more delay, a little more licence, let the people's passions be fanned by further impunity, and nothing, nothing, I warn you, Colonel Brereton,' he continued with emphasis, 'can save the major part of Bristol from destruction!'

Brereton rose to his feet, an added wildness in his aspect. 'Good God!' he exclaimed. 'You don't mean it! Do you really mean it, Vaughan? But – but what can I do?' He sank down on the bed again, and stared at his companion. 'Eh? What can I do? Nothing!'

'Everything!'

He sprang to his feet. 'Everything! You say everything?' he cried, and his tone rose, shrill and excited. 'But you don't know!' he continued, lowering his voice as quickly as he had raised it and laying his hand on Vaughan's sleeve – 'you don't know! You don't know! But I know! I was set in command here on purpose. If I acted they counted on putting the blame on me. And if I didn't act – they would still put the blame on me.'

His cunning look shocked Vaughan. 'But even so, sir,' he answered, 'you can do your duty.'

'My duty?' Brereton repeated, raising his voice again. 'And do you think it is my duty to precipitate a useless struggle? To begin a civil war? To throw away the lives of my own men and cut down innocent folk? To fill the streets with blood and slaughter? And the end the same?'

'Ay, sir, I do,' Vaughan answered sternly. 'If by so doing a worse calamity may be averted! And, for your men's lives, are they not soldiers? For your own life, are you not a soldier? And will you shun a soldier's duty?'

Brereton clapped his hand to his brow, and, holding it

there, paced the room in his shirt and breeches.

'My God! My God!' he cried, as he went. 'I do not know what to do! But if – if it be as bad as you say—'

'It is as bad, and worse!'

'I might try once more,' looking at Vaughan with a troubled, undecided eye, 'what showing my men might do? What do you think?'

Vaughan thought that if the other were once on the spot, if he saw with his own eyes the lawlessness of the mob, he might act. And he assented.

'Shall I pass on the order, sir,' he added, 'while you dress?'

'Yes, I think you may. Yes, certainly. Tell the officer commanding to march his men to the Square, and I'll meet him there.'

Vaughan waited for no more. He suspected that the burden of responsibility had proved too heavy for Brereton's mind. He suspected that the Colonel had brooded upon his position between a Whig government and a Whig mob until the notion that he was sent there to be a scapegoat had become a fixed idea; and with it the determination that he would not be forced into strong measures had become also a fixed idea.

Such a man, if he was to be blamed, was to be pitied also. And Vaughan, even in the heat of his indignation, did pity him. But he entertained no such feeling for the Honourable Bob, and in delivering the order to him he wasted no words. After Flixton had left the room, however, he remembered that he had noted a shade of indecision in the aide's manner. And warned by it, he followed him.

'I will come with you to Leigh's,' he said.

'Better come all the way,' Flixton replied, with covert insolence. 'We've half a dozen spare horses.'

The next moment he was sorry he had spoken. For 'Done with you!' Vaughan cried. 'There's nothing I'd like better!'

Flixton grunted. He had overreached himself. But he could not withdraw the offer, and Vaughan went out with him.

Let no man think that the past is done with, though he sever it as he will. The life from which he has cut himself off in disgust has none the less cast the tendrils of custom about his heart, which shoot and bud when he least expects it. Vaughan stood in the doorway of the stable while the men bridled. He viewed the long line of tossing heads, and the smoky lanthorns fixed to the stall posts; he sniffed the old familiar smell of 'Stables'. And he felt his heart leap to the past. Ay, even as it leapt a few minutes later, when he rode down College Green, now in darkness, now in glare, and heard beside him the familiar clank of spur and scabbard, the rattle of the bridle chains, and the tramp of the shod hoofs. On the men's left, as they descended the slope at a walk, the tall houses stood up in bright light; below them on the right the Float gleamed darkly; above them, the mist glowed red. Wild hurrahing and an indescribable babel of shouts, mingled with the rushing roar of the flames, rose from the Square. When the troop rode into it with the first dawn, they saw that two whole sides – with the exception of a pair of houses – were burnt or burning. In addition a monster warehouse was on fire in the rear, a menace to every building to windward of it.

The Colonel, with Flixton attending him, fell in on the flank, as the troop entered the Square. But apparently – since he gave no orders – he did not share the tingling indignation which Vaughan experienced as he viewed the scene. A few persons were still engaged in removing their goods from houses on the south side; but save for these, the decent and respectable had long since fled the place, and left it a prey to all that was most vile and dangerous in the population of a rough seaport. The rabble, left to themselves, and constantly recruited as the news flew abroad, had cast off the fear of reprisals, and believed that at last the city was their own.

The troop had not ridden far into the open before Vaughan was shocked, as well as astonished, by the appearance of Sir Robert Vermuyden, who came stumbling across the Square towards them. He was bareheaded – for in an encounter with a prowler who had approached too near he had lost his hat; he was without his cloak, though the morning was cold. His face, too, unshorn and haggard, added to the tragedy of his appearance; yet in a sense he was himself, and it was not without success that he tried to steady his voice, as, unaware of Vaughan's presence, he accosted the nearest trooper.

'Who is in command, my man?' he asked.

Flixton, who had recognized him, thrust his horse forward.

'Good Heavens, Sir Robert!' he cried. 'What are you doing here? And in this state?'

'Never mind me,' the baronet replied. 'Are you in command?'

Colonel Brereton had halted his men. He came forward. 'No, Sir Robert,' he said. 'I am. And very sorry to see you in this plight.'

'Take no heed of me, sir,' Sir Robert replied sternly. Through how many hours, hours long as days, had he not watched for the soldiers' coming! 'Take no heed of me, sir,' he repeated. 'Unless you have orders to abandon the loyal people of Bristol to their fate – act! Act, sir! If you have eyes, you can see that the mob are beginning to fire the south side on which the shipping abuts. Let that take fire and you cannot save Bristol!'

Brereton looked in the direction indicated, but he did not answer.

Flixton did. 'We understand all that,' he said, somewhat cavalierly. 'We see all that, Sir Robert, believe me. But the Colonel has to think of many things; of more than the immediate moment. We are the only force in Bristol, and—'

'Apparently Bristol is no better for you!' Sir Robert replied – and this time with passion.

So far Vaughan, a horse's length behind Brereton and his aide, heard what passed; but with half his mind. For his eyes, roving in the direction whence Sir Robert had come, had discerned, amid a medley of goods and persons huddled about the statue, in the middle of the Square, a single figure, slender, erect, in black and white, which appeared to be gazing towards him. At first he resisted as incredible the notion which besieged him – at sight of that figure. But the longer he looked the more sure he became that it was, it was Mary! Mary, gazing towards him out of that welter of miserable and shivering figures, as if she looked to him for help!

Perhaps he should have asked Sir Robert's leave to go to her. Perhaps Colonel Brereton's to quit the troop, which he had volunteered to accompany. As a fact he gave no thought to either. He slipped from his saddle, flung his reins to the nearest man, and, crossing the roadway in three strides, he made towards her through the skulking groups who warily watched the dragoons, or hailed them tipsily, and in the name of Reform invited them to drink.

And Mary, who had risen to her feet in alarm, and was gazing after her father, her only hope, her one protection through the night, saw Vaughan coming, tall and stern, through the prowling night-birds about her, as if she had seen an angel! She said not a word, when he came near and she was sure. Nor did he say more than 'Mary!' But he threw into that word so much of love, of joy, of relief, of forgiveness – and of the appeal for forgiveness – that it brought her to his arms, it left her clinging to his breast. All his coldness in Bond Street, his cruelty on the coach, her father's opposition, all were forgotten by her, as if they had not been!

And for him, she might have been the weakest of the weak, and fickle and changeable as the weather, she might have been all that she was not – though he had yet to learn that and how she had carried herself that night – but he knew that in spite of all he loved her. She was still the one woman in the world for him! And she was in peril. But for that there is no knowing how long he might have held her. That thought, however, presently overcame all others, made him insensible even to the sweetness of that embrace, ay, even found words for him.

'How come you here?' he cried. 'How come you here, Mary?'

She freed herself and pointed to her mother. 'I am with her,' she said. 'We had to bring her here. It was all we could do.'

He lowered his eyes and saw what she was guarding; and he understood something of the tragedy of that night. From the couch came a low continuous moaning which made the hair rise on his head. He looked at Mary.

'She does not suffer,' she said quietly. 'She does not know anything.'

'We must remove her!' he said.

She looked at him, and from him to that part of the Square where the rioters wrought still at their fiendish work. And she shuddered.

'Where can we take her?' she answered. 'They are beginning to burn that side also.'

'Then we must remove them!' he answered sternly.

'That's sense!' a hearty voice cried at his elbow. 'And the first I've heard this night!' On which he became aware of Miss Sibson, or rather of a stout body swathed in queer wrappings, who spoke in the schoolmistress's tones, and though pale with fatigue continued to show a brave face to the mischief about her. 'That's talking!' she continued. 'Do that, and you'll do a man's work!'

'Will you have courage if I leave you?' he asked. And when Mary, bravely but with inward terror, answered 'Yes', he told her in brief sentences – with his eyes on the movements in the Square – what course to take, if the rabble made a rush in that direction; and what to do, if the troops charged too near them, and how, by lying down, to avoid danger if the crowd resorted to firearms – since untrained men fired high. Then he touched Miss Sibson on the arm. 'You'll not leave her?' he said.

'God bless the man, no!' the schoolmistress replied. 'Though, for the matter of that, she's as well able to take care of me as I of her!'

Which was not quite true. Or why in after-days did Miss Sibson, at many a cosy whist party and over many a glass of hot negus, tell of a particular box on the ear with which she routed a young rascal, more forward than civil? Ay, and dilate with boasting on the way his teeth had rattled, and the gibes with which his fellows had seen him driven from the field?

But, if not quite true, it satisfied Vaughan. He went from them in a cold heat, and finding Sir Robert, still at words and almost at blows with the officers, was going to strike in, when another did so. Daylight was overcoming the glare of the fire, and dispelling the shadows which had lain the deeper and more confusing for that glare. Dawn laid the grey of reality upon the scene, showing all things in their true colours, the ruins more ghastly, the pale licking flames more devilish. The fire, which had swept two sides of the Square, leaving only charred skeletons of houses, gaping with vacant sockets to the sky, was now attacking the third side, of which the two most westerly houses were in flames. It was this, and the knowledge of its meaning, that, before Vaughan could interpose, flung at Colonel Brereton a man white with passion, and stuttering under the pressure of feelings too violent for utterance.

'Do you see? Do you see?' he cried brandishing his fist in Brereton's face – it was Cooke. 'You traitor! If the fire catches the fourth house on that side, it'll get the shipping! The shipping, d'you hear, you Radical? Then the Lord knows what'll escape? But thank God you'll hang! You'll— If it gets to the fourth house, I tell you, it'll catch the rigging by the Great Crane! Are you going to move?'

Vaughan did not wait for Brereton's answer. 'We must charge, Colonel Brereton!' he cried, in a voice which burst the bonds of discipline, and showed that he was determined that others should burst them also. 'Colonel Brereton,' he repeated firmly, setting his horse in motion, 'we must charge without a moment's delay!'

'Wait!' Brereton answered hoarsely. 'Wait! Let me—'

'We must charge!' Vaughan replied, his face set, his mind made up. And turning in his saddle he waved his hand to the men. 'Forward!' he cried, raising his voice to its utmost. 'Forward! Trot! Charge, men, and charge home!'

He spurred his horse to the front, and the whole troop, some thirty strong, set in motion by the magic of his voice, followed him. Even Brereton, after a moment's hesitation, spurred his charger, and fell in a length behind him. The horses broke into a trot, then into a canter. As they bore down along the south side upon the southwest corner, a roar of rage and alarm rose from the rioters collected there; and scores and hundreds fled, screaming, and sought safety to right and left.

Vaughan had time to turn to Brereton, and cry, 'I beg your pardon, sir; I could not help it!' The next moment he and the leading troopers were upon the fleeing, dodging, ducking crowd; were upon them and among them. Half a dozen swords gleamed high and fell, the horses did the rest. The rabble, taken by surprise, made no resistance. In a trice the dragoons were through the mob, and the roadway showed clear behind them, save where here and there a man rose slowly and limped away, leaving a track of blood at his heels.

'Steady! Steady!' Vaughan cried. 'Halt, men! Halt! Right about!' and then, 'Charge!'

He led the men back over the same ground, chasing from it such as had dared to return, or to gather upon the skirts of the troop. Then he led his men along the east side, clearing that also and driving the rioters in a panic into the side streets. Resistance worthy of the name there was none, until, having led the troop back across the open Square and cleared that, too, of the skulkers, he came back again to the south-west corner. There the rabble, rallying from their surprise, had taken up a position in the forecourts of the houses, where they were protected by the railings. They met the soldiers with a volley of stones, and half a dozen pistol shots. A horse fell, two or three of the men were hit; for an instant there was confusion. Then Vaughan spurred his horse into one of the forecourts, and, followed by half a dozen troopers, cleared it, and the next and the next; on which, volunteers who sprang up as by magic, at the first act of authority, entered the houses, killed one rioter, flung out the rest, and extinguished the flames. Still the more determined of the rascals, seeing the small number against them, clung to the place and the forecourts; and, driven from one court, re-treated to another, and to another, and, still protected by the railings, kept the troopers at bay with missiles.

Vaughan, panting with his exertions, took in the position, and looked round for Brereton.

'We must send for the Fourteenth, sir!' he said. 'We are not enough to do more than hold them in check.'

'There is nothing else for it now,' Brereton replied, with a gloomy face and in such a tone that the very men shrank from looking at him; understanding, the dullest of them, what his feelings must be, and how great his shame, who thus superseded, saw another successful in that which it had been his duty to attempt.

And what were Vaughan's feelings? He dared not allow himself the luxury of a glance towards the middle of the Square. Much less – but for a different reason – had he the heart to meet Brereton's eyes.

'I'm not in uniform, sir,' he said. 'I can pass through the crowd. If you think fit, and will give me the order, I'll fetch them, sir?'

Brereton nodded without a word, and Vaughan wheeled his

horse to start. As he pushed it clear of the troop he passed Flixton.

'That was capital!' the Honourable Bob cried heartily. 'Capital! We'll handle 'em easily now, till you come back!'

Vaughan did not answer, nor did he look at Flixton; his look would have conveyed too much. Instead, he put his horse into a trot along the east side of the Square, and, regardless of a dropping fire of stones, made for the opening beside the ruins of the Mansion House. At the last moment, he glanced back, to see Mary if it were possible. But he had waited too long, he could distinguish only confused forms about the base of the statue; and he must look to himself. His road to Keynsham lay through the lowest and most dangerous part of the city.

But though the streets were full of rough men, navigators and seamen, whose faces were set towards the Square, and who eyed him suspiciously as he rode by them, none made any attempt to stop him. And when he had crossed Bristol Bridge and had gained the more open outskirts towards Totterdown, where he could urge his horse to a gallop, the pale faces of men and women at door and window announced that it was not only the upper or the middle class which had taken fright, and longed for help and order. Through Brislington and up Durley Hill he pounded; and it must be confessed that his heart was light. Whatever came of it, though they courtmarshalled him, were that possible, though they tried him, he had done something, he had done right, and he had succeeded. Whatever the consequences, whatever the results to himself, he had dared; and his daring, it might be, had saved a city! Of the charge, indeed, he thought nothing, though she had seen it. It was nothing, for the danger had been of the slightest, the defence contemptible. But in setting discipline at defiance, in superseding the officer commanding the troops, in taking the whole responsibility upon his own shoulders – a responsibility which few would have dreamed of taking – there he had dared, there he had played the man, there he had risen to the occasion! If he had been a failure in the House, here, by good fortune, he had not been a failure. And she would know it. Oh, happy thought! And happy man, riding out of Bristol with the murk and smoke and fog at his back, and the sunshine on his face!

For the sun was above the horizon as with a full heart he rode down the hill into Keynsham, and heard the bugle sound 'Boot and saddle!' and poured into sympathetic ears – and to an accompaniment of strong words – the tale of the night's doings.

An hour later he rode in with the Fourteenth and heard the Blues welcomed with thanksgiving, in the very streets which had stoned them from the city twenty-four hours before. By that time the officer in command of the main body of the Fourteenth at Gloucester had posted over, followed by another troop, and, seeing the state of things, had taken his own line and assumed, though junior to Colonel Brereton, the command of the forces.

After that the thing became a military evolution. One hour, two hours at most, and twenty charges along the quays and through the streets sufficed – at the cost of a dozen lives – to convince the most obstinate of the rabble of several things. *Imprimis*, that the reign of terror was *not* come. On the contrary, that law and order, and also Red Judges, survived. That Reform did not spell fire and pillage, and that at these things even a Reforming Government could not wink. In a word, by noon of that day, Monday, and many and many an hour before the ruins had ceased to smoke, the bubble which might have been easily burst before was pricked. Order reigned in Bristol, patrols were everywhere, two thousand zealous constables guarded the streets. And though troops still continued to hasten to the scene by every road, though all England trembled with alarm, and distant Woolwich sent its guns, and Greenwich horsed them, and the yeomanry of six counties mustered on Clifton Down, or were quartered in the public buildings, the thing was nought. Arthur Vaughan had pricked it in the early morning light when he cried 'Charge!' in Queen's Square.

CHAPTER XXXVI

Forgiveness

THE FIRST wave of thankfulness for crowning blessings or vital escapes has a softening quality against which the hearts of few are wholly proof. Old things, old hopes, old ties, old memories return on that gentle flood-tide to eyes and mind. The barriers raised by time, the furrows of ancient wrong are levelled with the plain, and the generous beast cries '*Non nobis!* Not to us only be the benefit!'

Lady Lansdowne, with something of this kind in her thoughts and pity in her heart, sat eyeing Miss Sibson in a silence which betrayed nothing of her feelings, and which the schoolmistress found irksome. Miss Sibson could beard Sir Robert at need; but of the great of her own sex – and she knew Lady Lansdowne for a very great lady indeed – her sturdy nature went a little in awe. Had her ladyship encroached indeed, Miss Sibson would have known how to put her in her place. But a Lady Lansdowne perfectly polite and wholly silent imposed on her. She rubbed her nose and was glad when the visitor spoke.

'Sir Robert has not seen her, then?'

Miss Sibson smoothed out the lap of her dress. 'No, my lady, not since she was brought into the house. Indeed, I can't say that he saw her before, for he never looked at her.'

'Do you think that I could see her?'

The schoolmistress hesitated. 'Well, my lady,' she said, 'I am afraid that she will hardly live through the day.'

'Then he must see her,' Lady Lansdowne replied quickly. And Miss Sibson observed with surprise that there were tears in the great lady's eyes. 'He must see her. Is she conscious?'

'She's so-so,' Miss Sibson answered, more at her ease. After all, the great lady was human, it seemed. 'She wanders and thinks that she is in France, my lady; believes there's a revolution, and that they are come to take her to prison. Her mind harps continually on things of that kind – and not much wonder either! But then again she's herself. So that you don't know from one minute to another whether she's sensible or not.'

'Poor thing!' Lady Lansdowne murmured. 'Poor thing!' Her lips moved without sound. Presently, 'Her daughter is with her?' she asked.

'She has scarcely left her for a minute since she was carried in,' Miss Sibson answered. And to her eyes, too, there rose something like a tear. 'Only with difficulty have I made her take the most necessary rest. But if your ladyship pleases, I will ask whether she will see you.'

'Do so, if you please.'

Miss Sibson withdrew for the purpose, and Lady Lansdowne, left to herself, rose and looked from the window. As soon as it had been possible to move her, the dying woman had been carried into the nearest house which had escaped the flames, and Lady Lansdowne, gazing out, looked on the scene of conflict, saw lines of ruins, still asmoke in parts, and discerned between the scorched limbs of trees, from which the last foliage had fallen, the blackened skeletons of horuses. A gaping crowd was moving round the Square, under the eyes of special constables, who, distinguished by white bands on their arms, guarded the various entrances. Hundreds, doubtless, who would fain have robbed were there to stare; but for the most part the guilty shunned the scene, and the gazers consisted mainly of sightseers from the country, or from Bath, or of knots of merchants and traders who argued, some that this was what came of Reform, others that not Reform but the refusal of Reform was to blame for it.

Presently she saw Sir Robert's stately figure threading its way through the crowd. He walked erect, but with effort; yet, though her heart swelled with pity, it was not with pity for him. He would have his daughter, and in a few days, in a few weeks, in a few months at most, the clouds would pass and leave him to enjoy the clear evening of his days.

But for her whom he had taken to his house twenty years before in the bloom of her beauty, the envied, petted, spoiled child of fortune, who had sinned so lightly and paid so dearly, and who now lay distraught at the close of all, what evening remained? What gleam of light? What comfort at the last?

On her behalf, the heart which Whig pride, and family

prejudice, and the cares of riches had failed to harden, swelled to bursting.

'He must forgive her!' she ejaculated. 'He shall forgive her!' And gliding to the door she stayed Mary, who was in the act of entering.

'I must see your father,' she said. 'He is mounting the stairs now. Go to your mother, my dear, and when I ring, do you come!'

Mary's eyes met hers, and what they read, of feminine pity and generous purpose, need not be told. Whatever it was, the girl seized the woman's hand and kissed it with wet eyes – and fled. And when Sir Robert, ushered upstairs by Miss Sibson, entered the room and looked round for his daughter, he found in her stead the wife of his enemy.

On the instant he remembered the errand on which she had sought him six months before; and he was quick to construe her presence by its light, and to feel resentment. The wrong of years, the daily, hourly wrong, committed not against him only but against the innocent and the helpless, this woman would have him forgive at a word; merely because the doer, who had had no ruth, no pity, no scruples, hung on the verge of that step which all, just and unjust, must take! And some, he knew, standing where he stood, would forgive; would forgive with their lips, using words which meant nought to the sayer, though they soothed the hearers. But he was no hypocrite; he would not forgive. Forgive? Great Heaven, that any should think that the wrongs of a lifetime could be forgiven in an hour! At a word! Beside a bed! As soon might the grinding wear of years be erased from the heart, the wrinkles of care from the brow, the snows of age from the head! As easily might a word give back to the old the spring and flame and vigour of their youth!

Something of what he thought impressed itself on his face, but though Lady Lansdowne marked the sullen drop of his eyebrows, and the firm set of the lower face, she did not flinch.

'I came upon your name,' she said, 'in the report of the dreadful doings here – in the *Mercury*, this morning. I hope, Sir Robert, I shall be pardoned for intruding.'

He murmured something, as much no as yes, and with a

manner as frigid as his breeding permitted. And standing – she had reseated herself – he continued to look at her, his lips drawn down.

'I grieve,' she continued, 'to find the truth more sad than the report.'

'I do not know that you can help us,' he said.

'No?'

'No.'

'Because,' she rejoined, looking at him softly, 'you will not let me help you. Sir Robert—'

'Lady Lansdowne!' He broke in abruptly, using her name with emphasis, using it with intention. 'Once before you came to me. Doubtless you remember. Now let me say at once that if your errand today be the same, and I think it likely that it is the same—'

'It is not the same,' she replied with emotion which she did not try to hide. 'It is not the same! For then there was time. And now there is no time. Let a day, it may be an hour, pass, and at the cost of all you possess you will not be able to buy that which you can still have for nothing!'

'And what is that?' he asked, frowning.

'An easy heart.' He had not looked for that answer, and he started. 'Sir Robert,' she continued, rising from her seat, and speaking with even deeper feeling, 'forgive her! Forgive her, I implore you! The wrong is past, is done, is over! Your daughter is restored—'

'But not by her!' he cried, taking her up quickly. 'Not by her act!' he repeated sternly, 'or with her will! And what has she done that I should forgive? I, whose life she blighted, whose pride she stabbed, whose hopes she crushed? Whom she left solitary, wifeless, childless through the years of my strength, the years that she cannot, that no one can give back to me? Through the long summer days that were a weariness, and the dark winter days that were a torpor? Yet – yet I could forgive her, Lady Lansdowne, I could forgive her, I do forgive her that!'

'Sir Robert!'

'That, all that!' he continued, with a gesture and in a tone of bitterness which harmonized but ill with the words he uttered. 'All that she ever did amiss to me I forgive her. But –

but the child's wrong – never! Had she relented indeed, at the last, had she of her own motion, of her own free will given me back my daughter, had she repented and undone the wrong, then – but no matter! she did not! She did not one,' he repeated with agitation, 'she did not any of these things. And I ask, what has she done that I should forgive her?'

She did not answer him at once, and when she did it was in a tone so low as to be barely audible.

'I cannot answer that,' she said. 'But is it the only question? Is there not another question, Sir Robert – not what she has done, or left undone, but what you – forgive me and bear with me – have left undone, or done amiss? Are you – you clear of all spot or trespass, innocent of all blame or erring? When she came to you a young girl – a young bride – and, oh, I remember her, the sunshine was not brighter, she was a child of air rather than of earth, so fair and heedless, so capricious, and yet so innocent! – did you in the first days never lose patience? Never fail to make allowance! Never preach when wisdom would have smiled, never look grave when she longed for lightness, never scold when it had been better to laugh? Did you never forget that she was a score of years younger than you, and a hundred years more frivolous? Or,' – Lady Lansdowne's tone was a mere whisper now – 'if you are clear of all offence against her, are you clear of all offence against any, of all trespass? Have you no need to be forgiven, no need, no—'

Her voice died away into silence. She left the appeal unfinished.

Sir Robert paced the room. And other scenes than those on which he had taught himself to brood, other days than those later days of wasted summers and solitary winters, of dullness and decay, rose to his memory. Sombre moods by which it had pleased him – at what a cost! – to make his displeasure known. Sarcastic words, warrant for the facile retort that followed, curt judgements and ill-timed reproofs; and always the sense of outraged dignity to freeze the manner and embitter the tone.

So much, so much which he had forgotten came back to him as he walked the room with averted face! While Lady Lansdowne waited with her hand on the bell. Minutes were passing, minutes; who knew how precious they might be? And with them was passing his opportunity.

He spoke at last. 'I will see her,' he said huskily.

And on that Lady Lansdowne conceived a last act of kindness. She said nothing, she uttered no word of thanks. But when Mary entered, pale, and with that composure which love teaches the least experienced, she was gone. Nor as she drove in all the pomp of her liveries and outriders through Bath, through Corsham, through Chippenham, did those who ran out to watch my lady's four greys go by, see her face as the face of an angel. But Lady Louisa, flying down the steps to meet her – four at a time and hoydenishly – was taken to her arms, unscolded; and knew by instinct that this was the time to pet and be petted, to confess and be forgiven, and to learn in the stillness of her mother's room those thrilling lessons of life, which her governess had not imparted, nor Mrs Fairchild approved.

But more than wisdom sees, love knows.
What eye has scanned the perfume of the rose?
Has any grasped the low grey mist which stands
Ghost-like at eve above the sheeted lands?

Meanwhile Sir Robert paused on the threshold of the room – *her* room, which he had first entered two-and-twenty years before. And as the then and the now, the contrast between the past and the present, forced themselves upon him what could he do but pause and bow his head? In the room a voice, her voice, yet unlike her voice, high, weak, never ceasing, was talking, as from a great distance, from another world; talking, talking, never ceasing. It filled the room. Yet it did not come from a world so distant as he at first fancied; a world that was quite aloof. For when, after he had listened for a time in the shadow by the door, his daughter led him forward, Lady Sybil's eyes took note of their approach, though she recognized neither of them. Her mind was still busy amid the scenes of the riot; twisting and weaving them into a piece with old impressions of the French Terror, made on her mind in childhood by talk heard at her nurse's knee.

'They are coming! They are coming now,' she muttered,

her bright eyes fixed on him. 'But they shall not take her. They shall not take her,' she repeated. 'Hide behind me, Mary. Hide, child! They shan't take you. One neck's enough, and mine is growing thin. It used not to be thin. But that's right. Hide, and they'll not see you, and when I am gone you'll escape. Hush! Here they are!' And then in a louder tone, 'I am ready,' she said, 'I am quite ready.'

Mary leant over her. 'Mother!' she cried, unable to bear the scene in silence. 'Mother! Don't you know me?'

'Hush!' the dying woman answered, a look of terror crossing her face. 'Hush, child! Don't speak! I'm ready, gentlemen; I will go with you. I am not afraid. My neck is small, and it will be but a squeeze.' And she tried to raise herself in the bed.

Mary laid gentle hands on her, and restrained her. 'Mother,' she said. 'Mother! Don't you know me? I am Mary.'

But Lady Sybil, heedless of her, looked beyond her with fear and suspicion in her eyes.

'Yes,' she said. 'I know you. I know you. I know you. But who is – that? Who is that?'

'My father. It is my father. Don't you know him?'

But still, 'Who is it? Who is it?' Lady Sybil continued to ask. 'Who is it?'

Mary burst into tears.

'What does he want? What does he want? What does he want?' the dying woman asked in endless, unreasoning repetition.

Sir Robert had entered the room in the full belief that with the best of wills it would be hard, it would be well-nigh impossible to forgive his wife with more than the lips. But when he heard her, weak and helpless as she was, thinking of another; when he understood that she who had done so great a wrong to the child was willing to give up her own life for the child; when he felt the drag at his heart-strings of many an old and sacred recollection, shared only by her, and which that voice, that face, that form brought back, he fell on his knees by the bed.

She shrank from him, terrified. 'What does he want?' she repeated.

'Sybil,' he said, in a husky voice. 'I want your forgiveness.

Sybil, wife! Do you hear me? Will you forgive me? Will you forgive me, late as it is?'

Strange to say, his voice pierced the confusion which filled the sick brain. She looked at him steadily and long; and she sighed, but she did not answer.

'Sybil,' he repeated in a quavering voice. 'Do you not know me? Don't you remember me? I am your husband.'

'Yes – I know,' she muttered.

'This is your daughter.'

She smiled.

'Our daughter. Our daughter,' he repeated.

'Mary?' she murmured. 'Mary?'

'Yes, Mary.'

She smiled weakly on him – Mary's head was touching his. But she did not answer. She remained looking at them. They could not tell whether she understood, or was slipping away again. At last Sir Robert took her hand and pressed it gently.

'Do you hear me?' he said. 'If I was harsh to you in the old days, if I made mistakes, if I wronged you, I want you – to forgive me.'

'I – forgive you,' she murmured. A faint gleam of mischief, of laughter, of the old Lady Sybil, shone for an instant in her eyes; as if she knew that she had the upper hand. 'I forgive you – everything,' she murmured. Yes, for certain now, she was slipping away.

Mary took her other hand. But she did not speak again. And before the watch on the table beside her had ticked many times she had slipped away for good, with that gleam of triumph in her eyes – forgiving.

CHAPTER XXXVII

In the Mourning Coach

It is a platitude that the flood is followed by the ebb. In the heat of action, and while its warmth cheered his spirits, Arthur Vaughan felt that he had done something. True, what he had done brought him no nearer to making his political dream a reality. Not for him the promise,

It shall be thine in danger's hour
To guide the helm of Britain's power,
And midst thy country's laurelled crown
To twine a garland all thy own.

Yet he had done something. He had played the man when some others had not played the man.

But now that the crisis was over, and he had made his last round, now that he had inspected for the last time the patrols over whom he had been set, seen order restored on the Welsh Back, and panic driven from Berkeley Square, he owned the reaction. There is a fatigue which one night's rest fails to banish; and low in mind and tired in body, he felt, when he rose late on the Tuesday afternoon, that he had done nothing worth doing; nothing that altered his position in essentials.

For a time, indeed, he had fancied that things were changed. Sir Robert had requested his assistance, and allowed him to share his search; and though it was possible that the merest stranger, cast by fortune into the same adventure had been as welcome, it was also possible that the baronet viewed him with a more benevolent eye. And Mary – Mary, too, had flown to his arms as to a haven; but in such a position, amid surroundings so hideous, was that wonderful? Was it not certain that she would have behaved in the same way to the merest acquaintance if he brought her aid and protection?

The answer might be yes or no! What was certain was that it could not avail him. For between him and her there stood more than her father's aversion, more than the doubt of her affection, more than the unlucky borough, of which he had despoiled Sir Robert. There were her possessions, there was the suspicion which Sir Robert had founded on them – on Mary's gain and his loss – there was the independence which he must surrender, and which pride and principle alike forbade him to relinquish.

In the confusion of the night Vaughan had almost forgotten and quite forgiven. Now he saw that the thing, though forgotten, though forgiven, was there. He could not owe all to a man who had so misconstrued him, and who might misconstrue him again. He could not be dependent on one whose views, thoughts, prejudices, were opposed to his own. No, the night and its doing must stand apart. He and she had met, they had parted. He had one memory more, and – nothing was changed.

In this mood the fact that the White Lion regarded him as a hero brought him no comfort. Neither the worshipping eyes of the young lady who had tried to dissuade him from going forth on the Sunday, nor the respectful homage which dogged his movements, uplifted him. He had small appetite for his solitary dinner, and was languidly reading the *Bristol Mercury*, when a name was brought up to him, and a letter.

'Gentleman will wait your pleasure, sir,' the man said.

He broke open the letter, and felt the blood rise to his face as his eyes fell on the signature. The few lines were from his cousin, and ran as follows:

DEAR SIR,

I feel it my duty to inform you, as a connexion of the family, that Lady Sybil Vermuyden died at five minutes past three o'clock this afternoon. Her death, which I am led to believe could in no event have been long delayed, was doubtless hastened by the miserable occurrences of the last few days.

I have directed Isaac White to convey this intimation to your hands, and to inform you from time to time of the arrangements made for her ladyship's funeral, which will take place at Stapylton. I have the honour to be, sir,

Your obedient servant,

ROBERT VERMUYDEN

Vaughan laid the letter down with a groan. As he did so he became aware that Isaac White was in the room.

'Halloa, White,' he said. 'Is that you?'

White looked at him with unconcealed respect. 'Yes, sir,' he said. 'Sir Robert bade me wait on you in person. If I may venture,' he continued, 'to compliment you on my own account, sir – a very great honour to the family, Mr Vaughan – in all the West Country I may say—'

Vaughan stopped him, and said something of Lady Sybil's death; adding that he had never seen her but once.

'Twice, begging your pardon,' White answered, smiling. 'Do you remember I met you at Chippenham before the election, Mr Vaughan? Well, sir, she came up to the coach, and as good as touched your sleeve, poor lady, while I was talking to you. Of course she knew that her daughter was on the coach.'

'I learned afterwards that Lady Sybil travelled by it that day,' Vaughan replied. Then, with a frown, he took up the letter. 'Of course,' he continued, 'I have no intention of attending the funeral.'

'But I think his honour wishes much—'

'There is no possible reason,' Vaughan said doggedly.

'Pardon me, sir,' White answered anxiously. 'You are not aware, I am sure, how highly Sir Robert appreciates your gallant conduct yesterday. No one in Bristol can view it in a stronger light. It is a happy thing he witnessed it. He thinks, indeed, that but for you her ladyship would have died in the crowd. Moreover—'

'That's enough, White,' Vaughan said coldly. 'It is not so much what Sir Robert thinks now, as what he thought formerly.'

'But indeed, sir, his honour's opinion of that matter, too—'

'That's enough, White,' the young gentleman repeated, rising from his seat. He was telling himself that he was not a dog to be kicked away and called to heel again. He would forgive, but he would not return. 'I don't wish to discuss the matter,' he added with an air of finality.

And White did not venture to say more.

He did wisely. For Vaughan, left to himself, had not reflected two minutes before he felt that he had played the churl. To make amends, he called at the house to inquire after the ladies at an hour next morning when they could not be stirring. Having performed that duty, and learned that no inquiry into the riots would be opened for some days – and also that a proposal to give him a piece of gold plate was under debate at the Commercial Rooms, he fled, pride and love at odds in his breast.

It is possible that, in Sir Robert's heart also, there was a battle proceeding. On the eve of the funeral he sat alone in the library at Stapylton, that room in which he had passed so many unhappy hours, and with which the later part of his life seemed bound up. Doubtless, as he sat, he gave solemn thought to the past and the future. The room was no longer dusty, the furniture was no longer shabby; there were fresh flowers on his table, though the season was late; and by his great leather chair, a smaller chair, filled within the last few minutes, had its place. Yet he could not forget what he had suffered there; how he had brooded there. And perhaps he thanked God, amid his more solemn thoughts, that he was not glad that she who had plagued him would plague him no more. All that her friend had urged on her behalf, all that was brightest and best in his memories of her, this generous whim, that quixotic act rose, it may be supposed, before him. And the picture of her fair young beauty, of her laughing face in the bridal veil or under the Leghorn, of her first words to him, of her first acts in her new home! And but that the tears of age flow hardly, it is possible that he would have wept.

Presently – perhaps he was not sorry for it – a knock came at the door and Isaac White entered. He came to take the last instructions for the morrow. A few words settled what remained to be settled, and then, after a little hesitation –

'I promised to name it to you, sir,' White said. 'I don't know what you'll say to it. Dyas wished to walk with the others.'

Sir Robert winced. 'Dyas?' he muttered.

'He says he's anxious to show his respect for the family, in every way consistent with his opinions.'

'Opinions?' Sir Robert echoed. 'Opinions? Good Lord! A butcher's opinions! Who knows but some day he'll have a butcher to represent him? Or a baker or a candlestick-maker! If ever they have the ballot, that'll come with it, White.'

White waited, but as the other said no more, 'You won't forbid him, sir?' he said, a note of appeal in his voice.

'Oh, let him come,' Sir Robert answered wearily. 'I suppose,' he continued, striving to speak in the same tone, 'you've heard nothing from his – Member?'

'From – oh, from Mr Vaughan, sir? No, sir. But Mr Flixton is coming.'

Sir Robert muttered something under his breath, and it was

not flattering to the Honourable Bob. Then he turned his chair and held his hands over the blaze. 'That will do, White,' he said. 'That will do.' And he did not look round until the agent had left the room.

But White was certain that even on this day of sad memories, with the ordeal of the morrow before him, Arthur Vaughan's attitude troubled his patron. And when, twenty-four hours later, the agent's eyes, travelling round the vast assemblage which regard for the family had gathered at the grave, fell upon Arthur Vaughan, and he knew that he had repented and come, he was glad. The young Member held himself a little apart from the small group of family mourners; a little apart also from the larger company whom respect or social ties had brought thither. Among these last, who were mostly Tories, many were surprised to see Lord Lansdowne and his son. But more, aware of the breach between Mr Vaughan and his cousin, and of the former's peculiar position in the borough, were surprised to see him. And these, while their thoughts should have been elsewhere, stole furtive glances at the sombre figure; and when Vaughan left, still alone and without speaking to any, followed his departure with interest. In those days of mutes and crape-coloured staves, mourning cloaks and trailing palls, it was not the custom for women to bury their dead. And Vaughan, when he had made up his mind to come, knew that he ran no risk of seeing Mary.

That he might escape with greater ease, he had left his post-chaise at a side gate of the park. The moment the ceremony was over, he made his way to it, now traversing beds of fallen chestnut and sycamore leaves, now striding across the sodden turf. The solemn words which he had heard, emphasized as they were by the scene, the grey autumn day, the lonely park, and the dark groups threading their way across it, could not hold his thoughts from Mary. She would be glad that he had come. Perhaps it was for that reason that he had come.

He had passed through the gate of the park and his foot was on the step of the chaise, when he heard White's voice, calling after him. He turned and saw the agent hurrying desperately after him. White's mourning suit was tight and new and ill made for haste; and he was hot and breathless.

For a moment, 'Mr Vaughan! Mr Vaughan!' was all he could say.

Vaughan turned a reluctant, almost a stern face to him. Not that he disliked the agent, but he thought that he had got clear.

'What is it?' he asked, without removing his foot from the step.

White looked behind him. 'Sir Robert, sir,' he said, 'has something to say to you. The carriage is following. If you'll be good enough,' he continued, mopping his face, 'to wait a moment!'

'Sir Robert cannot wish to see me at such a time,' Vaughan answered, between wonder and impatience. 'He will write, doubtless.'

'The carriage should be in sight,' was White's answer. And truly as he spoke it came into view; rounding the curve of a small coppice of beech trees, it rolled rapidly down a declivity, and ascended towards them as rapidly.

A moment and it would be here. Vaughan looked uncertainly at his postboy. He wished to catch the York House coach at Chippenham, and he had little time to spare.

It was not the loss of time, however, that he really had in his mind. But he could guess, he fancied, what Sir Robert wished to say; and he did not deny that the old man was generous in saying it at such a moment – if that were his intention. But his own mind was made up; he could only repeat what he had said to White. It was not a question of what Sir Robert had thought, or now thought, but of what *he* thought. And the upshot of all his thoughts was that he would not be dependent upon any man. He had differed from his cousin once, and the elder had treated the younger man with injustice and contumely; that might occur again. Indeed, taking into account the difference in their political views in an age when politics counted for much, it was sure to occur again. But his mind was made up that it should not occur to him. Unhappy as the resolution made him, he would be free. He would be his own man. He would remember nothing except that that night had changed nothing.

It was with a set face, therefore, that he watched the carriage draw near. Apparently it was a carriage which had conveyed guests to the funeral, for the blinds were drawn.

'It will save time, if it takes you a mile on your way,' White said with some nervousness. 'I will tell your chaise to follow.' And he opened the door.

Vaughan raised his hat, and stepped in. It was only when the door was closing behind him and the carriage starting anew at a word from White, that he saw that it contained, not Sir Robert Vermuyden, but a lady.

'Mary!' he cried. The name broke from him in his astonishment.

She looked at him with self-possession and a gentle, unsmiling gravity. She indicated the front seat, and –

'Will you sit there?' she said. 'I can talk to you better, Mr Vaughan, if you sit there.'

He obeyed her, marvelling. The blind on the side on which she sat was raised a few inches, and in the subdued light her graceful head showed like some fair flower rising from the depth of her mourning. For she wore no covering on her head, and he might have guessed, had he had any command of his thoughts, that she had sprung as she was into the nearest carriage. Amazement, however, put him beyond thinking.

Her eyes met his seriously. 'Mr Vaughan,' she said, 'my presence must seem extraordinary to you. But I am come to ask you a question. Why did you tell me six months ago that you loved me – if you did not?'

He was as deeply agitated as she was quiet on the surface. 'I told you nothing but the truth,' he said.

'No,' she replied.

'But yes! A hundred times, yes!' he cried.

'Then you are altered? That is it?'

'Never!' he cried. 'Never!'

'And yet – things are changed? My father wrote to you, did he not, three days ago? And said as much as you could look to him to say?'

'He said!—'

'He withdrew what he had uttered in an unfortunate moment. He withdrew that which, I think, he had never believed in his heart. He said as much as you could expect him to say?' she repeated, her colour mounting a little, her eyes challenging him with courageous firmness.

'He said,' Vaughan answered in a low voice, 'what I think it became him to say.'

'You understood that his feelings were changed towards you?'

'To some extent.'

She drew a deep breath and sat back. 'Then it is for you to speak,' she said.

But before, agitated as he was, he could speak, she leant forward again.

'No,' she said, 'I had forgotten. I had forgotten.' And the slight quivering of her lips, a something piteous in her eyes, reminded him once more, once again – and the likeness tugged at his heart – of the Mary Smith who had paused on the threshold of the inn at Maidenhead, alarmed and abashed by the bustle of the coffee-room. 'I had forgotten! It is not my father you cannot forgive – it is I, who am unworthy of your forgiveness? You cannot make allowance,' she continued, stopping him by a gesture as he opened his mouth to speak, 'for the weakness of one who had always been dependent, who had lived all her life under the dominion of others, who had been taught by experience that, if she would eat, she must first obey. You can make no allowance, Mr Vaughan, for such an one placed between a father, whom it was her duty to honour, and a lover to whom she had indeed given her heart, she knew not why – but whom she barely knew, with whose life she had no real acquaintance, whose honesty she must take on trust, because she loved him? You cannot forgive her because, taught all her life to bend, she could not, she did not, stand upright under the first trial of her faith?'

'No!' he cried violently. 'No! No! It is not that!'

'No?' she said. 'You do forgive her then? You have forgiven her? The more as today she is not weak. The earth is not level over my mother's grave, some may say hard things of me – but I have come to you today.'

'God bless you!' he cried.

She drew a deep breath and sat back. 'Then,' she said, with a sigh as of relief, 'it is for you to speak.'

There was a gravity in her tone, and so complete an

absence of all self-consciousness, all littleness, that he owned that he had never known her as she was, had never measured her true worth, had never loved her as she deserved to be loved. Yet – perhaps because it was all that was left to him – he clung desperately to the resolution he had formed, to the position which pride and prudence alike had bidden him to take up.

'What am I to say?' he asked hoarsely.

'Why, if you love me, if you forgive me,' she answered softly, 'do you leave me?'

'Can you not understand?'

'In part, I can. But not altogether. Will you explain? I – I think,' she continued, with a movement of her flower-like head that for gentle dignity he had never seen excelled, 'I have a right to an explanation.'

'You know of what Sir Robert accused me?'

'Yes.'

'Am I to justify him? You know what was the difference which came between us, which first divided us! And what I thought right then, I still think right? Am I to abandon it? You know what I bore? Am I to live on the bounty of one who once thought so ill of me, and may think as ill again? Of one who, differing from me, punished me so cruelly? Am I to sink into dependence, to sacrifice my judgement, to surrender my political liberty into the hands of one who—'

'Of my father!' she said gravely.

He could not, so reminded, say what he had been going to say, but he assented by a movement of the head. And after an interval of silence –

'I cannot,' he cried passionately, 'I cannot, even to secure my happiness, run that risk!'

She looked from the window of the carriage, and in a voice which shook a little –

'No,' she said, 'I suppose not.'

He was silent, and he suffered. He dared not meet her eyes. Why had she sought this interview? Why had she chosen to torment him? Ah, if she knew, if she only knew what pain she was inflicting upon him!

But apparently she did not know. For by-and-by she spoke again.

'No,' she said. 'I suppose not. Yet have you thought' – and now there was a more decided tremor in her voice – 'that that which you surrender is not all there is at stake? Your independence is precious to you, and you have a right, Mr Vaughan, to purchase it, even at the cost of your happiness. But have you the right to purchase it at the cost of another's? At the cost of mine? Have you thought of my happiness?' she continued, 'or only of yours – and of yourself? To save your independence – shall I say, to save your pride? – you are willing to set your love aside. But have you asked me whether I am willing to pay my half of the price? My heavier half? Whether I am willing to set my happiness aside? Have you thought of – me at all?'

If he had not, then, when he saw how she looked at him, with what eyes, with what love, as she laid her hand on his arm, he had been more than man if he had resisted her long! But he still fought with himself, and with her; staring with hard flushed face straight before him, telling himself that by all that was left to him he must hold.

'I think, I think,' she said gently, yet with dignity, 'you have not thought of me.'

'But your father – Sir Robert—'

'He is an ogre, of course,' she cried, in a tone suddenly changed. 'But you should have thought of that before, sir,' she continued, tears and laughter in her voice. 'Before you travelled with me on that coach! Before you saved my life! Before you – looked at me! For you can never take it back. You can never give me myself again. I think that you must take me!'

And then he did not resist her any longer. He could not. And the carriage was stayed, and orders were given. And, empty and hugely overpaid, the yellow post-chaise ambled on to Chippenham; and bearing two inside, and a valise on the roof, the mourning coach drove slowly and solemnly back to Stapylton. As it wound its way over the green undulations of the park, the rabbits that ran, and then stopped, cocking their scuts, to look at it, saw nothing strange in it. Nor the fallow deer of the true Savernake breed, who, before they fled through the dying bracken, eyed it with poised heads. Nay, the heron which watched its approach from the edge of the

Garden Pool, and did not deign to drop a second leg, saw nothing strange in it. Yet it bore, for all that, the strangest of all earthly passengers, and the strongest, and the bravest, and the fairest – and withal, thank God, the most familiar. For it carried Love. And Love the same yet different, Love gaunt and grey-haired, yet kind and warm of heart, met it at the door and gave it welcome.

CHAPTER XXXVIII

Threads and Patches

THOUGH ENGLAND had not known for fifty years an outbreak so formidable or so destructive as that of which the news was laid on men's breakfast tables on the Tuesday morning, it had less effect on the political situation than might have been expected. It sent, indeed, a thrill of horror through the nation. And had it occurred at an earlier stage of the Reform struggle, before the middle class had fully committed itself to a trial of strength with the aristocracy, it must have detached many of the more timid and conservative of the Reformers. But it came too late. The die was cast; men's minds were made up on the one side and the other. Each saw events coloured to his wish. And though Wetherell and Croker, and the devoted band who still fought manfully round those chieftains, called heaven and earth to witness the first fruits of the tree of Reform, the majority of the nation preferred to see in these troubles the alternative to the Bill – the abyss into which the whole country would be hurled if that heaven-sent measure were not passed.

On one thing, however, all were agreed. The outrage was too great to be overlooked. The law must be vindicated, the law breakers must be punished. To this end the Government, anxious to clear themselves of the suspicion of collusion, appointed a special Commission, and sent it to Bristol to try the rioters; and four poor wretches were hanged, a dozen were transported, and many received minor sentences. Having thus, a little late in the day, taught the ignorant that Reform did not spell Revolution after the French pattern, the Cabinet turned their minds to the measure again. And in December they brought in the Third Reform Bill, with the fortunes and passage of which this story is not at pains to deal.

But of necessity the misguided creatures who kindled the fires in Queen's Square on that fatal Sunday, and swore that they would not leave a gaol standing in England, were not the only men who suffered. Sad as their plight was, there was one whose plight – if pain be measured by the capacity to feel – was sadder. While they were being tried in one part of Bristol, there was proceeding in another part an inquiry charged with deeper tragedy. Not those only who had done the deed, but those who had suffered them to do it, must answer for it. And the fingers of all pointed to one man. The magistrates might escape – the Mayor indeed had done his duty creditably, if to little purpose; for war was not their trade, and the thing at its crisis had become an affair of war. But Colonel Brereton could not shield himself behind that plea: so many had behaved poorly that the need to bring one to book was the greater.

He was tried by court-martial, and among the witnesses was Arthur Vaughan. By reason of his position, as well as of the creditable part he had played, the Member for Chippinge was heard by the Court with more than common attention; and he moved all who listened to him by his painful anxiety to set the accused's conduct in the best light; to show that what was possible by daylight on the Monday morning might not have been possible on the Sunday night, and that the choice from first to last was between two risks. No question of Colonel Brereton's courage – for he had served abroad with credit, nay, with honour – entered into the inquiry; and it was proved that a soldier's duty in such a case was not well defined. But afterwards Vaughan much regretted that he had not laid before the Court the opinion he had formed at the time – that during the crisis of the riots Brereton, obsessed by one idea, was not responsible for his actions. For, sad to say, on the fifth day of the inquiry, sinking under a weight of mental agony which a man of his reserved and melancholy temper was unable to support, the unfortunate officer put an end to his life. Few have paid so dearly for an error of judgement and the lack of that coarser fibre which has enabled many an inferior man to do his duty. The page darkens with his fate, too tragical for such a theme as this. And if by chance these words reach the eye of any of his descendants, theirs be the homage due to the memory of a signal misfortune and an honourable but hapless man.

Of another and greater person whose life touched Arthur Vaughan's once or twice, and of whom, with all his faults, it was never said by his worst enemy that he feared responsibility or shunned the post of danger, a brief word must suffice. If Lord Brougham did not live to see that complete downfall of the great Whig houses which he had predicted, he lived to see their power ruinously curtailed. He lived to see their influence totter under the blow which the Repeal of the Corn Laws dealt the landed interest, he lived to see the Reform Bill of 1867, he lived almost to see the *coup de grâce* given to their leadership by the Ballot Act. And in another point his prophecy came true. As it had been with Burke and Sheridan and Tierney it was with him. His faults were great, as his merits were transcendent; and presently in the time of his need his high-born associates remembered only the former. They took advantage of them to push him from power; and he spent nearly forty years, the remnant of his long life, in the cold shade of Opposition. The most brilliant, the most versatile, and the most remarkable figure of the early days of the century, whose trumpet voice had roused England as it has never been roused from that day to this, and whose services to education and progress are acknowledged but slightingly even now, paid for the phenomenal splendour of his youth by long years spent in a changed and changing world, jostled by a generation forgetful or heedless of his fame. To us he is but the name of a carriage; or is remembered, if at all, for his part in Queen Caroline's trial. While Wetherell, that stout fighter, Tory of the Tories, witty, slovenly, honest man, whose fame was once in all mouths, whose caricature was once in all portfolios, and whose breeches made the fortune of many a charade, is but the shadow of a name.

The year had waned and waxed, and it was June again. At Stapylton the oaks were coming to their full green; the bracken was lifting its million heads above the sod, and by the edge of the Garden Pool the water voles sat on the leaves of the lilies and cleaned their fur. Arthur Vaughan – strolling up and down with his father-in-law, not without an occasional glance at Mary, recumbent on a seat on the lawn – looked grave.

'I fancy,' he said presently, 'that we shall learn the fate of the Bill today.'

'Very like, very like,' Sir Robert answered, in an offhand fashion, as if the subject were not to his taste. And he turned about and by the aid of his stick expounded his plan for enlarging the flower garden.

But Vaughan returned to the subject. 'If not today, tomorrow,' he said. 'And that being so, I've wanted for some time, sir, to ask you what you wish me to do.'

'To do?'

'As to the seat at Chippinge.'

Sir Robert's face expressed his annoyance. 'I told you – I told you long ago,' he replied, 'that I should never interfere with your political movements.'

'And you have kept your word, sir. But as Lord Lansdowne cedes the seat to you for this time, I assume—'

'I don't know why you assume anything!' Sir Robert retorted irritably.

'I assume only that you will wish me to seek another seat.'

'I certainly don't wish you to lead an idle life,' Sir Robert answered. 'When the younger men of our class do that, when they cease to take an interest in political life, on the one side or the other, our power will indeed be ended. Nothing is more certain than that. But for Chippinge, I don't choose that a stranger should hold a seat close to my own door. You might have known that! For the Party, I have taken steps to furnish Mr Cooke, a man whose opinions I thoroughly approve, with a seat elsewhere; and I have therefore done my duty in that direction. For the rest, the mischief is done. I suppose,' he continued in his driest tone, 'you won't want to bring in another Reform Bill immediately?'

'No, sir,' Vaughan answered gratefully. 'Nor do I think that we are so far apart as you assume. The truth is, Sir Robert, that we all fear one of two things, and according as we fear the one or the other we are dubbed Whigs or Tories.'

'What are your two things?'

'Despotism or anarchy,' Vaughan replied modestly.

Sir Robert sniffed. 'You don't refine enough,' he said, pleased with his triumph. 'We all fear despotism; you, the despotism of the one: I, a worse, a more cruel, a more hopeless despotism, the despotism of the many! That is the real difference between us.'

Vaughan looked thoughtful. 'Perhaps you are right,' he said. 'But – what is that?' He raised his hand. The deep note of a distant gun rolled up from the valley from the town.

'The Lords have passed the Bill,' Sir Robert replied. 'They are celebrating the news in Chippinge. Well, I am not sorry that my day is done. I give you the command. See only, my boy,' he continued, with a loving glance at Mary, who had risen, and, joined by Miss Sibson, was coming to the end of the bridge to meet them, 'see only that you hand it on to others – I do not say as I give it to you, but as little impaired as may be.'

And again, as Mary called to them to know what it was, the sound of the gun rolled up the valley – the knell of the system, good or bad, under which England had been ruled so long. The battle of which Brougham had fired the first shot in the Castle Yard at York was past and won.

Boom!

NOTE – The honourable part in the suppression of the Bristol Riots, ascribed above to Arthur Vaughan, was actually played by Major, afterwards Sir Digby, Mackworth, aide-de-camp to Lord Hill. Major Mackworth, though present in an unofficial capacity, took upon himself to give the order to charge, which in the opinion of many saved the city.